The Fires of Edgarville

Also By Craig Joseph Danner

Himalayan Dhaba

The Fires of Edgarville

Craig Joseph Danner

Crispin/Hammer

THE FIRES OF EDGARVILLE. Copyright © 2009 by Craig Joseph Danner
HIMALAYAN DHABA, CHAPTER ONE. Copyright © 2001 by Craig Joseph Danner

All rights reserved. No part of this book may be used or reproduced in any form or by any electronic or mechanical means, including information storage and retrieval systems, without written permission except by a reviewer, who may quote brief passages in a review.

This is a work of fiction. All the names, characters, organizations, and events portrayed in this book are either products of the author's imagination or are used fictitiously for verisimilitude. Any resemblance to any organization or to any actual person, living or dead, is unintended.

Printed in the United States of America

First Edition

Publisher's Cataloging-in-Publication Data
Danner, Craig Joseph
    The Fires of Edgarville / Craig Joseph Danner.—1st ed.
    p.   cm.
    ISBN 978-0-9706405-7-4
  I. Title.
  Library of Congress Control Number: 2008909980
  813'.54—dc21

Printed on recycled paper

CRISPIN/HAMMER PUBLISHING COMPANY
www.crispinhammer.com

10 9 8 7 6 5 4 3 2 1

— for Beth, and our boys

Twin Tricks
December 1996

THE SIREN BLARED at three a.m. while Hank and Jessie snuggled close, waking them from different dreams of all the trouble there had been. They bolted up and wide-eyed to the siren's undulating scream, which was far away but loud enough to flood them with adrenaline. Their big dog started howling, which just added to their sense of doom, before Hank finally recognized the siren from the fire hall. They'd heard it half-a-dozen times, every Tuesday night at six, but this was not a test since it was long past middle-of-the-night.

Jessie tried the bedside light while Hank groped blindly for his pants: "Oh-my-god," she whispered to him. "Someone's cut the power off!"

Hank leaned toward the windowsill to pull the faded curtain back, squinted through the wavy glass at nothing but the black of night. Just before they'd climbed in bed he'd let the dog out one last time; looking at the sky he'd only noticed that the stars were gone. But now there was a yard of snow as dense as fresh divinity, blanketing the valley filled with rows of pear and apple trees. The snow took locals by surprise, so Hank and Jessie had no chance: silent after sundown, it snapped power lines and orchard boughs. There hadn't been a breath of wind or rain pecking the windowpanes, just flakes that fell as quiet as an old friend at a funeral. All this was so new to them: the silence of this lonely place, a small farm on a dead-end road, his mother in the room next door. Hank was used to waking up when ailing patients' parents called, rushing off to see a child whose bad heart wasn't beating well. But that life was now gone, and they had moved where Hank might not be found, living where the neighbor's house was half-a-mile down the road.

"Trouble, hush!" Hank scolded, but his words got stuck deep in his throat, and he stumbled on the black dog as he raced to head his mother off. He was cautious of the soft wood floors, the old fir splintery and worn; Myrna's bedroom shared a wall, and Lord-knows-what his mom might do. Hank wasn't used to creaking boards and ancient peeling wallpaper and window frames that rattled when the wind blew through the ship-lathe walls. His heart sank when he saw his mother, candle dripping in her hand, the hallway filled with trembling light, her shadow menacingly large. But his mom was only five-foot-two, slender as a twelve-year-old, and her bathrobe wasn't fastened so Hank reached to pull it closed for her.

"I hate that sound! Please turn it off," and she is speaking to a half-dressed man: his short hair salt-and-pepper and the face of someone Japanese. The loud cry of the siren makes her tense between the shoulder blades, her skin crawl up and down her spine, her chest flood with anxiety. Myrna freezes when this stranger reaches for her bathrobe cord, the act of someone intimate: I've never seen this man before!

"Mom, I'll go and turn it off, but first please get back into bed. There's nothing that you need to do. I'll take care of everything."

After settling his mom, Hank had to go investigate, couldn't sleep until he knew what made them set the siren off. Trudging through dark orchards with the wet snow nearly to his knees, he'd had to leave his truck stuck barely ten feet down his unplowed drive. The snowflakes were so large a single one could fill a catcher's mitt, the silence broken only by his big dog's jangling collar tags. Once out on the road he found the tracks of someone's four-wheel-drive, pushed on through one deep trench as it led him past the fire hall. It took Hank thirty minutes to walk far enough to see the fire, time spent lost in thoughts about what happened several months ago. He'd been seated on a wooden chair, a courtroom on the second floor, staring at the table while the jury coughed and cleared their throats. His heart had stopped the moment when the jury captain finally stood, and just like that Hank's lawyers reached to slap his back and shake his hand. He'd turned around to hug his wife, then suddenly was back again, high up on a cliff above the river and a raging fire.

Trouble gave a single bark at distant trucks and firemen; Hank breathed in then out again to clear his muddleheaded thoughts. A hundred feet below he heard the roar of river rushing past, the rumble of the fire trucks, the snap and pop of bursting sap. He saw an army's worth of volunteers all dressed in bulky fire suits, the flames shoot through the south end of the old mill where the roof collapsed. Hank inhaled the stunning smells of fresh snow, pine and Douglas fir all swirled around a stink like something nasty burning on the stove. Trouble leaned against Hank's thigh, so absently he stroked her ear; the steep sides of the riverbank were lit up by the raging flames. Then even from so far away, Hank heard a groaning blackboard screech as several thousand rusty nails popped from the folding metal roof. There were three blasts from a truck horn then the splitting of the timber beams, the crumpling of metal sheets, then under towers of bright red sparks the east wall of the mill collapsed. For a moment Hank experienced a night sky filled with shooting stars, a universe of sparkling embers rising brilliant red and orange. There were bright white spinning galaxies and gorgeous cloudy nebulae and comet tails and dying stars and novas bursting back to space. He watched for an eternity, the sparks and flames and flashing lights, until the snow turned back to rain, soaking through his overcoat.

...

By the time Hank got back home his feet were solid blocks of ice, his pants wet to the knees with streams of water running down his back. While he'd been out his thoughtful wife had brought more wood in from the shed, put a pot of water on the stove to make some cocoa with. So now she stripped him to his shorts and helped him towel off his hair, and then led him to the woodstove that was on the verge of glowing red. The power was still off and so the woodstove was the only heat; nearly standing on the stove, his teeth would not stop chattering. Jessie brought the thick red robe she'd given him a year ago; "Shhh . . ." she said, "it took almost an hour to get your mom back down."

...

At nine o'clock the morning after, Hank called from the kitchen door: the power was back on, so he could make his famous scrambled eggs. Coming from her bedroom, Hank could see his mom was neatly dressed; everything was buttoned right, face washed and her hair pulled back.

"I'd like mine over hard," but Hank had beaten half a dozen eggs, added fresh ground pepper, chopped cilantro, splash of Worcestershire.

"You like them better scrambled, Mom. Besides, this is my specialty." He put a cup of coffee near the place that he had set for her. He was glad to see she'd dressed herself, was up and out of bed so fast, a sign, perhaps, the day would go much better than some others had. It broke his heart to see his mother struggle with her memory: this woman who had raised him through the neighbors' stares and gossiping. So as he put her coffee down, Hank bent to kiss his mother's head, hand squeezing her shoulder as he turned back to his frying pan. While Myrna sipped her coffee Hank took bacon from the ancient fridge, laid it out to sizzle while he skinned and minced a garlic clove. The old stove was an ugly beast that only had two burners left; the light over the table was a bare bulb in a light socket. He'd never understood why Myrna chose to move out to this farm, had sold their place in Portland three short months after her husband died. But the house was slowly growing on him, even though it needed paint; the soft light off the wet snow filled the windows of the breakfast nook. He stopped to stare out at the yard, the rows of fallen orchard trees, thinking that he'd have to learn to use a chain saw pretty soon.

"The Edgar mill burned down last night," *but Myrna doesn't really hear,* looks up at this man who thinks he knows best how she likes her eggs. She doesn't want to argue over anything so trivial; the man seems fairly pleasant but one never can be sure these days. So she holds her peace about the eggs and thinks how she might leave the room, slowly push her chair back and sneak out now while his back is turned. She slides her chair a half-a-foot across the worn linoleum, just about to stand up when she feels a hand against her arm. Instinctively she screams and jerks her sleeve from her assailant's grasp, turns to find a sleepy woman wrapped up in a flannel robe. The man cooking the scrambled eggs has dropped his fancy spatula; shiny bits of green and yellow spatter out across the floor. The woman's look is horrified, her eyes wide as an open door, but the man just laughs and shakes his head.

"Mom, you scared me half to death."

"I'm sorry, Mother," Jessie said. "I didn't mean to startle you. . . ."

Searching for the paper towels, Hank looked beneath the kitchen sink; Jessie found them back behind Hank's aged balsamic vinegar. It was worthless trying to predict where Myrna might have put something; the day before he'd found a head of lettuce in the microwave. But overall their life was good considering the drastic change: moving in with Mother who was loony as a circus clown. Jessie got down on her knees to help him wipe up spattered eggs; their eyes met and Hank smiled at her and shook his head from side to side.

"We're not in Kansas anymore," which caused his wife to start to laugh.

"*Omm, Mani Padme Hum*," and Hank could tell his wife was fine.

...

Hank stood up to check his eggs, make sure the bacon hadn't burned, the wispy smoke reminding him again about the fire last night. The bacon strips were perfect so Hank took them from the frying pan, blotting with a paper towel to wick the saturated fat. His own doctor had told him that he had to get more exercise; his cholesterol was slightly high with borderline triglycerides. They'd gone over his history: his mother with her memory loss, the fact she needed insulin, his father dead at sixty-eight from cancer of the pancreas. But all that hadn't mattered since they weren't his *real* mom and dad: both of them were white while it was obvious that Hank was not. Looking in the mirror, Hank had often wondered what he was: mostly Japanese mixed with a whispered hint of something else. The people in Japan are famous for low rates of heart disease, but Hank had read the studies that said the benefits were diet based. Hank grew up on pot roast and spaghetti made with hamburger, macs-and-cheese with all-beef franks and triple-decker ice cream cones. The spatula he'd dropped was something he'd spent twenty dollars on: ergonomic handle and a shaft made from titanium. He rinsed it clean of dust and fur and used it to dish up the eggs: buttered toast and bacon with an orange slice and a parsley sprig.

"Go ahead and eat," he said, while washing up the frying pan, wiping down the counter before sitting with his wife and mom.

"Hank, this is delicious," but his mother didn't say a word; looked down at the plate as if he'd served her scrambled slugs and snails.

"It isn't going to bite, Mom," and Hank quickly reached his fork across, stabbed some of her eggs and held them up before her scowling mouth.

"Don't treat me like an invalid," and she pushes back his outstretched hand; she's finally recognized her son: so cheerfully solicitous. He's always been the caregiver, ever since he was a child: four years old and jumps out of the car to help her with the door. All her friends are jealous that she's raised a son so *damn* polite with homework done and table set and hair combed like an Eagle Scout. She loves him more than life itself, so proud of his accomplishments: honor rolls and service groups and academic scholarships. But she's always wished that Hank might act a bit more like her brother Sam, brave and bold and never seems afraid of doing something wrong. And all at once it's years ago and she is just a girl of eight: dirt path to a dark shed and a cow that she's supposed to milk. She doesn't want to go inside, with what the twins did yesterday: a half-a-dozen garter snakes in the bottom of her milking pail. There are spiderwebs and flitting sparrows, corners way too dark to see, stacks of empty apple crates could hide an angry grizzly bear. All she'd have to do is tell their father what the twins had done and Earl and Ed would be dragged past their mother's rhododendron bush. But a switching never slows them and she's begged the twins to stop their pranks; they nod their heads and wait a week then get her when she's turned her back. The twins have turned eleven years and Martin's thirteen-and-a-half, and Sam's the oldest sibling and is fifteen in another month. Today Sam's there to help his sister seek a little sweet revenge: all that Myrna has to do is be brave till their trick is played.

Sam's been planning this all week; everything has been prepared: coached her how to act like she has had an epileptic fit. She's not sure what the twins have planned, but Sam had seen them go inside; she walks into the dark shed and Sam slams the creaking door behind. Before the twins can pull their prank she falls down on a pile of hay, making sure the milk pail makes a clatter when it hits the ground. She's never felt so jittery, not knowing what the twins would do, the dark shed filled with cow smell and the sad coo of the mourning doves. Face against the hay she starts to flail her arms and legs about, then lies there still as death until the twins come to investigate. She's breathing in the smell of dung and mildew in the bits of straw, all this so familiar that it makes the waiting easier. It takes a couple minutes, but then Myrna hears them whispering, then slowly creeping from behind a stack of scrub oak firewood. She feels one shake her shoulder and hears Edward whispering her name; they turn her over slowly in the darkness of the door-shut shed. Their gasps are simultaneous, like startling a rattlesnake; her face is smeared with charcoal dust and streaks of drying chicken blood. She opens up her eyes and screams and thrashes like Sam told her to; they try to run outside but find the doors closed and the bolt is thrown. Sam bangs the north wall with a stick while Martin bangs against the south; scared to death, the twins race up the ladder leading to the loft. Sam has thought the whole thing through including two small animals; once the twins are upstairs Sam comes in and knocks the ladder down. Sam and Myrna rush back out, then Martin pulls the bailing string that roughly opens up the box and gets the baby skunks to stink. The twins both leap over the box right through the fog of burnt perfume and out the hay door down into what should have been a pile of straw. Myrna sees it clear as day, the twins waist deep in pasture pies and half a bin of rotten pears and sawdust from the chicken house.

"What's so funny?" Hank asked, since his mother had been snickering, staring like she'd seen a flitting sparrow half-a-mile away.

"What Sam did to the twins," and Hank had no idea who they might be, but smiled as Myrna dug into her breakfast like a teenager.

Three Short Blasts
December 1996

CHIEF GEORGE NAGOYA sat inside his office at the fire hall, feeling every day of all the years he'd been a volunteer. His head was resting in his hands, a tightness made it hard to breathe; familiar smells of smoke and sweat still lingered on his turnout sleeves. He rubbed the sore bridge of his nose, the headache right between his eyes, leaned back in the chair so he could stare up at the ceiling tiles. He was trying to remember all that happened as the mill burned down, trying to reassure himself that nothing he had done was wrong.

He pulled his chin and rubbed his eyes and stroked the stubble on his neck, wished that he'd retired back when he was only sixty-five. But teaming Jack and Jason was his only really big mistake; better to have paired them both to men who had more common sense. But once they'd gone around the back George couldn't see them anymore, and when he saw the wall would fall he blasted off the warning horn. If George could do it all again, he wouldn't even fight the fire; better if they all had cut some sticks and roasted marshmallows. They'd crept the engine down the hill through several feet of slushy snow and half the building's roof was gone with nothing to be saved inside.

Leaning from his chair George turned the small electric heater up, bone-chilled from the sight of all the snow melt dripping off the roof. He rubbed his hands before the coils that made a lovely rosy glow, his office walls the color found in old state mental hospitals. The desk was stained mahogany, its edges worn through thin veneer, a blotter pad showed twelve months that all happened several years ago. The carpeting was wall-to-wall and no one ever vacuumed it, lumped and stained beneath his desk from years of rolling back and forth. George no longer noticed how it always smelled of truck exhaust, like married men sometimes neglect to notice what their wives smell like. He settled back and took a pencil, drummed it on his little pad, looked down at a list of names with check marks next to most of them. The pad was in a leather case that George got from his Uncle Shige, back when he was young and couldn't keep track of his orchard bins. It stayed in his back pocket so it curved to match his buttock cheek; it held a list of family names George wrote down thirty years ago. Each check was made after a fire, each fire another home destroyed; with only one name left George wondered why the hell the mill burned down.

The last big fire they'd had was back a half-a-dozen years ago: allegedly the Stack's house burned when lint caught in the dryer vent. They hadn't saved a single wall and flames singed the surrounding trees and all that Stack had left was an old barn half-filled with pesticides. George had spent the next day sifting through the wreckage of the fire, looking for some proof to back his theory how these fires start. He'd climbed into the basement, tracing back the way the flames had spread, looking for the telltale signs of fuel and an accelerant. The Stack fire fit the pattern well and George checked off another name but still he kept his secret since his theory seemed impossible. Like all the other structure fires, he'd found no proof or evidence, just fabric lint or mouse-chewed wires or misdirected fireworks. He'd kicked through all the charred wood and the carcass of a dishwasher, twisted metal bed frames and the bike used by Stark's granddaughter. To George it still seemed obvious—the pattern unmistakable: *Every seventh year some bastard's house burns down in Edgarville.*

George drummed his little pad again, flipped the pencil in his hand, traced the unchecked box beside the only name left on his list. All the fires seemed innocent, just dumb mistakes or acts of God; until last night there hadn't been a single person scratched or harmed. It wasn't till the third house burned, way back in 1962, that George first noticed that the fires had been spaced out so evenly. But of course it was coincidence—he didn't think about it twice—but when the fourth house burned the odds of that became phenomenal.

Stepping from his office, George walked off to fill his coffee cup, down the dim-lit hallway to the kitchen of the fire hall. The coffeepot was on the counter, next to piles of paper cups, the frayed electric cord spliced with a few wraps of electric tape. The pot was almost empty, although George was all alone that day; the inside of his white cup stained the color of a chocolate bar. The air smelled of burnt coffee and the dank rag in the kitchen sink, something left reheated then forgotten in the microwave. The ceiling in the meeting room was high enough to keep giraffes, and all the warmth George needed was up melting snow off of the roof. The place had always felt like home; he'd helped to raise the roof and walls; remembered still exactly how it felt to lift a cinder block. For fifty years he'd volunteered, with twenty as the Fire Chief; in all that time they'd only fought one big fire every seventh year. There were always lots of little ones, the brush piles creeping through the grass, the flue fires in the fall each year from crusty layers of creosote. But last night's was the first big fire that didn't fit with all the rest: one year shy and no one at the mill had been on George's list. They'd always looked like accidents: an unwatched pot left on the stove; a candle tips; a lightning strike; a smoker falls asleep in bed. But the pattern stretched for fifty years, since George was still a teenager: three years from the war and coming home from the internment camp.

The first was Allen Tippler's place, who once had sicked his dog on George; the next was Alfred Petty, who'd refused to sell them diesel oil. The Maxon's place was after that, the one in 1962: wouldn't let his kids get on the school bus with the Japanese. Even though George couldn't see a pattern in the way they burned, he'd made a list of houses that belonged to certain families. And sure enough, the fourth house was the Hamsted's down on Collins Road, who'd leased the Soji's orchard but then never paid the rent they'd owed. A squirrel up in the attic had chewed through a few electric wires, sparking off a fire that took the whole house plus half of the barn. The fifth house was the Smatters' at the far end of O'Leary Road: July 4th in the evening of the nation's bicentennial. They thought it was a bottle rocket, lit by Smatters' daughter's son, landed on their shake roof after weeks without a drop of rain. But George could not find anyone who *saw* the bottle rocket land; everyone just figured since *what else would cause the shakes to burn?*

George had been named Chief by then, to lead the other volunteers, but half had gone to town that night to watch the fireworks display. His instinct was to rush right in to save the Smatters' burning house, burst up through the attic floor with fire hose and battle-ax. But he only had four sober men and two who seemed a little drunk, so George made sure that no one tried to go inside the burning house. Until they had a dozen guys, he'd kept them in defensive mode, fighting from the outside with two men on every water line. George wasn't going to risk his men by sending them inside the house of someone who had signed his name to ads placed in the *Hooster News*. They'd run them when the war was through: *You Yellow Dogs Aren't Welcome Back; This Valley Isn't Big Enough; Stay Away, You Stinking Japs.* He'd watched as flames dropped through the roof and started burning attic junk, spreading east and west until the house glowed like a birthday cake. The sky had held a trillion stars, a bright white band of Milky Way, the orange glow shining off the hills and mountains around Edgarville. By the time more help arrived there hadn't been much they could do but keep the fire from spreading to the woodshed and the tractor barn.

...

George leaned back against the counter, staring at the kitchen sink, watching water dripping on a plate that someone hadn't rinsed. The power lines had been repaired, but George had not turned on the lights, the room lit by the gray clouds and the wet snow of the parking lot. There was an echo in the meeting room each time a logging truck went by, the roads cleared by the county so the bus could take the kids to school. Sipping at the coffee that had simmered thick and syrupy, George tried once again to link the mill fire and the arsonist. His father worked the greenchain there before his orchard could produce, coming home with splinters in his hands for Mother to remove. His father was the first mill hand they'd hired who was Japanese: half the size of Swedes and Finns but still could do the work of three. As far as George remembered there were never any problems there; each man had an equal chance of cutting off an arm or leg. Before this, George's theory had predicted all the other fires, jotted down in pencil on the back page of his little pad. There was still a year to go before the next house on the list should burn: fifty years of sevens and *so why get so impatient now?* The watchman had described for George the way he saw the fire start: the heavy snow, the roof collapse, the blue arc from the conduit. For decades George had tried to paint a picture of the arsonist: Japanese and patient and intelligently devious. But *no one* could have planned this fire unless he was omnipotent: sparking wires and sawdust piles and broken sprinkler water pipes.

He poured his coffee down the drain and rinsed the aging dirty plate, tried to turn the handle on the faucet so it wouldn't drip. At least they'd kept the fire from spreading to the massive storage barn, hangarlike and filled with several forests' worth of plywood boards. But the mill itself had been destroyed with a fortune in machinery and at least a hundred jobs that fed a hundred local families. His cup now on the drain board, George could see the flames and sparks erupt, could hear the creaking timber beams, the screech of rusting metal roof. He still could not quite catch his breath or calm a sense of nausea; he'd made the calls he had to make and went to see both families. With the burning of the mill, they'd lost all trace of Edgarville, a town so small that once the only road in was the railroad tracks. It only took a hundred years from cutting down the Douglas fir to what was now a pile of ash that killed two of his volunteers.

Green Alder
January 1997

HANK SAT in the kitchen thinking he should just lay down the law: that two plus two is four and that there is no place called *Edgarville*. The day before she'd seemed all right, her mood no worse than usual, then once more she was telling lies and living in some fantasy. He'd help his mother make her bed and she'd say her mom had stitched the quilt; standing by the back door she would point out where the train tracks were. But no matter how much Hank cajoled, his mother was as adamant: *Listen, Mister-know-it-all, you could learn a thing or two!* She'd either stomp out of the room or look at him that certain way, deny she ever said it or demand that he apologize. Then perhaps three minutes later she'd forget that she had been upset, walk back in the kitchen and ask whether lunch was ready yet.

He was sitting at the table thinking what was he supposed to do, now that Myrna chased away the latest of three nursing aides. Hank listened to the quiet house, tried to hear where Myrna was, in case she might have climbed out of her bedroom window once again. There was an odor in the house somewhere Hank couldn't put his finger on: the old house hiding secrets in the sawdust in between the walls. It smelled a bit like tuna fish that someone mixed with camphor balls, all underneath the cleansing scent of Pine-Sol used to wash the floor. Scooting back his wooden chair across the cracked linoleum, Hank thought he might hide the smell by baking something sugary. He could quickly mix an apple cake that called for lots of cinnamon: ginger spice and nutmeg and a teaspoon of fresh lemon rind. He started looking through the cupboards filled now with his kitchen goods, mixed up with his mother's box of Bisquick and canned lima beans. The hinges on the doors were loose, the latches hadn't latched in years, the newspapers that lined the shelves were printed when Hank was a teen. Perhaps he could convince his mom to come help slice the apples up, sit and tell him once more how she used to live in "Edgarville."

His mother always had a strange relationship with truth and fact, so for the last few years Hank thought her problem had been carelessness. He hadn't paid attention in the middle of his jury trial: other things to worry about than whether Myrna's screw was lost. But she'd phoned to say the dog had died, and he told her that was years ago, then she said *of course* but she thought she should tell him anyhow. Then once when he was visiting, he found socks in the freezer chest; she said that she had done that to keep mice from chewing through the toes. And now she'd talk about a phantom past like it was yesterday: sunburns picking strawberries and sawdust in her underwear.

For fifty years Hank always thought his mother was an only child who grew up as an orphan with an aunt above a grocery store. But she'd never answer questions straight when Hank would try to pin her down: where had she been born and how old was she when her parents died? *You ask so many questions, Hank. I really don't remember them. That was all so long ago. What'd you do in school today?*

Perhaps when she moved out here she'd misheard someone say Edgar *mill*, and since had manufactured all these fantasies about herself. She'd told him of a big hotel with balconies on all four sides; a post office they built inside an old abandoned railroad car. Hank could not remember any stories about Myrna's past: Daniel only told him that it hadn't been a happy one. But now she'd claimed twin brothers *who once tricked me into eating snake*; her house burned down when she was small *so we lived out in the chicken coop*. Hank stepped from the kitchen down the hallway with the old wood floor, pictures on the wall he couldn't see because the light switch broke. Hank wasn't sure what Myrna did to make the aide leave suddenly; Clara grabbed her coat and said *your mother is impossible!* Stepping into Myrna's room, he asked her if she'd like to help. Myrna only glared at him, said:

"No TV for *you* tonight!"

Clara was the third to quit, so Hank sat down on Myrna's bed:

"Mom, the shots don't hurt that much, and you *have* to take your insulin."

She looks up at this stranger who is sitting just a bit too close, has a funny feeling she knows someone else who looks like that. On certain days it's all so clear, she knows exactly where she is: the old house on her father's farm she'd last seen before Hank was born. But other days she's not so sure: the furniture she knows is hers, *but who's this Japanese guy and why is he trying to lecture me?!* This man keeps going on and on, as if his train of thought's derailed; he either isn't making sense or she's missed a part she shouldn't have. She wishes he would finish up so she could then excuse herself: something about *blood sugar* and *damaged nerves* and *risk of stroke*. It's *fingersticks* and *blah-de-blah* and Myrna's finally had enough:

"Thank you. That was very nice. But I have to meet a friend for lunch."

...

It still could take Hank by surprise: he'd thought his mom was listening, when suddenly she stood up to go wander toward the laundry room. That morning he had checked the doors to make sure they were all still locked, and after breakfast he'd turned off the power to the kitchen stove. He was relatively certain Clara wasn't coming back again, and the agency would say they wouldn't send another nursing aide. He'd have to watch her by himself and place another classified and hope it wouldn't take long to find someone with a bit more spine.

He waited for a minute then he followed Myrna down the hall, remembering that last time she put soap into the clothes dryer. The laundry room was once a porch, the windows had been painted shut with several of the wavy panes replaced with squares of cardboard box. He found her standing at the window, nose pushed almost to the glass, staring out at all the gray and rain now drowning Edgar Flat.

"I remember when Dad planted those. After all his chickens died."

Hank's mom was looking east out toward the rows of old uprooted trees: knocked down by the county since nobody sprayed them anymore.

"I would have given anything to be allowed to work outside. My brothers laughed and laughed then never told me what they'd laughed about."

The words had almost passed his lips when he decided he should swallow them: unsuccessful so far in his efforts at correcting her. He remembered when he was a boy, he'd ask about his birth parents, and she'd frown and wrinkle up her brow then say something impossible. *Your mother was a geisha, Hank, so don't ask who your father was,* then, *no one knows because you were abandoned in a rice paddy.* But now and then she'd change her mind and squat so they were eye-to-eye, cup his chin inside her palm, say *Hank, I really am your mom.* And her look and voice seemed so sincere that he knew this was her biggest lie, since white moms don't give birth to little babies with such narrow eyes.

"Mom, how 'bout a cup of tea? Let's go put the kettle on."

"But since I was the only girl, I had to do the kitchen chores. God I hated canning beans. *Squeak-squeak-squeak* all winter long!"

Hank could feel that little wedge of *something* catching in his throat, the ghost sense of the nickel he had choked on as a five-year-old. He had to stop and swallow to make sure his epiglottis worked, eyes closed with a hand out on a stack of folded flannel shirts. He still could feel the way it raked his tonsils sliding past his tongue, lodging in his windpipe so the air could not go in or out. He'd been in the kitchen by himself and he couldn't call for Myrna's help, but somehow she just *knew* and she'd come rushing from the living room. He still could feel her shake his shoulders, make his head snap back and forth: a sharp smack with a closed fist hard between his little shoulder blades. But all that did was make the tears run down the edges of his nose, made him feel as if his mother maybe *wanted* him to choke. Then kneeling down in front of him, their noses now an inch apart, Hank could see the horror and determination on her face. With both hands she had grabbed his ears and pulled so hard he had to scream, which made the coin dislodge so Hank could finally take a breath again. He'd wanted desperately to cry, but he hadn't coughed the nickel out, and she'd asked him if he'd swallowed it: the best that he could answer was to meekly shrug his shoulders up.

Little Hank sat scared stiff for his father to come home from work, burst into the kitchen with his black bag and his stethoscope. Hank usually would rush to him and hug his dad around the hips, but this time Hank had sat and waited for his dad to notice him. Daniel had that clinic smell of cotton dipped in alcohol, the anxious stink rubbed off from children waiting to be immunized. Hank thought he might get mad at him for putting nickels in his mouth; his dad would turn him upside down and shake until the coin fell out. But Daniel was a gentle man, asked Hank if he could breathe all right; Hank remembers how Dan's hands felt warm and gentle on his neck. He'd listened to Hank front and back while cautiously Hank took some breaths, then looked inside Hank's throat using a mirror on a metal stick. Daniel laughed and kissed Hank's cheek and told him to stop worrying: *In two days, Hank, you'll flush this week's allowance down the toilet bowl.*

...

His mother still looked out the window, her words steamed up the wavy glass, looking out at trees she thought her father planted years ago.

"Martin sometimes told me things."

"Mother, help me fold this sheet."

"I never will forgive him, though. You'd think he'd have some loyalty."

When Hank was small he'd asked his dad if Myrna didn't lie sometimes, and Daniel only shook his head and said *she's unpredictable.*

—*If there's one thing to believe, Hank, it's that your mother loves you very much. Sometimes she might pull your leg. I wouldn't let it bother you.*

"What did Martin do?" Hank asked.

"My brother was a real scrub."

"I thought you were an only child."

"The twins were kind of mean sometimes. Did I tell you how they one time tricked me into eating garter snake?"

"Way too many times, Mom. And it tasted kind of chickenlike."

Myrna didn't answer back, just kept on staring past the yard: the dripping trees and hills beyond all shrouded in a cloak of clouds. She was seeing how it once was back when she had been a little girl, with houses made from mill scraps and the coyote's distant yap and howl.

...

Hank wandered through the old house trying to get his mother off his mind, noticing the sloped floor kept the closet door from staying closed. He kept reminding Jessie that he didn't own a screwdriver, much less know the difference between two-by-fours and studded tires. But she said it can't be rocket science; all he'd have to do is learn: go down to the library and read some books on carpentry. Looking at the buckled floor, he wondered what he'd have to do: crawl under the house with all the spiders, snakes and scorpions. He could maybe use the jack out of the truck to get the floor to raise, prop it up with concrete blocks and chewing gum and baling wire. But what if he did something wrong? The house would fall on top of him; better he should save himself for when they let him work again.

Instead Hank walked down to the room where he'd put his desk and table lamp, an oak chair and some filing drawers and a basket for recycling. He left his office door open, in case his mother did something: decides today's the day the leaking toilet needs to be replaced. He read again the letter from the board for doctors licenses: the members had decided that they'd need another interview. They wouldn't meet for three more months; they'd asked him for his *transcripts* now: proof that he had really gone to med school thirty years ago. He'd asked the Board to reinstate his license right after the trial, let him take a stab at getting back up on his feet again. But five months after asking they still wouldn't tell him yes or no, and he couldn't start a practice till the bastards finally said he could. His office had one window and the wind came howling from the north, so the raindrops pattered on the glass as the letter fell back on the desk.

He took a piece of paper out, a ruler and a triangle; might as well start sketching plans and looking for a contractor. In five years since she moved here Myrna hadn't had a thing repaired: peeling paint and rotting steps and *Lord-knows-what* that smell could be. He'd like to punch the south wall out and add a little sitting room; Jessie wants a shower in a bathroom off a master suite. He could put some dormers in the roof to better use the attic space: carpet and a skylight and a place to sit and meditate. That was where he'd take his wife when she'd ask for a back massage: small and warm and quiet where his mother might not bother them. He couldn't figure out why Myrna moved here after Daniel died: tattered roof and crumbling brick, an orchard of infested trees. He heard a gust of wind approach, battering their twisted limbs; he tensed up for the impact as it rattled through the window panes. The draft slipped underneath his shirt, its fingers wrapped around his chest, raking up his spine like sliding naked down a block of ice.

Once the gust had passed, Hank got the feeling there was something wrong: sixth sense that his mother had been quiet for a bit too long. She could be kneeling down to put a fork into a light socket, crawl beneath the bathroom sink to see what chlorine bleach tastes like. Or she might be on her bedroom floor, crumpled by a massive stroke; her doctor said she looked great now but couldn't say how long she'd last. She had the rapid-onset type, the change came on so suddenly: Alzheimer's dementia and some infarct on her brain CT. And Hank had no experience to tell him what he should expect; he hadn't seen a geriatric patient now for thirty years. His specialty was children's hearts: myopathies and birth defects, babies born with left-right shunts from septal ducts that wouldn't shut. He'd keep his patients' hearts alive till they were old enough to vote, then move them on to someone trained to take care of mature adults.

Stepping from his office Hank looked up and down the narrow hall, calling in a soft voice hoping that his mother would respond. He looked in through her bedroom door, the quilted spread she'd always had; the room was neat and smelled of talc and drawers of freshly laundered clothes. He peeked into the bathroom, though the light was off and door ajar; he found her in the living room, her feet up in her Lazy-boy. Her face was tilted to the left, her head held floppy on her neck, her mouth ajar about an inch, her tongue hung out like someone dead. He rushed then to his mother's side, watching for her chest to rise, heart skipped in his own because he didn't want his mom to die. She'd never been a beauty but the years had been kind to her face: laugh lines at her eyes the only hint she was past seventy. But what if Myrna's heart had stopped? What if she wasn't breathing now? Should he put her on the floor and puff into her mouth and nose? Opening her flannel robe, his hands would press between her breasts; already he could feel the snap and crack of ribs and cartilage. But she didn't give her son the chance to find out how he would respond: sleeping, Myrna scratched her nose and parked her tongue back in her mouth.

Hank found he could breathe again, and took a deep lung-full of air, held it for a moment and then slowly let it out again. The book that she'd been reading was splayed open in his mother's lap: the same book she'd been reading since the last one's binding fell apart. Carefully he picked it up and glanced down at the cover page: pirate with big bulging pecs, the buxom wench's bodice torn. Hank scanned the page that she was reading when she'd drifted off to sleep, thinking he could guess now what his mother might be dreaming of:

. . . the cutlass pressed against her throat, she slapped him with her steely glare.

"*Do it if you must,*" *she cried,* "*but never will I willingly!*"

It was time to buy another since the cover page was falling off; when Hank was young his mother used to hide them in her bedside drawer. So that was where he'd look when he was bored with reading Dick and Jane, not sure what it meant each time *the pirate's manhood was aroused*. Hank learned now that he only had to move the bookmark toward the front, and Myrna would be happy reading what she'd read a hundred times.

. . .

Trouble sprawled across the burnt-orange carpet of the living room, while Hank sat on the sofa near the pile of morning newspaper. He pushed the pile aside since there was nothing worth his time to read; looking at the dingy walls, he thought that he should buy some paint. There was the ghost-print of a rectangle where a picture must have hung for years; Hank imagined dogs around a table playing pinochle. On the coffee table there were several weeks of magazines, and Hank picked up the latest *Pediatric Cardiology*. Skimming through the abstracts, Hank found an article by Sandra Burns: a doctor who he'd met once at a conference down in Florida. Backed into a corner at an after-dinner gathering, Hank had felt her spittle every time she'd said the letter "p." She'd told Hank she was curious: *How come your name is Davenport? That's about as Asian as a hot dog made with sauerkraut. . . .* He'd tried to take a step back since her breath could run a lawn mower: *You wanna come up to my room? I'll bet you're really naked cute. . . .* He'd told her that he'd be right there, that he'd like to freshen up a bit; went back to his own room where he'd locked the door and gone to sleep.

He once had been a doctor, now he baby-sat his addled mom while this horrid woman's research got in all the periodicals. Hank got off the couch and picked the journals from the tabletop; ripping off the covers, they got crumpled in the fireplace. He stacked a pile of kindling—using branches that he'd trimmed last week—then went into the kitchen to the locked drawer where the matches were. Touching off the pages Hank found out they didn't burn so well; the chimney didn't draw and so the whole room filled with bluish smoke. Squatting down Hank fanned the fire, which made the situation worse; suddenly was pushed aside by Myrna with some newspaper.

"Mother, don't! You'll burn yourself!" But she got some pages crumpled up; coughing from the smoke she quickly shoved them up the chimney flue. Once the pages caught on fire the chimney flue could finally draw and slowly all the blue haze started clearing from the living room.

"How'd you know to do that?"

"Oh, this chimney's never drawn too well. Father built the thing himself, but he really should have hired someone."

Hank looked at his mother as she bent to fiddle with his fire, confused because her explanation seemed perfectly logical. How could she have learned this trick from reading torrid romance books? Maybe there was something to the stories she'd been making up. He felt the nickel once again slip sideways in his trachea, closed his eyes and pulled his ears till he could finally breathe again. Then he picked himself up off his knees and reached into the kindling box:

"That alder's much too green," she said. "There's dry fir in the shed out back."

He realized his mother's life had always been a mystery; he loves this woman so much yet she's never told him anything. There was not a single story from her past that he could verify; they'd always been so close and yet *who is this woman, anyway?* She was right about the alder branch, so green he still could bend it some, but going out to get more wood was risking everything he owned. The last thing he could do was trust his mom to tend the fireplace: five minutes alone and she could set the crumbling house ablaze.

Nothing To Look At
January 1997

HANK RECALLED his first time, pulling off the slender needle cap, filling up the glass syringe, sliding the sharp needle tip beneath the bright orange puckered skin. The room had filled with citrus smell, tainted with formaldehyde, the sound of nervous laughter because next they'd practice on themselves. He hadn't been too keen on being punctured by his lab partner, a pasty-colored brain who acted like he was in middle school. He remembered how this young man wiped his nose against his lab-coat sleeve, smirking as he'd filled the hypodermic with the cold saline. His partner hadn't washed his hands before he'd started touching things, neglected to wipe Hank's arm with the cotton dipped in alcohol. But Hank did not object because he didn't want to make a fuss, hoping that this guy would end up being a pathologist.

But now Hank had unlocked the drawer, selected a brand new syringe, filled it with ten units from a half-full vial of insulin. He flicked the shaft with middle finger, squirted out a tiny stream, breathed a deep chest full of air, the exhale lasting twice as long. He was trying to imagine all his tension flowing out his nose; he'd like to open up a window, get some air into the room. The kitchen filled with nervous dread, a stench that didn't have a smell; he walked into the living room:

"Mother. It's that time again."

Hank's mom was in her easy chair, charming in a flowered robe; he was glad she was reclining so she couldn't bolt so easily.

"Time for what?"

"Your vitamin shot. Remember?"

"No."

"Well, they're good for you. Vitamin eye. Keeps you from going blind."

"Lot of good it does me."

"Why? What's the matter?"

"There's nothing to look at."

He was amazed she was behaving since she often put up quite a fight; the capped syringe between his teeth, he took a pillow off the couch.

"What's this for?"

"To hit me with."

"Why would I want to hit you?"

"I don't know, but you always do."

It was Thursday, which was left thigh day, and she let him push her nightgown up; Jessie said she envied how good Myrna's slender legs still looked. He'd done this several hundred times, she got a needle twice a day; he pulled it from between his teeth: stab-plunge-done, *it's over with*.

"Bugger!" she said, hitting him, his glasses scratched across his nose; most times he was fast enough to get his face out of the way.

"You told me that it wouldn't hurt!"

"I never said that."

"Well, you should have. *This won't hurt a damn bit!* That's what you're supposed to say. You're the doctor, aren't you?"

"Not currently."

"Peckerhead."

The swearing only just began and it was difficult to not react; sometimes it was funny but sometimes he found it hard to laugh. He was careful where he put his feet, his glasses somewhere on the floor; to get the needle safely capped he had to wear his bifocals. One temple arm was bent so they were crooked when he put them on, but he didn't want to stab himself, inoculate his finger with whatever made her talk like that. He couldn't conjure memories of Myrna using dirty words, but one day like a switch was thrown she was cursing like a truck driver. It was half a week ago when they were sitting down for Sunday brunch, Hank had cooked a perfect plate of French toast with some fresh-squeezed juice. Jessie took the plate from him and put it down before his mom, who shoved the plate off of the table, clattering across the floor.

"I said *eggs*, you stupid slut!"

Jessie looked at Hank in shock, neither sure what they should do; Jessie left to take a walk while Hank had stayed to clean the floor.

He'd thrown the broken plate away and checked his mother's blood sugar, fixed a slice of toast for her with homemade apricot preserves. His heart beat like a hummingbird's, worried by this sudden change: was she suffering a stroke or merely in a nasty mood? He'd thought that he should take her in, a visit to emergency: a blood count and an EKG, a spinal tap and head CT. But what would he have said was wrong? *She called my wife an awful name.* She was sullen and demented and there was nothing they could do for her. She was barely in her seventies, though hadn't aged in twenty years; he was battling the thought she should be locked up in a home somewhere. But Hank was haunted by an act of kindness Myrna once had done: in 1942 she got a baby from an orphanage. He knew what his life would have been if Myrna hadn't been so bold, if he had been *the Jap* among the bullies in a home for boys. He owed this woman more than Sunday visits once or twice a month; her language wasn't pleasant but at least she still was continent. She just had *old timer's disease,* a fairly nasty case of it: Type II diabetes and a worthless short-term memory. And he knew that it was catching since he felt some symptoms of his own: fifty-five and couldn't cap a needle without bifocals. He'd developed a small tremor that came on when he was stressed or tired; worried it was MS or the early signs of Parkinson's. Or maybe he sick of having Myrna knock his glasses off, always scratching arms and face, and calling him a *peckerhead.*

"It's time to get dressed, Mom. I put some things out on your bed."

He helped her get up from the chair, got her pointed down the hall.

"Second door, on the right."

"I know where my damn bedroom is."

Good Days
January 1997

ON GOOD DAYS things seem bright and sharp: a clarity of thought and sight, a vision of the here-and-now that's different than most other times, when there is no here-and-now but just the past like it was yesterday, the present only mist and murk, the caustic smell of boiler smoke. She is barely in her seventies, though some days she feels twenty-eight, but today's not one of those days and Myrna's sensing that she's getting old: already past her prime and all the years keep going by so fast, as if time were a logging train that's rolling down toward Edgar Flat. It started oh-so-slowly but the train keeps picking up more speed, brakeless down a steep grade and now virtually unstoppable.

There are good days when she sees her son, his black hair mixed with strands of gray, cheeks could sometimes use a shave, crow's feet 'round his worried eyes. She is not sure how he got so old and grown from such a little sprout: her lamb-chop-sweetie-little-buddy-darling-snookums-honey-pie. He's always looked so Japanese and Myrna wonders where *she* is: ears, perhaps, stick out like hers; maybe has the Capo chin. But the rest looks like his father, though some days the man is all a blur: did Frank have such a broad nose, or was that his little brother George? Today she doesn't see the man, remembering her stoic boy: so well behaved it's sometimes to the point of being worrisome. At six he was adorable, she'd watch to give her heart a thrill: practicing piano twenty minutes every afternoon. But she wishes he'd surprise her sometimes: run out from between parked cars, hit somebody back at school, give himself a haircut with a pair of stolen pinking shears. She can even now predict his tears, know right when he'll come crying home, sit out on the front stoop trying to keep his mom from noticing.

—*What?* she asks.

—*Dirty Jap. And Chink.*

She dearly wants to strangle someone, slap some bully's soft pink face; she sits beside him on the step, smears his tears back with her thumbs.

—*Of course they did. I said they would.*

And today is one of those days, when the here-and-now is far away, remembering the warm front stoop, her son home from first-day-of-school. She feels his strong ambivalence, how he does and doesn't want her there: sitting close so she can feel the hiccups Hank gets when he cries. More than anything she wants to be the mother he deserves, say whatever good moms say to ease their tenderhearted boys. But she can't think what might make him laugh or think up some convincing lie, and it seems the truth would make things worse so she sits and doesn't say a word.

The Missing Chapter
February 1997

THIS WAS WHAT Hank missed the most: a young boy sitting on his table, might be four or five years old; mom says he's not growing right and *always looks so pale and tired.* She'd brought him to Emergency because she couldn't stand to wait; the doc had heard a *rub* or *thrill* so sent the boy to Doctor Hank. It's supposed to be Hank's lunch hour but his schedule's always filled for weeks, and the mom had been so anxious that his nurse had booked his only break. He doesn't mind skipping his lunch for someone who is really ill; already he has seen enough to know this kid is one of those. As he climbed the table Hank could see the boy's distended veins, the palest blue around the lips, the pause he needs to catch his breath. He looks like he is half the size of healthy kids about his age; his mother says he doesn't really like to do much exercise. She radiates an anxious sense, a slightly hostile attitude, as if she is expecting Hank won't listen to a word she says. But the part that frustrates Hank the most is that they've come in all alone: a family should be more than just a mother and her six-year-old. *Where the heck's the father?* But Hank doesn't bother asking yet, knowing that the answer won't help fix this young boy's ailing heart.

It was evening now and Hank was in a classroom at the fire hall, not at all surprised he couldn't keep his mind from wandering. It was drill night —every Tuesday—and he'd only been to one before, coming since the day the other volunteers filled up his yard. He'd thought he'd learn to squirt a hose, to turn the fire hydrant on; instead, the first thing that they did was teach a class on CPR. The room smelled of carcinogens, of inorganic truck exhaust, the anxious sweat of grown adults who don't like taking written tests. There were six around the table, plus a nurse whose name was Natalie: she drove the twenty twisting miles up from the Hooster hospital. Already Hank had grown concerned by things that she was telling them: the class can last four hours but she'll try to cut it down a bit. *What's she trying to teach,* he thought, *transthoracic surgery?* Flipping through the workbook: *This should take about a half-an-hour!* The nurse looked like a teenager, a nervous quiver in her voice: a quarter of Hank's age and he was the second youngest volunteer. But this was all there was after the mill became a pile of ash: a handful of old-timers who had lived their lives on Edgar Flat. The smell inside the room gave Hank the strongest sense of déjà vu: strange and unfamiliar and yet somehow oddly comforting. Hank sat at the table, drummed a pencil on a yellow pad, wondered if this nurse had ever *actually* done CPR. She'd drawn a heart up on the board: transposed the veins and arteries; it was hard not to correct her *when she's wrong on half of what she says.* But he hadn't told the volunteers that he'd been a cardiologist: *I'm just the quiet guy who's got that orchard where the trees are dead.* Already he'd decided that he'd tell them if they ever asked, but didn't feel the need to wear a scarlet letter on his chest. The last thing that he wanted was more questions asked about the trial, to listen to the silence when they learned he was *that* Doctor Hank. He'd sold his clinic, moved away, abandoned everything he'd made, all because a nurse said Hank did something *really, really bad.* He'd noticed that when Natalie could drag her eyes off of her notes, *she knows* because she looked at all the volunteers except himself.

It hadn't once occurred to Hank he'd ever have to take *this* class: a million things to do and he would rather clean a septic tank. But he'd walked into the fire hall expecting to help check the pumps; instead was greeted at the door by mannequins on tabletops. When Chief Nagoya asked him if he'd like to be a volunteer, he'd seen them dragging hoses, squirting foam across his burning yard. One reason that he'd moved here was to make a brand new start in life and *what could be more different than to learn to drive a fire truck?* He really couldn't have refused with four old-timers in his yard stomping muddy boots across the charred grass and the blackened snow. He'd spent the first months on the farm out hacking back the berry vines, the Scotch broom from the pasture and the branches off the orchard trees. The pile had grown enormously, was over fifteen feet across, and the thought of lighting it on fire had scared him so he'd put it off. He'd never burned a pile of leaves, could barely light a Presto-log, so he'd left it until January, waiting for the snow to fall. There had been two weeks of chapping cold, the temperature down in the teens: that short break in mid-winter when the dry wind blows out of the east. That morning started beautifully, a cloudless, bright-blue sunny sky; he'd never been a Boy Scout but he knew that he should *be prepared*. He had a can of diesel fuel, a shovel from the garden shed, a canvas coat, a woolen hat and a glove-box fire extinguisher.

There hadn't been a breeze when Hank had thrown the match onto the pile; he'd used most of the diesel since he thought the pile was wet inside. The ground had scattered bits of snow with clumps still frozen in the trees and he never would have guessed how things can burn when it's so cold outside. As if it were a jumbo jet, the fire taxied on the ground, then suddenly was taking off: a hundred-fifty-miles-an-hour. The scotch broom flared and crackled sending vicious sparks across the yard; the wind picked up and pushed the flames out thirty feet into the air. The grass between the piles of snow had dried out in the arctic cold, and the sparks had landed on the shed: six cords of pear and apple wood. Hank ran all around the yard, shoveling snow on little fires: racing toward the house and barn, the pickup and the lawn mower. *Stupid! Frigging! Idiot!* and he'd thrown the shovel on the ground, cursing that he'd given up his cell phone when his clinic closed. So he had to run into the house to punch the buttons on the phone, wake his snoring mother who was napping in the Lazy-boy. He'd almost yanked the cord off as he'd stretched to look back out the door: voice rose as he gave his address to the fire dispatcher.

Please stay in the house! he'd told his mother as he'd slammed the phone; barely out the door he'd heard the siren from the fire hall. His mother hadn't listened, but came out into the freezing cold, dressed up in a housecoat and pajamas that she always wore. Hank had trouble trying to decide what things to try to save, running back and forth so that he wasn't saving anything. The fire station siren blared, rising up and down the scale; his mother beat at spot fires with the lid off of a garbage can. It seemed like several hours passed before he'd heard the fire trucks: the rumbling of the diesel engines racing past the neighbor's house. Then suddenly his yard was filled with fire hose and flashing lights, the fire fighters acting *like a bunch of bumbling nincompoops.*

They were all dressed up in bulky suits and shouting orders back and forth, rummaging through truck compartments, doors flapped like a wounded bird. To Hank it was bad comedy, watching as one slipped and fell; he couldn't see the humor while his farm was burning to the ground. *What the blaze is wrong with them?* and he was having trouble watching this: someone got a half a mile of hose in a spaghetti knot. His dog was going crazy, barking at the clumsy firemen, and Hank scanned for his mother who was beating with the garbage lid. There were flames now in the woodshed with the grass fire halfway to the house; the pile of burning brush still shot its sparks up into outer space. His eyes burned and his lungs ached and the temperature was twenty-two; he'd dropped a glove and couldn't feel his left hand's frozen fingertips. It was like they were in quicksand as they fumbled in their fire suits, and he'd wondered if these clowns had ever really fought a fire before—when suddenly they'd done the job, were rolling up the muddy hose: they'd doused the pile of brush and filled the woodshed with a dense white foam.

...

Natalie was creeping through the chapters on anatomy, warning signs of heart attack and how to help if someone chokes. *What if the victim vomits?* and Hank was having trouble listening, didn't need instructions how to wipe his mouth across his sleeve. He hadn't yet learned all their names, but he thought that he sat next to Ben, and from the corner of his eye he saw Ben's head begin to nod. He looked then at the mannequins all lined up on the tabletop; a modern little family: mother, brother, baby girl. *Where the hell's the father?* and Hank was back inside his clinic walls, listening to the mom as she describes one of the fainting spells. As she speaks Hank reaches out to open up a bottom drawer, glancing at the mom so that she knows that he's still listening. The drawer glides out on nylon wheels, the handle brushed aluminum; Hank proud of his clinic since he'd picked the furniture himself. He rummages until he finds the latest version of the game, a little plastic box that blinks when Hank inserts the battery. The young boy's swinging feet stop: he has recognized it instantly: *Double-whammy-max-o-million-spitfire version 2.4*. Pushing several buttons so the darn thing won't make so much noise, Hank hands it to the waiting boy:

—*See if you can beat my score.*

...

Natalie was talking about where the hands go on the chest, how to finger-sweep the mouth and when to call the ambulance. She'd started with the ratios: how many times to thump the chest for every time you bend to give the pulseless body one more breath. The numbers drive Hank crazy since they change them every other year and *who can think of ratios when their loved one's crumpled on the floor?* This class could be a nasty joke, a prankster's sick, sadistic trick: to lure Hank to the fire hall and make him sit through CPR. It wouldn't have been bad if he could make this woman go away, then stand before the volunteers and teach them some reality. It doesn't help to tell them there is magic in the *thump and puff,* that pounding on a dead man's chest will somehow bring him back to life. But he'd have to then explain himself, how he'd learned this from experience: *that sometimes when a boy is dead there's no more you can do for him.*

...

Once they got the fires out, Hank stood and stared across his yard: the smoking pile, the blackened grass, the frozen chunks of blowing foam. As he watched them rolling hose, one of the men walked up to him; tilting back his helmet shield, Hank thought the man looked Japanese. They both took off their leather gloves to shake hands in the bitter cold, and Hank could see the man was maybe ten years older than himself. He said he was the Fire Chief, that he'd meant to stop by earlier: *It's good to know your neighbors since there's not too many left up here.* He said his name was George Nagoya, owned the orchard one road down, and he pointed out the others who responded to the fire call. Ben Espeth lived on Alder *with an orchard full of D'Anjou pears;* Evan Smith lived with his mom *who just turned eighty-one-years-old.* The other two were Paul and Brenda Thompson down on Punch Bowl Road; the only one not there was Roger Noji, who still worked in town. They used to have at least another dozen fire volunteers.

—*I'm sure you heard what happened,* he said. *We still try to do the best we can. . . .*

...

The boy's feet dangle motionless as he's concentrating on his game, but Hank knows he is all ears as his mother gives his history. Hank rolls his chair across the squares of red and blue linoleum; he takes notes with a pen that Jessie gave him twenty years ago. Hank asks the mother questions about illnesses her son has had: *Any family history of heart problems or lung disease?* He learns he was adopted, that she got him as a three-month-old, that his birth mom was a crack-head and the rest she really didn't know. Already Hank had read his chart: the minimum of routine shots, stitches on his forehead once, a nasty case of chicken pox.

—*We don't believe in doctors,* she says, staring Hank straight in the eyes; Hank has heard all this before and nods as if he understands. He is right up there with *leprechauns* and *Santa Claus* and *Tinker Bell*; his job is to convince her there is magic in his stethoscope. *Has he ever had a seizure? Any passing out or dizzy spells?* She tells him of a time her son was playing in the neighbor's yard.

...

Natalie was asking questions: *Which foods have lower sodium? What's the average heart rate of an active, healthy two-year-old?* She was going 'round the table so that everybody had a turn: *If the victim's wearing dentures, what are you supposed to do?* Hank finally had to think because he'd never come across this one; all his patients without teeth were nursing in their mother's arms. He was imagining a scene where some old man is on the bathroom floor, his prunelike lips have disappeared inside a toothless cavity. The wife is standing in the door, the paramedic kneeling down: he's wedged between the bathtub and the round edge of the toilet bowl. He thinks of his adoptive father, died about eight years ago: still a perfect set of teeth, a full, thick head of silver hair.

...

Hank has started his exam, his hands around his patient's throat, feeling for suspicious nodes while the kid pretends he's somewhere else. He listens as the mother tells the story of the fainting spell, nodding every now and then while palpating a body part. The kid was playing *army;* Hank can see the backyard tragedy: he squats to dodge a bullet then jumps up to toss a hand grenade. The boy's still concentrating on the buttons on the plastic box; his only movements are the random twitches of his nimble thumbs. But Hank can see him in the yard, he's aiming but his friend shoots first: he grabs his chest, his eyes roll back, *a very realistic death.*

—*How long was he out for?*
—*A minute. Maybe less.*
—*Was he incontinent? Did he mess his pants?*
—*I think he might have wet himself.*
—*MOM!!*

Hank feels his patient's trembling throat, how deeply he has been betrayed; he sees the glance from son to mom: a lethal dose of Krypton Rays.

—*I told you, I spilled orange juice!*

This patient's name is Nathan but it's okay if Hank calls him Nate; he's six-years-and-a-quarter and his ears stick out a little bit. He's way down on the growth chart and his weight is barely forty pounds, his favorite food is sushi and he wants to be a fireman. Already Hank has made a guess at what the diagnosis is: undoubtedly a virus has destroyed his myocardium. He's seen his bulging jugular, his pursed and cyanotic lips; how climbing on the table caused him rapid, doglike panting breaths. Hank knows that they will have to bond to get him through the years ahead; that if he doesn't trust Hank then he won't always cooperate. Because he's on his lunch hour Hank can take some extra time with him, can let Nate finish with the game before he takes it from his hands.

—*Did I beat you?*
—*No.*
—*Shit!*
—*Nathan!*
—*You need to get undressed,* Hank says.

...

Hank listened to the crackle of the radio in George's hand, watching as the Chief told dispatch they were in *the mop-up stage.* The grass would grow back in the spring, they'd stopped the fire before the house, the woodshed slightly blackened *but good thing it's only firewood.* He knew his neighbors saved his butt, that he'd been *a stupid idiot,* when the Chief said:

—*You're in okay shape. We could use you if you're interested.*

Now he was in the fire hall and listening to Natalie: just two-thirds through the workbook and already nearly nine-fifteen. She was doing every single chapter: *warning signs and risk factors, heart and lung anatomy, sudden infant death syndrome.* He'd started taking notes to try to keep his mind from wandering, was having trouble following the woman's droning monotone. He got distracted by the way her eyebrow on the right would twitch, the way she stroked her workbook like a cat asleep across her lap. He was flipping through his copy counting all the chapters left to do, hoping Jessie won't forget to check his mother's blood sugar. They'd done the *drowning* chapter and the *risks of high cholesterol, actions for survival* and then *proper hand positioning.* But Hank discovered one they'd missed that barely covered half a page: *Why would she have skipped the only chapter that means anything?* Scanning through that chapter he saw words like *Good Samaritan* and *legal case* and *in good faith* and *no one's sued successfully.* The only reason Hank could think why Natalie would pass this by was that she'd recognized him from the TV and the newspapers.

...

Standing in the yard George said to wait another month to burn, a weekend when it's raining *and the volunteers are all at home.* It was really only half a joke and Hank could only nod and smile, silently acknowledge being chastised for his big mistake. The Chief was last to leave, the others gone to wash and dry the hose, fill the truck with water, hang their helmets at the fire hall.

—*Sorry that it took a fire, but I'm glad we finally got to meet. I've seen you in your rig but didn't realize you live so close.*

—*We moved here in October. It's actually my mother's house.* Hank could see by George's face he'd seen his mother's skin was white.

—*Adopted.*

—*Ah . . .* is all George said, standing awkward for a while, taking off his helmet so that he could scratch behind an ear.

—*Tuesday nights at six,* George said.

—*I'll be there. Thanks for everything.* Hank watched this man climb slowly up into his battered pickup truck.

With the engine idling, George cranked his spattered window down, told Hank it was kind of strange to meet another Japanese.

—There used to be a lot of us who lived up here on Edgar Flat. Back when things were good before the war and the internment camps. He told Hank they were mostly gone, *we didn't get much welcome home,* and *it's nice to see a new face that could pass for an original.*

The brakes squeaked as George backed it up to get his old truck shifted 'round: *I guess it's time I took it in and paid to have the rotors turned.* Hank watched as George pulled from his drive then turned to face his blackened yard, the patches of mud-ugly snow, the half-burned brush still smoldering. Hank started gathering his tools, his empty fire extinguisher, feeling the familiar sense of something stuck inside his throat. He bent to pick his shovel up, the garbage lid from off the ground, when he saw a single bedroom slipper resting on a pile of snow. His chest filled with a sudden dread, pushing on his pounding heart: his mother's barmy as a hen and *God-knows-where she's wandering.*

...

The table had been pushed aside, the mannequins were on the floor, with Natalie instructing them on how to seal the mouth and nose. George was thumping on the chest while Roger did the rescue breaths, while Evan Smith made jokes about how jealous Roger's wife can get. They were working on the plastic mom, and Hank was trying not to pace: can't watch the placement of the hands, the ineffective sternum thrusts. *Mouth closed, Roger, no tongue* and the jokes weren't funny anymore, wishing they would *shush-up* so that they could get this over with. Too soon it would be his turn, and they'd moved on to the mother's son: the plastic eyes are painted blue, the cheeks both have a healthy glow. He could be four or six years old, and this was what Hank missed the most: the crinkling paper, swinging feet, how Nathan glances up at him. He'll learn this patient loves to read, has allergies to cats and dogs; they can't afford insurance now; there's no *damn father* anymore. In time the three of them will bond, the mom will trust Hank's magic powers, and that he'll do all that he can to keep her little boy alive.

It was Hank's turn to get on his knees beside the middle mannequin, check for a carotid pulse, a puff of breath against his cheek. He was thinking about IV lines and chest X-rays and vent settings, orders for the pediatric nurses in intensive care. He has done all this now countless times, the nature of his specialty: the one the nurses shout for when a patient crashes on the ward. He's calling out for *lidocaine,* for *epi* and *bretylium,* paddles placed across the heart: *little shock, big shock, shock shock shock!* He can't stand watching anymore, he pushes someone's hands away, his own press down on Nathan's chest, the angry scar the surgeon made. His patient looks like five or six but he's made it all the way to nine, and Hank had thought for sure that he'd brought Nathan through the danger zone. But this must be why Natalie had skipped the chapter in the book, breezed right past the only bit of knowledge Hank could really use. Perhaps she'd done it to be kind, to save Hank from embarrassment, knowing what the TV and the newspapers had said he did. But if she'd wanted to be kind she should have skipped through all the rest and gone straight to the chapter that says *when it's finally time to quit.*

The Chicken Coop
February 1997

SINCE THE ONLY THINGS on Myrna's feet were one slipper and a pair of socks, it didn't take too long before she'd tumbled on the snow and ice. She'd gone out for a little stroll among the pear and apple trees: was such a lovely blue-sky day and ages since she'd stretched her legs. She couldn't quite recall the last time she'd gone out to test the air, a morning constitutional to chase the clutter from her brain. But she wasn't dressed for so much cold and her slipper didn't give much grip; she'd fallen on a patch of ice and struggled to get up again.

"Son . . . of . . . a . . . *dog!*" she says through gritted teeth, sharp grains of ice pressed in her palms, and she has to crawl five feet to use a pear tree to support herself. It hurts to put weight on the right, she'd landed on her hip and thigh: not much padding there but thin pajamas and her morning frock. She finds one of the sticks they use to prop up branches in the fall when pears get big and limbs can break and fruit goes tumbling to the ground. With something now to lean upon she limps between the snow and ice, following as best she can a shortcut down an orchard row.

The dormant trees are clean of leaves so she sees the mountain to the south, the winter sun so low a shadow's cast across the glacial face. Except for being cold and bruised, she is happy as a meadowlark: the wind flips through her housecoat but the crisp air smells immaculate. She is trying to recall the last time she'd been walking through the trees, noticing that someone hadn't pruned this section very well. They'd lopped off all the suckers but they'd left the dense interiors, branches crossed so that the trees would choke themselves with too much leaf. She can hear her father's scolding voice, *it's Martin who's the lazy one:* these trees would harbor codling moths and apple mites and fire blight. But ever since the incident that tipped the cow onto its side, his hearing hasn't been so good so the scoldings haven't helped too much. Martin is the family clown, is always trying to make her laugh, the only one who tells her what the men say when they're by themselves. There was talk about a mill strike or a cougar spotted near the ridge, *I'm not supposed to tell but Bishop Fulton took another wife.*

"Dad says the Greens are giving up. And you can bet who's gonna buy their place."

Martin makes a funny face: his eyes crossed with his cheeks pulled tight, sucking in his lower lip, smacking on his upper teeth. Myrna's only six and this routine has always cracked her up; she tries to say her line but Martin's tickling her bony flanks. Her brother's nearly twice her age and they're wrestling in the sunny yard, and she's mortified she's passed a drop of urine in her underwear.

"Say it!" he goads. "*Say* it!"

She can't quite catch her breath to speak around her laughs and hiccupping, knowing that he won't stop till she says the words he wants to hear.

"What is it that you *rike?*" he says, his legs are locked around her thighs, and she gasps the words one at a time:

"I . . . rike-y . . . lice!"

...

The air is tart as Pippin juice, though flavored with a hint of smoke, the faint drift of a burning stump, the slow work of the orchardist. Leaning on the stick she'd found, she's only out meandering; she stops to turn a circle so that she can get her bearings straight. The landscape's so familiar, she is startled when she looks around: somehow she'd forgotten that this place could ever look so nice. The naked pears are wretched with their branches gnarled and insectlike, but she looks out past the orchards to the valley and the mountaintops. She'd thought the hills were clear of trees, the loggers leaving only stumps, but somehow they've grown thick with firs, their branches graced with snow and frost. Looking west she sees the valley rising up to Lost Lake Pass, turning north and south she can see Adams, Hood and Chinedere. Martin used to tell her he was leaving when he got the chance, that Edgarville was certainly the armpit of the universe. They'd all been down to Hooster where the houses are two stories high, with *Penny's* and *The Paris Fair* and *The Grand Rialto Theater*. But all four of the older boys have been to Portland with their dad: sixty miles of highway carved along the wide Columbia. They told her there were trolley cars and buildings fifteen stories tall, the roads paved so they didn't have to wipe their feet to go inside. So she always had imagined that she grew up in a stinking pit, that anyplace was better than the slab of mud called Edgar Flat. She couldn't say what day it was or how long she had been away, but something must have changed that she just can't quite put her finger on.

She remembers how each morning she'd walk down a steep and muddy trail, wedged between the twins so they could catch her if she slips and falls. The trail dropped a hundred feet down to the rushing riverside, winding through the stumps and shrubs and glossy leaves of poison oak. Edgarville was just the mill, the hotel where the loggers stayed, a boxcar with a desk where Mrs. Eckles handed out the mail. Perhaps a dozen houses stand along the rusty railroad tracks: a nice one for the Eckles and the others are all cracker box. The rain's been coming down for weeks, an endless misty drizzling, the color washed out of the trees so everything looks brown or gray. The mill dust settled in the rain, the boardwalks slick with sawdust paste, the one street ankle-deep in mud and stray dogs barking back and forth. The schoolhouse has a bell tower and the mist gives it a lonesome sound; she hears it clanging as they slide along the trail to Edgarville.

With every vision blurred by rain, they shuffle toward the two-room school, underneath the dripping eaves, giant firs half hidden right across the river raging past. Across the wooden covered bridge they climb the steps into the school, greeting Mr. Janeway throwing mill ends in the tin-box stove. To get the schoolroom warm enough to dry their dripping slickers out he has to make the stove glow red and warn them not to walk too close. Myrna can remember still the essence of the little school: six-year-olds and fourth-grade girls and young men learning how to shave.

It's damp and cold and Mr. Janeway throws more scraps into the fire, and she takes her muddy boots off as she watches him across the room. She's hoping that he'll look her way and notice that she's taller now; she likes his friendly mop of hair and eyes big as a puppy dog's. If only he were Mormon then perhaps one day he'd marry her and she'd never have to worry she'll get stuck with someone uglier. But Martin says that Teacher is a *gentile* and an *infidel*, that in the end *he'll go to hell with all the other Lamanites*. He tells her that she has no choice of who she'll marry anyway: *As soon as you grow tits,* he says, *the Bishop has his eye on you.*

She sits down on the same bench she's been sitting on for seven grades, with Peggy Smith and Molly Imai, Myrna in between the two. Looking at her two friends Myrna knows she hasn't got a chance: Peggy's cute and Molly's smart and Myrna's neither one of those. Peggy's got a button nose and a mother who wears store-bought clothes and a house that has an upstairs and a bathroom and a telephone. But it's Molly who she wants to be, even though she's Japanese: sharp and sweet with perfect teeth, her homework always done on time. She once asked Molly what it's like to look out through such slanty eyes; Molly laughed and said that it makes everyone look short and fat. She'd heard her brother's rude remarks, but the Japanese all seem so nice; their men will stop their work and smile and wave when she walks home from school. But she really doesn't have a clue what life for Molly must be like: desk-mates since the first grade but she's never been in Molly's house. She knows she has a mother since somebody makes a lunch for her, even if it's always rice and *smelly little pickled things.* This woman starches Molly's clothes and teaches her to play the flute, but Myrna's only seen her in their doorway from across the road. Martin told her that's because their houses don't have furniture: *They eat right off the floor and don't want strangers walking on their food.* He says they cook disgusting things, like *fish heads stuffed with seaweed paste* and *juice squeezed from fermented bugs* and *meat that normal people don't.*

"That's why they kind of smell like dog."

She smiles at him and nods her head as if she really understands, then wonders since they sit so close if she'd merely gotten used to it. For years while Molly shared her desk she'd lean to whisper in her ear, but never could sniff anything but wood smoke mixed with lavender.

...

It was Molly who had raised her hand to ask if they could go outside that morning when the sun came out, the first time in a month of rain. The rain had kept them in for days, all fidgety and miserable: restless hands and cramping calves and pigtails screaming to be pulled. It started out all gray and cold and Mr. Janeway stoked the fire; the smell inside the classroom was of eighteen pairs of soggy socks. Then suddenly the sun came out like top-milk splashed across the floor, Teacher standing in the puddle pouring through the windowpanes. He was looking at a patch of sky like something no one's seen before and Molly raised her hand and asked the teacher *can we go outside?* He'd turned his head to look at her, his eyes not really focusing; the class held its collective breath:

"Good lord, yes," he'd finally said.

It was like a flushed covey of quail, sudden burst of beating wings; Earl had been the first outside, neglecting to put on his shoes. She's remembering how good it felt, the air still damp with dripping eaves, the dogs still barking back and forth, the sun warm on her shoulder blades. She hadn't yet stepped off the porch, not ready to engage the mud; she likes to keep her clothes clean now that she is in the seventh grade. But the twins have tripped Jim Ishiro so that he's filthy head to heel, and already she can smell the smoke of fire where it shouldn't be. It's Tuesday morning, January, second week of '36, and the smoke she smells reminds her it's the last day of the two-room school. There are urgent shouting voices as the men rush buckets from the mill, the hollow ring of boot steps as they run across the covered bridge. But even though the sun is warm, her feet are getting awfully cold, and the shouts aren't from the mill hands but from migrants pruning orchard trees.

All this makes her head spin as she tries to sort out here-and-now: she is standing in an orchard when she should be on the porch at school. The voices that distracted her are workers pruning two rows down, up three-legged ladders made of shiny bright aluminum. Martin said that all these men were *Godless heathen Lamanites* and *I know what they'll do if they should ever catch you by yourself.* She is startled by her shadow stretching long across the ice and snow, northeast toward Gilhouley so she thinks it must be two o'clock. *What the heck is happening? It's time for Math and*

Algebra. Maybe this is Saturday. Father's going to clobber me. She is frightened not for being late or that her father might be mad but that she isn't sure why she is in the orchard by herself. Leaning on the stick she found she takes her bearings from the hills: *Snowshoe, Blowdown, Mt. Defiance;* home is over there a ways. She's guessing that between these rows she'll come out close to Sarah's house, a little stretch down Green Road then she'll take the shortcut through the woods.

Wishing she was not so cold she looks down at her morning clothes: a housecoat with a flowered print, pajamas and a pair of socks. *Cheese-and-crackers! Why have I got just one stupid slipper on!* Her feet feel like two solid bricks and *the ice is slick as baby snot!* She takes a deep breath in because she shouldn't get excited now, best to move off slowly so the *Lamanites* won't notice her. Keeping one eye on the men and one hand on her walking stick, she inches down the orchard rows of D'Anjou, Bosc and Comice trees. But her toe's caught by a chunk of ice and all at once she's down again and the *Lamanites* all turn to look at what the devil's brought for them. One man climbs down from his ladder, scampers toward her through the snow, speaks to her with strange words in a smooth voice meant to soothe and calm. But Martin told her she should never trust a single word they say, that *Lamanites* have forked tongues and long tails tucked in between their legs. So to Myrna he's a maniac who should be in the county jail for trying to molest a girl gone out to catch a breath of air. The man looks so lascivious with dirty coat and stocking cap and skin brown as the water in the river when the glaciers melt. Martin says that all these men have only one thing on their minds: to take the flowers of little girls out wandering the orchard rows. She didn't quite know what he meant since she was barely five years old *and no one's picking flowers in the winter with a foot of snow.*

...

It was Martin who taught her to swear out in the second chicken house, the one where all the chickens died, feathers thick with poultry lice. It nearly broke her father's heart to slaughter his entire flock, county agent standing with an order from the government. They piled the bodies on the ground and she hasn't eaten chicken since: the stench of burning fat and feathers wafting over Edgar Flat. The agent made them fumigate with some green deadly pesticide, and Father didn't have the cash to raise another poultry flock. So the chicken house became the place for storing junk and apple crates, where Martin took her when he had a secret that just couldn't wait. He's thirteen and she's seven and he's made her promise not to tell: that she'll never, ever say out loud the nasty words he's teaching her. She's not sure where he learned them but he's got a dozen words apiece for what the loggers do for fun and things that shepherds do with sheep. There's wrestling and tickling and giggling till the hiccups start, and even though the play is rough it never hurts enough to stop. She loves to feel his full attention beaming from on top of her, the sense that there is no one else that Martin likes to tussle with. He's coaching her inflection till she's sounding like a lumberjack; every time she gets it right he laughs as if his sides will split. *Knuckleheaded-pie-artist* and *jungle-buzzard-nincompoop;* the game is she's to say these things with grunts and spit and vehemence. *Misery-whips* and *fiddling-Swedes* and *dogger-ups* and *dizzy-bints;* she has to say them over if she lets a smile across her face. He doesn't offer to explain, so the words are only gibberish: *meat-burner* and *scuzz-bucket* and *can-inspecting-timber-beast.* She's only seen a *nigger* once and she's never met a *dirty kike* and she likes all of the *stinking Nips* who smile and wave when she walks past. He won't give her the slightest hint for terms like *putz* and *schmuck* and *schlong,* words he made her swear to never tell who she had learned them from. She loves that she can make him laugh by simply acting serious: *Chicken-choking-chowderhead! Jobber-jabber-pantywaist!* He's got her on the cement floor, straddling her bony knees, wrists held tight so that her hands are at the level of her ears. The light inside the chicken house comes through the space beneath the eaves, and it's summer so the hard cement is cool after the heat outside. Martin's maybe sixteen now but scrawny as an apple stem and even though she's barely ten she's just gone through a growing spurt. Martin can't release her wrist or she'll jab him underneath his arm, and he's laughed so hard a strand of spit hangs from the corner of his mouth. And this is too hysterical, it's swinging like a pendulum; there's no way she can say it straight: *You-lollygagging-fart-knocker!* She does something she's never done, she manages to buck him off, rolling over on the ground so *she's* the one who's now on top. Her posture feels precarious, and he's hanging on to both her wrists, but still this is the first time that she's ever been on top of him. They both are breathing heavily and Martin looks a bit alarmed; she hawks some spit into her mouth, says:

"Tell me! What's a *cocksucker?!*"

She thinks the potent threat of drool has given her the upper hand, but with a burst of effort Martin knocks her off onto the floor. Her head smacks on an apple crate hard enough to make her cry, and Martin's on his feet already standing with his back to her. He doesn't ask if she's okay or even turn around to look:

"That's it," he says, "you broke the rules. *And don't EVER call me that again!*"

...

Now Myrna looks up at a face she couldn't say she'd seen before, listens to his foreign words, an accent soft and musical. There is something in his soothing voice that makes her feel not so afraid; already she's forgotten he might try to take her flower away. Her wrist hurts and her feet are cold and she can't think why she's standing there; she'd stopped to look around to try to get her bearings straight again. There's Middle Mountain, Broken Top and Mount Defiance to the west, so if they keep on down this row they'll end up near the Collins' place. It's best if she gets home soon since she's not quite sure what time she left, and even though it's Saturday she'll have to make some lame excuse. It's dangerous to be so bold, out walking in the light of day, and she worries what the twins might do if they find out who she's walking with. But she loves how safe Frank makes her feel when his hand is on her upper arm, firm but gentle pressure as they walk between the orchard rows. She can't believe she let her brother fill her head with nasty lies: she knows now that they don't eat cats or beetles fried in gopher fat. In fact, she's learned to like the taste of *smelly little pickled things* and loves the candied ginger treats Frank sneaks into her coat pocket. And if she looks at him again she knows she'll want another kiss, but they're too close to the Collins' place *and that would be the end of it.* If her father ever found out he would label her a *dirty whore;* the twins would search for ax handles to beat the lust out of the boy. So she just enjoys the pressure of his hand against her upper arm, his steady reassurance as they walk between the ice and snow. Her arm was where he touched her first, the first time that he saved her life: the last day of the Edgar school when he pulled her off the burning porch. That was in the seventh grade, January '36, the first sun after weeks of rain, the children like a flush of quail. Mr. Janeway stoked the fire until the stove was glowing red, and Myrna's on the front porch watching all the others caked with mud. Molly Imai rescued them by asking *could they go outside?* But Myrna had smelled something so she went to turn the damper down. She was three steps in before she heard the first pops of the timber beams: something in the attic where the glowing stovepipe disappeared. It was then she saw the strangest thing there in the waxed linoleum: the floor was brown and tan but it reflected yellow, red and orange. She scanned the room to find the source, for something bright and colorful, when suddenly somebody pulls her backwards by the upper arm. She's barely back up on her feet in the muddy yard outside the school when she sees the bell and tower sucked straight down into the burning roof. The mill hands rush with buckets but the best that they can do is watch, and the older students have to keep the younger back where it was safe. In minutes it is smoke and ash, the bell sunk glowing in the coals, and no one knew but her that Frank Nagoya had just saved her life.

...

Now they're walking through the trees, a cold but bright blue sunny day, and she's thinking maybe she should dare to ask him for a kiss good-bye. The sound of gravel under tires brings Myrna from her reverie, and the driver's door swings open several yards before the truck has stopped. Suddenly she's face to face with someone she remembers well; she feels her heart race in her chest, uncertain what she's supposed to do. She knows that she's in trouble, wishing that she could faint dead away: *How can this be possible? I should have told Hank years ago!* She takes a breath to calm herself, and wishes she could have a drink, closes both her eyes and turns to get the damage over with.

Standing now before his mom, Hank's heart was flooded with relief that he had yet another chance to give back what she'd given him. But he also could have wrung her neck or turned around and left her there, angry that she'd wandered off with just one stupid slipper on. She held her arm as if it hurt, so he asked her if she felt okay.

"Hank, it's time you met your dad." But there was no one standing next to her.

The Big Suburban
March 1997

HANK WAS IN THE ORCHARD cutting through the dead uprooted trees, one by one he figured this would take a half-a-dozen years. It was bitter cold but sunny with a blue sky and bright patchy snow, a nice break from the last six months of gray clouds and a constant rain. The sawdust from the pear trees didn't smell as good as fir or pine, but the crisp air made his head clear and the hard work helped him settle down. The man who ran the farm store had convinced Hank of the need for power, so Hank held a big chain saw with more horses than a little car. At first he had regretted it, his arms could barely hold the thing, but now he'd gotten stronger and the big saw made things easier. He was wearing his protective gear, the chaps and boots with safety toes; already there were two nicks where he'd slipped and cut the hard lug sole. Nine acres was a lot of ground and he was only on the second row: two weeks into March and still the forecast was continued cold.

The only way he got things done was with the help of Lidia: that patron saint of patience who could somehow make his mom behave. But today was Lidia's day off so he'd snuck out during Myrna's nap, which gave him just an hour and there was maybe twenty minutes left. Looking at the gopher mounds all scattered out between the trees: *Those freakin'-little-rodents do more damage than a bulldozer.* At fifty-five he'd never had to kill a furry animal: he almost hit a 'possum once and nearly flipped his minivan. But now if he could catch the things he'd gladly wring their scrawny necks then cut their stinking heads off and impale them all on sharpened sticks.

He was imagining the heads on stakes all scattered out around the farm, till all the other gophers knew exactly who was now in charge. But he'd set the traps a dozen times and only caught one little guy, and the trap had merely snagged a paw so it was suffering and terrified. He stood there with the little stinker dangling from the vicious trap: drowned it in a bucket since he couldn't beat the thing to death. But the varmints ate his tulip bulbs and the garlic Jessie planted out, and those healthy rhodies that he bought were dead before his gloves were off. The state extension service said the orchardists all poison them with little strychnine pellets or a gas made out of cyanide. But they pumped their water from a well and he'd rather keep the poison out; he didn't want to kill the cats that ate the rodents that they catch. The traps, though, were discouraging: the gophers always seemed to win; looking down one row Hank counted fresh mounds every couple feet. Trouble sometimes dug for them, but today she must have wandered off, and he turned back to the dead trees and his numbing *Sisyphycious* task.

He glanced back toward the house to quickly check there was no plume of smoke, that Myrna hadn't lit a stack of kindling in the kitchen sink. The house looked like it leaned left toward a grove of giant cottonwoods, as if the trees said something that the house would like to know about. There was no smoke from beneath the eaves, no sound of rushing fire trucks, no smell of leaking propane but he noticed something worse than that. Above his buzzing chain saw Hank had missed the gravel-crunch of tires; parked before the house he saw a car he didn't recognize. It brought the gall up in his throat: a white Suburban four-wheel-drive, the kind used by the TV news with room for all their camera gear. He'd hoped that it was over, that those creeps had all forgotten him: newspapers and Channel Two and broadcasts live by satellite. He wondered were they snooping 'round, sneaking back behind the house, hoping they might catch him doing nasty things to nanny goats. They'd get it all on video and run it on the evening news: *caught at his new hideout skinning pelts off bludgeoned baby seals.* He'd always been more than polite, doing what his lawyers said; but now he'd like to tell them where to shove their stinking microphones. Hank thought perhaps his chain saw might help make him look more threatening, wishing that his dog was there and that she was a Doberman. But no one was behind the house and they hadn't tried to hide their car, and it suddenly occurred to him *they're inside talking to my mom.*

God knows what she's saying! and Hank rushed back to the kitchen door; pausing in the mudroom, he could hear a young man's droning voice. He was gearing up to give them hell, to read them out the riot act: *Get out of my house now or I'll have to punch you in the nose!* But it only took a second till he'd figured what was going on: he could have spent another hour out doing work around the farm. He took a breath to calm himself: he'd heard that tone of voice before; pulling off his gloves he flipped the breaker for the stove back on.

Glancing in the living room, he saw the two men on the couch, wide ties over white shirts and a seam pressed in their dark blue slacks. He was hearing terms like *peace* and *joy* and *knowing everlasting love;* he might as well start fixing lunch and let these nice boys watch his mom. He got the griddle out to make a pair of grilled cheese sandwiches: Imported Gouda, homemade bread, and drizzled virgin olive oil. These young men had no video or microphones or cable feeds, just some glossy pamphlets and a mandate to bring in the sheep. He tore some lettuce in a bowl, a mix of fresh organic greens; mixing up his special dressing, he warmed it in the microwave. He assumed the boys were Mormon since they always came in same-sex pairs, but didn't know if that meant they were Adventists or LDS. Someone tried explaining once the differences between the two: one set won't drink coffee and the other's vegetarian. He took a set of plates out and then flipped the grilling sandwiches, noticing he hadn't heard a word out of his mother yet. He had filled the kitchen up with smells of freshly ground black peppercorns, the bread he'd baked that morning and the pungent melting Gouda cheese. He wondered if she was asleep and if the boys had noticed this and *would they try to wake her up or quietly excuse themselves?*

Hank never much liked missionaries, but he grudgingly admired them, thinking of the time that he and Jessie spent in Ecuador. It was right after his internship, a year spent at an orphanage: seven hundred kids and most had never had a goodnight kiss. They both had studied Spanish but the first few months were challenging: trying to ask questions with the grammar of a four-year-old. He'd seen the pairs of Mormon boys out canvassing on bicycles, nametags on their breast pockets and black books underneath their arms. He watched them from across the street as they stood and talked at people's doors, their conversations more complex than simply *does your tummy hurt?* They can't be more than twenty-one and speaking in a foreign tongue, trying to convince these heathen papists that they've got it wrong. One evening they knocked on Hank's door, and he asked them in and offered tea: politely they declined but were excited he's from Oregon. *That's practically in Utah*, and they pumped Hank for the latest news, so thrilled to speak in English that they never thought to proselytize.

The one who did the talking now was lamenting *how we've lost our way*: teenage sex and gangsta rap and violence on the movie screen.

"The Mormon faith is different. Our main focus is the family."

Hank finally heard his mother's voice:

"Don't tell *me* what Mormon's think. Bunch of blasted hypocrites! You know what they once did to me? Threw me out! Burned my bed! Just for one stupid mistake!"

Her voice was so convincing that Hank almost thought her words were true: had to cover up his mouth to keep his laugh from being heard. *Where does Mother get this stuff?* though he was feeling sorry for the boys, certain they had no idea they'd walked into a loony bin. The young men didn't say a word, though the air felt like she'd dared them to: the only sound inside the house was the beeping of the microwave.

"If you think Joseph Smith's a saint, I'd like to show you boys some real estate."

His mother's voice had raised a notch; it was almost time to interrupt:

"All this time I thought you boys were trying to sell me magazines."

Hank stepped in the doorway, was about to say *it's time for lunch*, when the young men stood up off the couch:

"We'll go, ma'am, if you want us to."

Hank had to give them credit for the courage they showed under fire; the bravest thing to do sometimes was cut and run while still alive.

The young men glanced at Hank and so he nodded while he winked an eye; a silent way to let them know *My mother likes to joke around*. The younger looking of the two now had the car keys in his hand; the other put a pamphlet on the table as they backed outside.

"I'll just leave this here, in case you want to read it later on," and Myrna picked the pamphlet up and quickly tore the thing in two. The boys left and she threw the pieces in the old wood-burning stove; Hank turned to his mother and asked, "What the heck was that about?"

Then Myrna gave an answer that Hank took as a non sequitur:

"My brothers once convinced me I should never change my underwear."

The Fireball
March 1997

LIDIA WAS TRYING to link the stories that this woman tells, to get a picture of her life back in this town called Edgarville. Lidia came every week on Tuesday, Thursday, Saturday: an evening now and then so Hank and Jessie could go out somewhere. She thought Myrna was a *character,* her language more than colorful: every day a new one for her list of words she shouldn't say. Lidia had learned a trick to keep their conversations smooth: never telling Myrna that her stories might be less than true. She knew that she would go insane if Myrna had gone on and on, repeating twenty times a day a story she'd already heard. So she kept their visits interesting by focusing on long ago, by realizing Myrna was incapable of here-and-now.

"What was your mother like?" she asked.

"Oh, she was just your average mom. But one time I remember when she took the sled down Lost Lake Hill..."

Then Myrna would go rambling on, a story of an accident: Sam took Mother on the sled and ran into a barbed wire fence. There wasn't any doctor so the postmistress had sewn her up: a gash across her forehead and her lip cut by her bottom teeth. She remembered how her mother screamed the whole way sliding down the hill, laughing as her oldest son tried steering from in back of her. But once they hit the buried fence her mother didn't make a sound, not the slightest whimper as they rushed her to the post office.

"It was actually a boxcar. Mrs. Eckles was the postmistress," and the stairs her husband built were slick with ice and sawdust from the mill.

"My brothers had to carry her. Poor Sam felt so responsible."

They had her by the arms and legs, rushed across the covered bridge, the snow was maybe three feet deep, so the boys were all exhausted by the time they reach the icy steps. The four sons held their bleeding mom as they tried to navigate the stairs, when Martin slipped and fell and "It was just like playing dominoes..." Then UPS would ring the bell or the dog would start to bark outside, and Lidia would see the story vanish right before her eyes. The house might make a popping sound, a bird might hit a windowpane, and Myrna would be brought back to this last part of the century. Lidia would know that she might never hear the story's end, that once she'd been distracted she could not remember where she'd been.

"How many brothers did you have?"

She was learning—very slowly—how to navigate poor Myrna's mind, that every journey would depend on what her mental weather's like. It was futile to start out each day with a destination set ahead; a plan to go from A to B would somehow get to Y or Z. She'd ask about her brothers but she'd hear about the neighbor's dog; *What kind of apples did you grow?* got a tale about a swimming hole. But at least she didn't often have to listen to a story twice; when Myrna would repeat herself she'd simply cough or clear her throat. She'd compliment her pretty scarf or show her the new brooch she bought, and Myrna simply smiles and wonders *who the hell this woman is? It doesn't help to get upset* but she wishes she could find a clue for why this woman thinks she has the slightest interest in her brooch. But the woman's accent's lovely and her manners are impeccable, and so Myrna nods and smiles and wonders when this interview will end. She listens to the woman's questions, answers each one pleasantly:

"I'll bet you peeled a lot of apples when you were a little girl...."

"The apple peeling wasn't bad. What I really hated were the *beans!*"

Myrna started up again: *The beans! the beans! those putrid beans!* Now it was Lidia who smiled: this story struck her funny bone. There were canning beans and runner beans and all those *stinking* jars to wash; the sweat dripped from her brow from standing near the boiling water bath. She could hear her *peckerheaded* brothers laughing working in the trees;

could hear the *blasted squeak squeak squeak* of eating beans all winter long. But if the dog was quiet, if no starlings landed on the eaves, then Myrna might just chuckle as another story would evolve. Done now with the beans, *the beans!* her laugh would be an early sign, an indication of her mood, her clarity of memory. Laughing made her cheeks turn red and her eyes would add that spark of light, and Lidia would swear this woman's nowhere near her seventies.

"There were four. Earl and Edward and ... they were twins, those two...."

Lidia imagined she was fishing from a drifting boat; no telling what might strike her hook: a dogfish or a leather boot. So patiently she trolled until she felt a tug against the line; slowly reeling in a barracuda or an old truck tire.

"They were the youngest, next to me, and they both had quite a nasty streak...."

The story Myrna told was of the time the twins got whipped the worst; a nasty trick that went too far, past mischief straight to federal court. She told her of the kindling stick gripped tight inside her father's hand, his trembling knuckles white as the twins followed him like frightened calves. The twins were used to taking turns for which of them would get the blame for jokes and tricks they played on older brothers when their guards were down. But this time Father led them both across the hard dirt of the yard; usually he'd stop behind their mother's rhododendron bush. Her oldest brother, Sam, was standing out beside the tractor shed, tending to the milk cow that was injured by the brothers' prank.

"Sam was the only one brave enough to follow. He was worried Dad might kill them this time."

Myrna had been witness to the accident the twins had caused, watching from the garden as she dug potatoes on her knees. She'd seen the cow go over sideways, the shatter of the shed windows, the look on the twins' faces as they picked themselves up off the ground. She was maybe eight or nine and so the twins were twelve or thirteen years; she'd watched them trying to decide the best direction they should flee. Martin was their victim, sent to burn the garbage in the pit.

"The twins had mixed gas in the can of diesel used to light it with."

It was a time between pear harvests, the Bartletts finally all were picked, the Comice nearly ready and the D'Anjou would come after that. The garbage pit was full and Martin doused it liberally with fuel, carefully put down the can, then used his thumb to light the match. The morning had been rather cold, the first clouds they had seen in weeks, the air smelled of the dew-damp grass and the soil that Myrna's hands were in. She was elbow deep in hills of dirt her mother had just spaded up, searching for potatoes that the gophers hadn't eaten yet. She liked this part of gardening, the reaping what had once been sown, and she looked up at the instant that poor Martin tossed the lighted match.

She saw it all: the toppled cow, the bursting of the window glass, Martin thrown against the shed, a giant bright red ball of fire. She was knocked down by the boom of heat and sound that came across the yard, got up just in time to watch the twins decide which way to turn. One decided to go north, but the other grabbed him by the shirt, pulled him 'round the corner to drag Martin from the burning grass.

Lidia was silent as she looked at Myrna's vacant stare, her eyes were focused on some distant memory inside her brain. They were standing in the kitchen, peeling apples for an apple pie; Myrna could remove the peel in one unbroken twisted line. Lidia was worried that a logging truck would cross the flat, use its bleating air brakes while descending to the riverside. Then Myrna would look startled as she wondered *what the crap was that?!* Lidia would never find out how they got the cow back up.

"Sam said worst of all was watching Dad dish out the punishment," trembling as he led the twins beyond the second chicken house. The twins were both good Mormon boys, knew all about authority; knowing what was coming they knew running would be even worse. Sam heard their father tell one boy to drop his drawers and stand up straight, saw their father give the stick of kindling to the other twin. He told the one twin not to stop until the stick was stained with blood, knowing if he did the job himself he might not stop so soon. When both ends of the stick were red he told the boys to wipe their eyes, that they would both do Martin's chores until the cow gave milk again.

"Martin wasn't hurt too bad. His hair was singed along one side, and he lost the hearing in that ear. But the twins had really saved his life. The deafness made him 4-F, so he didn't have to go to war. All my other brothers went, but none of them came back again."

Every Seven Years
April 1997

HANK ASSUMED they all knew but were too polite to point and stare, to whisper when he's in the room or ask *how was the food in there?* He could picture them in easy chairs, staring at the evening news: lawyers trying to shield Hank's face from pushy news photographers. They might recall the story of the doctor and the ICU: *Whatever happened to that guy, the one who killed that little boy?*

He was underneath a fire truck, searching for some blasted stick, the one he'd had to find last month to check the pump's oil level with. It was a Tuesday night in April and was time to do equipment check: make sure all the tires were round and that they'd filled the water tank. He felt like such a total fraud, unsure what he was doing there: fifty-five and all dressed up pretending he's a fireman. He knew the stick was near some pipe all coated with an inch of grit: *How could they design a truck so that this was so difficult?* He groped along the rough edge of the chassis with an ungloved hand, couldn't see to look with all the road grime falling in his eyes. There was a toxic stink of truck exhaust, the rumble of the tanker rig, and he'd done this once before and really didn't want to ask again.

"You're too far south. Scoot up a bit. It's right there by the manifold."

Hank turned his head a few degrees to see a pair of lace-up boots; scooting half a yard he finally saw the dag-nab oil stick.

"Thanks, George. I can see it now," and Hank pulled the stick out of the sleeve, rolling toward the boots he held it out to show the Fire Chief.

George was looking down now at the pant-legs of his new recruit: *Two months on the team and still can't find the stupid pump-oil stick.* He wished that Hank was younger since it takes a lot to train a man, but half his volunteers were gone and he'd take whatever he could find.

"That could use a little oil. Nondetergent thirty weight. You'll need some help to fill it since it's hard to reach the opening."

Ever since George met this man he'd wondered what his story was: hadn't spent a lot of time with dirt beneath his fingernails. But though the man was awfully green, he was clearly not an idiot: asked a lot of questions about the different fire extinguishers. George was playing with the thought that Hank could be the arsonist: the right age and a Japanese and was certainly intelligent. It fit with the conspiracy, the way Hank joined the volunteers: lit his yard on fire so that the volunteers would come to him. George tried to imagine how someone could be so devious: taking seven years to plan each fire so that it burned down right. From the very first he noticed Hank was not too talkative, never volunteering to say anything about himself. He had a sense of humor but there was something he was holding back: a good joke made Hank snicker when it made the others belly laugh. He wondered where Hank came from and what made him move to Edgar Flat: not because his mother's farm was ever going to earn a lot. And what was going on with her? Why did his mother buy that farm? After Capo died it never listed with a realtor. There were lots of questions George could ask, but men don't talk that way up here: prying into past lives was what women did while sipping tea. The weather and the size of fruit and *what the road conditions are* was all that you should ask about until you'd known a man a while. He found it disconcerting each time Davenport came in for drills: something in the way he'd tilt his head when he was listening. This was more than a reaction to the thought Hank was the arsonist, but George felt he was looking at a younger version of himself.

It was quite a strange coincidence that Hank moved to the Capo farm, washing dishes in the sink of George's lifelong nemesis. Three times Capo shot at George's dog for stepping on his land: kept a rifle in his truck in case he got another chance. It was never quite as classic as a burning cross in George's yard or messages in spray paint written on the siding of his barn. But every now and then he'd find a dead skunk in his mailbox, step up on his tractor to find dog crap smeared across the seat. Just before they herded all the Japanese off Edgar Flat, George's older brother searched for someone to take care of things. Their father had been dead for years, and Frank had learned to run the farm, keeping all the trees pruned and the mortgage and the taxes paid. Frank went to the Capos since their orchard was the one next door; Martin said he'd lease it but would pay them half what it was worth. Then every month while in the camp George watched his mother's hopes collapse: never got a cent of rent or word how many bins were picked. Every now and then they'd get an answer from the Mathesons, two farms to the west who'd say *the trees aren't looking very good*. His mom would take the letter after Frank had finished translating, staring at the lines of ink that looked to her like scribbling. He'd see her face drop to her hands, the letter crumpled in her lap, the plywood walls and tin-box stove and steam with every breath she took. George could see Frank's nostrils flare, his deep breaths to control himself, knowing there was nothing in the world that he could do to help. Frank brought the blanket from his bed and wrapped it 'round her like a shawl; kneeling down, in Japanese, said *everything will be all right*.

...

"Evan, go help Davenport. The pump needs half a quart of oil." George looked 'round to make sure Brenda double-checked the booster truck. The volunteers were dragging butt since no one got much sleep last night, up at two a.m. to save their newly budding trees from frost. Last night eating dinner, George had seen the clouds begin to break, out beyond his TV and his picture window facing west. He'd stood between the curtains watching lipstick reds and cobalt blues, the valley walls around the flat reflecting lovely violet hues. The sunset didn't make him sigh or rush to find his Polaroid, but sit back on the sofa between his dinner and remote controls. His plate was on a stack of mail he hadn't found the time to sort; remotes topped off a three-foot pile of newspapers and magazines. One was for the TV and the other for the VCR, a third one for the Betamax he hadn't used in fifteen years. A clear night sky meant all the trees would lose their heat to outer space; unless the clouds rolled back, the buds would freeze before the sun came up.

All his life he'd thought of spring as being filled with *grumpy* months: April, May and June when all the orchardists are sleep deprived. Last night

George rolled out of bed at one to sit out in his truck, idling the diesel so that he could keep the heater on. He'd parked so he was facing west, a kitchen timer on the dash, hoping by some miracle the clouds would all roll back again. With the rumble of the engine and the dry heat flowing from the vents, George was thinking he should buy a truck with nice reclining seats. Startled by the timer-ding, he blinked at the thermometer: sleep too late and he'd wake to a hundred-thousand-dollar loss. At two-fifteen the mercury had dropped to thirty-one degrees; George put his truck in gear to race the clock to start his orchard fans.

The fan blades were each twelve feet long, could push ten acres' worth of air, make the orchard sound like it's a helicopter landing pad. They helped protect the tender buds from three or four degrees of frost; more than that and he'd be forced to ask his men to light the pots. He'd always found it scary, starting up the monstrous twirling blades: what if one should twist and break and fly off only *God-knows-where?* The north-block fan rumbled to life, and he throttled to accelerate; the ground beneath his feet shook like a rocket ship was taking off. Buffeted by blasts of air each time the fan rotates around, the windchill burrowed through the canvas coat he'd worn for thirty years. He was worried what would happen when he tried to start the south-block fan: overhauled and freshly tuned and still was unreliable. He got out of his truck again, mud caked on his rubber boots, ice skinned on the puddles of his road between the orchard blocks. Of course the damn thing wouldn't turn so he had to pull the starter off, gloveless fingers fumbling with his wrenches in the truck headlights. Cursing at his foreman who said yesterday he'd fixed the thing, he shook his head and swore he'd never trust another Mexican. It only takes one freeze and all his yearly profit could be lost, and staying up till dawn won't stop another freeze tomorrow night.

He pulled himself into the cab, his hands thrust toward the heating vents; left hip hurt from all the cold and climbing in and out so much. He had at least five hundred pots and each held nine gallons apiece so every night they burned cost George the mortgage on a city block. But the temperature kept dropping and he saw flames from the other farms; he really didn't want to but he really didn't have much choice. So at three he knocked on all their doors, his foreman and two hired boys, sent them off to light the pots and keep them full of diesel oil. George didn't *'ablo* much *'spanol* and his foreman's English wasn't great, so he had to wave his arms and shout to make sure they would do things right. He was anxious as the pots were lit in lines around his orchard rows, black smudge rising through the leafless branches of his livelihood. It seemed like such a dumb idea to try to heat the great outdoors; the flames jumped from the smudge pots and made all the trees dance back and forth. It hit a low of twenty-eight, could easy freeze the tender buds; by quarter-after-sunrise he told Julio to shut things off. The tension drained as one by one the orchard fans began to slow, the noise and smoke drift down the valley, clearing as the sun came up. He was hoping that they'd done enough to keep the damage minimal; asked his foreman once again to fix the starter on the south block fan. He told the men to get some sleep but that they'd start again at eight: try to get the west block sprayed before the wind picked up again.

...

When George would try to twist an arm, recruiting a new volunteer, the man would show a time or two then that's the last he'd see of him. But Davenport seemed like the type who just might stick around a while: *If he lasts another month I'll show him how to engineer.* George saw Evan Smith come from the storeroom with a quart of oil, a funnel and a greasy rag to wipe what they were going to spill. It shocked George how old Evan looked, though well into his fifties now; George could still remember back when Evan was a teenager. He had a funny, loping gait, like one leg wasn't long enough, though Evan claimed that all was fine since both his feet could touch the ground. The man had been around so long George rarely thought about him now: quiet guy too shy to ever talk into his radio. Except he wasn't Japanese, he'd peg him as the arsonist: a volunteer who'd been at every major fire for thirty years.

"This is kind of tricky, Hank. You'll probably get dripped on some," and Evan dropped the plastic funnel, kicked it underneath the truck. Hank was mystified by the instructions Evan gave to him: put the *fantail* in the *dog's mouth* then the *flapper* on the *Cuisinart*. If Hank knew only one thing it was pumps and how they operate: the ventricles and atria, the mitral and tricuspid valves. If a pump malfunctions he might challenge with a fluid load, add a beta-blocker or digoxin or some dopamine. But the panel on the pumper truck had labels that could be in Greek: knobs and dials and levers that nobody'd tried explaining yet. Hank was trying to get the funnel up above the greasy pipe, but the thing was over two feet long and there was not much room beneath the truck. He couldn't get his head back far enough to use his bifocals, and with the road grime in his eyes they wouldn't help him anyway. It smelled of dirt and diesel and the faintest whiff of body-stink; arms above his head, Hank knew exactly who the culprit was. He hadn't slept too well last night, came wide-awake at two a.m., sat up next to Jessie to the sound of the apocalypse. All around the farm they heard the beat of helicopter blades; out the window Hank watched as the flames spread through the neighbor's trees. It took a few beats of his heart to think of all those giant fans, the lines of rusty smudge pots running up and down the orchard rows. Somehow Evan reached around the battery compartment wall; he'd blindly pour the can of oil if Hank could get the funnel set. This all seemed so ridiculous: *What stupid ditz designed this thing?* Evan started pouring and Hank felt it dripping down his sleeve.

...

Standing near compartment three, George was feeling old today: just turned sixty-eight and up all night for three nights in a row. He should be taking inventory, making sure the tools were there; instead was staring at the box of fusies and the Halligan. There were tire chocks, a hydrant wrench, an out-of-date extinguisher, a burlap bag of wooden dowels, forgotten what they use them for. But he was thinking about Davenport, the quiet, thready voice he had, the fact he joined the force after a fire on his property. The Capo farm was now the last place on his list of families, but the grass fire wasn't big enough to make a check mark by the name. When Capo died eight years ago, George thought to cross him off the list, since who would plot revenge against some bastard who's already dead? But if any place deserved to burn, it was the last farm on Paul Partlow Road: the county had condemned the trees when Martin had stopped spraying them. Capo lived all by himself for years after his parents died: three brothers killed by Hitler and a sister who had disappeared. George had heard the legend that his sister's in an unmarked grave, back behind the barn where one night Martin might have strangled her. There were contradicting motives that depended on the gossiper: that Martin was the father of the baby she was carrying. But others said his sister was the victim of a jealous rage: that Martin heard that she'd been seen once kissing someone Japanese.

The Fire Queen
April 1997

IT WAS THE SMOKE that woke Myrna, not the jostle of her mother's hand, not her hushed, urgent voice, not the pounding of her brothers running up and down the narrow hall: the squealing of the rusty hand pump croaking in the dusty yard. It was smoke that tore her from her dream, in her dream they're by the riverside: a campfire and her father's lap, the smoke drifting into her eyes.

"The smoke just thinks you're beautiful," and her face was in her father's shirt, his sawdust smell and body heat, and even though her eyes burned she's as happy as she's ever been.

"Hold a piece in your mouth," Lidia says. "It will keep away the tears."

She's in the kitchen chopping onions, with this stranger standing next to her, and this woman reaches out to place some onion in between her teeth. For a moment it relieves the burn and stems the flood from Myrna's eyes, but it keeps her from her story, from the campfire by the riverside.

"Better to light a candle," Myrna says. "It helps burn off the onion oils."

Myrna puts the big knife down and wipes her hands off on a towel, blotting at her weeping eyes with the long sleeves of her cotton blouse. Myrna's thinking about candles, that they're in the second left-hand drawer, but all she finds are gadgets that she knows she didn't put in there. She pushes past a garlic press, a wheel for cutting pizza crusts; sifting through the twist-ties and the wine corks and a pastry brush. *Who put this crap in here?* she thinks, pulls the drawer out all the way, picking up the biggest stupid corkscrew that she's ever seen. *Who's been in my kitchen!*

and she's starting to get really mad. *Why is someone doing this?* She throws the corkscrew on the floor. She quickly glances to her left, this woman standing next to her, whose skin and eyes and strange perfume all say that she's a foreigner.

"You were telling me a story."

Lidia gently reached out then and put a hand on Myrna's wrist, slowly led her from the drawer back to the onion by the sink. In the month that she'd been Myrna's aide, she'd learned to quickly intervene, distract her from the fact that Myrna's memory was scatterbrained. She reminded her of Grandmother, her *abuela* on her father's side, who shared her bedroom growing up but called her by her mother's name. Myrna was still worse than that, this woman could forget to breathe; every other day she'd tell the story of the beans, *the beans!*

"You were telling me a story, when your house burned down when you were small."

Myrna looks at Lidia, cataloging who she is: a pleasant smile with sparkling eyes, her makeup just a little thick. Her long black hair's done in a braid, her accent soft and lyrical; every time she speaks it sounds like some exotic melody. Beneath the flowered apron she is dressed in something sharp and neat: a silky blouse and tailored skirt and shoes with half-an-inch of heel. There's not the slightest hint of threat, looks solid upper-middle-class; the music in her voice makes Myrna think she should behave herself. So she lets this woman lead her to the onion on the cutting block; the hand against her wrist is light and gentle as a kiss goodnight.

"But that was a long time ago."

She starts at the beginning, once again describes the river scene: her father and her brothers and the smoke that followed her around. It was the smoke that woke her from her dream, not the nudging of her mother's hand; her face pressed deep into her pillow, breathing through the quilt and sheets. She heard the sound of rushing footsteps pounding up and down the hall, her father shouting to his sons, the splash of water being thrown. Over all this noise there was a voice she'd never heard before: the full-throat roaring of a bear, the bellow of a hurricane; it shook the house, rattled her bed, smacked the windows in their frames. She wasn't more than five years old, her mother nudged her shoulder blade, whispering above the noise that everything will be okay.

—*Don't be afraid, hon. We'll be fine.*

Lifted from the tangled sheets, her knees embraced her mother's hips, the air was dark and stung her eyes, she hid them in her mother's hair. She remembers breathing in the scent of lavender and fireplace, the dark tang like his kisses when her father didn't brush his teeth. Wrapped up in her quilt her mother rushed them down the smoky hall, through the kitchen to the yard where her mother finally put her down. It was a time of day she'd never seen, a purple rim behind the hills, a tiny sliver of a moon, the Milky Way bright overhead.

"I remember it like yesterday," she tells this woman listening, whose birthmark on her neck makes Myrna think they'd met somewhere before. She tells her how the sparks and flames shot up out of the chimney top, celebrating embers like confetti on a birthday cake. The bright orange sparks rained down and danced against the wood shakes of the roof; in all her life she can't recall a sight more beautiful than that.

—*Don't move an inch. I need to help.* And her mother left her there alone, sitting on a tree stump in a distant corner of the yard. She watched the wooden roof ignite as the black-and-purple sky turned blue, the clouds from red to pink as smoke rolled from the fire's leading edge. She saw right when her father knew the fire was unstoppable, ordering her brothers to stop filling buckets from the well. Trying to save all they could, they ran into the burning house, pulling out the pots and pans, the braided rugs and table lamps. They dumped it all before her as she sat there quiet on her stump, wrapped up in her dark-red quilt, awestruck by the fireworks.

"The yard looked like a rummage sale," with piles of coats and underclothes, whole closets emptied on the ground, the few books scattered 'round like trash. Lidia was amazed how Myrna pulled out every last detail from something from so long ago: three-quarters-of-a-century. The images all seemed so real, she felt the heat on Myrna's face, the caustic smell of blackened smoke, the anguish in her father's voice.

"You must have been so scared," she said.

"It was exciting! I'd never seen so much commotion."

Myrna watched the flames consume the roof, drop down into the living room, her oldest brothers trying to wrench the spinet through the narrow door. It was hung up on the threshold, and her brother Sam was caught inside; her father pushed the twins away but still he couldn't make it move. She hears the echo still today, the roaring of the chimney fire, the flaming ceiling crashing down, her shouting father's anxious voice. The yard was filled with haunting music, pounding chords from high to low, Sam's bare feet against the ivory keys as he escaped the flames.

The neighbors started to arrive, stumbling through the purple light, men and women thick with sleep, startled with adrenaline. There was nothing they could do except throw spades of dirt against the house, back away as it got hot, each room a glowing rose of fire.

"I could feel the heat across the yard, and there were burning embers everywhere."

Shrouded in her quilt she started darting all about the yard, beating at the embers with a stick she picked up off the ground. For years her brothers told this tale, the story of the Fire Queen: how an ember landed on the patchwork of her royal robe. Beating with her scepter she chased harmless bits of soot and ash, unaware behind her she was lighting everything they'd saved. But what she most remembers is the high note of her mother's scream, that morning's only taste of fear: how her mother snatched the quilt up as the flames began to singe her hair. She looked up at her mother who was holding up a ball of flame, and it now seems she was mighty Atlas, standing with the world ablaze.

Never Been Sick
April 1997

"Good morning," Jessie said, turning around. "You're up kind of late."

"Where's Daniel? Isn't it Sunday?"

"Almost. It's Saturday. And Daniel is gone, Mom. He died six years ago. Pancreatic cancer. Remember?"

"Yes, of course," Myrna says, but she doesn't, and she can't, and she feels the need to sit down.

"I miss him, is what I mean."

"We all do."

For a moment Myrna's silent; Jessie brought her coffee.

"That's kind of you to say."

She doesn't want to say more because she doesn't remember, doesn't want to embarrass herself; can't recall the last time she watched Daniel pulling on his socks. She knows there must be something wrong, but can't think what the heck it is: *Didn't I come in here to chop two cups' worth of celery?* She does remember Jessie, though; was pleased Hank found a pretty wife; glad she likes to laugh and smile and makes Hank loosen up a bit. But Jessie's aged a lot in just the few days since she'd seen her last, as if she'd disappeared and been replaced by Jessie's spinster aunt.

"You look tired," Myrna tells her.

"Gee, Mom. Thanks. That means so much."

Jessie turned back to the stove, told Myrna she would cook today; she had a choice of rye toast or a bagel with Hank's marmalade.

"Hank and I ate earlier. But I could make you anything you want."

"Just don't fix me any beans."

"You don't have to worry, Mom."

Jessie's voice sounds light and sweet, and Myrna's feeling more awake: *scrambled* she remembers now, but can't think what the question was. She looks up at the kitchen clock, same one she's seen half her life;

"I think I'll wait till Daniel's home. He should be finished rounding now."

"Mother, Daniel won't be home. I wish you could remember that."

"Remember what?"

"About Daniel."

"He'll be home soon. Then we'll have pancakes."

"Myrna, Daniel's dead. For six years. But I'll gladly make you some pancakes."

"Don't be ridiculous. No one eats pancakes for lunch."

She gets up from the table since she isn't hungry anyway, eye caught by a photo stuck by magnets to the Frigidaire. The picture is her husband Daniel, next to his adopted son, arm around Hank's shoulders and they're both in sweaty hiking clothes. A baseball cap shades Hank's dark eyes and hides how short he keeps his hair, but Daniel's face is brightly lit and it shows how old and pale he is. His face looks well past middle age and his hair has lost its reddish-orange but his smile's as big as ever and there's still a sparkle in his eyes. She can't tell how old Hank is but her husband looks like sixty-five, and her throat feels tight as if she's trying to swallow an unbroken egg. Daniel's only fifty and next week they're going to Florida, getting on a cruise ship for a tour of the Caribbean. Jessie stood behind Hank's mom and put her hands on Myrna's back, fingers on her shoulders while her thumbs rubbed up and down her spine.

"I've always loved that photograph. Hank thinks it's from '87, the year before Dad got sick."

Jessie felt Myrna's shoulders stiffen. Myrna stares at the photograph, at her two handsome men, but there's something wrong, she feels annoyed, this woman's pressing much too hard.

"That's a lie," she snaps. "Daniel's never been sick a day in his life."

...

For Jessie, all this mess confirmed how life was unpredictable; never in a million years would she have guessed she'd end up here. Myrna left the kitchen, but she wasn't going to chase her down: didn't want to add to Myrna's growing list of phobias. The poor thing was miserable enough, living in the present tense, sections of her past erased like expletives from White House tapes. Jessie heard a friend describe her father who had Alzheimer's: defecating on the carpet, curtains used to wipe himself. The worst things that Hank's mother did were hiding matches in her room, pushing plates onto the floor and swearing like a lumberjack. Hank had put a smoke alarm on every ceiling in the house, searched her room from time to time to find the hidden candle stubs. But Jessie was disturbed the most by words that spilled from Myrna's mouth: *pea-brained-little-diddly-squat* and *double-fisted-bum-sucker*. Being called a *stupid bitch* felt just as bad as *cunt* or *whore*; could hear her father yelling at her mother through her bedroom wall. She'd have liked to learn to turn off the reaction that she always had: deep down like a glowing ember burning through her abdomen. At times Myrna was nice as pie, then instantly turned paranoid: *Someone's stealing all my socks! I'll bet it's you, you flea-bit tramp!* Every now and then Myrna would hit her in the solar plexus: *Jesus-fucking-Christ,* she'd say, *You greedy stinking hook-nosed kike!*

If she were a Buddhist she could simply clear her mind and breathe, invite the bad to pass through on its way to being something good. But that still seemed too much to ask, her grounding wasn't firm enough; the bad came in and knocked her down and kicked while it was going past. She'd have to leave the room to let her tremor settle down a bit: that tiny twitch below one eye that no one ever saw but Hank. If he was home, she'd leave the house, take the dog out for a walk, climb into her monster car and make the short drive to the lake. But today she'd promised Hank that he could have the morning off to work: outside in the orchard cutting dead trees into firewood. Myrna wasn't all that bad, just ornery as usual; tried to scratch but missed when Jessie poked her for her blood sugar. She'd left her in the living room, settled in her easy chair; odd how she could be so daft yet still could sit and read all day.

But Jessie couldn't concentrate; was wandering from room to room, cataloging all the places mice could get in through the walls. She'd lived in an old house before, their Northeast Portland bungalow: three baths and a kitchen made with polished granite countertops. Their dream had been to fill that house with children once things settled down: thesis done and loans paid and Hank's practice finally taking off. She'd loved that house but every year the extra bedrooms echoed more; one doctor said the problem was she's acid and Hank's alkaline. But Myrna's house was so beat down that a 'possum wouldn't live in it; Hank wanted to remodel but her vote had been to torch the place. Maybe if it had good bones there'd be some point in fixing it, but she laid odds they skimped on nails by building with wallpaper paste. Now looking out the kitchen window, past the rows of torn-up trees, Jessie was imagining the garden she could plant someday. There was lots of room for vegetables and herbs close to the kitchen door, a row of birch to shade a place to sit out in a summer breeze. Hank was out two acres off, engulfed in light-blue chain saw smoke, the revving buzz of cutting wood came through the cracks and crevices. Ignoring all the negatives, the property was beautiful; she liked the sound the wind made as it blew through all the cottonwoods. She filled a glass up from the sink with water from the shallow well: loved the taste but worried about coliform bacteria.

It was coming on a year now since the bailiff handed back their bail and Hank and she were free to try to build a life back up again. She knew it was irrational to worry that they'd change their minds, but still she'd wake from dreams they'd come to take Hank for another trial. With every deposition she had watched her husband's stature fall; every court appearance dropped him further into bitterness. Sipping from the water glass she watched as Hank cut up the trees, anxious that the saw might slip and rip right through his denim jeans. He'd never done this kind of work, but from this far she couldn't tell; he was handling the chain saw with respect yet some *laissez-faire*. He'd always been a doctor, but they'd yanked that rug from under him; there had never been a kinder man, yet the nurse claimed that he'd killed someone. He'd gone from fixing children's hearts to cutting up infested trees and living in a rotting shack while listening to Myrna swear.

The whole mess lasted two full years of watching Hank pace back and forth: couldn't work and few friends dared to be seen with him having lunch. They'd actually arrested Hank and stained all of his fingertips: wallet, watch and pager in a big manila envelope. The nurse was this religious freak who claimed she knew what God would say; the D.A. saw a case like this could bring lots of publicity. She watched her husband whittled down, his kindness slowly turning sour: a healthy ego that had always stayed this side of arrogant. She listened now to see if Myrna still was in her easy chair, and not deciding it was time to reupholster all the furniture. Everything was quiet but the buzzing of Hank's chain saw blade, as one by one Hank limbed the trees to burn them in the fireplace.

...

"Let's play cards."

Hank took the deck out of the drawer, pulling off the cellophane, asked his mom to drop her book and sit down for a little game. Hank dealt the cards out, five apiece; his mother taught him how to play: five card draw with nothing wild and ante-up a nickel each. She liked to play for money and Hank always made sure that she won, knowing it was unfair to take advantage of forgetfulness. He'd rather they played Scrabble but she'd lost all her attention span, would wander off before Hank got a chance to lay his tiles down. He hadn't picked his hand up when she was giving him a dirty look, threw her cards across the table, stood up so her chair fell back.

"You cheat," she said. "I don't play cards with cheats."

Hank watched his mother as she stormed across the silent living room, turning 'round to let him know exactly what she thought of him:

"Cable-choking horse thief. You must take me for an idiot. But I've been around the block, you know. Can't pull the wool over *my* eyes."

Hank let her go off down the hall, heard the toilet flushing twice, the opening of cupboards and her rummaging beneath the sink. Gathering the cards, he put the new deck back inside the box; eyes closed and a big breath and his head was shaking back and forth. Months ago they'd emptied out the cabinet full of medicines: nothing now but band-aids and a digital thermometer. So he didn't have to rush to keep his mom from poisoning herself: the acid-blocker for his stomach, the *Keflex* for his sinuses. He heard her swear beneath her breath, cabinet doors swung slamming shut; she came back to the living room, temples rubbed by fingertips.

"I've got a headache. Where's the damn aspirin?"

She'd been this way all afternoon, she couldn't seem to settle down, refused to take a walk because she said her *stinking feet* were sore. *They itch!* she had complained and then she'd paced the whole house back and forth, sat down with her romance book but then got right back up again. He'd tried to stay out of her way, then thought he'd try distracting her; nothing seemed to work and she'd already hit him twice today. The first was for her insulin, the shot went in her upper arm; the second just because she didn't like the way he'd looked at her. She'd even kicked once at the dog, poor Trouble simply in the way; she missed and Hank had watched her slipper sail across the living room. He'd felt like he should take her out and lock her in the garden shed, walk her to the river for a swim above the waterfall. Instead he'd made a quiche for lunch and read the newspaper out loud, tried to start a jigsaw puzzle, a movie in the VCR. Hank reached in his pocket now for the key to open up the drawer where he kept her thin syringes and the big bottle of *Tylenol*.

After they'd moved in Hank had to empty out a kitchen drawer, fill it with their medicines and screw a hasp and padlock on. It was like having a two-year-old, latches on the cabinet doors, a strap across the toilet so she wouldn't accidentally drown. Deep inside, the drawer was filled with matches that they've had to hide, out-of-date prescriptions for his ulcers and his blood pressure. Once while waiting for his trial he woke up with his back thrown out, suffered bad from migraines like big ice picks through his frontal lobes. So there were lots of different drugs to help his back muscles from spasming, sleepers for the week before the jury brought their verdict in. Except for her syringes and a refill of her *glyburide*, most of it was Hank's except for Jessie's extra bee-sting kit. His mom was diabetic and was suffering from Alzheimer's, but otherwise as robust as a slender sumo wrestler. He came across a bottle that was nearly full of *Percocet*, something that a friend prescribed when the *ibuprofen* hadn't worked. He'd never thought he'd do this but it was one way he could calm her down: something strong for pain and he could use a couple hours off. *It's only a narcotic* and the standard dose was safe enough: something for her headache and might make her want to take a nap.

It's not like she could be more confused.
"This isn't aspirin."
"It's stronger. It'll work faster."
"You're probably trying to poison me."
"You said you had a headache."

He watched as she was swallowing, the undulations of her throat, imagining the two pills tumbling down her pink esophagus. The pills were quickly broken up, dissolved into her gastric juice, rapidly absorbed before they passed through her duodenum. It was as if he'd swallowed them himself, waiting for the drug's effect, the tension in the metal bands released around his head and chest. It felt like someone backing off the screws sunk in his occiput, the first time since he woke up he could finally get his lungs to work.

"Mom, why don't you sit down, put your feet up in your Lazy-boy..." and with every heartbeat Hank could feel the screws backed out another turn.

Doughnuts & Nachos
May 1997

NOT ONCE in Hank's entire life had he dreamt of being a fireman, of pulling cats down out of trees or babies from their burning cribs. He'd dreamt of being a film critic, a newspaper photographer, a diver for Cousteau, and then a children's cardiologist. But there he was on hands and knees, crawling down a smoke-filled hall, dragging on a heavy hose and huffing year-old bottled air. With smoke so thick he couldn't see a headlight inches from his face, he knew if he got lost he wouldn't ever get back out again. His airtank weighed a thousand pounds and the hose at least a couple more; he was out of breath and scared to death and it was getting really, really warm. He was trying hard to concentrate on hunting down the source of fire, making sure he didn't lose his bearings in this burning house. But he was also standing four feet back, his eyes cut through the smoke and soot, could see himself on hands and knees, his partner crawling close behind. He knew that he was crazy to be battling a structure fire, crawling through a building where he'd die if he ran out of air. The hallway stopped abruptly with two doorways heading left and right: one room filled with dense black smoke, the other glowed bright red and orange.

"Hit it! Hit it! Hit it!"

Evan slapped Hank's back the way they'd done in drills a dozen times: saving life and property, a blazing room-and-contents fire. Hank hesitated briefly as he stared into a preacher's hell, engulfed in brimstone's lashing flame like nothing that he'd ever seen. The room was filled with serpents' tongues, the crimson fingers of a ghost, the tendrils of a giant squid, the hot blast of a dragon's cough. But even so, it wasn't bad, protected by his fire suit, breathing through his face mask with the hose line as his battle-ax. Hank was now the armored knight supposed to slay the fiery beast, but why would someone want to kill a dragon oh-so-beautiful?

"*Hit it!*" Evan shouted, which drove Hank out of his devil's trance; he grabbed the nozzle in both hands and pulled the metal lever back. The hose bucked as he turned it on, once more when the valve was shut; they hunkered down while waiting for the steam to cool the searing heat. For a moment it snowed flakes of fire, saucers made of soot and ash, darkening the flesh tone of his brand-new Nomex fire suit. The smoke thinned and Hank now could see exactly where the fire was: a stack of wooden pallets in the corner of an empty room. The floor was warped, there was shattered glass, the wallpaper was peeling off, a cord hung from the ceiling but Hank knew the power wasn't on. Evan pointed at the pallets, telling Hank where he should aim:

"Don't put it out. There's still two kids who haven't got to practice yet."

...

Hank had now passed all the tests: ropes and knots and nozzle streams, blindly searching smoke-filled rooms, how to roll up fire hose. Officially he was qualified to run into a burning home, climb up on the roof to cut a vent hole with a power saw. They'd all said that he'd tested well, but Hank was feeling not so sure: the next time that the siren blares he's certain he'll be killed somehow. It was a job for twenty-four-year-olds, for fire-eating bucks and does, sturdy youths with time to spare and lots of energy to burn. Hank was sitting next to Evan, who must be in his fifties now, and George could be retired and Hank was well past half-a-century. They were resting on the open gate of Evan's massive pickup truck, and Hank stared at his mud-caked boots and soot-stains on his pants and coat. Evan only then began to rib him for his helmet shield, melted when Hank stood up in a hot room when he shouldn't have. He'd had to come outside to rest when he'd felt his knees begin to shake, when the thought of dragging one more hose gave him visions of a heart attack. They were sitting on the tailgate near a box with just one doughnut left, torn-up bags of nacho chips and empty cans of soda pop.

"Nice work, Hank."

"Thanks," he said. "You're a good instructor."

"No. I mean your appetite. You're like a human vacuum cleaner."

He'd devoured half a foot-long sub, and was on his second can of Sprite, a big bag of Doritos and that doughnut had his name on it. The last time Hank had felt this drained was right after his honeymoon: cells used up their ATP and couldn't run the Krebs Cycle. There was a big hole in his stomach he was trying hard to fill back up; the sugar in the Sprite was helping raise his sagging blood glucose. His tremor was slowly clearing with the lactic acid from his legs, his breathing was so hard he'd been afraid he'd aspirate his food. And if he'd had the strength to think he'd tell the Chief he had to quit, that no one over seventeen should ever have to work like that. They were watching as the remnants burned, at the others standing 'round the fire: volunteers from other towns who weren't much more than teenagers. But Hank felt really stoked to know he wasn't quite a geezer yet; perhaps he'd take up jogging to start building up his stamina. Standing from the tailgate, he bent to stretch his aching back, fingertips could barely reach a foot above his rubber boots. Perhaps a little yoga and a long soak in a scalding bath, have his spine taken apart and scrubbed off with a bristle brush.

Hank was startled by a crash above the crackle of the fire, turned around to see the last wall of the cabin falling down. There were lots of younger volunteers, though none of them from Edgar Flat; several came from Hooster and the rest of them from Hillendale. They were standing close around the fire, armed with pikes and water streams, asked to help burn down a house to practice putting fires out. The cabin that they'd just destroyed was an old dilapidated thing that the owners wanted burned so they'd have room to place a doublewide. Hank watched the others joke around, spitting out tobacco juice, looking big as fullbacks in their helmets and their fire suits. What better way to spend a Sunday morning than down on your knees, praying to the God of Fire while crawling through the smoke and flames? They'd been waiting for this wall to cave, pushing with the ten-foot poles, bets placed which direction the stone chimney was going to fall.

...

Brushing chip crumbs off his pants, George stood up from the tailgate to go ask Brenda Thompson how much water was in the tender truck. The crashing of the falling wall had caused him to feel sick inside, a burning indigestion and a growing sense of nausea. He was not sure how much longer he could keep on being Fire Chief, surprised that all these youngsters came to help them burn the cabin down. He didn't have to hear them to know what was said behind his back, and if they'd said it to his face he still would not defend himself. He was pretty sure if he quit they might get a few more volunteers, but as it stood there wasn't anyone he felt could take his place. Evan could take over but he wouldn't use the radio: every time he tried he got some paralyzing phobia. Brenda would be great except her focus wasn't broad enough: once she started on one task, nothing else got through to her. Maybe attitudes had changed since she joined fifteen years ago, but *how would all these guys feel taking orders from a grandmother?* His indigestion now was worse and he'd swallowed half a roll of Tums and he knew he'd get an ulcer from the stress of staying on the job. It was not like he was being paid or vested in a pension plan, but spending all his free time doing something no one thanked him for. His hopes were now on Davenport, though Hank was somewhat awkward still, but maybe in a year or so he'd let him be the one in charge.

Elvis Hits
May 1997

JESSIE ALWAYS LOVED to drive on steep and winding mountain roads, so now her after-work commute was better than it used to be. She missed driving a smaller car down closer to the yellow line, but Hank thought when they'd moved that she should get a car with four-wheel drive. So she let herself get talked into a leather-seated behemoth, with CD and remote locks and the engine of a business jet. Just climbing in the driver's seat was enough to start her nose to bleed, but she loved how when she punched the gas she was pushed back hard against the seat. So she'd kind of gotten used to sitting up so high above the road, and it was nice to drive a rig that had the guts to pass a logging truck.

Whenever they went out somewhere she always let Hank take the keys: she hated when his knuckles blanched, his black hair sprouting strands of gray. But when she drove home after work she liked to crank the stereo and let the noise and speed drive out the stories that she'd listened to. This afternoon she'd heard a crying woman forty-eight years old who wished to rip the balls off of a husband who'd been screwing 'round. Jessie passed the box of tissues as the woman sobbed and wailed, made all of the mandatory sympathetic groans and nods. She truly felt bad for her and she thought the man deserved her wrath, but for some time now she'd lost at least three quarters of her empathy. She hadn't really trained for years to help those who weren't really sick; this woman's only problem was she trusted life to treat her straight. The woman hadn't thought the man she'd loved for over twenty years would get the urge to strut around with someone near their daughter's age. So now she felt the rug pulled out; why did she ever trust this man? All those years of business trips and flowers when he came back home. The woman didn't need a shrink to help her through this tragedy, but someone who could watch the kids while she ran up his credit card.

Now Jessie had the windows down, the radio was turned up loud, going over sixty past the dairy farm at mile post nine. She was listening to oldies tunes, remembered maybe half the words: *endless love* and *holding hands* and *never having to be alone*. It was all so complicated, how the human species can survive: *How did we evolve to be both devious and gullible?* This woman who sat on her couch had trusted grunts and syllables: the vows her husband made that he would keep his stupid zipper closed. But her husband was a man and men don't have much of a track record: studies showed that half of them would cheat if given half a chance. So why'd this woman blubber on about a lie that's so mundane? Because she had imagined he was different from the rest of them.

Her rig was doing seventy—she soared across the railroad tracks—breathing in the sweet smell of a sunny slope of clear-cut fir. She knew she was a hypocrite for how she felt superior: she never gave a second thought to Hank and infidelity. Her husband was good looking with his olive skin and trim behind; after all these years he still fit nicely in a pair of jeans. He'd grown a little tummy once, but lost it going to the gym, and now with all his farmwork she had noticed muscles on his arms. But in thirty years of marriage she was certain that he'd never strayed, that Hank's whole constitution was built on the rock of loyalty. That was why it hit him hard when the nurse had claimed he'd killed the boy: Hank had been the one to recommend she head the ICU. He always thought she was a friend, that they had formed a tight machine and did the very best they could for children in intensive care. Jessie still could not believe her testimony at the trial: said she'd always thought Hank had a massive Doctor God complex.

Jessie had to hit the brakes, a rock had fallen on the road; she swerved into the other lane then back on her side of the line. She let up on the gas a bit as she began a stretch of twisting curves, glad for the distraction from the pain of thinking of the trial. But it dominated everything for more than two years of their lives; Hank stayed home and cleaned the house and planted lots of garden starts. She reached out then to punch some buttons, fix the crackling radio, try to find some music that would fill her mind with pleasant thoughts. She'd listened for an hour to the woman with the wandering spouse, another session with a man who last year tried to kill himself. There was not much choice of stations but for oldies and a talk-show host, the only one that came in clear was playing nonstop Christian rock. So she fumbled for the CD box that was stashed beneath the right-hand seat, one eye on the road as she tried finding something that she liked. Her husband's tastes were classical and easy listening pop and jazz, but Jessie needed something to get the day's bad taste out of her mouth. She found a disk of Elvis hits she'd first heard back in second grade, took both hands to get the disk out of the stupid CD case. Once she had it in the slot she chuckled at the irony: of all the songs that Elvis sang the first tune up was *Jailhouse Rock*. But it had a driving, catchy beat so she sped up as she sang along, didn't notice that she'd passed one of the sheriff's speeding traps.

The radar gun read seventy so the deputy pulled out behind, spraying bits of gravel as he raced to catch the SUV. He turned the flashing blue lights on but hadn't touched the siren horn, calling in to dispatch that he was going to stop a speeding car. Then all this happened suddenly: a deer stepped out across the road, Jessie hit the brakes so hard the deputy ran into her. She heard screeching tires and shattered glass and crushing autobody parts, the sickening thud of something solid pounding into something soft. Before her big car stopped the deer had rolled across the crumpled hood, smashing through the windshield so the deer became her passenger. She was off the road and in the ditch—was lucky that she didn't flip—cracked into a power pole that sheared off just above the base. The snapped lines fell into the trees and started arcing instantly, quickly lighting crisp leaves of a scrub oak's mossy canopy. Before the deputy climbed out the side door of his totaled rig, he'd radioed for extra help: the fire trucks and an ambulance.

Cup Half Full
May 1997

HANK LOOKED at his mother sitting silent on a kitchen chair, the room filled with the pleasant scent of cinnamon and citrus peel. He'd fixed her a midmorning snack to keep her blood sugar in line, now wondered should he leave her be or stay to keep her company. On the kitchen table was a steaming cup of herbal tea, most of a biscotti Myrna'd barely had one nibble from. Staring at the china cup and unaware that Hank was there, she was trying to remember what it was she has to do today. The problem is she really needs some coffee mixed with half-and-half, two heaping spoons of sugar and a Bismarck from the doughnut shop. She needs some kind of pick-me-up, a fresh tank-full of premium: what she'd give right now for one good deep drag off a cigarette! *That* would get her heart rate up, clear the cobwebs from her brain, help her to decide which of her chores to do this afternoon. Daniel asked, if she went out, to dash into the dry cleaner's; they're out of milk since Hank is going through another growing spurt. It seems like it was yesterday that Hank was wearing Buster Browns; now every time she blinks it seems he needs a longer pair of pants. She's not sure what is wrong but she can't get herself up from her chair, can't quite get her eyes to focus: sitting staring into space. If she could only stand up she'd go take another Dexedrine: give herself a boost while helping shed a couple extra pounds. But now that it has crossed her mind, a cigarette is all she needs: to fill her lungs and clear the fog and get her butt up off this chair.

Hank had wiped the counters down and emptied out the dish drainer, happy that the sun was out and streaming through the windowpanes. It was now the third day in a row that Myrna hadn't hit him once, hadn't called his wife a slut or *fat-assed-little-two-bit-tramp*. He thought not to disturb her since she was lost somewhere in reverie, glad to see that Valium worked as well as methocarbamol. He poured himself a mug of tea, deciding that he'd go outside: throw the dog a ball so that poor Trouble got some exercise.

Myrna racks her brain for where she might have stashed a pack of smokes: back behind the hatbox on the top shelf of the laundry room. There might be some in the garage, way back in a cupboard drawer, bottom of that stack of pants and shirts Hank grew out of last year. She knows one day she'll quit for good but life is really stressful now with vacuuming and making beds and picking Hank up after school. And *yeah yeah yeah*, she knows that's life, but it's the only real vice she has: every now and then she sneaks a smoke beneath the bathroom fan. She doesn't drink, tries not to swear, and hasn't cheated even once; dinner's on the table when Dan comes home from the hospital. She tries to be the wife and mom her husband and her son deserve, to pack Hank's lunch and iron clothes and make love every Tuesday night. But in her purse she always keeps some matches and a roll of mints, since sometimes she just has to have a lung full of tobacco smoke.

...

Hank flipped the breaker for the stove and whistled for his big black dog, heard the scratch of claws against the wood floor in the living room. It was only quarter after ten, but the air felt nice and warm outside, the sun above the cottonwoods had dried the dew off of the lawn. It already needed mowing and the blackberries had grown a yard and he'd need at least two hours to set a dozen stinking gopher traps. Lidia would come at one so he could work all afternoon, whacking weeds and cutting grass and breathing lots of toxic fumes. He'd like to hire some laborers to take care of the dirty work, but couldn't justify the cost since he wasn't earning money yet.

He had almost given up on ever hearing from the stupid Board: two months since he'd gone in for a second formal interview. Every time he called he would get put onto eternal hold; he'd leave another message for the stinking bastards to ignore. He wondered what would happen if they never let him work again; if he'd find satisfaction simply raising pear and apple trees. He was thinking of this all the time now: what else could I learn to do? Garbageman or grocery clerk or maintenance of county roads. But every time he dwelt on it he fell into a funky mood, and right now he had sunshine and a big black dog anxious to play. So he focused on these simple things like what he'd like to fix for lunch, how nice it was that so far Myrna hadn't hit him yet today.

She can't remember how long now she's gone without a cigarette: Daniel says she'll do fine if she makes it past the two-week mark. When Daniel came back from the war he'd kindly asked if she would quit, that he'd prefer she didn't set a bad example for the kid. She almost told him he could leave, that she knew what was best for Hank, but that was all he'd asked for and so how could she begrudge him that? It took Daniel about a year to get over his war fatigue, to not sit up in bed each time a dog would bark out in the street. The afternoon they'd married he had sworn that he would not come home, that all his family's cursed and he was certain he would die at war. But all he'd done was sprain an ankle stepping off a transport plane; nasty rash under his arms from high heat and humidity. The Greyhound is an hour late, waiting for Daniel's return, and Myrna hopes Hank doesn't see how everybody stares at them. She keeps her own eyes on the floor, her four-year-old between her knees, knowing everyone who's seen would love to know the story here.

The station is now filled with children watching for returning dads, anxious women waiting for their families to be whole again. Myrna opens up her bag, removes a box of Cracker Jacks; pulling back the top she doles them out into Hank's waiting hands. Every other minute she decides that she's an idiot; any man with half a wit would not acknowledge knowing them. She'd married a young man she'd been engaged to for a half-an-hour: a tender boy with orange hair and a face pitted with acne scars. It's all so convoluted since she can't predict what Dan might do, and four years is a long time even if she'd known him earlier. But he'd only asked, before he left, if she would like to marry him, and the only thing she knows now is she can't imagine why he did. The depot's filled with bus exhaust and freshly atomized perfumes on women hushing children while they sit together visiting. Hank twists in-between her knees so that he looks up at her face; Myrna doesn't hear the first three times her son whispers her name. He looks so much like Frank that she sees nothing but his Japanese: eyes and skin and straight black hair she combs back with her fingertips. She feels he knows she's anxious and his eyes reflect all her concern, then in his funny voice Hank tells her *you can have the peanuts, Mom.*

...

Outside Hank had finally found a tennis ball that he could throw, and Trouble's ears had perked up and she was bouncing like a puppy dog. He pitched the ball off underhand, protecting his rotator cuff, sprained while pulling hose out from a crosslay on a Tuesday night. Tossing it between the trees, he watched as Trouble chased the ball, couldn't quite explain why he was proud his dog was beautiful. She had a handsome blocky head and fur like polished ebony and her big brown eyes got even bigger every time she looked at him. Evenings around nine o'clock she'd put her muzzle on his lap, pushing back the pages of the book that was putting him to sleep. He'd feel her tail thump through the floor, her hot breath warm against his crotch, roll his eyes because he knew he can't deny her anything.

...

Myrna finally finds the prize deep in the box of Cracker Jacks, takes it out and reads the joke that's printed on the envelope. She's not sure if Hank gets it since his laughter seems a bit too forced; he takes the prize and puts it in the pocket of his little suit. She thinks he looks adorable with short pants and a clip-on tie, a jacket with a turtle patch embroidered on the breast pocket. He looks like such a little man, ready to take on the world:

"Aren't you going to open it?"

"I'm saving it to give to Dad."

...

It's half-an-hour later that they hear the Greyhound's parking brake: a hiss of air like opening a soda that's been shaken up. Dragging Hank up on her lap, she squeezes him around the chest, whispers in his ear that there's a chance he won't be on the bus. All the other women are now gathering their children near, pinching cheeks and slicking hair so that they're more presentable. Myrna kept her seat and put her arms around her patient son, trying to recall a face from three days back four years ago. She loves Hank more than life itself, but he doesn't make life easier: if not for him she'd still be living quietly in Edgarville.

...

Trouble finally dropped the ball and flopped down tired on the ground; using his back pocket, Hank wiped slobber off his throwing hand. He thought that he should go inside to see if she was still okay, double-check that what he gave her wasn't causing side effects. It seemed that all she'd need was just a whisper of *diazepam,* a tiny taste of *Percocet* or a quarter of a *Flexeril*. He hadn't told his wife yet but she'd noticed Myrna had improved, commenting to Hank she was surprised how quiet Myrna'd been. If all it took was medicine, then he'd bring her for a checkup soon, ask her doctor for whatever dose kept her from hitting him. Squatting next to Trouble, Hank grabbed fur behind her floppy jowls, pulled her head up toward him so his chin was on her blocky skull. The orchard lay in ruins around this old dilapidated house; if Myrna weren't a problem he could salvage something from this mess. Imagining the dead trees gone, he saw long rows of blueberries: friendly little bushes you can harvest standing on the ground. His mind's eye saw the house re-sided, chimney mortar now repaired, insulated windows and a workshop over the garage. He'd have them build some trellises so Jessie could grow table grapes, a bunch of climbing roses and a handsome pink wisteria. The dog made quiet snoring sounds whenever Hank was petting her, hands sunk in the loose flesh of his amiable Labrador. Above the panting of his dog, Hank heard the fire siren blare, starting down at bass and quickly rising up through baritone. Standing, Hank patted his leg so Trouble knew to come with him, glad to have one friend who didn't think he might have killed someone.

...

Myrna's sitting at the table, sips the funny-tasting tea, doesn't like the licorice in this dried-up biscuit she's been served. But she's noticing how still it is, the families having been rejoined, the soldier's have been welcomed and then quickly trundled off for home. If he doesn't show up she will take her son back to their room, tell the guys downstairs that her poor husband's prophecy came true. She's looking at a future cooking dinners for the firemen, Hank with lots of "uncles" but nobody wants to be his dad. She doesn't hear her son's voice till the third time that he says her name, and she looks up from the floor to see they're not the only ones still there. A man stands with his duffle hanging from his shoulder epaulet; not the lanky boy she'd been remembering for several years. He'd taken off his cap as he'd approached them on the station bench, eyes show that he's unsure if she even recognizes him.

"I was afraid you wouldn't wait," Dan says, his eyes at last connect with hers, and she realizes all this time she'd thought her husband's eyes were blue.

The Deer & The Elephant
May 1997

CHIEF GEORGE NAGOYA was first on scene, arriving in the booster truck, told dispatch he would be Command and that he'd need Pacific Light *right now!* to cut the power off. There was fire climbing up a tree and the cop had a big forehead cut and the woman in the SUV was complaining that her neck was hurt. But he couldn't reach to hold her head with a power line draped on her car and a jillion volts of juice just waiting for a solid path to ground. Using his best Fire Chief voice he told her not to climb outside, that *everything is fine* but she would have to stay put for a while. She wasn't looking too convinced with the windshield sparkling on her lap and the antlers of a six-point buck still twitching in the right-hand seat.

"Dispatch, send a second ambulance. Have law enforcement close the road. There's fire in the trees so you should notify state forestry."

George gave the cop a wad of gauze to press against his bleeding cut, asked him nice if he would sit still on the bumper of the truck. But of course he wouldn't listen since he's not supposed to be a wimp, insisting that the bleeding gash was just a superficial scratch. So George decided he could wait until the sheriff got on scene to order him to let the firemen fit him with a C-collar. George wanted to pull two-inch hose and squirt some water in the trees, but even that was not safe till the power lines had been shut down. He ran back to the woman who sat petrified inside her car, making sure she really knew she couldn't step down on the ground.

Her big rig was a totaled wreck, the front and back accordioned, the airbag hung deflated like the scrotum of a neutered dog.

Jessie tried to calm herself, her chest hurt with each breath she took, sitting in a pool of glass, a dead deer as a passenger. In all her years of driving fast she'd never had an accident; she gently wiggled hands and feet, afraid they might not work quite right. She slowly took an inventory, arms and legs, her knees and hips; everything seemed a-okay until she tried to turn her head. A sharp pain took her breath away and shot her with adrenaline: *Oh my god I broke my neck!* She wished that Hank was with her now. A man stood with a radio and told her to stay in the car, said the buzz she's hearing means her car's touching a power line.

George asked if she was still okay, if anything had changed at all, thinking that the buck would make a freezer full of venison. He'd been on scene two minutes but already it felt like an hour, and George was desperate to keep track of traffic on the radio. Dispatch said Pacific Light had a truck in the vicinity, guessing that they had about a fifteen minute ETA. Hooster had an engine rolling, but that was twenty miles away, and he hadn't heard a word yet from the other Edgar volunteers. He was getting too damn old for this, his back hurt and his elbows creaked, prostate so enlarged it took him half-an-hour to take a leak. Pulling out a preconnect he had to stop to catch his breath, feeling like the canvas hose weighed twice as much as usual. He rushed up to the booster truck to bring the water pump to life, cranking up the pressure to one-hundred-fifty psi. The water filled the flaccid hose that snaked beside him on the ground; George could hear, still miles away, the siren of their pumper truck. The driver would be Evan Smith who won't talk on the radio, a good man but sometimes George thought to tell him *just get over it*! He hoped Evan was not alone, they were going to need a lot of help; the deputy was dripping blood while pulling fusies from his trunk. George looked at the trees again, the fire spreading limb to limb; six o'clock was when the evening breeze would start back up the hill. Above the smoke and truck exhaust was a whiff of something horrible; beneath the crumpled SUV George saw a drip of gasoline. Already he could see how this disaster was about to play; that something really bad was going to happen any minute now. He was trying to ignore the giant elephant on top his chest, the aching pain now moving down his left arm through his scapula.

...

He'd seen a lot of wrecks and fires in twenty years of being Chief, but ever since the mill burned he had lost some of his confidence. George couldn't get his breath back since he pulled out all the fire hose, and he was trying to make his mind up how to deal with the gasoline. The best thing was to smother it with half-a-foot of Class B foam, but that might ground the vehicle and fry the woman trapped inside. If he only could remember which: if foam conducts or insulates; he didn't want to risk a life to find out he was wrong again. So he planned to simply watch and wait until the power was shut off; pray-to-God that some stray spark won't drift down from the trees above. The bleeding cop was lighting flares on the road north of the accident, and from the south at last he saw the red lights of their fire truck.

It was now at least five minutes since George pulled up to the crumpled cars and he radioed to dispatch *we are going to need more help up here*. The awful feeling that he had was high stress and anxiety; his legs felt made of lead; he rubbed a fist against his aching chest. He stepped back to the SUV, made sure the woman was okay; told her since her neck hurt it was vital that she didn't move. The power buzz had disappeared beneath the pump and engine noise, and he was having trouble breathing with a band of steel around his lungs. He felt a wave of nausea, a sudden flood of drenching sweat; Jessie hadn't moved an inch, sat rigid in the driver's seat. She heard the fire in the trees and smelled the dripping gasoline; she tried to keep from panicking by focusing on little things.

Without turning her head she tried to get a good look at this man: ghastly shade of ashen gray, a sick expression on his face. For the briefest moment Jessie had been startled by something she saw: this man could be her husband's brother, older by a dozen years. Their noses were identical, the color of their skin the same; Hank looked just as sick before the jury's verdict at the trial. But when the man turned 'round so he could talk into the radio, she looked down at the sparkling bits of glass spread out across her lap. It was like somebody dropped a sack of diamonds from a jewelry heist, a fortune worth of precious stones spilled on the leather bucket seats. She turned her head a little so that she could take a better look: a lethal-looking antler rack, an eye big as a chicken egg. Mercifully the deer seemed dead, as still as lilies on a pond, and she'd never been this close before except once at a petting zoo. The deer was specked with broken glass, but there wasn't any blood involved, and Jessie reached a hand out to discover what its fur felt like.

She was startled by how warm it was, her mind was thinking dead and cold, but also thinking soft and smooth though it was scratchy as a kitten's tongue. The coat felt full of grit and sand, like a dog out rolling on the beach; she picked at something in the fur that was squishy as a shriveled grape. It came loose from the deer so she could hold it up before her eyes: it looked like a big blueberry with tiny, moving legs and arms. As her eyes got round and wide she screamed and threw the thing aside; the dead deer's coat was crawling with bloodsucking little parasites. Pressing hard against her seat, her instinct was to run away, fumble for her safety belt and reach out for the door handle. But it was not until a sudden pain went bolting down her neck and spine that she remembered she was not to move or touch her feet down on the ground.

Her heart now beating twice as fast, she scanned the scene before her car, across the crumpled hood out through the place the windshield used to be. A fire truck came howling up and stopped two dozen yards away; two firemen climbed from the cab, and one was her beloved Hank. She'd never seen him dressed up in a helmet and a fire suit; was certain now she'd be okay since there was no one she could trust as much. But he barely even looked her way though she was desperate for eye contact; she watched her husband struggle getting hose down off the fire truck. He should have rushed right to her side to save her from the ticks and fire, instead of placing tire chocks to keep the truck from rolling off. The other man was telling Hank what he was now supposed to do, pointing to compartments filled with fusies and orange safety cones. This was Hank's first real fire since he became a volunteer; the only other call they'd had was to help an old man off the floor.

Hank could not think where things were or what he was supposed to do; there was fire in the trees but they said not to squirt the fire hose. Evan pointed out how wires were arcing in the flaming limbs, told Hank to take flares and block the south end of the accident. There were other volunteers arriving in their private cars and trucks so one side of the road looked like a party at the neighbor's house. It took Hank half-a-minute till he found the box of fusie flares, another one to sprint the hundred yards to lay them on the road. He liked the way the flares ignite, a snap across the plastic cap: a satisfying sudden pop of bright red light and sulfur smoke.

    Hank hustled back to Evan to get more instructions what to do, was told to grab a stop sign and an orange vest and a radio. He'd rather try squirting the hose or help to get the victim out but knew that stopping traffic was as vital as the rest of it. Evan said that Hank should take the north end past the accident, hold all of the traffic but the ambulance and power truck. Hank was worrying about his mom, hoped Lidia got there on time; left Myrna in the house alone complaining of the siren noise. Walking past the accident he finally got to rubberneck: the cop car's nose was flattened with the SUV a mangled mess. It dawned on Hank now all at once: the color of the SUV, the special order alloy wheels, the woman in the driver's seat. He dropped the two-way radio, the stop sign clattered to the ground; rushing to his wife's side he felt someone grab his turnout sleeve. He pulled his arm violently away, about to grab the door handle, when George Nagoya blind-sides him and yells *the car's electrified!* George was pushing on Hank's chest, who strained to reach his injured wife; he pointed to the power line that was complicating everything. Hank stopped pushing back so hard, then walked past George up to the car, horrified his wife was trapped with nothing he could do for her. Jessie seemed all right except for looking tense and terrified; was sitting staring straight ahead, a death-grip on the steering wheel. Hank was not sure what to do but stand and ask if she was fine:

    "It hurts to move my neck but it's this filthy deer that bothers me!"

...

George looked up to see the fire had spread south into three more trees, the pressure pounding on his chest, the pain spread further down his arm. Pushing Hank back from the car took all the energy he had; his legs were weak, was hard to breathe, he couldn't think straight anymore. The last thing that he did was hand his radio to Evan Smith, tell him he was in command *while I sit down and rest a bit.*

Evan didn't understand, he never talked to radios; he turned to give it back to George but George was staggering away. That was right when Brenda brought the pike-pole from the fire truck: twelve feet long, a metal hook, a handle made of fiberglass. She'd been a volunteer for years and didn't pussyfoot around; she boldly snagged the power line and flipped it off into the ditch. The wires cracked and sparked another fire in the underbrush, but at least they now could touch the car and get the victim stabilized. And later George would wonder why he hadn't thought of that himself; embarrassed that he stood there demonstrating more incompetence. The car's door wouldn't open and so Evan got the Halligan; Brenda's husband Paul had brought the backboard and the spider straps. Roger Noji tried to pull the deer out of the other side; the antlers catching on the empty airbag for the passenger. Hank was mostly in the way, he'd never seen this done before, desperate to help Evan pry the door off with the metal bar.

Jessie had been watching all this from the corners of her eyes; someone reached inside to put a plastic collar 'round her neck. It was tightened half-a-turn too snug so she couldn't swallow very well, her right ear folded down but then her neck feel better right away. Someone else had climbed in back and held her head still from behind, she wished that she could turn around to see who was taking care of her. It was like two disembodied hands had clamped themselves around her ears; a quiet, gently soothing voice said *everything will be okay*. The voice narrated how they'd slide the backboard underneath her butt, then swing her 'round and lay her down and strap her so she couldn't move. She was not supposed to help at all, but let them do the dirty work; her only job was stay calm and imagine safe in bed at home.

—*Better yet, imagine that you're lying on a sunny beach: a chaise lounge and a good book and a favorite sweet umbrella drink. . . .* The voice said to relax her arms, to gently drop them to her sides, to concentrate on breathing and the sunshine on the sparkling waves. *And every time a wave comes in it reaches up to bathe your feet, then as the wave retreats again you feel yourself relax a bit. . . .* She knew what it was trying to do, the voice was trying to hypnotize; she sometimes used this trick herself on patients with anxiety. It really was a good idea, to let herself relax control, allow the firefighters someone nice and calm to take care of.

—As the waves reach up the beach you slowly fill your lungs with air, and as the waves go out again you gently exhale through your nose. . . .

The sun gleamed off each cresting wave like diamonds mixed into the foam; each time the breakers washed the beach she felt her shoulders drop some more. The hands holding her head were firm but gentle so she couldn't move, and she let the hands protect her neck, the calm voice whisper in her ear. She knew that they were frantic to remove her safely from the car, then put her in an ambulance and take her to the hospital. She'd been in trances lots of times while training in psychology, but this time something kept Jessie from giving up her vigilance. Her eyes had not completely closed, she knew the deer was next to her, that Hank was half-a-yard away while wrestling with the stubborn door. Every time a wave came up to touch her feet with salty foam, she got the feeling she should open up her eyes and look around. The scene was filled with energy, the air charged with adrenaline, the crackling of the blazing trees, the smell of dripping gasoline. And when she cleared her bleary eyes, backing off the sandy beach, this was what she finally saw: a man out kneeling on the road. No one else could see him since their focus was on saving her; the man pitched forward on his chest, his face against the yellow line. Willing Hank to look her way by hoarsely whispering his name, she tried to speak above the noise of breathless grunting volunteers. At last she heard her husband's quiet voice ask if she was all right; he wasn't in her field of view, but she whispered *someone else is hurt!* Motioning with chin and eyes, she sensed that Hank had turned to look, knowing he was battling his instinct not to leave his wife. *Go!* was all she had to say, and Hank was bolting up the road, yelling for a volunteer to bring another medic bag.

...

There aren't that many things that cause someone to crumple to the ground; statistics said that only one cause dropped excited firemen. Kneeling down beside the Chief, Hank put a hand against his neck: the skin was damp without a pulse, the diagnosis obvious. This was what Hank trained to do, not stopping cars or pulling hose, but bringing people back to life after their ailing hearts had died. He gently rolled George on his back, his face the gray of newspaper, saw Roger Noji rushing the defibrillator from the truck. Hank put his lips around the mouth, the taste of salty, clammy skin; he felt the lungs expanding then his own hot breath come out again. The last time Hank felt his own breath was back about three years ago, when Nathan had reached nine years old and had a brand-new heart installed. The boy had spent a half a month at a San Francisco hospital, the closest place to Portland with a heart transplant facility. Everything went beautifully until Nate finally made it home, spiked a fever even with the massive steroids he was on. Hank put him in the ICU, was doing early morning rounds; didn't want to wake the mother sleeping in the folding chair. The boy had opened up his eyes when Hank had gently touched his arm, gave Hank a brief, authentic smile then slowly closed his eyes again. Hank had stepped out of the room to ask the aide for Nathan's chart when the monitor in front of her started making an unpleasant sound. *He must have pulled a chest lead off* and the aide went in to check the boy, and Hank was waiting for the chart when the aide yelled *Doctor Davenport!* Already she had pushed the button on the wall above the bed: a flashing light, a ringing bell, the sound of running down the hall. He looked like he was sleeping and Hank shook his arm to wake him up; the monitor above the bed looked like an earthquake seismograph. The boy smelled soft as baby sweat as Hank filled Nathan's lungs with air; so strange to smell his own breath strong with coffee from the cart outside. *There's no reason for this at all,* there was something else that must be wrong; the boy now had a brand-new heart: a teenage girl from Iowa. The room filled up with nursing staff, two interns and a resident, but Hank had full command and hoarsely called out for which drugs to push.

There was no way Hank would let him die, they'd been through way too much for this; fourteen months of waiting for a heart to fit his narrow chest. Hank had a hundred other patients nicer than this little brat, but Hank's heart lost the battle when the boy said he liked *lobster bisque*. His favorite dish was calamari, loved the taste of escargot; his mother rolled her eyes and said *I shouldn't have indulged the boy.* Every now and then Hank took the boy out to a sushi place where little plates went slowly 'round a never-ending carousel. Hank loved the way Nate's eyes got wide when something strange went sliding by, scanning all the dishes for the next one that had tentacles. Nate was two parts black-and-white and two parts no-one-knew-for-sure, adopted as an infant by a couple couldn't have their own. When Nate was nearly eight he could have passed for maybe four or five, and Hank got too involved because Nate made him think about himself. It was not that they were so alike, since they were total opposites: Hank could never talk back even if his mother asked him nice. Hank was calling out for *epi* and another dose of *lidocaine,* inspecting all the leads again to double-check the monitor. The intern placed an ET tube; already had a central line; with every dose of *epi* there was a squiggle on the dark-blue screen. Hank couldn't stand it anymore, he pushed somebody's hands away, his own now thumped the skinny chest, the ropy scar the surgeon made. Every time Hank shocked the boy he bucked like this was rodeo; Hank could taste the air charged with electrons flying everywhere. He'd helped the mom with fundraisers to pay for Nathan's medicines; pulled a lot of strings to get his name moved up the transplant list. The boy was a celebrity: a full-length feature article, his picture on the front page of *The Sunday Oregonian.* Hank ran the code for two full hours, a dozen rounds of protocol; whenever he would try to stop, some muscle in Nate's leg would twitch. The screen would flash a tiny blip, a nurse would see a finger move, and Hank would call for yet another big dose of *bretyllium.* If Hank had been a surgeon he'd have opened up the healing scar, thrust his hand into the chest and squeezed some life into the boy. He was sensitive enough to know the staff wished he would call it off, but Hank could not believe that little Nathan's life would end like this. He'd never run a code so long, at most they only last an hour; he'd shocked the boy a dozen times and doubled all the drug doses. Half of Hank could not accept that he had failed to save the boy; the other half knew there was no point hoping for a miracle. He leaned his head against the wall and asked the staff to mark the time; he pulled the breathing tube himself, the nurse turned off the monitor. It was just Hank and the PICU nurse, the mother crying in the hall, when Nathan's chest twitched once like it was gasping for a breath of air. Hank knew the boy was truly dead and the twitch was muscle memory, and he stopped the nurse from reaching up to turn back on the monitor. But he couldn't stand imagining that Nate was somehow trapped inside, that he had tried too hard to simply keep the corpuscles alive. The boy's face was so small Hank's hand could cover both the nose and mouth, and the nurse stared as Hank stood for several minutes with his hand clamped tight.

...

Jessie's eyes were still half-closed, she saw the crest of breaking waves, her husband placing paddles on the smooth chest of the crumpled man. It only took a single shock, the man trying to get back up, the waves came rushing up the beach to help her shoulders to relax. She hadn't been abandoned, they had almost got her door open, the hands still firmly held her head, the tick-bag of a deer was gone. They were prying on the door hinge with a nasty-looking metal bar; she finally heard the wailing of the ambulance they'd sent for her. And when they got the door to move, it sounded like a haunted house, some gruesome horror movie when they open up the coffin lid. It was fingernails on blackboard and the sandy beach had disappeared, and she saw the ambulance back up to take the other man away. She was giving in to panic that the medics had forgotten her, as if she'd been abandoned at the altar on her wedding day. Hank was with the other man, they'd put him on the stretcher now, and as they rolled the man in back Hank stopped to look across at her. She wanted him to be with her but the other man was critical, and it took all of her selflessness to let him leave her there alone. Her head nodded a half-an-inch, she read the words that crossed his lips, then watched a medic tell Hank that *we don't have room for passengers.*

They were sliding something under her, was scary as they pushed and pulled; all done on the count of three and she was out and safely on the ground. Evan Smith was in command, he watched them quickly put her down; at last he saw Pacific Light come 'round the corner to the south. His hand was on the radio and dispatch had been calling him; he had to press the button but he couldn't think what words to say. There were half-a-dozen volunteers and a cop who had a forehead cut and they'd need at least two tow trucks and more help to put the forest out. They'd spread a layer of foam across the gas the SUV had spilled, but the wind had blown the foam so that the puddle was exposed again. Evan glanced then at the deer they'd dragged a few feet from the wreck; he looked because he thought he saw the back leg twitch a little bit. An ember wafted from the trees and landed on the leaking gas: a momentary burst of flame that knocked two firefighters down. This was what he told them later sitting 'round the fire hall: the big buck got up on its feet just as the gas leak caught on fire. He *swore-to-God* that this was true, though no one else saw anything: the buck leaped through the ball of fire and bound into the flaming trees, the sharp tips of ts rack ablaze like candles on a birthday cake.

Beneath The Bed
May 1997

SOMETIMES SHE FORGETS she's old, surprised by creaking brittle bones, the gray hairs broken by her comb, how urgent when she has to go. Myrna wakes up from a nap and can't remember where she is, knowing that she's going to leak if she can't find a bathroom quick. She gets up from the bed or chair—she can't believe the aches and pains—starts racing 'round from room to room although she's merely shuffling. *Where the hell's the bathroom!?* She is searching for the echo sound, the vague increased humidity, the lingering smell of flatulence. It's naps that get her all messed up, erasing recent memory; she can't remember lying down: *morning or late afternoon?* The carpet in the hallway has a pattern she's not seen before, and the living room is furnished with somebody else's furniture. The only thing familiar is a picture hanging on the wall remembered from a trip they took when Hank was eight or nine years old. Maybe it was yesterday, and maybe fifty years ago; the photograph is black and white with brown-red tones of sepia. She was seated in a straight-back chair, her son and husband next to her: Hank dressed in a cowboy suit and Daniel in old farmer clothes. They'd made her wear a long white dress with bonnet and a petticoat, and this is what's confusing her: she's not sure if it's real or fake. Her mother had a dress like that, and her father could have worn those clothes, the twins once had a matching set of cowboy hats and cowboy boots. But that was when she was a child—*God knows how long ago that was*—and Myrna can't just stand and stare: she's leaking in her underpants.

She finds a door that leads outside—perhaps a privy in the back—and she's startled by how late it is, the whole day nearly over with. The sun is low on Blowdown Ridge and the temperature is early June, the cottonwoods are blowing bits of cotton over everything. It drifts down through the slanted light like snowflakes in a winter storm; the wind is warm and from the west in gusts that nearly knock her down. The cottonwoods are massive beasts that tower high above the yard; the rustle of their leaves is like the ocean when the surf is rough. She hears each gust of wind approach as it rushes through the flashing leaves and she feels the warmth against her face as the sound comes crashing over her.

Even though the wind is warm it raises goose bumps on her arms, and Myrna can't hold back the tide: she hikes her housedress, squats and pees. It soaks into her right sock then the green grass that she's balanced on; a chill runs up and down her spine as the burning urgency subsides. All of this upsets her as she stands and glances left and right; she straightens out her housedress for the two cows in the neighbor's field. She leans against a picnic table, bends to reach her yellowed sock, knees popped when she squatted down and now her hips and low-back ache. She feels about a hundred but she can't remember how she aged; the skin around her ankle is as flaky as a well-baked pie. She's so stiff she can barely reach, but at last she hooks a fingertip, slides the damp sock off her foot, distressed how poorly she has aged.

Myrna looks across the field and suddenly knows where she is: she's standing in the backyard of the *widow-witch* of Edgarville. She and Margaret Beechnut would go walking through the woods nearby, the witch-lady would stand out on her porch and scream obscenities. *You two girls should be in school!* and *Don't you dare walk through my yard!!* and *Both of you will burn in hell! The Lord will make you pay for this!!* The first time that this happened they both turned around and ran back home, but after that they'd sprint past for the safety of the Douglas fir. Now Myrna looks across the field at cottonwoods and evergreens, the underbrush of vine maples, the thorny brambled blackberries. Fearing that the widow might soon burst out of the kitchen door, she flings her dirty sock behind a clump of big chrysanthemums. The grass is cool against her foot and beckons for a little stroll; she reaches for her other sock: can barely stand to bend that far.

As she starts out of the yard a big black dog comes bounding up, sniffs her hand, looks at her face, then trots a yard or two ahead. Across the field she finds the trail that leads down to the little creek where she would hide when Mother had another batch of *beans* to can. In June it could get plenty warm, the winter mud all turned to dust so Edgarville was brown and gray and grit would make her molars crunch. But the air along the creek was cool—a patch of trees they hadn't cut—and she'd wade in so the silky mud would squish up in between her toes. She'd pull her cotton dress up but the hem would still get soaking wet and snag on twigs and branches as she gleaned a thimbleberry bush. Sometimes she would be alone and sometimes Peggy Smith would come; they'd sit and watch the twigs and leaves float down the irrigation ditch. The smell today is just the same, the musky scent of skunk cabbage, the sweet breeze flowing down the ridge, the spicy hint of distant fire. She doesn't recognize the trail, but otherwise it's all unchanged: the fern and wild ginger floor, the canopy of cedar boughs. The black dog seems familiar and she's glad to have the company, watching as the bitch dog sniffs the air then dashes off the trail. Then Myrna steps on something sharp and looks down at her bunioned feet, wonders why she's walking in the woods without her shoes and socks.

She might have taken off her shoes while wading in the muddy creek, maybe left them somewhere back along the logging railroad tracks. The train divides the woods in two, brings logs down from the upper slopes; she's young and barefoot feeling all the coolness of the metal rail. She'd grip her toes around the lip, her arms held straight out from her sides; she'd walk along until she felt the big train coming down the hill. It starts out as a tiny hum—the vaguest little tickling—and she stops and closes tight her eyes and puts her hands over her ears. As the train comes closer she can feel it vibrate through the rail, climbing up her ankles to the soft spot just behind her knees. She knows how far away it is by how far up it's tingling: a couple hundred yards when it starts tickling between her legs. She doesn't open up her eyes until it climbs her spinal cord, bursting through her head so that she hears it from inside her brain. She trusts that God is on her side because she's of the chosen faith, protected by her prayers at night, the prophesies of Joseph Smith. The train is twenty yards away when Myrna opens up her eyes, jumps off as the blast comes from the big train's rusty steam whistle. She stands beside the rushing train—there's nothing like it in the world: the massive weight, the pulsing hum, the smell of freshly fallen trees. The engineer sticks out his head and curses her for scaring him, although he's never hit the brakes in all her years of doing this. His fear is that the brakes will spark and start a fire in the brush; the train is speeding down the hill at over fifteen miles an hour.

...

She's thinking that the railroad tracks are off the trail a dozen yards, and even though she has no shoes she's heading through the underbrush. There's perhaps an hour of evening left before the woods start getting dark, and her brothers told her lots of times: *Be careful when you're in the woods, they're filled with wild animals and wicked gentile sodomites.* Myrna's startled by the sound of something crashing through the brush: a big black bear is charging at her, leaping over fallen trees, scares her half-to-death until she sees the bear is just a dog. She watches as it sniffs a branch then looks at her and wags its tail, waiting for a sign of which direction they'll be going next. Myrna's trying to ignore the dampness in her underpants, remembering specifically one time after the train went past. Years ago she's all alone and standing by the railroad tracks; she still could sense the tingling thrill that's spread between her slender breasts. It takes another minute for the sense to slowly dissipate so it isn't for some moments till she feels the eyes upon her back.

It's nothing that she can explain, a feeling that she gets sometimes; she slowly turns around to find a coyote with its hackles up. She knows she shouldn't be afraid—the coyote's more afraid of her—but still there might be pups nearby so who knows what the bitch will do? The animal looks horrible with shaggy variegated coat and dull black eyes and tattered ears just twenty feet away from her. The coyote put a front paw out and slowly took a forward step and Myrna slowly reaches down to pick a stick up off the ground. The coyote's lips begin to curl and show an inch of yellow fang; Myrna looks for bits of foam around the black edge of its mouth. Her heart is rising in her throat, she's not sure what she's supposed to do; she'd run but doesn't want a chunk bit from the backside of her leg. The coyote takes another step, its ruff stands stiff along its back, and suddenly the stick she holds does not seem nearly big enough. Is she supposed to stand up tall and shout and wave her arms around? Or crouch and slowly back away and try not to look menacing? She knows that if a bear attacks she's not supposed to kick and scratch, but playing dead won't help fight off a creature that eats carrion. The coyote's fangs are wet with drool, surprised it doesn't lick its chops; Myrna's indecision has her mouth as dry as Edgar dust. She wants to throw the stick now but she's always had such crappy aim: the stick will land behind her in the bushes several yards away. She doesn't even know Frank's there until she hears the rifle pop; aiming for the coyote's head, he hits the shoulder blade instead. This will be the second time that Frank Nagoya intervened, walking with a rifle hunting rabbits in the afternoon. The rifle's barely big enough to dent the soft skin of a squirrel, but still it makes a noise and hurts enough to make the coyote turn.

The boy is obviously proud, he's saved a damsel in distress; he's sixteen with a rifle and his feet a foot above the ground. He hunts off through the bushes, finds the fresh-dead carcass of a deer: the reason that the coyote wanted Myrna not to walk that way. They both know that a year ago he'd pulled her from the burning school; twice he's saved her life and Myrna wants to pay him back somehow. She tells him that she thinks he's brave; he says *don't be ridiculous;* she says that he's a good shot but he says *I couldn't hit a barn.* They walk along the railroad tracks where no one ever comes around; the train's been by and won't be back until they've cut more logs to haul. They're walking back to get her shoes, still barefoot balanced on the rail, and Frank is wearing clunky boots bought from the store for Japanese. Myrna's not sure what to say, so she keeps on piling compliments, remembering the time Frank came in second in a running race. It's starting to get challenging, he won't accept a single one: *I only came in second because Donny wasn't there that day.* He *isn't* brave and he *isn't* fast and his teeth *aren't really* all that straight; when she says he's really smart, he says *that's just the Japanese.* Battling her butterflies, she plays the last card in her hand: *I think that you're the cutest boy of all the boys in Edgarville.*

She likes the way he turns so red beneath the dark tan on his face; he says that he's not cute at all *but you're the one who's beautiful.* There's no one for a quarter mile, the woods so dense they can't be seen; she leans over to kiss his cheek; her bare feet slip off of the rail. Of course he reaches out to grab, his left hand briefly touching breast, and she lets her weight rest in his arms while she gets her feet back underneath. There are magnets in Frank's pockets that are pulling in her hips to his, and she can't quite find the strength to put more space between the two of them. Maybe it had been the train that got her body tingling, the shot of fear back when the coyote showed its snarling yellow fangs. But perhaps she has some special power that turns this young man's cheeks so red, that makes him rather walk with her than shoot at helpless furry things. She finally gets to kiss his cheek, a tiny corner of his mouth, and she doesn't understand but it feels like a grand accomplishment.

    Myrna's feet back under her, Frank quickly takes a small step back, looking like a dog behind a fence who wants to be let out. She's certain if he had a tail she'd feel it thump against her leg and if his ears were like a dog's she knows that they'd be long and soft. She asks to try another kiss but Frank steps back another foot, worried that they might be seen, the train might somehow reappear. He's looking up and down the tracks, the skinny rifle in one hand, then says *okay, but make it quick* and she puts her lips against his mouth. This time it's not a simple peck but long enough to taste his breath, the scent of pine and summer leaves from hunting through the underbrush.

...

Myrna, in the here-and-now, is standing in a clump of trees, lost out in the woods she once knew better than her living room. But her mind has gone back years ago, remembering the railroad tracks, a nice boy who kept blushing every time she gave him compliments. He's not much taller than herself and a grade ahead of her in school and he doesn't smell of dog or cat the way her brother said they did. The thrill is still deep in her chest—the thunder of the logging train—but this time from a simple kiss she's stolen from a Japanese.

...

She walks to school now by herself, the twins finished the year before; halfway down the hill she's joined by Margaret and two younger girls. They're going on about the crushes they all have on little boys: braggarts puffing out their chests with talk of going off to war. *The Krauts are getting out of hand* and *Those stupid Frogs don't stand a chance* and *Churchill is the only one in Europe who has any balls!* But Myrna now has secrets that she's not allowed to talk about: meetings in the woods to kiss while sitting on the railroad tracks. She's not sure what she's supposed to do, but he's such a sweet and tender boy, and when they kiss she likes the way his mouth tastes just the same as hers.

…

And in her mind she's eighteen and it's midnight and the rain has stopped; the living room is silent since the radio has been switched off. She still can hear that quiet click, the small knob on the wireless, the radio announcer's voice still echoes through the stuffy room. Her family's huddled 'round the set and dumbstruck by the news they'd heard: *sneak attack* and *hundreds dead* and *stinking little yellow Nips*. Her brothers start to pledge revenge, they'd like to go enlist tonight: *But what about the local Japs? They're probably all in on it!* And maybe they should go right now and put them under house arrest, confiscate their guns and knives and search for hidden shortwave sets. They could be sending signals now to ask for orders what to do, sent here by their government to spy on pear and apple trees. Their plot is so nefarious, all planned out years and years ago: the Japs planted their orchard rows to spell out secret messages. They're pointing out the reservoir, the farmers' irrigation flume, the warehouses for storing fruit, the Grange Hall that was built last year. Her father's face is getting red, the twins both pace around the room; he leaves three boys to guard the house while he and Sam investigate. She's not sure how long they were gone since her mother sent her off to bed, whispered underneath her breath *this whole thing is ridiculous!* Lying in her darkened room, she's too excited now to sleep, waiting for the sound of guns, the bombs to drop on Edgar Flat. Instead she hears a window tap, so faint she's not sure that it's real, then just a little louder till she pulls her bedroom curtain back. She almost screams to see a man there, hands around a rifle stock; finally recognizes Frank, the gun he shot the coyote with. She slides the window carefully, he's whispering in urgent tones, asking if she'll keep his gun, *my father says get rid of it.* The sheriff had already come to tell them not to leave their farm; his mother spent the evening burning letters they'd received from home. All the Japanese are scared the whites will try to take revenge, that any weapons that they find will justify mistreating them. She's flattered that he came to her—that *she's* the person he would trust—but knows the twins have gone outside to guard them from the likes of Frank. She puts a finger to her lips and listens to the dripping trees, waiting for the telltale snap of twigs beneath four creeping feet. She knows that if they catch him here they'll beat him till he's nearly dead: there's nothing that they'd rather do than catch a sneaking-yellow-Nip. She hears what might have been a cough and she drags Frank through the window frame; there are footsteps in the hallway so she orders him beneath the bed. It's good her mattress doesn't squeak since she's barely in-between the sheets when the doorknob slowly turns again and Martin sticks his head inside. The curtains flutter in the breeze and Martin walks across the room to slide the window closed again, protect her from the blustering. She wonders what he would have done had Martin glanced beneath the bed, stared into a young face with the black eyes of the enemy.

...

Someone calls her name again and Myrna turns around to look: not a dozen yards away a woman's walking through the woods. Her voice is warm and musical, an accent she can't recognize, but as she calls her name out there's a guarded sense of urgency. She doesn't know this woman and she can't imagine what she wants and the tension hidden in her voice gives Myrna a slight sense of dread. So she doesn't move or answer her, but lets the woman walk on past, calling Myrna's name out in the evening as the woods get dark.

Double Solitaire
May 1997

HANK ASKED the nurse out in the hall to kindly turn the volume down, the constant *beepbeepbeep*ing of the monitor in George's room. For years Hank had ignored the sound, the ticking of his patients' hearts, but now that he was visiting he found it hard to concentrate. The nurse had scowled and heaved a sigh and Hank would swear she rolled her eyes; she fiddled with the buttons but the beeping had stayed just as loud. He was cringing at the IV pump, the crackling pages overhead, the carts *squeak-squeak*ing down the hall, the grounds staff whacking weeds outside. He was not sure how the Chief could sleep through all this racket going on: *That was why the doctor ordered painkillers and sedatives.* Perhaps he'd come back later on when George had had more time to rest; he'd stopped to say *hello* and make sure everything was going well. But the nurse had only said *he's fine,* Hank couldn't look at George's chart; he'd like to know his CPK, the numbers from this morning's blood. He couldn't claim to be his kin, although he knew they looked alike; the nurse said George would have to sign permission forms in triplicate. So he sat there twiddling his thumbs and counting the obnoxious sounds, rising from his chair when George's eyes came open all at once.

"I had the strangest dream," George said without a hint of preamble; he dove right in and told Hank of the flood that wiped out Edgarville.

In the dream George said that he was eight *though maybe I was nine or ten* and he was fishing at the place down where the two forks of the river met. He was down below the Punchbowl and the dam that formed the Edgar Pond and he'd cast his line out upstream when it caught up on a sunken log.

"With every ounce of strength I've got I'm pulling on my fishing pole, when suddenly the log pops like the cork out of a wine bottle." He watched the log go floating past, and then a massive jumbled pile, knowing that the log he'd pulled had caused the mill pond to collapse.

"The whole damn town starts floating by! Folks I haven't seen for years!"

George began describing things: the hotel where the loggers stayed, its balcony on all four sides, a pair of copulating dogs, a section of a lumber flume, the canned goods from the Randal's store. Mrs. Eckles waved at him with a fist of undelivered mail, then floating at an angle came the bell tower from the school that burned.

"And I know that I'm responsible, but they all look like they're having fun." He described a group of loggers playing cards up on a pile of logs. There were saw blades and an Oldsmobile, the teacher like a drowning rat, and the girl who cleaned the hotel rooms *though everybody knows the truth*.

"But then I see my parents on some fruit bins tied into a raft." He waved as they went floating by, his older brother paddling. He'd been alone since he was sixteen, orphaned one kin at a time, but there they were out on the river: didn't even notice him. His dad died falling off a ladder, top rung in a Bartlett tree; his mother had a stroke the second summer in Camp Manzanar; and Frank had been killed in the war, six months before Hiroshima: shot while helping save a bunch of white guys in the Philippines. His family finally saw young George and they started waving happily, but he couldn't hear their greetings with the river rapids rushing by.

...

It was not till he had finished that George took a good look at the man, sitting in a folding chair and backlit by the window frame. It took another minute before George remembered where he was: he'd died two days before but somehow Davenport had brought him back. There was a plastic tube stuck in his arm and he must be on some kind of drugs since he couldn't get his head quite clear enough to shake the dream he'd had.

"How's your wife?" he finally asked.

"Oh, Jessie's fine. Her neck's just sprained."

Hank now stood beside the bed and looked down at this muddled man who rubbed the space between his eyes, his salt-and-pepper hair a mess. No one ever looks good when they're dressed up in those stupid gowns: different colored little wires sneak out around the neck and arms. The nurse had fiddled with the knobs but the monitor still seemed too loud; Hank noticed the dancing line showed a brief run of *bigeminy*. There must have been some illness that was spreading through the elderly, for once again he'd listened to a fantasy called "Edgarville." But there wasn't any place like that, there were only pear and apple trees, a bridge over the river near the place the old mill used to be. He gave George time to clear his head, then asked if he was okay again:

"Fine, but I'd be better if they'd turn that stupid beeping off."

Hank thought about what Jessie said, how he and George both looked alike: the same sharp chin and broad-based nose, the earlobes with the funny notch. There were times when he was young he used to fantasize a family: a mom and dad and siblings who all shared the same genetic traits. He'd daydream they were in a park, a formal garden in Japan: his mother dressed traditional, his father as a samurai. Hank might have his mother's eyes, his nose is from his father's side, how good he is with languages, the fact he's red-green color blind. But he couldn't dwell on it for long, he always felt such guilty pangs, that even simple fleeting thoughts might put a knife through Myrna's heart. *Dan and Myrna Davenport;* Hank couldn't have been luckier: a doctor and a homemaker, the perfect modern family. So every time his mind would start to dwell on where he got his chin he'd slam that door and throw the lock: ungrateful little orphan kid. *So what?* his mother fibbed a lot and his father came home late from work; at least he had a roof and food, a bed and books and undershirts. He understood that they could always change their minds and send him back, that being bad was not the option that it was for normal kids. Hank had always envied all the kids who weren't *unnatural*, who didn't have a guilty sense for taking space up in the house. So he brushed his teeth and made his bed and got his homework done on time and Myrna sweetly kissed his cheek and asked *what did you do today?* He'd start his recitation till he saw her eyes begin to glaze, then he'd say it was his bedtime and he loved the meatloaf that she made.

Occasionally they would play cards, a game of Double Solitaire, waiting up for Daniel to come home late from the hospital. Even though he was a kid his mother never let him win, whining when he got ahead and cackling when she clobbered him. He might be in the second grade—coordination still not great—and Myrna could put up her cards much faster than an eight-year-old. So once more she was winning, but was running up her cards too fast, fouling up the whole damn game so she could play her eight-of-spades. He looked across the tabletop, his cards in neatly ordered rows, realized that he could see the ending from a mile away. It was not that Myrna wasn't smart, she merely didn't like to lose: if she puts up her eight-of-spades then Hank can't reach his buried queen. Without the queen the game would stall, they might as well just give it up, but Myrna didn't see this as she gleefully put up the eight.

George asked Hank for water—there was a plastic pitcher near the bed—and Hank removed the lid to sniff to make sure that was what it was. George's head had cleared some and the dream sense had begun to fade, replaced by flashing visions of what happened only days ago. *The doctor said I almost died.* It was slowly coming back to him; the last thing he remembered was the woman trapped inside her car. But Evan Smith came earlier, said Davenport had saved his life: had filled his lungs and thumped his chest and shocked his fibrillating heart. He remembered then the ambulance, the drugs that took the pain away, the mask across his nose and mouth, the dusty taste of oxygen. His glasses must have fallen off since he wasn't seeing very well, and the man they said was Davenport he thought had been somebody else.

"I thought you were my brother," and he told Hank when he was a boy how his mother had died slowly of a stroke in the internment camp.

"They let Frank have compassion leave from the military language school, but they only gave him three days and it took two days to get him there."

She took another month to die, but Frank had just an afternoon, and the part that George remembered most was the way he said *good-bye* to her. Frank was in his uniform—the new stripes of an officer—but the camp guards wouldn't let him in till they got the word from base command. George was waiting in the shade beside the guardhouse near the fence, could hear Frank argue with the guards, his words all sounding strained and terse. His train back left that evening with his mom a hundred yards away but the stupid guards had barred him from a locked camp filled with Japanese. They wasted half the morning keeping Frank outside the barbed-wire door while George sat worried any minute that their ailing mom might die. Finally getting through the gate, Frank strode across the empty yard—the white dust and the searing heat—whispering beneath his breath *it doesn't help to get upset!* George had never seen his brother ever looking half that mad; never in his life had Frank pretended that George wasn't there. His brother walked so fast that George imagined he knew where to go: half across the camp Frank said *they've moved the damn infirmary!*

It was back four rows and to the left; Frank stopped to light a cigarette.

"I'd never seen him smoke before, but he said that's how he'd learned to cope."

There were *Issei* standing in the doorways—tarpaper-and-plywood shacks—the men and women bowing to the *Nisei* in the uniform.

"And even though I know the way I'm rushing to keep up with him."

Everybody knew Frank was the soldier with the stricken mom. They wanted Frank to stop and talk, to tell what it was like out there, but wouldn't dare delay a man who was rushing to his mother's side. The infirmary was one big room, some curtains 'round their mother's bed; they couldn't keep the flies away; the desert heat was stifling.

"She mostly wouldn't even eat, but she let me sit her up for Frank. I had to borrow pillows from the patients in the other beds."

Their mother listing to one side, the spittle dribbled from her mouth; George placed her limp arm on her lap, her chin wiped with his fingertips. George was barely fourteen and his brother had turned twenty-two, their mother only forty-six, their father dead three years before. Frank had always been his pal, the older sibling idolized, but now his face had somehow changed: a smile but all the sparkle gone. If their mother died George knew there'd only be the two of them, and with Frank in the army he'd be all alone inside the camp. Before they went inside Frank stopped to finish off his cigarette, had brushed the dust off of his pants, a peppermint popped in his mouth. *Don't tell Mom I smoke,* he said, then gave the roll of mints to George; first time since arriving that he looked his brother in the eye. And as they stepped behind the curtain, suddenly Frank's back again, bowing to their mother with a pleasant smile across his face. Their mother couldn't speak with all her words incomprehensible; someone brought a chair for Frank, some tepid water in a glass. He sat all through the afternoon, their mother slightly leaning right, and Frank told stories that George knew were told to reassure their mom.

...

The floor nurse came in George's room, wearing someone else's smile, pushing in a cart that held a twelve-lead EKG machine.

"I need to get a heart tracing," and she unsnapped George's flimsy gown; Hank got up to go but George insisted he should stay a while.

"I need you for a chaperone," and he gave the nurse a feeble wink, and Hank could see the woman having trouble being nice today. She placed all of the sticky leads and told George to breathe quietly then pushed a blinking button till the tracing paper started through. But George couldn't help but reach his hand to scratch at something on his nose so the tracing came out fuzzy so she'd have to do it one more time.

"Please don't move again," she said, not trying to hide how tired she was: working through a second shift and been there nearly fifteen hours.

"You've got the chest leads placed all wrong," and Hank just couldn't help himself; the nurse gave him a stare that could have sobered up a stumbling drunk. But it had always been a pet peeve when a nurse would bring an EKG where it was obvious to Hank that she had put the leads on sloppily. So even with her icy stare Hank couldn't bring himself to stop; Hank reached over George's chest to place the stickies properly. Then trying to defend himself, he lectured her on vector points:

"The R-wave in V-3 is tall, so you know the ventricle's enlarged . . . the QRS is widened so there's infarct in the bundle branch. . . ."

"I'm sorry, but I've got to go. The Doctor wants this right away." She ripped the leads from George's chest like price tags off of cellophane.

The head of George's bed was raised, and he leaned back as he rubbed his chest: his ribs sore from the CPR, the skin raw from electric shocks. He was certain he was missing flesh that came off with the sticky leads, and he'd meant to ask the nurse today if lunch could be a hamburger. He once more was reminded of the arsonist of Edgar Flat, how Hank was living in the only house left on the list he wrote. The strange dream made him think how there was nothing left of Edgarville; it soon would be the year he thought the Capo house was going to burn. He was thinking about telling Hank about this theory that he had; could watch his face to see if there was something Hank was trying to hide. George paused when Hank sat down again, his ankles crossed in front of him; Hank stared blankly at the wall: some artwork and a crucifix. The only noise inside the room was the droning of the IV pump: the dogs were gone, the weeds were whacked, the mute pushed on the TV set. He was on the verge of telling when George remembered where he'd seen Hank's face: the front page and the TV and the news over the radio.

"So you're that cardiologist. The one who killed that little boy."

"No," Hank said, not looking up, "I just couldn't keep the boy alive."

Fried Potatoes
June 1997

WHEN LIDIA wasn't feeling well she liked to take a steamy bath with scented oil and candlelight and music on the stereo. Today the cause was menstrual cramps, a headache from mid-term exams: taking classes part time for a license to sell real estate. The problem was she didn't have a bathtub in her little house; she had to go next door and ask Lucia if *the jerk* was out. Lucy didn't mind at all, but her husband was an idiot: drank and smoked and strutted 'round like God's gift to the universe. So Lidia had waited till she saw his truck had left the yard to ask if she could use the tub to soothe her aching uterus.

Lucy was the best there was and barely twenty-three years old, with three kids and *the jerk* and still the sweetest smile she'd ever seen. Lucy said she loved *the jerk*, that he was deeper than he looked, hinting that his strut was caused by something God endowed him with. Her girls loved trading houses since they'd not yet got a satellite, and Lucy led them cross the yard to watch the one at Lidia's. Lidia had her ritual: a basket full of oils and salts, a dozen scented candles and some headphones for the radio. She rinsed the battered tub and hung her robe up on a rusted nail, stepped into the scalding water, pulled the vinyl curtain closed.

It was nine o'clock in mid-June, the stars out and the air was cool; a light breeze blew the curtains, made the flames dance on the windowsill. The heat helped almost instantly, the muscles of her womb relaxed; she slid the headphones on her ears: soft music from some decade past. The bath oil smelled of lavender with subtle tones of rose and bay; wafting in the steam, it filled her lungs with sweet humidity. Even with her eyes closed she could see the candles flickering, shadows on the peeling ceiling dancing 'round like butterflies. She was trying not to think about the test on rates and mortgages, her spoken English excellent but still some words she didn't know. And she didn't want to think about the calls her boyfriend hadn't made: six weeks back in Mexico, his last call several weeks ago. She had the normal aches and pains of trying hard to get ahead: two jobs and a ton of school and her period on top of this. But at least she wasn't pregnant —she was practically a whole month late—her boyfriend left the day after the condom's business end had broke. So even though she was sick and tired, the pressure had decreased two-thirds, surrounded by the smell of herbs, the aura of the candle glow.

She didn't notice how the light had changed then momentarily, as the headlights of a pickup swept the house while rolling through the yard. She didn't hear the squeaking brakes, the rusty hinges of the door, the banging of the metal screen, *the jerk* home earlier than usual. Instead she had her eyes still closed and listening to something smooth, thinking it was for the best the boyfriend wasn't calling her. She wasn't pregnant after all and she didn't have to marry him and *if he doesn't call this week I'll manage to get over it.*

The vinyl curtain billowed some and the candle flames nearly went out, but she was chin deep with her eyes closed and the headphones kept her ignorant. Bernie came in through the door—the lock broke several months ago—and stumbled to the toilet bowl and unzipped what he was famous for. While he was pissing on the seat he finally glanced around the room: "What the fuck's all this?!" he muttered, head thick from the beers he drank.

Lidia was miles away sunk deep inside her steamy bath, thinking of the story of the woman that she baby-sat. Today was rather difficult, with tests and cramps and splitting head, the afternoon spent with a woman can't remember who she is. At times Myrna was charming, but could also be a bitter pill: chatting in the kitchen or she'd bite and scratch and spit on her. Today was sort of in-between: she'd slapped her hand and called her names, then suddenly was sweet and warm as flan her grandma used to bake. They went out to the patio—it cooled down after six o'clock; at first the woman sat and stared, but then she couldn't shut her mouth. *These words have never crossed my lips, but I've got to get this off my chest...* and Myrna told a story she told Lidia three times this week. *I think I was in second grade...* and Lidia had only smiled, not quite in the mood to try to steer the conversation 'round. Her head had hurt and her bowels were loose and she hadn't been good company; she would have tried some aspirin but it always made her stomach burn. It was nearing time to draw up Myrna's evening dose of insulin; Doctor Hank said give the shot a half-hour before dinnertime. He paid her ten bucks extra on the days she had to stab his mom, put up with a slap or scratch and some new name she'd never heard. But Lidia enjoyed the chore, a challenge that took skill and care, and except for Myrna's brief abuse, she liked the extra bit of cash.

She'd wondered what it would be like if she could go to nursing school, imagining the starched white dress, the clunky-looking nursing shoes. She's drawing up a huge syringe, she's scrubbing up for surgery, she's comforting a crying child who's mother has just passed away. But she'd have to get a bachelor's, with three more years of studying; in only two semesters she'd be licensed to sell real estate. Half the population of the valley was now Mexican, and as their lot in life improved they'd all start buying houses soon. Even though it was kind of dull—long contracts full of legalese—it seemed it was the best way to make sure she'd buy one, too, someday.

Myrna had gone droning on, the story of the bicycle, the twins and Margaret Beechnut and the bear inside the chicken coop. Then almost like the smell of something burning in the other room, she realized that something in the woman's storyline had changed. She'd thought they were in second grade, the tale about the yawning frog, the big dog with the missing leg, the day they got a telephone. But Myrna now was talking about a room next to a firehouse, a baby in a fruit box and the sirens middle-of-the-night. Myrna said she worried they might try to take her child away; they'd rounded up the Japanese and sent them off to *God-knows-where.*

Lidia had tried hard to imagine which parts could be true: that Myrna had this sordid past of bastard kids and firemen. Myrna's husband was at war, and knew her baby wasn't his; she'd met him on a Greyhound bus the day her father kicked her out. Of course this guy sat next to her—a young girl traveling alone—but when he saw her eyes were red he didn't bother her at all. He fiddled with his floppy hat: the flat, green army envelope; the patches on his sleeve meant he was supposed to be a gentleman. She was absolutely scared to death; she'd never been away from home; her father'd called her names that even Martin hadn't used before. Myrna wasn't sure where she would go since she'd been sent away; Martin put her on the bus, some small bills in an envelope. And even Martin was unkind, had told her he'd expected more, that *if you're giving it away, at least give to a Mormon boy.* They were almost to Multnomah Falls before the soldier cleared his throat, offered her a stick of gum, said *might help if you're motion sick.*

    He wasn't being coy or shy but he didn't say more for a while, and corner-of-her-eye she'd watched him watch her watch the scenery. *How long till the big day?* and he had a pleasant baritone; when she turned to look the soldier glanced down at her abdomen. *Mom thinks late November* but she was too scared to say any more, guessing he was probably a *Godless-heathen-Laminite.* He was not the greatest-looking guy, but he had a pleasant, bashful smile: orange hair in a crew cut and his eyebrows were a bit too pale. But she'd just been kicked out of her home and told she couldn't be a Mormon now: the gates of heaven slammed shut when she'd loved someone she shouldn't have. The soldier asked where she was going: *Off to visit relatives?* All she did was shake her head and try to keep from sniffling. He said he was a doctor now, had nearly finished internship; ordered to Fort Lewis then was off to fight the Japanese. This doctor-soldier told her he could help her find a place to stay: *Portland can be kind of rough; the cheap hotels aren't really safe.* She'd wondered how he knew these things, he barely looked past twenty-three; she'd only met one doctor once: an old man with an ether stink. This doctor's name was Davenport, *but Daniel is okay with me;* the bus stopped at the train station: he stored his duffel bag away. She had an anxious feeling that this man must be an *infidel,* but now that she'd been kicked out of the church it didn't matter much. She'd always been told what to do by men with God's authority, so she'd followed like a puppy when he led her from the train depot. He took her gently by the arm, her satchel in his other hand; three blocks from the station and they passed a red-brick fire hall. The building right next door had a small sign up on the second floor: *You'd be plenty safe up there!* Then: *Let's go get the kid some food.*

Right around the corner was a café with a window seat: *Order anything you want. I'll be back in a couple shakes.* Sitting there all by herself she'd wondered if she'd live or die; no one loved her anymore; her suitcase wasn't even full. She'd felt a gnawing in her gut, the thought the soldier won't return; her family put her on a bus and told her *God is through with you!* Peeking in the envelope, there were sixteen dollar bills inside, a fortune for a girl who'd lived her whole life up in Edgarville. She asked first for a bowl of soup, which helped calm down her butterflies: a grilled-cheese and some home fries and an Apple-Betty a la mode. She wasn't all that hungry but the gnawing wouldn't go away; she'd asked the waitress if she could please have another slice of pie. *I guess you're eating now for two* and the waitress winked above a smile, told her not to worry, *you'll look pretty when your cheeks are round.*

She didn't want people to stare, so she didn't ask for any more, but the gnawing didn't settle till the bell rang on the café door. Breathlessly he'd slid into the narrow bench across from her; smiling Daniel told her he was sorry that it took so long. *But I think I've got things all worked out. . . .* A room next to the fire hall. *The firemen are always there . . .* so she'd never have to feel alone. The landlord was six blocks away and he'd had to run the distance twice: *The guy said that he'd clean the place for two months rent paid in advance.* He'd said he met the firemen, to tell them she was moving in: *I told them that I'm shipping out, and I want you near a hospital.* He'd hoped she wouldn't get mad at him for something he'd said to the men: *I let them think we're married so they don't get any strange ideas. . . .*

. . .

Lidia was startled when the ads came on the radio; they cranked the volume up so that she can't miss what they're selling her. But instead of sitting up and trying to fiddle with the volume knob, she slipped the headphones off her ears until the music came back on. The water now was cooling down but still was plenty comfortable; her only parts that stuck out were her head and knees and wrinkled toes. The bath was having an effect, her cramps had nearly disappeared, her headache wasn't gone but just a fraction what it used to be. But then she heard a grunting sound; her first thought is a grizzly bear; something was behind the curtain, snuffling and breathing hard. Her heart jumped and her breathing stopped and she stifled a strong urge to scream; about a half-an-inch or so, she pulled the curtain back to see. *The jerk* was sitting on the toilet, pants bunched 'round his cowboy boots, head down in his hands, his elbows leaning on his bony knees.

The jerk looked up when Lidia let out a stream of expletives, his eyes wide as a 'possum in the headlights of a semi-truck. She was naked standing in the tub, he stood up from the toilet seat—still so drunk the sudden movement made the walls move back and forth. He fell back toward the toilet with his pants still down around his knees, arm knocked over candles that were sitting on the windowsill. The window curtains caught the flames, *the jerk's* head hit the toilet tank; Lidia was so enraged she hoped the bastard bled to death. Lucy stood out in the hall, her husband's feet blocking the door; she'd seen his truck out in the drive while cooking French fries for the girls. She rushed across the yard to tell him not to bother Lidia, that if he needs the toilet he can step behind the cottonwoods. But Lucy hadn't reached the porch before she heard the crash and thump, words she never would have thought could come out of her best friend's mouth.

She'd left the girls glued to the set, the French fries in the bubbling oil, and she knew the bathroom didn't lock so she gave the door full body weight. She never will forget the scene: her husband bleeding on the floor, his pants bunched down around his knees, while her naked friend stood beating flames. And what was she supposed to think? *She'd asked his help to scrub her back?* Could not believe her eyes or ears: *my husband really is a jerk.* The curtains Lucy made by hand were burning in the window frame; Lidia had soaked a towel and swung it like a maniac. The bathroom had filled up with smoke so she was coughing as she flung the towel while Lucy dragged her husband's sorry ass across the splintered floor. Lidia was coughing as she finally backed out of the room, modesty demanding that she grab her bathrobe off the nail.

While Lucy tended to *the jerk,* she ran out to her small red car, knowing somewhere in the trunk was a matching fire extinguisher. But she didn't have her keys, left on a hook beside her kitchen door; running up her back steps, she saw the kitchen window glowing orange. She thought it was reflecting from the fire that *the jerk* provoked; glancing back it looked more like the bathroom fire was almost out. But her kitchen window still was orange, and the doorknob was a little warm, when she heard a desperate anguished scream for years she'd hear again in dreams. ¡*Las Fritas!* And she was pushed aside by Lucy rushing through the door; a wave of heat and smoke enough to stop a charging elephant. The fresh air only made things worse, and Lucy staggered back outside; hands wrapped in her skirt she held a sloshing pan of flaming oil. Already with her blouse on fire, the handle burning Lucy's hands, the pan dropped to the porch dried by an early summer without rain. Lucy screamed and started running, but Lidia had grabbed her arm, pulled her to the ground and rolled her back and forth across the yard. Beating what was smoldering, poor Lucy's eyes were terrified: ¡*las niñas!* she was whispering around her coughs and sputtering. Lucy struggled to get up, but Lidia still had more breath; rushing past the burning porch she pushed in through the kitchen door.

Pink Ones
June 1997

WITH JESSIE'S HEAD against his chest, Hank watched it rise with every breath: the sweetness of her skin and hair, a hint of fruit and spiciness. He loved inhaling Jessie's scent while nuzzling behind her ear; they'd done this now for centuries: their nightly bedtime ritual. His wife had always read in bed a book she'd gleaned a thousand times; he'd throw his clothes onto a chair and slide in naked next to her. Slowly she would close the book while Hank rolled over on his back, pulled her with him as he went so she was tucked against his hip. They'd both release contented sighs; the best place in the universe: naked and alone in bed, the whole world just the two of them. This time he pulled her carefully, her injury still stiff and sore; the X-rays showed she'd merely strained some muscles when she'd wrecked her car. So once her head was on his chest he felt she wasn't quite relaxed, but with each cycle of his breath some tension would evaporate.

"You're not allowed to move," she said, her whisper barely audible; at last he felt her head's full weight, her own breath warm and delicate. They'd climbed in bed at nine o'clock once Myrna stumbled to her room; his mother still exhausted from her evening lost out in the woods. He wasn't sure now what to do to keep his mother safe at night; he put a bell above her door to wake him when she opened it. This was not what he envisioned when they thought to move to Myrna's farm, startled from his fitful dreams each time his mother's bladder filled. It used to be his job to take the late-night calls from anxious moms all certain that the end was near when Johnny wasn't feeling well. But that was all so long ago, the trial was like a mountain pass: the mule died and two broken spokes but he got the wagon safe across. And now he's on this little farm, pretending he's a pioneer, laying wood up for the winter, salted meat and mealy flour.

He would have liked to put in fences, learn to build a chicken coop: dig some holes and plant some trees and calluses across his palms. But every time he'd go outside his mother somehow wandered off, said she's going swimming or to visit Margaret Somebody. He ought to put her on a leash, a ball-and-chain around her leg, perhaps one of those collars that give shocks when bad dogs run away. He wonders *why this burden now? Why didn't she have heart disease, bad rheumatoid arthritis or a crippling anxiety?* Instead she had to lose her mind. *She can't remember sitting down!* He knew by how she smiled the times she didn't recognize him now. He'd say it was July 16th and nearing the millennium; she'd tell him that he's full of crap: *You're off by half a century!* Harry Truman's president. *A disappointment all around!* Something would distract her, then she'd ask Hank *what's your name again?* He was totally bewildered by her changing personality; one moment she's his mother and then suddenly she's horrible. The thing that bound them now was all her years of tender loving care, showers of affection just as if he was her very own. But each time she met someone new she made sure that they weren't confused: her little boy looks Japanese because he's an *adopted* child.

He was not sure why this bothered him since they were very different specimens: Myrna's hair was brownish-black and Daniel's was a reddish-orange; nothing to suggest they would produce a little Asian boy. But every time she'd tell the truth to someone at the grocery store, it made the life they led at home seem even more a blatant lie. Sitting at the breakfast table, steam comes from the waffle iron; Daniel would suggest that Hank should try out for the baseball team. *I used to have a decent arm,* implying Hank should have one, too: *Next Saturday I'm not on-call I'll show you how to throw a curve.* Each time Myrna called him *son* he'd see the letters in the air, the word always surrounded by a bold set of quotation marks. He tried to squelch the fantasy of having been born in Japan, that somewhere was a mom and dad out searching for their long-lost boy. The first time he asked Myrna she said that his parents drowned at sea, other times it was the plague, a train wreck and a burglar. He could tell the questions bothered her, she'd answer in a snippy way; he learned it's better not to ask than risk an awful brooding mood. And he only asked his father once, remembered Daniel squatting down so that the man was eye to eye with a boy who was a six-year-old. *As far as I'm concerned, son, I'm the only father that you have. If someone tells you different then don't listen to them anymore.*

So he had to train himself to stop from wondering about his past: the circumstances of his birth, how things could have gone differently. Instead he mowed the big back yard and did his homework after school; never learned to throw a curve but got to play in center field. He'd be standing at his locker when the Bronson twins would start again, feigning conversation about stinking filthy chinks and Japs. He wouldn't turn around till it progressed into a punch and shove: head banged on his locker so the echo filled the locker room. He'd keep his arms in close because his goal was to protect himself; when the coach would break things up, Hank said *we're only roughhousing.*

Teacher's conference junior year, Hank's parents met his counselor: *Based on all his test scores, Hank is smart enough for Ivy League.* Daniel said he could apply but Harvard was too far away; thought that Stanford offered Hank more chance of meeting *Asian girls.* But Hank had always liked the pink ones with their long blond ponytails; liked to watch the coeds playing intramural volleyball. But Jessie wasn't pink or blond, her skin a silky olive brown, her dark hair long and wavy and an Eastern European nose. The second week of physics class, she sought him out for extra help: *I understand the basics; it's the details I find difficult.* At first she drove him up the wall, just *why?* she couldn't understand; but then he figured out she didn't really need his tutoring. They were sitting at a table in the basement cafeteria, both their plates half eaten since the meatloaf hadn't tasted good. He had tried explaining *quantum jump* with his forehead on his fingertips, head over a textbook while he tried to keep his mind on work. But this girl who sat beside him had the sweetest arms he'd ever seen: nicely tapered, downy hair, and biceps with a little form. *I play a lot of tennis* and her knee pressed on his outer thigh and he was suddenly aware it might be chemistry they're learning now. He thought that she must wear perfume:

the faintest hint of something nice; he glanced up from the book to find her staring at his shaggy locks. *You should let me cut your hair* and she reached to brush it back in place and since then Hank had never once felt lust for anybody else.

...

That was thirty years ago, her head now on her husband's chest, thinking of his heart and how she hoped his arteries were clear. That was how her father died, a sudden massive heart attack; same age as her husband now but overweight and smoked a lot. She couldn't bear to think someday his tender heart would finally stop, praying for another fifty years of sleeping next to Hank. He didn't smoke and didn't drink; his blood cholesterol was fine; his weakness was the jo-jos at the Windmaster convenience store. If he had a gut at all it wasn't more than half a basketball, and now that they were on the farm he got a lot more exercise. The only thing they didn't know was how healthy was his DNA; cancer killed his father and his mom had rapid Alzheimer's. But he wasn't blood kin to his dad and he didn't come from Myrna's womb so his mother's diabetes didn't mean a thing genetically. They'd passed a law that said Hank had the right to open up his file, find out who his parents were and learn about his risk factors. Perhaps he had genetic traits that led to early skin cancer, polyps in his colon or some Asian Lou Gehrig's disease. Jessie said she'd do the work, he'd only have to sign his name; Hank said that he felt he'd be invading someone's privacy. *There's nothing I'd do differently;* he didn't smoke so couldn't quit; he went without complaint for Doctor Gary's yearly finger poke. So she finally gave up on the plan to search out who Hank's parents were; to find out if his mom or dad gave Hank his stupid stubborn streak.

While Jessie listened to his heart her fingers traced his abdomen, circling his navel and then down to touch his private parts. She was always pleasantly aroused to find her husband *capable:* like looking for a midnight snack and finding a big slice of pie. His hair was salt-and-pepper and his face had just a hint of jowl, but the rest of him looked thirty-five and holding now for twenty years. She'd never met a sweeter man, as tender as a daffodil, but if somebody threatened her she knew he'd rip the man in half. The way he took care of his mom was bordering on saintliness; he'd listen to her call him names then fix her something nice for lunch. It seemed like Hank could let them slide as if her words were compliments: *you bug-eyed little pissant* said to warm the cockles of his heart.

Jessie told him not to move, her tender neck finally relaxed; he was trying not to get his hopes up as her hand ran further south. He was pretty sure she didn't really mean to get him all riled up, that sometimes her hand wandered 'round while she thought about something else. But it was over two weeks now since the last time they had fooled around: patiently been waiting for her injured muscles to improve. Even if it was a tease, he didn't want her hand to stop; better things go halfway than to not go anywhere at all. There was no place half as nice as bed, the perfect body temperature, the softness of the flannel sheets, the firm weight of the comforter. The farm was always cool at night, even when the days were warm: all the windows opened so the sound of crickets filled the room. Slowly reaching out his hand, and clicking off the bedside lamp, Hank put his hand against her head and stroked her long-dark-wavy hair.

She was breathing slow and steady and her hand had lost most of its grip and thinking she was fast asleep Hank lost all hope for sex tonight. He put one arm behind his head, the other hugged his sleeping wife; he listened to the crickets and the breeze out in the cottonwoods. The wave sound of the leaves made him think longingly of traveling; next winter when it rained they could go someplace warm like India. Imagining the Taj Mahal, the white sands of a Goan beach, walking 'round the temples while being careful where he put his feet. They both loved traveling overseas but hadn't since before the trial and now he had his mother like a fifty-kilo ball-and-chain. The last time Myrna smacked his face he'd had to stop and count to ten, the impulse strong to slap her back then wash her mouth with kerosene. He knew he couldn't blame her for the nasty things she'd say or do: her mind more like a chicken's brain with random neurons firing. But even with a pill it was a fight simply to brush her teeth, to help her trim her fingernails and try to get her PJs off. This was now a constant struggle, mostly he would let her win: she was vehement she had to wear pajamas underneath her clothes.

It says so in THE BOOK! she'd scream, then call Hank a long list of names: *dirty yellow Satan-loving wicked heathen Lamanite!!* Her screw got looser every day and the *yellow* reference struck a nerve; all his life he'd never heard one hint his mom could think that way. *The Book* must be the bible but there weren't pajamas way back then; of course he knows the other words, but he'd never heard of *Lamanites*. Assuming it's some reference to the fact he wasn't blonde and white, he had to tell himself again it was not his mother saying this. But even with the Alzheimer's she was not completely innocent; at some point in her life she must have thought about his *yellow* skin. He'd like the words to float away, pretend she'd spoken gibberish, but every time she spewed them out a spring was tightened in his chest.

If Lidia was not around, Hank's mother would be dead by now: he'd beat her with a baseball bat then toss her down the basement stairs. Lidia was the only one who Myrna would let help her bathe, strip off her pajamas so that Hank could put them through the wash. He'd finally bought some extra pairs, which had to be identical, since Myrna had a fit each time she thought somebody'd stolen them. Lidia deserved a raise, a big bonus at Christmastime: *Perhaps she might be willing to start coming in an extra day.*

Hank was startled when his wife's hand stirred down in the nether-lands;

"I didn't mean to fall asleep. Do you think you might be interested?"

All he'd have to do was rid his brain of certain images: thinking of his mother was an anti-aphrodisiac. This morning she got up too soon, her doorbell woke him from a dream; he found her in the kitchen trying to light the burner on the stove. But the stove was an electric range and he turned the circuit off each night; she had a book of matches and was searching for the pilot light. *What stupid prick designed this thing?* and she'd pulled out half the elements; Hank couldn't figure out where she kept finding matches in the house. Trying to erase his mind of thoughts of Myrna's latest deeds, he conjured up some images of losing his virginity. Jessie was the only woman Hank had ever had in bed; starting in their junior year: a motel near the interstate. They'd been together half a term and hadn't moved past fondling: no place but the backseat of the Buick Daniel bought for Hank. He was trying to remember what they'd called the motel manager: *Dwight* or *Ike* because he looked a little like the president. Brazenly they'd signed the book as *Hank & Jessie Davenport*, Ike not looking happy with the mix of racial heritage. Jessie took the tarnished key while Hank paid fifteen dollars cash: two nights in a lumpy bed with grains of sand between the sheets.

"My neck is still a little sore, so maybe we could take this slow."

In all their years of having sex he'd never failed to be amazed how absolutely perfect it felt when he finally slid inside. Everything would melt away, now just the urgent need to push; nothing else existing outside the Hank-and-Jessie Universe. He loved it when she'd start to dig her fingernails into his back; the pleasure made him gasp until he heard the bells start going off. Everything began at once: the siren from the fire hall, the shrill sound of his pager and his mother's shouts outside their door. *Holy shit!* he thought as his heart leapt high up into his throat; instantly deflated and as soft as butter near the stove. He was rolling out of bed and desperate-searching for his underwear; a voice came on his pager telling Edgar Flat they had a fire.

"R.P.'s speaking Spanish, but I think she says there's kids inside."

He pulled on pairs of socks and shoes, asked Jessie if she'd mind his mom, stumbled over Trouble howling as he rushed out through the dark. His mom was in the living room. *I can't find my baby boy!* She was hunting under cushions on the sofa and the easy chair. *Jessie's going to help you look* and he finally found his ring of keys; had to lock the door behind him so she wouldn't go outside.

As his truck ran down the road he tried to clear his muddled mind, trying to recall the address dispatch gave out for the fire. He hadn't felt this way since his first night alone in internship: sitting in the on-call room he'd jumped each time the phone would ring. But he didn't need the address since already he could see the glow: orange and red and billowed smoke all coming from down Alder Road. His instinct was to go straight there but knew that wouldn't help at all; he needed both his turnout gear and a backpack filled with bottled air. He pulled into the parking lot, forgot to turn his headlights off; Brenda Thompson had the truck out, sitting in the driver's seat. *Let's go! Let's go!* she screamed at him, no other volunteers around; kicked his shoes and stepped into his waiting pants and rubber boots. He grabbed his bulky coat and gloves, his helmet with his name in back; he didn't get the door shut before Brenda had the clutch pulled out.

Better put your seat belt on but it was only half-a-mile away, and she drove it like a racecar with a thousand-gallon passenger.

Brenda spoke into the mike, said *Engine Seven-six en route,* turned the wheel with her left hand, the other shifting through the gears. *I wish there were some more of us. There's not much two people can do.* Reaching for the mike again, said, *we need mutual aid.* And this was what they saw out through the windshield of the fire truck: two small houses side by side with one of them all flame and smoke. Yellow fire spit from the windows, red flames licked out through the roof: *Somebody's alive in there* she whispered as she set the brake.

In Flames
June 1997

THERE WERE PEOPLE standing in the road all stepping backwards from the flames; Brenda yelled to pull some hose while she put on more fire gear. Hank was still not good at this, was stumbling like a puppy dog: the rubber boots were clumsy and the thick gloves made his fingers huge. He grabbed the cross-lay from one side and dragged the hose into the road, trying to remember which three levers on the pump to pull. There were all these people standing 'round but no one offering to help, assuming now that they'd arrived the two of them could handle it. But the hose had to be stretched out so it wouldn't get all kinked and snarled; someone had to stand and watch the pressure on the monitor. The closest help was miles away, the water truck from Hillendale, the ambulance from Hooster and some extras in their private cars. They were not supposed to go inside until they had four firemen: two to stand outside the door while two crawled through the leaping flames. Hank was certain there could be nobody still alive inside; such a tiny wooden house with windows spilling smoke and fire. But Brenda had an air pack on, the far end of the fire hose, dragged it to the front door where she hunkered down on hands and knees. It was dark out so that all Hank saw was Brenda's bulky silhouette, crouching on the front stoop like a long-tailed baby buffalo. She signaled him to fill the hose, to pull some levers on the truck; Hank could not remember *Does this prime the pump or drain the tank?* He grabbed one that said *tank fill* and another that said *tank to pump*, thankfully watched as the water filled the snakelike canvas hose.

As soon as she had water Brenda pushed against the wooden door, opened up the nozzle but the water barely dribbled out. Hank looked at the flames behind her, smoke thick as a lava flow, inches from disaster and he had the levers pulled all wrong. He couldn't hear what Brenda yelled since her face was covered with a mask, and the gesture she made with her arm looked just like strangling a cat. He looked back at the pump panel, the gauges for the preconnects, a half-a-dozen handles all with labels didn't make much sense. He'd never been so ill prepared for doing an important job; even as an intern he at least knew what the parts were called. With all these people watching Hank, he felt like such an idiot; his partner's life depending on his knowing how this damn thing works. Trying hard to concentrate, to conjure George's blemished hands that pulled the knobs and levers as he showed Hank how to engineer. But Hank had always figured there'd be other volunteers around, that there'd be someone nearby who could tell him what he's doing wrong. He looked back up at Brenda, who still choked the nonexistent cat, knowing he was going to have to figure this out by himself. Hank pushed hard on the *tank to pump* and pulled the *tank fill* all the way; the pressure dropped down further so he quickly did the opposite. The pressure gauge jumped eighty pounds and the hose line gave a sudden jerk; he turned around to see that Brenda'd gone inside all by herself.

The smoke was like a concrete wall that Brenda boldly crawled in through; a yard inside and Brenda could see nothing past the mask she wore. She was breathing in the bottled air that tasted like a rubber tire, her only thought was dispatch said there might be children trapped inside. The light clipped to her helmet didn't penetrate the smoke at all; she rolled onto her side and swept the ceiling with the fire hose. The heat turned all the drops to steam and she shut the spurting nozzle down, hunkered on the floor while she got rained on by the fire debris. The steam brought down the temperature and turned the smoke from black to white; couldn't see a thing still but a flame-glow coming from the left. She wasn't trying to stop the fire, just save whoever's still inside, knowing they'd be in the room the furthest from the smoke and flames. Sometimes they fall near the door, a few feet from the outside air; she reached in all directions, spreading wide her bulky arms and legs. She only found an end table, a sofa and a padded chair, knocked into a wooden stool and something crashed against the ground. She was trying to imagine where she'd find a frightened four-year-old: hiding in the bedroom in the closet under dirty clothes. There was no sense crawling toward the room that was already a ball of fire, like looking for survivors in a ship sunk fifty years ago. She crawled until she felt the wall, then worked her way around the room, reaching through the blackness for some object that was soft and warm. Brenda now was thinking of her precious little grandbaby, way back when her daughter was still doing lots of crack cocaine. Her daughter would take off for weeks so the court gave Brenda custody, and she swore this time she would avoid mistakes she made with Gabby's mom. She taught Gabby to spell her name, count all the way to thirty-nine; could make her bed and get dressed but for trouble telling left from right. *Not bad for a four-year-old!* and Brenda was so proud of her; one day they took Boomer for a walk down by the riverside. She still can hear the thud-and-scream of head against a mossy rock, the splash into the river and the big dog jumping after her. Brenda stood as carved from stone and couldn't think what she should do: jump into the river and they'd all three go over the falls. She was desperate for a stick or log, for something that the child could grab; Boomer had the toddler's sleeve but drifted past the eddy line. The water swept her granddaughter and Brenda swore *never again:* standing doing nothing while her precious dropped over the edge.

Ten years later Boomer died, all gray and stiff and smelling bad; Gabby'd gotten pregnant by the boy who took her to the prom. Thankful for the kayaker who fished them out below the falls, Brenda taught herself to swim and never pussyfoot around. It took all of her discipline to never stand and hem or haw, drag her feet or beat a bush when something needed doing *now*. So she was crawling on her belly trying to drag a heavy fire hose, searching for a child or two here hiding deep inside the smoke. She was past the room all glowing red and found another opening, down a hallway several feet to what must be the bedroom door.

...

Hank was standing at the pump with one eye on the pressure gauge, the other on the front door watching for the fire hose to move. It only had to move an inch for Hank to know she's still alive, that Brenda was still crawling 'round for victims of this holocaust. Each airtank had a small device that beeped when it stopped jostling so that whoever listened could tell if a volunteer was down. But Hank thought he might miss the blare above the pump and engine noise, and *what am I supposed to do if I can't see what's happening?!* Should he follow Brenda in? Or wait until more help arrives? Better to be ready so he tried to put an air pack on. The tanks weighed forty pounds apiece, enough to make his shoulders sag, plus harnesses and Passport tags and all these dangling straps to pull. He couldn't think which goes on first, *the face mask or the Nomex hood?* No one stood beside him to make sure he had no skin exposed. He finally thought *I'm ready* and was breathing in the bottled air, but with his fire gloves on he couldn't work his helmet's strap buckle. It was nearly more than he could stand, like living a frustration dream: the more he tried to rush the more things worked to try to slow him down. This helmet cost a fortune but the buckle was cheap plastic crap; some cretin counting beans had tried to shave a nickel off the cost. He was ready now to kill himself, to plunge a dagger through his heart: *What the hell is wrong that I can't pull this blasted buckle off?!* His breathing was so heavy now he'd fogged the inside of his mask, ripped it off his face before the claustrophobia began.

The door had been left open so the bedroom air was thick with smoke; above the hiss of air-tank Brenda heard the crackling attic space. She knew she didn't have much time before the ceiling would collapse, yelled out through her face mask for whoever might be hiding here. Still down on her aching knees, she ran her hands across the bed: nothing but the rumpled sheets and blankets and a pillowcase. Moving off the bed she felt her tank hit something breakable; guessing from the sound she must have knocked over a TV set. A big hose filled with water weighs at least a half-a-million pounds; Brenda's arms were aching from the massive effort dragging it. But she knew it was her safety line and not for putting out a fire, but what she'd follow when she had to rush back out the way she came. She left the nozzle by the bed so she could search the tiny room, a boot always against the wall so she could trace it out again. She knew she'd find them in the closet, huddled with their teddy bears, screaming if they were alive when Brenda stuck her mask inside. She finally felt the skinny door but didn't find the victims there, the closet was so crammed full that she couldn't push a finger in. That was when her alarm bell rang and thumped against her lower back, told her she was running out of air and had three minutes left. She had to turn around *right now* or risk the wrath of *Fire God*, but she wasn't going to leave because *I haven't checked under the bed!* Trying hard to hold her breath, to make her air last long enough, she quickly crawled along the wall to the nozzle by the bedroom door. Kneeling on the shards of glass that used to be the TV set, she slid down on her belly so her reach was long as possible. Pushing past the dust-bunnies and broken parts of plastic toys, her heart jumped when her gloved hand came across a tiny, lifeless arm.

Hank could finally hear the sound of a siren several miles away: the booster truck from Hillendale down where the big mill used to be. They'd be here in about three minutes, someone who knew what to do; Hank still looked for movement from the fire hose that Brenda dragged. He finally got the face mask on, the buckle underneath his chin, was crouching at the front door watching flames lick through the living room. Above the crackling of the fire, the rumblings of the pump and truck, he thought he heard the sound of Brenda's air-tank running out of air. But at least the sound was coming closer: *Brenda's on her way outside!* He saw her light shine through the smoke, a baby tucked beneath her arm. *I'm such a stupid idiot!* He should have pulled the first-aid bag, ready with some oxygen and saline for the baby's burns. Reaching through the smoke, he grabbed the baby out of Brenda's arms, horrified by what he felt: there was something obviously wrong. Stumbling off the front steps Hank was ripping off his foggy mask; lips around the baby's mouth, he puffed but no air went inside. Brenda stumbled next to him; they both stared at a plastic doll:

"That's all that I could find inside," she coughed out between gasps for air.

Apple Juice & Oatmeal
June 1997

ALL THAT MYRNA WANTS to do is find a comfy place to sit, plop down in an easy chair and read another romance book. She can't think where the day has gone, it seems she just got out of bed, already feeling sore and tired: *Could really use a cigarette!* She'd love to feel the smoke go in and wake up all her sleepy nerves like mothers in the morning getting all their children off to school. Imagining how good it feels to pull the smoke deep in her chest, filling every inch of lung with richly fragrant stimulant. This room could be somebody's den, a wall of books and bric-a-brac, but no place for someone to sit with feet up on an ottoman. And what has she accomplished yet? She hasn't done the grocery list, and Nona should be here today to do the floors and ironing. She'd really like to have a smoke to burn the cobwebs from her brain, but Daniel says the filthy things cause lung cancer and heart disease. Why do they keep finding out the best things are all bad for you? Cigarettes and sausage links and French fries with your hamburger? She'd never had to watch her weight until her husband made her quit; she's never had to work so hard to find a place to rest her feet. Hunting through the cluttered shelves she's looking for a hiding place, a stash kept for those dinner guests who haven't kicked the habit yet.

Myrna sees a small box in the front drawer of an end table: heart beats fast until she finds it holds two decks for pinochle. *So much for the gracious host*, but she does find something she can use: way-back-of-the-drawer there is a matchbook from a restaurant.

"What have you lost *this* time?" and she nearly jumps out of her skin, turns around to find a strange man holding out a coffee mug. She slips the matchbook in her pocket, coughing in her other hand, takes the offered cup of coffee, asks him how his day has been.

"No complaints so far," he says. "I've got your breakfast ready now."

Feeling slightly more confused—she thought that it was afternoon—but now that he has mentioned food she notices her hunger pangs. She follows slowly down the hall into a sunny kitchen nook to a place set at the table with a great big bowl of oatmeal.

"Aren't you having any?" but he said he'd eaten earlier.

"Jessie had to go to work. I got up to keep her company."

He starts telling her about a fire, some woman's house burned to the ground, how another woman braved the flames to save the children trapped inside. But the kids were watching from the road beside someone named Lidia: no one harmed except their clothes all smelled like they'd been barbecued. It's actually quite interesting to hear this talk about a fire, reminding her of all the stories she'd heard down at the fire hall. Remembering how scared she was of all the brawny firemen, sensing that they'd hate her when they saw her baby's racial blend. But they helped her to the hospital when her labor pains had started up, helped her up the long stairs when the two of them came home again. They bought her a big bassinet when they saw the fruit box where Hank slept, a baseball and a leather glove, a homemade set of wooden blocks. But she didn't let them see his face till Hank was nearly four weeks old, claiming that the light's too bright, afraid of all their nasty germs. Until he was asleep one day when another check from Daniel came and Myrna thought that she'd have time to run to get some groceries.

She'd hoped they wouldn't notice as she stepped off the front stoop alone; "Where's our little buddy?" asked a Captain smoking by the door. "I didn't want to wake him up. I'm only going to the store," but the line inside the bank was slow so the whole trip took her twice as long. She's rushing down the sidewalk with a half-full bag of groceries, reassured that all is well by silence as she climbs the stairs. Her hand is on the banister when she gets up to the second floor, gasps to see the jamb all splintered, locked door half-a-foot ajar. Instantly she's certain someone's busted in to harm her son, taken him to be shipped to a Japanese interment camp. She runs into the little room, almost knocks a fireman down who holds a vicious-looking tool for bludgeoning her baby boy. The Captain's got Hank in his arms and swings to block him from her grasp; "Shhh . . . shhh . . . shhhh," he whispers softly, "finally got him settled down."

Hank could see his mom was gone by the vacant look now in her eyes, halfway through his story of the blaze last night at Lidia's. The flames took all the woman's clothes, her kitchen things and furniture, left her with a little car with blistered paint along one side. But at least the fire didn't spread and Brenda saved the plastic doll and nobody got hurt since all the kids ran out the backyard door. The Red Cross brought a brimming bag so Lidia would have some clothes; worst thing was she'd lost the only picture of her grandmother. He told her not to come to work until she'd found a place to stay, *take whatever time you need to get back on your feet again.* Already he and Jessie had discussed the extra room in back; Hank had put his desk there but could move it for a bit more space. Lidia was the only help that Myrna hadn't chased away; if she lived here full time Hank felt their lives would be much easier.

His mother wasn't listening and she hadn't touched her oatmeal; his story not important but he'd like it if she ate some more. So he asked if it was hot enough, if she'd like some cream instead of milk, a pat of butter for the top, some raisins or some chopped-up nuts. She looked up like he'd startled her, a blank expression on her face; he watched as Myrna's brain engaged:

"Raisins would be rather nice."

He wondered where it was she went when she was in some reverie: *Living in the past or thinking up new ways to torture me?* He got up from the table to fetch raisins from beside the stove, came back to find Myrna spooning coffee on her oatmeal.

"I'm not sure that will taste too good," and he took the bowl away from her. "How about some scrambled eggs," his voice starting to sound annoyed. Hank hadn't slept at all last night, his thoughts revolving 'round the fire: all the things that could have ended in some huge catastrophe. Climbing into bed at four, the little house now soggy coals, after filling up the truck and cleaning all the fire hose: what if Brenda had been hurt or somehow trapped inside the house? *Would I have been brave enough to crawl inside and search for her?* When Jessie's radio went off he hadn't had a wink of sleep, watching as the early morning slowly lit the bedroom walls. He thought he might as well get up while she was still under the shower, make her something hot for breakfast, try to think of something else. Jessie said how proud she was—*my brave and handsome fireman*—even after Hank confessed he'd pulled all of the levers wrong.

Myrna wonders why the waiter took away her oatmeal: learned to like it that way when she once found all the milk was gone. This man has got an attitude, he makes a show of being polite; but by his tone of voice she knows he thinks she isn't good enough. Hank flipped some butter in a pan, got eggs out of the Frigidaire, reminded he still had to give her morning dose of insulin. He put a couple slices down, then grated some fresh Parmesan, turned around to find his mother heading for the living room.

Jesus Christ Almighty! Is it gonna be one of those days? He raced around the table till he got her by the upper arm.

"Your eggs are almost ready," but she turned around and clobbered him: closed fist hard against his face, which knocked him up against the door.

He was too stunned to react till she was almost halfway down the hall: impulse was to drag her back and chain her to the blasted chair. But instead he let her disappear: she won't remember anything; give her fifteen minutes and she'd ask him where her dinner was. She'd never hit that hard before, his glasses all bent up again, a scratch across his left cheek and his jaw hurt when he opened it. He went back to the kitchen to wrap ice inside a paper towel, hold it underneath his eye, which felt like it was going to swell.

—*how'd ya get that shiner, Hank?*

—*my mother throws a nasty hook*

He sat down at the table and sipped coffee from his mother's cup, patted Trouble on her head now resting warmly on his lap. Deep inside he felt a burning numbness spreading through his chest, thought he might unlock the doors and hope his mother wandered off.

...

The last time someone grabbed her arm was over fifty years ago, when Myrna's father found out who his daughter's baby's father was. He'd grabbed her arm and slapped her face and pushed her down onto the floor;

didn't matter who the boy was, just that he was Japanese. Looking at his livid face, she was absolutely petrified: he'd reached out for the kindling box but grabbed a poker from the fire. He wasn't going to wait to drag her past the rhododendron bush, but right there in the living room where blood would stain the carpeting. The poker only came down once before her mother grabbed his arm, begging him to stop and let *God* be the one to punish her. *Go get all your things!* he snapped, *and put them outside in the yard!* Her mother let her pack a bag: her quilt and clothes and underwear. All the rest went in the pile: her dolls and all her books from school; the stack had not been large until he made her put the mattress on. She dragged it down the hallway past the kitchen through the living room; Martin didn't help but simply sat out on the porch and stared.

—*Martin, take her into town and drop her at the bus depot.*

Hank came in the living room to find a pile of Myrna's clothes; "What the heck," he whispered as he walked down to his mother's room. She had her bed all pulled apart, the mattress halfway on the floor; tears welled in her eyes, she said, "Well, look who's come to say *good-bye.*"

"Mother, don't get so upset."

"Just how am I supposed to feel?"

"I just want you to eat something."

"I'm not exactly hungry now."

The man she's looking at is Frank; she thought that he'd been sent away; it's been so long she's not exactly sure she even likes him now. It was all infatuation, that he gave her funny little gifts, like the candy-coated ginger that she had to learn to like to eat. But she loved to walk and hold his hand, enjoyed her power over him: touch him where she shouldn't and it makes his breathing difficult. But she missed him since the war began, the Japanese confined to home; several times a week they had been meeting near the railroad tracks. He came to her house only twice, each time the middle of the night: the day the Japs began the war then just before internment camp. She heard the tapping at her window, every night expecting it; second time he visited she didn't have to drag him in. They're standing on her braided rug, her bare feet starting to get cold, whispering tomorrow they'll be loaded on a special train. He's got to get back to the farm before his mother notices; the sheriff said they'd shoot first *if we see one of you out at night.* Holding out a little box that's papered with a simple bow; he's not sure where they're sending them or how long they'll be kept away. She takes the box and opens it, the ribbon floats down to the floor: a tiny dragon carved from jade, the stone cool in her open palm. Even in the darkness she can see how beautiful it is; eighteen years and no one's ever given such a grown-up gift. She leans forward and kisses him, wraps her arms around his neck, makes his breath completely stop by pressing in against his hips. Moving both hands to his belt, she fumbles with his button fly; the only forward thing he did was lift her nightgown up a ways. They've done this only twice before, and she's thrilled how hard and smooth he is; leaning back against her bed it only hurts a little bit. But she barely gets the rhythm down before he's started shuddering; footsteps in the hall and Frank is climbing out the windowsill. He doesn't even say good-bye; her brother's opening the door; her nightgown's fallen back in place: *I thought I heard a voice in here.*

Martin glances 'round the room, asks *why are you up out of bed?* He takes two steps across the floor to push the window closed again. Not sure which one saw it first, the moonlight on the Asian lace: *How did this thing get in here?* as he stoops to pick the ribbon up.

Hank was looking at his mom whose face now had that vacant stare, standing still for several moments till Hank roughly cleared his throat.

"What were you just thinking of?" but she didn't care to answer him. "Let me help you turn the bed," and she let him push the mattress back. Again he wondered where she went: *Is she having little seizure spells?* He told her, "In the living room there's some laundry you could help me fold." They put the sheets and blankets back as if it were a normal chore; halfway down the hall she asked Hank if they might be eating soon.

"I don't know why I'm hungry, since I ate so much at lunch today. If I keep pigging out I'll soon be fatter than an elephant!"

Hank told her if she'd fold the clothes he'd fix her up a little snack; he was way late for her insulin but she had to eat some breakfast first. Already it was half past nine, most days she got her shot by eight; the oatmeal went down the drain and Trouble got the scrambled eggs.

"Mom, how 'bout some cereal?" he called while pulling down a box; she liked it kind of soggy with some sugar sprinkled over it. Hank had never seen the charm of such a boring bowl of food: *I'd rather eat a plate of air and save two hundred calories.* She was always going on about how much she overate at lunch, but she really only picked at food and criticized how it was cooked. So Hank had made a mental list of how she said she liked her food, hoping to avoid the scenes where plates got broken on the floor. She liked a steak cooked bloody-rare and mustard on her hamburgers; he'd never serve another green bean even if she begged him to. He didn't hear an answer so he went ahead and filled the bowl, stopped to grind another half a cup of fresh espresso beans.

Hank called that it was ready but he didn't hear if she replied, *maybe she's gone to the bathroom,* thinks he'll do her insulin. He kept the vial in the fridge, the needle locked up in a drawer that was filled with all the other things that Myrna shouldn't get into. Drawing up a new syringe he flicked it with a fingertip; about to lock the drawer but had his eye caught by the *Vicodin.* He'd given her some earlier, when he'd first roused her out of bed; perhaps she needed more because the first dose wasn't big enough. He called his mother one more time; her hearing wasn't very good; he thought she might have answered though he was thinking about side effects. The label said you're not to drive or operate machinery: *I'll have to take her keys and call her boss down at the gravel pit.* Sliding out one of the knives, he pulled the wooden cutting board, taking out a tablet thinking he could cut one into halves. But the pill just crumbled into dust, scattering across the board; he didn't want to waste it since there was only half a bottle full. *It's really not that big a dose,* and he scooped the dust into a glass, filled it full of apple juice then tested if it tasted right.

It didn't help to call again, he'd have to track his mother down; try once more to herd her to the table for her cereal. He was not yet to the living room when he noticed a strong sulfur smell; found her standing near the mound of clothing she'd spilled on the floor. There were at least a dozen matches lying dead among the pile of clothes, half of all her blouses scarred with blackened half-inch little holes. She didn't look him in the eye but spoke in quiet mumbled words; scared expression on her face:

"I couldn't find the kerosene."

She's not sure what he'll do now that she couldn't get the clothes to burn; maybe he will change his mind and not send her away from home.

Remembering the way it smelled, the black smoke from the kerosene, the curling pages of the books as flames consumed their binding glue. But once the mattress caught on fire, then Martin put her in the car, Father watching from the porch and Mother's face inside her hands.

Martin didn't speak till they were halfway down the Hooster road, across the river safely on the new bridge over Tucker Falls. Martin must be twenty-six, rejected by the army docs, sent back home so someone's there to help get all the apples picked. Glancing sideways at her brother, death-grip on the steering wheel, face a mottled pink and red: *You might as well have fucked a goat! There are things that people JUST DON'T DO!!* Then he takes a deep breath through his nose, holds it till his shaking stops and doesn't say another word.

Hank stared at his mother standing by the pile of ruined clothes; it was one thing burning candles but this could have been their funeral pyre. He'd searched the house for matches and then locked what he'd found in the drawer: *I brought my wife to live here with a raving pyromaniac.* He grabbed the matchbook from her hand—a fancy Portland restaurant; he and Jessie ate there last a half-a-dozen years ago. He gave the matchbook back to her—she'd used all of the matches up—and she slipped it in the pocket of the housecoat that she liked so much.

"I've got your breakfast ready."

"I don't think I'm hungry anymore."

"Well, I don't really care!" he said, and grabbed her upper arm again. She didn't try to fight this time but let herself be dragged along; Hank pulled out her chair and set her down with more than just a shove. Her bottom only glanced the seat, which tipped her down onto the floor, head hit hard against the fake brick print on the linoleum. Myrna didn't move because she's waiting for the poker strike; Hank's breath now was caught behind the nickel sideways in his throat. The sound of death was in the house: nothing but the ticking clock; Hank stared at his mother for the longest seconds of his life. He was thinking that they should have found him guilty for the death of Nate, put him into prison *since I can't seem to control myself.* It was not until he saw her breathe that he broke from his paralysis, quickly bent to make sure that his mother wasn't badly hurt. He got her sitting upright and then checked for equal pupil size; already he could see the growing goose egg where she hit the floor. He helped her up into the chair, asked her if she felt okay; Hank now had a shiner and his mother had a forehead bruise. He watched as she picked up her spoon and took a bite of cereal, horrified to see he'd left a handprint where he'd grabbed her arm.

"This is all I need!" he whispered. *Now what am I going to do?*

"Here, Mom, drink your apple juice. It's time you got your insulin."

Cold Soup
July 1997

THERE WERE FOUR around the kitchen table, bowls of chilled *gazpacho* soup, summer sun was filtered backwards through the windows facing north. The sandwiches were salmon salad, lightly toasted Jewish rye, the soup made from the vegetables that Jessie picked an hour before. Lidia told Myrna it was her family's secret recipe, that Hank had sworn he'd never tell a soul what made it taste so good. But Myrna isn't in the mood—just woke up from a two-hour nap—to listen to some *brown-skinned heathen* dresses like a *worthless tramp*. She takes a big spoonful of soup and puts it quickly in her mouth, spits it back into the bowl: *How come my stinking soup's not hot?!* Lidia was mortified and Jessie's head shook back and forth, Hank sat right across from Myrna, wiping soup off of his shirt.

"That's the way it's supposed to be."

"Well, I'm not going to eat this crap."

"Then you just eat your sandwich," and he took the bowl from Myrna's place. But he hadn't even sat back down when he saw the tears well in her eyes; looking 'round the table, she says:

"Why don't I get any soup? Everybody else has some."

"No one's having soup, Mom." And he took the other bowls as well.

Lidia had seldom had much chance to watch them interact; before when she came over Hank and Jessie would go rushing off. Hank was obviously trying to be patient with his addled mom, but not far underneath she saw he'd really like to strangle her.

"Her blood sugar is low again. That's why she's acting ornery." She watched as Hank got up to get a jug out of the Frigidaire. He poured a glass of apple juice, unlocked one of the kitchen drawers, took a pill out of a bottle, crushed and poured it in the glass. Lidia saw Jessie giving Hank a certain kind of look.

"Don't you think she's had enough?"

"Obviously not," he said.

"She slept most of the morning…" but Hank gave her back a tired stare, put the glass down on the table:

"Mother, drink your apple juice."

They all watched as she took the glass, obliged him with a healthy sip; once she'd finished half Hank finally let the breath out of his chest.

"Let's just get this over with," and he brought all of the soup bowls back. "Lidia, I'm sorry, but sometimes things get a little tense."

whatzamaddayou?
July 1997

HANK WAS THINKING of his mom, though not the one sprawled in a chair, with eyes closed and her lips apart, about to lose a string of drool. He was thinking of his *real* mom, the one he was imagining: the perfect mom who didn't snore or slap him when she got confused. She was wrapped in a kimono, wooden sandals on her tiny feet; she slid a room partition back and stepped in with a tray of tea. He was not sure if she ever speaks, she still looked thirty-two years old, with black hair and romantic eyes and skin smooth as a polished stone. She walked with tiny, measured steps across the spotless wooden floor: tatami mats and paper walls and paintings with calligraphy. The room smelled strong of cooking rice and steaming bowls of miso soup, the sound of someone in the kitchen chopping on a wooden block. The window screens were pulled back to expose a stunning mountain view: Fuji framed in cherry blossoms, bamboo and a deep-blue sky. Gracefully down to her knees, balancing the polished tray, bowing as she put a cup before a handsome samurai. If his father stood up he would tower over six feet tall with a sword tucked in a belt of silk and his long hair in a ponytail. But the two of them sat on the floor, his mother served her men some tea; they were seriously talking over manly and important things. They talked about the family name, of honor and integrity, how Hank had to imagine what his every action told the world. His father spoke of ancestors, a line that spanned a thousand years, how all their ghosts were watching to make sure Hank didn't ruin things. And even though Hank was fifty-five, his father looked just thirty-nine and Hank might weigh a hundred pounds, his voice not yet begun to change. He looked up at his father with desire burning through his chest, was mesmerized by how his mother seemed to float across the room. This was Hank's alternate life, the way things were supposed to be: the product of a family of aristocratic samurai. The fantasy was elaborate, beginning when he was a child, built around an entry in the "J" encyclopedia.

Hank would have looked in books at school, but someone would have taunted him: more evidence that Hank was not American as God Himself. But at home they had a volume for each letter of the alphabet so when he thought he was alone he'd get out the *Britannica*. He'd only skimmed the article, a boring list of industries, a chart on population growth, a picture of Hiroshima. But what kept Hank's attention was a portrait of a family, a handsome-looking couple with a son who could have been his age. Their clothing was traditional, the backdrop was a painted screen: this is who he would have been if Myrna hadn't interfered. They all had the same kind of hair, their skin-tones were identical; the boy looked like the father only he'd been done in miniature. Sitting on the floor he'd act like he was browsing randomly; each time Myrna passed he'd flip to *Jupiter* or *Jimson weed*. He thought that he was clever but one day she stopped behind his back; handing him another book, said *Hank, you'll wear that volume out*. Her voice had sounded casual but Hank could always tell her mood; felt like she had caught him in the act of pleasuring himself.

The few times Hank had ever stopped to analyze this fantasy, he'd seen it made no sense at all that someone might have stolen him. They would have asked a ransom but a samurai would not have paid; his father would have tracked them down and whacked their heads off with his sword. And how'd he end up in the States with a name as white as Davenport? Why would Dan and Myrna want a boy who didn't look like them? Born the first year of the war, while people rationed food and gas: raising Hank was just like giving comfort to the enemy. He was more likely the product of a Park Blocks business accident: some wretched girl brought from Japan to rent in fifteen-minute slots. His father was anonymous, a sailor or a laborer: a skinny, squint-eyed, buck-toothed Nip with four-bits paid to scratch an itch. Myrna never answered Hank why she and Dan adopted him; why they would have taken on the stigma and embarrassment. But they treated him like family, as if he was their flesh and blood, except when meeting someone new: *...and Hank is our adopted son.* He always wondered why they never had a baby of their own; wondered how it would have felt if there had been a *real* one.

Myrna made a quiet snort and Hank looked at his sleeping mom, her jaw relaxed so that her lips were open in a perfect "O." The string of drool was hanging like the small line in the letter "Q," and he wondered if he tried if he could wipe it without waking her. He wanted her to stay asleep, deciding he should leave her be; he picked up a *New Yorker* that he'd read a half-a-dozen times.

On one of the end tables, there was a little dragon made of jade, something Hank remembered from as long ago as he could think. It was the only thing his mother owned that looked like it was Japanese, besides, of course, a son she might have picked out of dumpster bin. He once asked where she got it and she'd said *a present from a friend,* and he'd asked her who it was and she'd replied *someone you've never met.* When she wasn't in the room, he sometimes used to finger it, knowing if she caught him he might miss out on dessert that night. But the smoothness of the stone was often too much for a six-year-old, calling to his fingers since there's nothing else that felt that cold. He'd hold it in his hand and marvel at how intricate it was, knowing someone Japanese had carved and polished it by hand. His father once had walked in when Hank held the dragon in his palm, told him to be careful since the thing was irreplaceable. Daniel sat down on the couch and pulled Hank up onto his lap, said *someday when you're older I think your mom will probably give you this.*

Hank now thought of Daniel, how his father tried to give him time: outside in the backyard with a football or a baseball bat. There was nothing else to do so Hank gave in to random, idle thoughts: weekends Daniel took him to do rounds down at the hospital. Hank couldn't visit patient rooms so Dan parked him at the nurses' desk, remembering white dresses and the funny little nursing caps. The nurses fawned all over him: the doctor's shy adopted son; they'd whisper that his father was the nicest doctor on the staff.

Trouble got up off the floor and asked to have her back end scratched, pushed her hip against Hank's knee and started rocking back and forth. Hank looked at his mother who'd been sleeping for at least an hour, wondered why his father had to be the first of them to die. What if it was Daniel who was napping in the Lazy-boy? Later on they'd go outside and try to fix the lawn mower. The man was never shy on jokes, his timing was impeccable: *whatzamaddayou?* he'd ask when Hank would look too serious. He learned when Daniel got that tone—*there's something that you have to know*—it always meant that what came next was going to be another joke. But even though his father joked, Hank knew he did important work, every day he'd come home tired from cutting some kid's tonsils out. He'd almost always walk in late, hug Myrna with a noisy kiss, then mix himself a highball drink and ask Hank *homework finished yet?* Hank wondered why he had to ask: *Of course I've got my homework done! And made my bed, hung up my clothes, and helped Mom get the table set!* Then he'd ask about his father's day, the many worthy lives he'd saved: *A young boy picked his nose so deep his finger poked into his brain!* Daniel worked until he died, the perfect doctor-patriarch: hair still full and brilliant white and knew his patients' names by heart. Hank always meant to *talk* to him, to finally have a man-to-man, but every time he thought he might, Hank's beeper would go off again.

Myrna's drool was longer now and reached an inch below her chin; Hank could see it clearly from the sofa clear across the room. His mother looked much younger than a woman in her seventies: *What would she be like now if she didn't have the Alzheimer's?* All his life she'd told him she was born in 1923, in Denver, Boston, Pittsburgh and one time in Philadelphia. *My parents both died of the flu just after I had finished school. I met Dan on the stagecoach when the horses stopped in Idaho.*

"But where did you get *me?*" he asked.

"I'll tell you when you're older, Hank."

It made more sense to Hank she should be ten years *older* than she said: *Why would they adopt me if they could have had one naturally?* If Hank was fifty-five then she was nineteen when she brought him home, with Daniel in the army pulling shrapnel out of dirty wounds. Maybe well before the war they'd tried at first the normal way, then picked out Hank before Dan left so Myrna would have company. But the numbers never worked out right when Hank would try to think it through, so he'd drive the thoughts out of his head with homework done right after school. Hank thought back how his mother must have suffered several miscarriages, those times when she got "sick" and Hank was banished to the neighbors' house. Daniel had stayed home from work—Hank saw his car parked in the drive—but Hank was not allowed home till the neighbor lady said he could.

Myrna gave another snort and Hank looked over at his mom: halfway through a two-arm stretch, her face distorted by a yawn. She's looking at her only son, the boy grown up into a man; she's trying to remember when his beard had started turning gray. And what had they been talking of? She must have lost her train of thought. Probably some patient since that's all Hank ever thinks about. It seems like it was just last year that Hank was such a little guy: eight going on eighty and lighthearted as a grizzly bear. Perhaps it was his Asian blood that made him act so serious; she took him to the movies but he didn't laugh like other kids. Maybe she's responsible—for hiding who his father was—but Myrna didn't want the boy to think his mother was a slut. So the only ones who knew the truth were the doctor who delivered her, Daniel and the nurses and the men down at the fire hall. She'd always planned to tell Hank when he reached an understanding age, but after he was eight or nine he never brought it up again. Except for being sensitive, he really was the perfect child: didn't sass and chores were done and never started fights at school.

"How was your nap?" Hank asked his mom.

"I barely even closed my eyes."

"Maybe we should have some lunch."

"There's something I should tell you, son."

Hank had heard this line before, it never came to anything: the dog would bark, the mail would come; she'd tell him that her feet are cold.

"When I was just a girl," she said, "this boy I knew was Japanese..." but that's all that she said before the thought had slipped away from her.

What He Wants To Be
July 1997

IT WAS YEARS AGO on morning rounds two weeks past Nathan's surgery: Saturday at six a.m., ICU room seventeen. The surgery had gone quite well, a San Francisco hospital, the new heart from a young girl floating facedown in a swimming pool. But after Nathan came home from the California hospital, his mother called to say Nate had a fever and his throat was sore. Hank stepped in the curtained room where Nate's mom slept curled in a chair; he didn't want to wake her since he knew she hadn't slept for days. He'd seen the blood culture results and narrow sensitivities, changed antibiotics but Nate's fever hadn't gone away. There were monitors and IV pumps and wires from Nathan's healing chest; drinking cups with bendy straws and half-a-dozen plastic trucks. It smelled of rubbing alcohol and antiseptic floor cleaner and off-gassing from cathode rays and half-full plastic urine bags. Unconsciously Hank noted that Nate's heartbeat was irregular; the constant beep-beep-beeping not as steady as the night before.

The boy was just a skinny runt who had a funny, winning way: could barely run a dozen steps but not afraid of anything. He'd march in through Hank's clinic doors, go straight to the receptionist: in a breathless voice he'd tell her *Doctor Hank can see me now.* And they sat once on a bench outside the new home for the elephants: a swimming hole and fake bamboo and rocks made out of concrete mix. Eating lunch Hank packed into the backpack with Nate's oxygen, occasionally they'd thrown a peanut to the swaying pachyderms. The boy had won Hank's heart to a degree that was embarrassing, constantly imagining when next he'd get to see the kid. It almost felt like an affair; he'd stop on his way home from work, anxious to see Nathan's face and check the beating of his heart. Nate had thrown a peanut but it didn't even reach the fence; Hank had wondered how much something like that must have bothered him. The boy was such a skinny runt; he didn't have an ounce of fat; Hank imagined what he'd be like if they found the boy a heart. Then Hank asked what Nate wants to be: a doctor or a fireman? Perhaps a famous scientist? A teacher or an astronaut? The boy looked up at Hank and had to catch his breath to answer him: *I've been thinking that I'd really like to be a teenager.*

In the ICU room Hank was fiddling with the IV pump, pushing several buttons so the damn thing wouldn't wake the mom. He tried to warm his stethoscope by rubbing it between his palms, then put it light against the chest when Nathan opened up his eyes.

"*Whatsamattayou?*" Hank whispered, still concerned he'd wake the mom, heart ached when he saw the faintest smile cross Nathan's tired mouth.

"My throat still hurts."

"I'm sure it does."

Hank could barely hear his words. He brought a straw within his reach.

"Try to drink a little bit."

Nathan gently licked his lips then lifted up his head a bit; lips around the plastic straw he winced as he was swallowing. His head fell on his pillow and his eyelids slowly closed again; in the faintest whisper he said *Hank, I don't feel very good.* Hank put down the cup and snugged the blanket underneath his chin, ran his hand over the top of Nathan's light-brown, kinky hair.

"Just go back to sleep," Hank said, then gently patted Nathan's thigh, stood up from the bed where moments later his young friend would die.

The Hero
July 1997

HANK HAD GRABBED his beeper and was holding it up to his ear, stepping to the kitchen for a pad to write the address down. It was somewhere along Collins Road, an old man feeling short of breath; dispatch said that Hooster didn't have an ambulance to send. Their backup was the next small town, at least a forty minute drive if traffic wasn't heavy and their crew remembered where to turn. It really could be anything: pneumonia or a sudden stroke, cardiac or asthma or he got up from his chair too fast. Edgar had no medical, the volunteers were first-aid trained, except for a physician who they'd all seen on the evening news. Hank's choice was to ignore the call and let the others handle it, or lock his mother in the house and hope that she behaved herself. But neither option felt okay and sometimes no one else responds; how could he just sit there while some old man slowly crumped and died?

"Mom, how 'bout a little drive?" and his shoes were in the entryway; Myrna was in her housecoat and her slippers were already on.

"That would be delightful. But I need to use the Ladies first."

"We're going to a neighbor's house. We'll do it over there," he said.

She simply shrugged and said *okay* and followed Hank out to his truck; traffic on his beeper said that Brenda had the booster rig. Ever since the Chief's collapse she'd taken over all his chores: checking trucks and running drills and making sure the tanks were full. So Hank could go straight to the scene and shave two minutes off the time since Brenda would be there first with the oxygen and AED.

"Aren't you driving kind of fast?" and Myrna's seatbelt wasn't on: "Buckle up," he told her, but she was having trouble with the latch. There was a corner where the Lake Road turned and Alder Road continued south, and the yard in Lake Road's elbow was all overgrown with bushy shrubs. He was halfway through the intersection going fifty miles an hour, realizing that this was a *really* stupid thing to do. If another car had come, an RV or a logging truck, he wouldn't have a clue until the air bag knocked his glasses off. Just because he'd volunteered, he was not the one responsible if some old geezer gasped his last while Hank drove sanely to his house. So even though he was safely through, Hank brought his foot up off the gas, took a breath and let it out; *Get a grip* he told himself.

Coming up to Collins Road he wasn't sure which way to turn: *fifty-seven-twenty-nine* should be the right side of the road. As Hank was making up his mind his beeper crackled back to life, Brenda Thompson speaking in a voice all firm and businesslike:

"Dispatch, seven-one on scene. Seven-zero-two command. All responding units, this is Chief Nagoya's residence."

All at once Hank felt a jolting surge of fresh adrenaline: racing heart and breaking sweat and the nickel sideways in his throat. Hank knew where he was going now: an old house with a covered porch, built by George's father back before George even learned to walk. It was the friggin' farm right next to Hank's, but the house faced toward a different road: a fence defined their properties with sixty acres in between. George had lived there sixty years and Hank had been to visit twice, checking in to see how George was doing since his heart had stopped. George lived there all by himself and Hank stepped back down on the gas, braked for Evan Smith, who ran the stop sign at O'Leary Road. They both raced down the gravel drive and stopped inside a cloud of dust; Evan barely stopped his truck before he ran into the house.

"Mom, I have to go inside. I want you to wait here for me."

"I need to use the Ladies' . . ."

"I'll be back as quickly as I can."

The house had a nice Craftsman feel but well into a downward slide: the porch steps void of paint or stain and one-half of the roof was moss.

Apparently George hadn't ever thrown a magazine away, with stacks of them along the porch weighed down with rusting tractor parts. But there was still a pathway to the door that opened on the living room; Brenda had George on the couch and measuring his blood pressure.

"Thank God you're here," she whispered, then, "one-fifty over one-o-two," moving to one side so Hank could do whatever doctors do. George's hand was on his chest, his face a mottled ashy-gray, a bead of sweat above his lip although it wasn't hot inside.

"*Whatsamaddayou?*" Hank asked, and George gave him a little smile.

"The elephant is back again."

"How many *nitros* have you had?"

Brenda had the oxygen, the green mask with the floppy bag.

"Fifteen liters," Hank said, "and could someone get the AED?"

George's eyes closed while he took a few breaths from the O2 tank; Hank could feel a decent pulse at George's slightly clammy wrist.

"How many have you had?" Hank asked.

"Those pills just make my head explode."

"It's your choice, George. You either get a headache or a heart attack."

The bottle was beside the couch, he hadn't even opened it: tiny little pills that he'd been told to take at times like these.

"Rate your pain from one to ten."

"It's kind of like the other time."

"Hold this underneath your tongue." Hank slipped a pill in George's mouth. What he wanted was an EKG and to stick an IV in his arm, but all the first-aid bag had were some latex gloves and bandages. If George started to fibrillate, they'd shock him with the AED, with little more that they could do until the ambulance arrived.

"Where do you keep your aspirin?"

"I think there's some behind the mirror."

Evan went to hunt it down while Brenda filled a water glass.

"You're supposed to take one every day."

"I know. I just can't stomach pills."

"How's your chest now, one-to-ten?"

"The elephant's moved to my head."

Hank saw the flush on George's face, the *nitro* dilating his veins; he wrapped the cuff around his arm and took his blood pressure again.

"One-thirty over eighty-six," and Brenda wrote the numbers down; Evan brought the aspirin.

"Chew before you swallow it."

It had been about five minutes since they all ran into George's house, twice that since the dispatcher had set their fire beepers off. They had done all they could do but wait, so Brenda called the dispatcher: *The ambulance from Skyline says they've just turned on to 35.* That was still a thirty-minute drive, even with their siren on; Hank took out another *nitro*, slipped it under George's tongue. His impulse was to put him in the back of Evan's pickup truck, get him to the hospital before the ambulance arrived. But George had pulled this stunt before: dropped dead right on the yellow line; what if George's heart should stop while they were driving him to town? They'd have to lay him in the road and shock him with the AED and hope no logging trucks came by while they were doing CPR. The best thing was to let his heart enjoy the bottled oxygen; every couple minutes pop another *nitroglycerin*.

"One-to-ten. How's the pain?"

"It's better," is all George would say.

Patting George's shoulder, Hank had trouble getting off his knees, let himself glance 'round the old Chief's claustrophobic living room. The first time Hank came over he was shocked by how the house was kept with every surface covered by a stack of worthless dusty junk. The front porch had seemed bad enough, but inside was a rabbit's den: foot-wide pathways ran between the five-foot stacks of magazines. There were tractor parts, a bicycle, recycled piles of Christmas wrap, never-opened gadgets sold on television late at night. The house was diagnostic of a nasty case of OCD: somewhere was a tin with every toothpick George had ever chewed. Hank thought about the fire hall, how everything was normal-clean, how George had somehow managed to control his rogue compulsive gene. The house smelled like a used bookstore, of crumbling yellowed paperbacks, the dark-and-dankest corner of a warehouse full of mice and crates. Hank looked for a kitchen chair so he could sit down next to George, keep a finger on his pulse until the ambulance arrived. But every chair was stacked high as a cairn up on a mountaintop: catalogs and junk mail selling window shades and nursery stock. Apparently the only place George ever sat was on the couch; every chair and tabletop was stacked until it might collapse.

George breathed through the clear green mask and felt a wave of nausea, the throbbing of the headache from the pill Hank put under his tongue. The pain began that morning while he dried himself after a shower, then faded after he was dressed and drinking coffee on the couch. Though it never really went away—like the memory of a missing tooth—he didn't want to take a pill for an ache that seemed so trivial. But now he wondered if he'd die from angina and heart disease: the doctors said he had a spastic coronary artery. After lunch he'd gone outside to check the firmness of his pears, had to stop three times before he made it to the tractor shed. Then he did what he's complained about, what people in the country do: instead of calling 911 he thought that he would rest a spell. He knew if he called dispatch that they'd have to set the siren off, bothering the neighbors when it all might be a touch of gas.

"You want to check his blood pressure?" and Brenda jumped to do the task, anything but stand around and wait for George's heart to stop.

Mother! Hank remembered, and he whispered that he'd be right back: out the door and down the steps and certain she'd have wandered off. That was all he'd need right now, to call a search out for his mom; which victim would he rather lose? His mother or the man inside? But he saw her in the driver's seat; he wondered if she'd wet herself:

"This stinking thing won't start!' she said while pounding buttons on the dash.

"You've got to have the key," he said, and Myrna stopped to contemplate.

"I knew that," she said, then let her hand drop down into her lap.

Hank opened up her door and sniffed to see if she had ruined the seat, but all he smelled was Myrna's mix of lavender and baby talc.

"Let's go find the Ladies' Room."

"I'd think you'd want to find the Men's."

"I thought you said you had to pee."

"Oh, that was days and days ago!"

Hank thought *what's gotten into her?* as he leaned to get her seatbelt off; she couldn't get it latched and so she'd wedged it tight between the seats. Leaning over, Hank got a strong feeling of impending doom, realizing that his face was right there in the danger zone. He was conditioned not to stand too near, to keep a full arm's length away, in case she had a sudden urge to sink her teeth into his ear. *She really should be in a home. It's not good that I feel this way.* But Hank feared that the nursing staff would treat her like a rabid dog. Yanking on the seatbelt clip, he finally got it free and clear, and as he leaned back out he felt her lips caress his bearded cheek. He looked back at his mother who was blushing like a schoolgirl; "Thank you. That was sweet," he said, and she let him help her from the cab.

She feels a bit unsteady, like she's had a sip too much to drink or after lying down a while she's gotten to her feet too fast. But Frank holds steady to her arm and lets her take what time she needs because he knows it's not just any day she meets his family. She's worried looking at the house, the years have not been very kind: the porch needs paint, the roof's a mess, the yard was once a paradise. She's seen his house a thousand times but never closer than the road; she's only seen Frank's mother standing in the shadow of the door. But apparently today's the day; she's finally going to see inside, where Martin says they don't wear shoes because they eat rice off the floor. She hopes they won't expect her to, especially the way things look: as if no one has cleared the porch since Noah loaded up his ark. Frank is also looking tense and older than he's supposed to be, his handsome Asian baby-face can't hide the fact he's middle-aged. Of course his parents must be getting well into their seventies and haven't got the energy to keep the house up anymore. Frank leaves her at the bottom step to help his parents get prepared; he bounds up through the front door in between tall stacks of magazines.

"Everything okay in here?"

"His pressure's stayed about the same."

"How's your pain, George, one-to-ten?"

"I've felt worse a couple times."

Tapping out another pill, Hank put it under George's tongue, wishing he could push a little morphine in the old man's vein. Calculating from his watch, *the ambulance is halfway here,* leaning 'round the corner near the Windmaster convenience store.

"I had to bring my mother, George. Okay if she comes in to pee?"

"Anything you want," he said, "But I'm not sure if the seat is clean."

Hank went out to find his mother standing on the middle stair. "Maybe you could help me, Frank. I'm more anxious than I thought I'd be." Managing the last two steps, the front door and the narrow paths, Myrna thinks that this is not at all how she'd imagined it. For sure it would be neat and clean, a table not far off the floor, with paper walls and woven mats and smells of steaming rice and tea. Frank's father's lying on the couch, a nurse taking his blood pressure; he looks an awful shade of gray like skim milk mixed with axle grease.

She whispers, "Is your mother home?"

"Not that I can tell," Hank said.

"You should have said your dad was ill."

"I think you're just a bit confused."

Hank watched his mother step across the steeply cluttered living room, stand before the couch and bow her body forward from the waist.

"*Konichiwa, Nagoya-san,*" and Myrna kept her formal bow.

"*Konichiwa,*" George said back while he gave his head a little nod.

Then Myrna said a few more words in perfect-sounding Japanese; Hank could feel the stupid nickel shift and make it hard to breathe.

"Let's leave George alone," and Hank took Myrna gently by the arm. "He isn't feeling very well. The bathroom's right here down the hall."

It suddenly occurs to her she's got a burning urgency, quickly as she can she follows Frank between the magazines. And though the hallway's filled with junk, the bathroom's reasonably clean; orange streak in the basin where a drip has stained the porcelain. Hank put down the toilet seat and checked to make sure it was dry, left the room so Myrna could enjoy a little privacy. Hank was flabbergasted by the scene out in the living room: *Where the heck would she have learned a single word of Japanese?* And how did she know George's name? Why would she have bowed like that? Something weird was going on but Hank was stumped what it could be. Every time she called him *Frank* was like a knife stabbed in his chest: not her fault but still hurt that his mom could not remember right. And what had she been on about some boyfriend when she was a girl? Perhaps she'd had a secret thing for Asian men all of these years. Maybe this explained a lot, her crush on little Asian boys: couldn't have one by herself so got one from somebody else. But why would she have married Daniel? So clearly just the opposite: freckled arms and bright-orange hair and eyes like dirty emeralds.

Hank stood in the crowded hall, staring at the piles and stacks; that was when he noticed what was really weird about this mess. George must have had subscriptions to four-dozen different magazines: *Rolling Stone* and *Seventeen* and *Popular Photography*. There were two full stacks of *Mother Jones* and half a wall of *Modern Bride: Penthouse, Gunsmith, Cats&Dogs*, and catalogs from *L.L.Bean*. He picked a random issue up to find it was the latest one, and underneath that issue they went backwards chronologically. He stepped into the kitchen with the table covered thick with mail: every single letter was an offer for a credit card. The chairs were segregated into sweepstakes from a clearinghouse, in-home carpet-cleaning ads and windshield crack-and-chip repair. It was like the biggest ball of string, the longest chain of paper clips, the man who broke the record for the most jumps on a pogo stick. George had sorted every piece he'd ever gotten in the mail; piled near the sink was maybe fifty years of Christmas cards. It was one thing if George was a slob who never threw a thing away, another if he kept junk thinking that it might be worth something. It must have taken lots of work to keep it all so organized; it didn't look too neat but Hank felt sure there was a system here. He went back to the living room and asked how George was feeling now:

"On a scale of one-to-ten…"

"Kind of comes and goes," he said.

He was feeling somewhat better now the headache started going away, the band around his chest had finally loosened up a turn or two. George was wishing that he hadn't had to call his volunteers, interrupt their afternoons on such a bright-blue, sunny day. But he also didn't want to die before he'd learned who lit those fires, figured out who had the brains and so much smoldering desire. Looking up at Davenport, the chest band tightened up a notch, knowing that this guy was neither dewy-eyed or innocent. Thinking of the latest fire, which wasn't on his check-off list: *Could be a distraction so the pattern isn't obvious.*

Kneeling down beside the couch Hank took the Fire Chief's pulse again, listened to his heart and lungs, the arteries along his neck. Looking at his watch Hank thought the ambulance should be here soon; just to be complete he did a quick check of the abdomen. George's face looked better—with some pink beneath the ashen-gray—the sweat gone from his upper lip and his breathing sounding easier. Hank checked the bottled oxygen to make sure it wouldn't run out soon: still eight hundred pounds of pressure, five more minutes more or less.

"Where'd your mother grow up, Hank?"

"I think in Philadelphia."

"What's her maiden name?" George asked.

"She's always claimed her name was *Jones*."

All this got George thinking that it couldn't be coincidence: a Japanese whose mom is white, both living on the Capo place.

Hank's knees popped as he got back up: *It shouldn't be much longer now*; a path led to the window so that he could reach the window blinds. The window looked across the drive, a hundred yards of Collins Road, and standing nose-close to the glass Hank saw the mountain to the south. He wondered why they built it so the picture window faced the road; shift it forty-five degrees and the view would be spectacular. But perhaps in 1923 it wouldn't have occurred to them: who would want to look outside when they'd spent the whole day pruning trees? Imagining what life was like for George when he was growing up: long walk back and forth to school and weekends filled with orchard chores. His parents had been immigrants; their English wouldn't have been good; even now George had a different way of saying certain words. The first time Hank came visiting, a few days after George came home, they sat here on the couch and Hank asked George about his growing up. What was there to do here for a young boy who was Japanese? George said he was only twelve the year the second war began. His father died two years before, so his brother Frank had been in charge, and he still could feel the thrill and fear of climbing up onto the train. The window shades had all been drawn and the soldiers told them not to peek so they couldn't tell their spies which way they went to the internment camps. In some ways George had felt relief, at least they weren't so all alone; ever since the first attack they weren't allowed to leave their farm. The train was filled with George's friends, with all the valley's Japanese; everybody's voice was hushed while soldiers paced between the seats. He'd seen his mother's look of fear, his brother's blank and constant stare; he had to go so bad till someone said there was a toilet stall. But after several hours had passed George started getting really bored: twelve years old and on a train and can't look at the scenery.

Myrna gets up off the seat and sets her clothes and housecoat right, turns to push the lever so her nasty business flushes down. The water at the basin takes a long time to start getting warm, and she barely gets a lather from a sliver of a bar of soap. The towel hung beside the sink has thoroughly been petrified; she's guessing that Frank's mother isn't up for laundry anymore. She can't leave with it smelling bad, especially Frank's parent's house: what if Frank's mom is waiting? She'll know who made the bathroom stink. So she looks behind the filmy mirror, opens up the cabinet doors, looking for a can of something she can spray into the air. The only thing behind the mirror is a tube of muscle liniment; beneath the sink are several hundred empty toilet paper rolls. But a drawer beside the basin has some tweezers and a shaving brush, several safety razors and some matches and a candle stub. She puts the candle on the counter, holds a match against the wick, thinking that she'll let it burn a moment then she'll blow it out.

Hank was at the window when he heard the distant ambulance; Evan Smith ran to the road to wave them left instead of right. When Myrna hears the siren she puts cupped hands over both her ears, mutters underneath her breath how much she hates that awful sound! It takes her to the fire hall, next door on the second floor, the sudden siren's climbing pitch when Hank has finally settled down. It only lasts two minutes, rising eight times up and down the scale, but every second hurts and then her baby screams for half an hour. It doesn't happen every night, it's sometimes quiet several days, but always when it starts to blare it's the last thing Myrna wants to hear. She has to pick the baby up, back and forth across the room, stick an aching nipple in to get him back to sleep again.

The siren got much louder as it raced the dust up Collins Road, shutting off completely as the ambulance turned in the drive. The dust was barely catching up when they had the stretcher from the back, the paramedic rushing with the med box and the monitor. Hank started giving history, a month since George's first attack; he doesn't but he's supposed to take an aspirin and a pressure pill. He'd had some chest pain yesterday, was feeling slightly short of breath, but thought it was the Polish sausage that he ate too fast for lunch. Hank told the paramedic that the *nitro* helped relieve the pain, but George refused to say how he would rate it on a sliding scale.

"Hey George, my name's Christopher. Your son here says you've had some pain. On a scale of one-to-ten, how'd you say the pain has been?"

"It got up to at least a nine, but now it's down around a two." Hank turned red because George now had totally embarrassed him. Hank thought to tell the paramedic that he wasn't George's son, that he wasn't just a volunteer: *I'm a bloody cardiologist!* The paramedic looked like he was barely old enough to drive, with his partner a young woman who had pink hair and an eyebrow ring. They hooked George to the monitor and popped an IV in his arm and had him on the stretcher before Hank had time to turn around. They all helped get George down the stairs and rolled into the ambulance; Hank wanted to go but he was told *there isn't room back here.*

"It's better if you drive yourself. But we'll take good care of your dad." Hank then had to swallow hard and hope they could do CPR.

It wasn't till the ambulance had pulled out of the dusty drive that Hank remembered that his mom was still inside the house somewhere. He turned around to see that Brenda had the bag and oxygen; Evan, starting up his truck, said,

"I guess I'll see you later, Hank."

Brenda walked up to the rig, the Number Six compartment door, put the first-aid bag away and clipped the metal bottle in. She turned around and Hank could see her eyes were brimming red with tears.

"Do you think he'll be okay?" she asked.

"If he'd take his stinking medicines."

Brenda was a solid rock, but obviously cared a lot; Hank gave her an awkward hug, as clumsy as a sixth-grade kiss.

"I think he's punishing himself . . . the whole thing with the mill collapse." She rubbed her sleeve against her eyes. "This place is disappearing fast."

Climbing in the driver's seat, she rolled the booster's window down, leaned her elbow on the door and wiped her eyes another time.

"Did you know that there was once a little town up here called Edgarville? I'd bet there's not a half-a-dozen people who remember it."

Hank felt the ground move under him, a momentary balance shift, had to put a hand up on the fender of the booster truck. She said there'd been a score of houses, front doors faced the railroad tracks, a grocery with a bar in back, a school for maybe twenty kids. But they needed to expand the mill, add presses for the hardboard plant; they'd finally paved the highway so the mill hands could live further off.

"I was maybe sixteen, and my father worked the greenchain then. He took us down to watch them run a 'dozer over everything."

A chill spread up Hank's spine until it rang a bell inside his head; how would Myrna know that there was once a little mill-town here?

"I heard my mom say *greenchain* once. I thought she must have made it up."

"*Greenchain* is the job of pulling lumber right after it's cut."

Through the booster's window Brenda looked out at the scenery, took a breath of air that smelled of diesel smoke and orchard spray. George's yard had one of the best views in all the universe: gorgeous orchard filled with fruit, a mountain rising out of it. There was dirt-road dust and drying grass and warm air off the valley walls, and Brenda thought how glad she was to live here where the air was clean.

"The mill burned down at least three times, but the owners kept rebuilding it. They promised they would this time, though it doesn't seem too likely now."

Brenda put the truck in gear and Hank stepped back a foot or two;

"I'll go put the truck away. Could you make sure the house is closed?"

Again Hank had forgotten he'd left Myrna in the *Ladies' Room*; probably would find her braiding rope from George's dental floss. He was bounding back up George's steps before the booster turned around: "Mother!" he called out to see if she was even in the house. The bathroom door was open and he quickly peeked his head inside: *Oh-my-god* she'd left a burning candle on the countertop. He blew the stub of candle out and drowned the wick beneath the tap; looking at the mirror he saw his angry face reflected back. *Jesus H. Christ!* he thought, *this is going to have to stop!*

"Mother!" he called out again back in the narrow, cluttered hall.

He still got no reply from her: *God help her if she went outside!* Three more doors he hadn't opened: one hid folded sheets and towels. The next door must be George's room with more tall stacks of magazines, a wicker basket full of clothes, a bed with rumpled pillowcase. It all seemed awfully lonely-sad: the room of someone unattached: a man who'd spent his whole life in the same house where his parents lived. He found her in the next room, but it could have been another house: a single bed, a desk and chair, but nothing stacked on anything. At first the scene seemed straight out of a movie where a child has died: a stranger finds a bedroom full of dusty memorabilia. There should be pennants on the wall, a model plane and baseball glove, a dresser top with treasures found while digging in the big backyard. And any moment now the dead child's mother should storm down the hall, shouting at them to get out, slam the door and throw the bolt. But it was really just a normal room, with fresh bills open on the desk, remarkable because this was the only room not filled with junk.

His mom was sitting on the bed, she didn't turn when Hank came in; was looking at a yellowed clipping taped inside a picture frame. He wanted to grab Myrna by the arm and drag her to his truck, find the nearest nursing home and shove as he slowed driving past. He was trying to collect himself, to gather up his resources: *George can't take a stupid pill and Mom's a pyromaniac.* His hand against the doorframe Hank took several deep breaths in and out, counting ten he tried to think of *eating chicken soup with rice*. And now that he had found his mom there wasn't any rush to leave; he took two steps into the room and sat down softly next to her. She was having a rare moment when the here-and-now was crystal clear; she realizes that the man beside her is her full-grown boy. Still she doesn't look at him, but moves the frame so he can read: *Edgar Son Dies Hero's Death* above a fading photograph. The caption reads that Frank Nagoya died on February 9th from mortal wounds inflicted in a battle in the Philippines. The story says the soldier had been trained as an interpreter; had learned about a deadly plot interrogating prisoners. His radio was broken and his captain was two miles away, and the hero had to rush across the front lines of the enemy. He'd died of shrapnel to the chest, but not before he reached the post, whispered what the plan was and so saved at least two-dozen lives. The photo is a portrait of a young man in a uniform: corporal's stripes and solemn face and eyes that look a lot like Hank's.

"I knew he was a hero. Frank once pulled me from a burning school. I'd always hoped you'd meet your dad. I'm sorry that won't happen now."

Noise & Stink
August 1997

HANK WAS with his chain saw, hacking dead trees into firewood; Mother was with Lidia, safe beyond his anger's reach. She was keeping Myrna in the house—*God-knows-how she manages*—knitting scarves or some such crap Hank couldn't give a damn about. It was the kind of day that should have made Hank think he was in paradise: warm breeze blowing sweet air from a sky as blue as Crater Lake. But the chain saw drowned the sound of passing ruby-throated hummingbirds, the drumming on a poplar of a Pileated Woodpecker. Any other time he would have gasped at the magnificence, with snow capped peaks and starry nights and ripe fruit waiting to be picked. But he wasn't in the here-and-now, couldn't hear the chain saw buzz, now he knew his mother hadn't moved here for the scenery. The breeze had no effect on him and the sky could have been lavender; the canned soup that he'd fixed for lunch had tasted like wallpaper paste. Instead of throwing it away and making something they'd enjoy, he simply didn't care and dared his mother not to finish it.

This morning he heard from the Board that issues doctors' licenses: more delays and legalese and *peckerheaded bureaucrats*. His interview delayed again by some unforeseen circumstance; he'd be on the agenda when the Board met in a few more months. All he really wanted was to lie down for a nice, long nap, sleep until his mother died or somehow he got over this. Every time he tried to think, he had to stop to catch his breath, felt the nickel twisting to block off his swollen breathing pipe. The chain saw bucked against a knot and nearly jumped out of his hands;

Hank's entire body quickly flooded with adrenaline. The sudden surge of hormone caused a tremor in his arms and legs, and as it faded it drained all the strength from his appendages. He couldn't find the energy to lift the chain saw up again, deciding to sit down until he got his concentration back.

Jessie was on hands and knees out weeding the tomato patch, crawling in the rows between the garlic and the brussels sprouts. When he turned the chain saw off, she looked behind and waved a glove, and waving back felt like he'd had to lift a hundred pounds of lead. The breeze cleared out the choking smoke and Hank sat on the biggest round, took the plastic helmet with the face shield and the earmuffs off. Once the tremor settled down Hank looked back at his working wife, and now a sense of guilt and shame replaced the hormone in his blood. He wasn't sure why he could not tell Jessie all the things he'd learned while sitting with his mother in the spare room of his *uncle's* house. All he knew was that he'd had a headache since that afternoon; if he tried to smile right now he thought his face would crack in two. Sitting on the spare bed with a clipping from a newspaper, he'd listened to his mother tell about a boy she used to know. Before she'd been distracted by a food stain on her housecoat sleeve, she'd cleared her throat and told Hank what she'd meant to tell him years ago.

Hank knew asking questions would send Myrna's mind off *God-knows-where:* telling him once more how many stinking jars of beans she'd canned. Instead, he kept his mouth shut as he followed her around the room, looking at the family pictures framed above the single bed. *I'm guessing that's your grandfather... Look at how much snow there was! I think this was the winter that the irrigation flume collapsed....* Hank had held the picture of the man she claimed to be his dad: a handsome man with honest eyes who shared Hank's facial bone structure. A pit grew in Hank's stomach as he followed her around the room: *If she knew my father then she must know who my mother was.* He'd waited for her to point out the picture of his father's bride, dressed in a kimono with two chopsticks holding up her hair. Guessing the scenario, Hank thought he saw the story here: Myrna had been friendly with the girl Frank got in trouble with. But George had told him all about the Japanese internment camps, that all the Edgar Japanese were forced to leave in early May. Hank was born December 10th, a full year since the first attack, so his mother would have given birth inside an eight-foot barbed-wire fence. But if he'd been born in a camp, then how did Myrna get him out? It didn't make a lick of sense and Hank had finally asked her straight:

"I got you out by *pushing*. And there's nothing that hurts worse than that!"

...

He was looking at the orchard grass that was growing thick between his feet, deciding he'd sulked long enough: was time to make more noise and stink. The saw took two hard pulls to start, and he yanked back on the safety brake, stepped up to another tree and bit the teeth into the bark. His arms were feeling heavy but were better than they were before; months ago the chain saw felt like wrestling a crocodile. He started cutting off the little branches from the bigger limbs, anything much smaller than the broad part of a gopher's neck. The limbs he cut up short enough to fit into the firebox, and later he would take them to the woodshed in a garden cart. And if the trees were standing they'd have reached upwards of sixteen feet; instead they all laid helter-skelter, root balls looked like dens of snakes. Their leaves were gone and so the orchard felt more like a battlefield, the twisted limbs like mangled bones of weathered soldier skeletons. The biggest of the tree trunks had a twenty-inch diameter, their size and bark reminding Hank of the stout legs of an elephant. Hank tried counting rings once on a trunk he'd cut up into rounds; wasn't sure because he lost track somewhere around sixty-five.

Hank wondered how the farm had been allowed to reach this sorry state: some brother of his mother must have really been incompetent. He never got an answer asking Myrna why she'd moved up here, but now at least he knew the reason why her family made her leave. All the things he thought were lies he now imagined must be true; so all the truths he'd once believed he couldn't trust now anymore. She hadn't come from Pittsburgh but was raised right here on Edgar Flat; he sees his mother bossed around by brothers in blue overalls. And what about this Mormon thing? Polygamy and Joseph Smith? Hank wanted to know why she kept calling him a *Lamanite*? Tomorrow he should go down to the courthouse where the records were, find out who first owned this place and if it was his grandfather. He put his chain saw down again but didn't shut the engine off, pulling on a branch he'd cut stuck underneath a bigger log. The branch gave with a sudden jerk so

Hank was thrown a few steps back; his boot stepped on the long blade so the chain saw flipped and sputtered out. He knew that Jessie'd been concerned that something suddenly had changed, that he'd been less than pleasant to his mother for the last few days. She was always going on about how dangerous a saw could be, that if he wasn't careful he could amputate an arm or leg. And sure enough, she was halfway there before he even hit the ground: landing on his rear between the chain saw and the can of gas. Trouble had come running and was barking too close to his ear, even though he still had both the face shield and the earmuffs on. The branch was sitting in his lap and Jessie helped to move it off; he tried to reassure her that he still had everything attached. Hank didn't bother getting up, knowing that he was okay; Jessie knelt beside him with a look of horror on her face.

"I'm fine," he said. "There's nothing wrong."

"Hank, you could have killed yourself."

"I just tripped pulling out this branch."

"Maybe you should give this up."

Her look changed then from horrified to steely eyed and furrowed brow, transformed from *thank God you're safe* to *don't ever pull that stunt again!*

She was kneeling down in front of him, he watched her try to calm herself: eyes closed and her shoulders back and deep breaths from her diaphragm.

"Hank, I can't keep on like this…" and she said what he would not admit: that he's a mess and she's too tired to keep on taking care of him. He'd been like this since Nathan died and it kept on getting worse and worse and he wouldn't talk and he seemed depressed and she'd help if he'd just tell her things. For Hank it was a litany of offenses and reprimands, hearing *everything's your fault!* and *what's wrong with you anyway?* She was saying that she understood how awful things had been for him: Nathan's death and fingerprints and feeling utterly betrayed. But three years was a long time and there was half their lives ahead of them and if he didn't get a grip she was not sure how it all would end.

Hank sat with his arms wrapped tight around his knees pressed to his chest.

"If you only knew . . ." Hank said.

"I'm pretty good at listening."

The Salesman
September 1997

IF EVERYTHING had gone as planned, then what would Myrna's life be like? A passel of brown-headed kids as green-eyed as a mountain lake. She knew that it was Daniel's fault she never had another child: Frank Nagoya's seed took and they'd only done it once or twice. She might have had a dozen children spaced about a year apart, a big house filled with Mormon Saints and homework needing finishing. They're gathered all around her—she is sitting in her Lazy-boy—Cindy, Sally, Betty Lou; Matthew, Mark, Luke and John. She tells the girls *go do the dishes,* boys *go play out in the yard. Let me put my tired feet up, close my eyes and rest a spell.* So Myrna's suddenly alone, can hear the housework being done, can't believe today her kids might actually behave themselves. Normally they're fighting curs, especially the older boys: every time she turns around they've caused another bloody nose. But she loves that they're high-spirited, throttling the neck of life, wouldn't want all of her boys as meek and mild as little Hank.

The thought of Hank disturbs her vision of her Mormon family, staring out the window at a blustery September day. That's what she had thought would happen when she was a little girl, teased she'd be the third wife of some farmer out in Idaho. She has to stop and think a while: which part of her life was real? Seven boys and seven girls or just one little Japanese? She's guessing that it must be Hank or why would she remember him? Just as clear she sees the others: maybe Hank's the neighbor's kid. But Hank's the only name that sticks, the others she was guessing at: Annie, Cory,

Sarah and the baby might be Jennifer. Looking out across the yard, the full leaf of the cottonwoods, slanting sunlight from the west casts highlights on their fluttering. It must be toward late afternoon and she hasn't been outside all day, but it's like she's tied into her chair and she doesn't really give a damn. On her lap she finds her book; the bookmark must have fallen out. She opens it at random to a page she hasn't read before. Searching for some energy, a quarter-ounce of *giddy-yup;* what she finds is *I-don't-care* all mixed with lethargy and sloth. She leans back in the Lazy-boy, takes a half a breath of air, feeling drugged she finally finds the strength to let it out again.

...

Hank was in the kitchen doing dishes leftover from lunch: ginger shrimp with golden raisins on a bed of jasmine rice. Today it was the two of them, both Lidia and Jessie gone; Hank was in the blackest mood he'd felt in his entire life. The cloud above his head was dark with sleet and hail and thunderbolts; already scolded Trouble when she'd simply asked to be let out. The morning started out okay, with fresh socks and clean underwear, breakfast in the kitchen with his wife and mom and Lidia. The house had smelled of sausages, the sound of grinding coffee beans, the pleasant morning-after-ness of having quiet sex last night. He'd learned a dish from Lidia: chorizo cooked with scrambled eggs, wrapped up in tortillas with a spicy, fresh tomato sauce. Everybody liked it so Hank thought to make it once again; this time Myrna looked at it, said *I'm not going to eat this crap!*

"You ate it just the other day."

"Maybe I was being polite."

"I made it specially for you."

"That's your problem, pencil-dick."

Hank quickly took her plate away, before she sent it to the floor, said he'd fix her something else if she first drank her apple juice. Jessie gave one of her looks—*how many did you use this time?*—then wiped her mouth, pushed back her chair and said *I have to get to work.* She might as well have come right out, said *try a little patience, Hank!* But all she did was shake her head: *I'll be a little late tonight.* When she walked behind his chair he felt her briefly kiss his cheek, one hand gave a tiny squeeze between his neck and shoulder blade. The muscles there were so tense that her fingers barely made a dent: sympathetic now that Hank had told her who his mother was.

...

Hank was not sure what he'd do now that he'd finished klettering: dried all of the dishes and he'd run the vacuum down the hall. His mood had not improved a bit—in fact had gotten slightly worse—a bad taste in his mouth as if he'd bit into a rotten peach. He'd have really liked to go outside and do a little gardening: rip some weeds out by their roots and gas a bunch of gopher dens. How satisfying it would feel to hack back at the blackberries, to cut that stupid walnut tree that dripped sap over everything. But Jessie liked the walnut meats and Myrna was in the living room: he didn't want to go outside until she fell asleep again. He thought about more apple juice, a little snack of *Vicodin*, perhaps a half a *Xanax* mixed with 25 of *Benadryl*. He had quite a collection now of different-colored medicines, Myrna's doctor happy to prescribe the drugs Hank recommends. He took her every other week and asked to try a different drug; the last one that they tried had several unexpected side effects. With such a wide assortment he could vary each one's time and dose; thinking he should keep her body guessing which drug's coming next. Today was a narcotic and tomorrow a barbiturate, yesterday a nice sedating dose of antihistamine. The last thing that he wanted was to make his mom a drug addict, but needed her on something so he wouldn't bludgeon her to death. The first drug worked for three days, but then Myrna wouldn't sleep at night; two more days of *Percodan* and she was constipated for a week. The *Xanax* was a miracle—he thought of taking it himself—but didn't last a fortnight till she started getting worse again. To temper guilt he'd tell himself the drugs were all prescribed for her, and nobody could argue his intentions weren't defensible. So he gave a random schedule of medicines to match her mood, watching her for side effects and slowly escalating need. He felt he was the engineer of an old dilapidated train, fiddling with cranks and valves to keep her running under steam. If her pressure got too low the train would fail to make the hills, and if he let her run too fast the boiler likely would explode. It was too bad they were in the mountains, always going up or down, constantly adjusting knobs and shovels full of colored pills.

...

He walked into the living room: Myrna's staring at the floor: *Perhaps,* he thought, *she might have had a little bit too much today.* But it was better than the opposite, especially with his black mood: better that her train creep slowly past his vicious thunderstorm. He was constantly obsessing on the fact of Myrna's massive lie: pretending she's the archangel of selflessness and sacrifice. Instead she was a teenage girl got knocked up by the neighbor boy, surprised she hadn't tossed him in a dumpster in some alleyway. And how did Daniel get involved? Was he mixed up in Myrna's lies? Or had he been as big a dupe as Hank was for believing her? He tried to shift out of this trance, to see her as his loving mom, and not *the lying little tramp who stole away my childhood.* But he couldn't find his way back to the feeling she was on his side, to somewhere in the future when he'd look back on all this and smile. The best that he could do right now was try to bottle up his rage, stuff his anger back into his mental cracks and crevices.

He was trying hard to sort out how he possibly could be her son; if he was born December 10th, then she'd conceived in early March. That was 1942, the war was only three months old, so it was just two months before they opened the internment camps. George said it was early May when they'd been forced to board the trains, before that all the Japanese had curfew when the sun went down. So Myrna really had to sneak around to manage an affair: meeting in the tractor shed at midnight when the moon had waned. It all seemed sweet and innocent, a love ignoring racial bounds, his biologic father simply couldn't keep his trousers on. But that was not what upset Hank, that she'd conceived prenuptially, but that she thought that Hank should be the one to have to pay for it. Hank's anger smothered the whole house: the curtains and the end tables; he'd have to get out mops and brooms and change the vacuum cleaner bag. If he stopped to think it through, she'd barely given anything; he'd had to make himself from scratch and even that was ruined now.

He used to have imaginary parents somewhere in Japan, a line of ancient ancestors that went back a millennium. But now he kept on catching himself staring at the bathroom mirror, trying to see someone who looked like Myrna staring back at him. The worst part was he saw her there, the sharp cut of her lower jaw, the way her forehead wrinkled when she was thinking up another lie. It had all been there since he was born, he simply hadn't looked before: half a century of never noticing the obvious. But then the shower steam would slowly clear off of the bathroom mirror and all that Hank could see now was a face that he no longer owned.

...

Myrna has now noticed that somebody's in the room with her, standing near the doorway staring at her like he wants something. She slowly puts her book aside and looks up at the man and frowns, guessing that he's probably a vacuum cleaner salesman. If he is he's in for a surprise when she shows him the door: she doesn't waste an ounce of charm on people trying to sell her things. The most she'll ever buy sometimes is candies from the Camp Fire Girls; if they're selling more than that she glares until they leave the porch. Especially those selling God, the Moonies and the Adventists, the time two pious Mormon women ambushed her one Saturday. She thought the two were neighbor ladies coming by to say hello; Dan and she just bought the end house on a lovely cul-de-sac. The sidewalks are nice poured cement and Hank can ride his bike to school and Daniel's now a partner in a clinic near the hospital. She asked them in for tea or coffee, should have known when they refused: *Juice or water would be nice. The stronger drinks we're not allowed.* Hank came in the living room and asked if he could have a snack; Myrna saw the looks the women shot each other back and forth. She'd prayed that Hank would stay upstairs; she didn't want to lie again, but knew she had to make a good impression on the neighborhood. *You can have one cookie, Hank, but lunch is in a little while.* Once Hank left the room she whispered: *Hank was orphaned by the war. . . .* They nodded like they understood, made that little *tiching* noise, then started telling Myrna how the Mormons were the chosen ones.

Myrna got her taste for coffee downstairs at the fire hall; smoked the firemen's cigarettes till Daniel came home from the war. All that started gradually, at first she didn't have a clue: nineteen and she'd never been that many miles from Edgarville. For weeks she stayed up in her room and watched the traffic down below, every now and then go to the café down the block a ways. The firemen were older guys who sat around and smoked for hours: inside when the weather's cold and outside in the summertime. She'd watch them wash the fire trucks and roll up lengths of canvas hose and argue whether Roosevelt had ovaries or testicles. She didn't have much money—just the check that Daniel sent each month—and she only had a hot plate so she didn't feel like cooking much. Thankfully she'd already gone through the weeks of nausea, since lots of awful odors would come drifting from the fire hall. Each time they started up the trucks the stairway filled with diesel smoke, and every morning right at six the bacon for the morning shift. They fried a lot of meat and eggs, spaghetti every Wednesday night, after lunch the acrid smell of ten men smoking cigarettes. Then one day she came down the stairs behind her swaying, pregnant hump; a man stood in the stairwell said his name was Captain Richardson.

—*Before your husband left he asked if we would keep an eye on you, and some here think that maybe you aren't putting on the weight you should....*

She felt her cheeks turn scarlet red, a sense she's breaking out in hives; all these weeks and all these men were guessing how much weight she'd gained. The Captain was as red as she, if not a slightly brighter shade: *We know it's not our business, ma'am, but your husband made us give our word....*

The doctor that they found for her said that she had anemia, that what she needed most were lots of liver steaks and spinach leaves. The doctor told her *stay in bed* and *don't go climbing any stairs;* the firefighters brought her meals at six and twelve and six again. Everyone was twice her age with all the young men off to war; some would bring the food and leave and some would visit for a while.

—*Gosh, it's awfully nice today.*
—*I sure wish I could go outside.*
—*Doctor said you shouldn't...*
—*Thanks for bringing me my lunch today....*

She got the Virgin Mary treatment, like her belly's filled with God, tiptoed up and down the stairs and always kept their voices soft. They never really bowed but always seemed like they were going to; the ones who stayed to chat would ask her if she's sure she's comfortable. They'd ask her how she liked the food; today they'd *boiled* the liver steak: *Actually, I think I might be over the anemia....* She's having awful labor pains, she's made it halfway down the stairs: first time in the six weeks since the doctor ordered her to bed. She's absolutely scared to death: the pains would take her breath away; someone heard her gasp when Myrna felt her bag-of-water break. She was carried down the last few stairs by overly excited men; they put her in the fire engine: clanging bell and siren. Racing to the hospital, barely slowing down for lights, Myrna thinks for sure that she will die before the baby's out. Every time the pains come she bites down hard on her lower lip, trying not to say words Martin taught her in the chicken house. They carry her in through the doors, the two nuns at the check-in desk: the small one asks them rudely *could you all keep down the noise a bit?*

...

Hank was looking at his mother, knowing she was off somewhere; he was trying to remember which damn pills she'd had that afternoon. A logbook would have helped but Hank's subconscious wouldn't write things down, didn't want to know exactly how much he was giving her. But he had never seen her quite like this: she was biting on her lower lip, every now and then a funny grimace flashed across her face. It's possible the *Haldol* dose was making her hallucinate; sometimes neuroleptic drugs would cause a sudden facial tick. If this didn't stop soon he would give her more *diazepam*, to counteract the side effects of drugs she'd taken earlier. But all he did was clear his throat and Myrna came back to the room:

"You can talk all afternoon, but I'm not buying anything!"

Because Hank was not expecting this, it broke right through his awful mood; a light came on inside his head—*my life is totally absurd.* How could he be angry with a woman who had lost her mind? Hold a grudge against someone who didn't know what year it was? It started out a grimaced smile, a tiny snort out of his nose, then shaking back and forth his head while watching his pathetic mom. He wondered what she'd answer if he asked her *who's the president?* How would she explain the saying *rolling stones don't gather moss?* His snort became a chuckle then evolved into a full-blown laugh; Trouble got excited and was barking while her tail wagged. He hadn't laughed like this in years and the dog was near hysterical; what really struck him funny was the stern expression on her face. She was absolutely serious she wasn't going to buy a thing; he wondered who she thought he was and what he might be peddling. He put the vacuum cleaner down, an arm out to support himself; the sternness faded from her face as she began to laugh as well. The two of them were laughing hard and he wondered which was funnier: Myrna looking serious or this crazy woman giggling. Tears were welling in his eyes, stomach muscles aching tight; what if he asked *now* why Myrna lied about adopting him? Would she even know the truth: *afraid what other people think? That sweet young Myrna let some Japanese boy in between her knees?* The black clouds moved back in again, he was not sure why they went away: *My mother's reputation meant more to her than my happiness.* He slowly took two deep breaths while his mother's laughing tapered off; his question had to cross the room:

"Mother, why'd you lie to me?"

For just a moment Myrna knows exactly what he wants to know: she's staring at her full-grown son, the question she's been waiting for.

Hank already knew the truth, had simmered it for several weeks, that Myrna simply tried to hide the fact she'd made a big mistake. So she let Hank take the brunt of it by telling unconvincing lies: all that he'd believed was it was brave that she'd adopted him. But there was nothing in his code book that said *this is what good people do*: make their children suffer to avoid the checkout-lady's stare. He'd lived his life believing that his parents had been honorable; that Dan and Myrna took him in to save him from the orphanage. He'd tried to emulate them both to pay back his adoption debt: floss his teeth and study hard and fix poor ailing children's hearts. Now he'd found it was a ruse to keep the neighbors ignorant; how would he have turned out if he'd known she was his *real* mom? He might have taken drugs in school and tried to have sex earlier, stolen candy from the store and vandalized the neighborhood. Or he might have simply said out loud he couldn't stand her casseroles: *I'd rather learn to play the trumpet than the stupid violin.*

What she had denied him was the sense of *unconditional;* every time she hugged him he knew she was only being nice. All the things they did for him were added debt he'd have to pay: dental checks and birthday cakes and times he'd missed the bus to school. The debt grew to enormous size, they paid all his tuition bills, a new car for his eighteenth birthday, all those graduation gifts. He wanted just to tell them *no!* He didn't have the resources: *How am I to pay you back for all the things I owe you for?* The time he'd dented Myrna's car while squeezing in a parking space; tipped a glass of grape juice on her brand-new linen tablecloth. He had been this skinny boy of eight and sitting on the back door steps, trying not to cry out loud though Myrna heard him anyway. She came and sat down next to him, asked him how he hurt himself: skin scraped off his hands and knees out on the grade school parking lot. The older boy had called him *Jap!* and *slant-eyed yellow piece of shit! Don't ever touch the tetherball! You stinking cowards killed my dad!* Hank's the only kid at school who was not as white as chalkboard dust, hadn't any friends yet who would help him to defend himself. He tried to turn around and leave, knew he couldn't win a fight; suddenly pushed from behind and face down on the gravel yard. His mother told Hank he should just ignore them when they called him names:*That boy's sad about his father. Best to stay away from him.* But he *had* tried to ignore the boy, and wasn't he an orphan, too? No one felt too sorry for a *Jap* who lost his mom and dad. It was not his hands and knees that hurt, it was how *alone* he always felt; Myrna said *let's go inside and we'll put on some iodine.* That was all he needed now, another *chit* he'd have to pay: medicine that stung and made his skin look even yellower.

...

Myrna looks at Hank and tells him *maybe you should have a seat,* knowing that what comes next isn't going to make him feel great. Because she's in the Lazy-boy, the nearest seat's the sofa's edge, hoping he'll sit close enough to hear what she'll be whispering. She's had about five decades now to figure out her strategy, how she can convince her boy *there really was no other way.* She didn't want to think how he'd be treated if the neighbors knew: *That half-breed bastard Jap's mom is a whore who screwed the enemy.* Daniel and the firemen were the only ones that knew for sure, and Daniel only after he first met Hank at the bus depot. Her letters to him said she couldn't make the stupid camera work, that's why the pictures of her son were too dark and not focused right. The day the firemen broke her door and found a boy with slanted eyes, she went from *Virgin Myrna* to just another of the guys. *Everybody makes mistakes* and *can't hold that against the kid,* and *all you have to do is say you got him from an orphanage.*

...

She always thought it funny how the men had suddenly relaxed, didn't seem to think they had to watch their manners anymore. They told her if she wants to she can come downstairs and eat with them; if she'd like to cook and clean there's ten men who could baby-sit. That's when she first began to smoke, mostly out of self-defense: either learn to like the smell or gag and cough and choke to death. It was after dinner, playing cards, language started getting rough; Myrna's finishing the dishes, Hank is on a fireman's lap. The baby was learning to stand, a poker chip gummed in his mouth; one man folds his cards and lets rip with a string of expletives. *God-damn-stinking-little-putz! Who's the dick who dealt this crap?* Half the table starts to laugh; Captain Richardson leans back: *Edwards, watch your language! There's a woman and a child here!* He tells him to apologize, but Myrna says she doesn't mind: *I'll bet you all a dollar I know more words than the lot of you!* The table's quiet for a moment, then they all reach for their chips; the Captain picks up Hank and says *we'll step out for a breath of air.* . . .

There are five men seated at the table, two more standing by the door; if she loses Myrna's not sure where she'll get the seven bucks. There's no discussion of the rules; the men know that they're going to win; Myrna waits for them to start by tossing out a dirty word. She's standing back against the sink, apron still around her waist; someone finally takes a breath: *numbskull* is the word he picks. The whole table lets out a groan, complaining that the word is lame; Myrna waits a couple beats before she whispers: *peckerhead!* The room is silenced suddenly, everybody's face turns red, then one of the firemen snorts and everybody laughs again. Just like they don't belch or fart or sometimes scratch between their legs, mothers of young children aren't supposed to know *that* sort of word. The advantage Myrna has is that the men are still a little shy, can't quite bring themselves to say their nasty words in front of her.

Dingbat . . .
. . . *bollocks!*
knucklehead . . .
. . . *eejit!*
fatso . . .

. . . dizzy bint!
Geezer . . .
. . . lard-ass!
Stumblebum . . .
. . . dicksmack
Gombeen . . .
. . . scuzzbucket!

Now it's getting serious, the men see how they're at some risk: dig a little deeper for some words more inappropriate.

Lunkhead . . .
. . . poontang!
Pantywaist . . .
. . .you guys already said that one!
Yahoo . . .
. . . wanker!
Doolally . . .
. . . can-inspecting timber beast!

This goes on for quite a while, then finally Myrna tops them all:

You hellacious halfwit gobshite douche-bag chicken-choking fart knockers!

...

Hank was thinking he was going to hear his mom apologize, seated on the couch near Myrna resting in the Lazy-boy. Instead she hit him with a string of words he'd never heard before, spat out like a logger who'd just dropped an ax-head on his toes. For Myrna all the men lean back, groaning while they shake their heads, push the chips across the felt they'd laid out on the tabletop. Randal offers her a chair, *we'd like a chance to win some back:* deals her in to five-card stud and tells her what the chips are worth. Marvin slaps her on the back and offers her a cigarette; Myrna puts one to her lips and coughs before she's got it lit.

The Really Gnarly Stuff
September 1997

THE SIREN only went off about every other week or so, and half the time for car wrecks on the straight stretch down by milepost nine. But it seemed to Hank the calls all came when he was talking to his mom so that he never learned the truth about his dark and sordid past. The last call was a false alarm, a barrel burning after dark, and someone driving home saw flames she thought came from the neighbor's house. It was toned out as a structure fire, automatic mutual aid: dispatch tripped the sirens off for Edgar Flat and Hillendale. But this time it was late afternoon and Myrna's drugs were wearing off and Hank just heard his mother tell him he's a *cacky-scuzz-bucket*. Hank kept falling for her traps, hoping for a miracle: that she might tell him why she'd made him suffer for her all these years. If she didn't settle down Hank felt he'd hyperventilate; every couple minutes had to slow his respiration rate. He listened to his beeper tone, deciding what he'd want to do: stay and take her foul abuse or run off to the fire hall.

...

Jessie would be home at five, and Lidia some time before: *How much damage could she do at home alone for half an hour?* She started to complain, of course, as soon as the alarm went off: siren climbing through the open window in the dining room. He had a bit of difficulty hearing over Trouble's howl, squinting with his ears to hear what other people's problems were. The beeper said that someone tumbled from a ladder near his house; he ran to flip the breaker off that cut the power to the stove. The dead bolt was keyed from both sides and the front and back doors were the same;

Hank thought if he took the keys his mother would be locked inside.

"Yes, I know, you hate that sound . . . I'm going now to turn it off. I have to lock the door behind me. Don't go outside while I'm gone."

It was barely two full minutes before Hank was starting up his truck, his mother in the kitchen yelling *shut that God-damn siren off!*

The siren trips a memory that Myrna has suppressed for years: the loud noise wakes her to a heart that's pounding like a sledgehammer. In twelve months living right next door, she's grown fond of the firemen: Larry, Erick, Steve and Gary; *Captain Andrew Richardson*. She'd grown up as the only girl, was used to living close with boys: it felt like having brothers only these men were more civilized. Her brothers used to tease her hard and tell her every kind of lie, convince her that one bite of snow will cause her pee to freeze inside. *Never open up your mouth, especially during snowball fights; it takes about two days to get the frozen pee to finally melt.*

She's thinking of her brother Martin, told the most convincing lies; Earl and Edward weren't so good because they'd contradict themselves. She's thinking how could she have been so innocent and gullible: the time they had convinced her that she can't take off her underclothes. All the boys were in on it, her underthings were sacred garb: *Once you turn eleven you can't ever take them off again.* They said that *it's the Mormon way* and that they'll keep her safe from harm: rattlesnakes and logging trains and men who prune the apple trees. She's not supposed to tell a soul: *It's just like when you pick your nose. Everybody does it, but it's nothing you should brag about.* The bottoms came down to her knees, the top a cotton camisole: *That's why women wear perfume, to keep from smelling really bad. . . .* The hoax lasted nearly a week, her mother finally catching on: *They told me if I took them off my cherry blossom would fall off. . . .* That's when Myrna learned about the vestments that she'd one day wear: *But only once you're married, dear. And you get to take them off to bathe.*

. . .

She's so glad to be living now with men who show her some respect: taught her to play poker and blow smoke rings from her cigarettes. They're paying her to cook and clean, enough to make her rent upstairs, so now she's saving money from the checks that Daniel's sending her. The checks come tucked inside his letters telling her his latest dream: big house on a dead end with a picket fence and grassy yard. He's looking forward to the day he finally gets to meet his son: *If we have a girl next time I'd like to name her for my mom.* She's not sure what it means that Daniel always signs his letters *love*; certainly he's nice enough, but still she barely knows the guy. The marriage was a legal thing, so she could have his benefits: his parents dead, an only child, with no place else to send the checks. It made such good sense at the time, her baby'd be legitimate; Daniel was convinced he wouldn't live to make it home again. *My family has got rotten luck. My father was hit by a bus. When I was six my mother died by eating tainted tuna fish.* So why not help a young girl out? Would barely cost him anything: five bucks at the courthouse and some cheap rings from a jewelry shop. And the only thing it cost her was the fact she had to change her name, a late walk through the park blocks and three long nights in a single bed. He took her to a restaurant—*ask for anything you want*—ordered her a drink with an umbrella and a swizzle stick. Speaking in excited tones, he told her all his history, though never asked her anything, like: who her baby's father was. He'd grown up with a widowed dad who liked to move around a lot: *My old man was a wheeler-dealer, never could sit still for long.* So he'd had to learn to make friends fast, to size up people right away: *That's why I sat down next to you. You've got a very honest face.*

The first day they'd been to the courthouse, eaten at the restaurant, then walked around the park blocks till it got too dark and dangerous. Daniel didn't say a word about where he would sleep that night: she worried he won't leave and worried just as much perhaps he might. It was technically their honeymoon, the county judge had bent the rules since Myrna had been showing and her boyfriend was in uniform. He'd walked her to the room he'd rented next door to the fire hall, clomping as they'd climbed the stairs so no one thought they're sneaking 'round. He whispered that it wouldn't look right if he didn't spend the night: *I'll just curl up on the floor. Kick me if a snore too loud.*

And now it's three nights later and tomorrow Daniel's leaving her; she's listening to how he breathes, the pounding of her aching heart. And absolutely everything has changed over the past three days: most of her belongings are now ashes in her parents' yard. Her father tore into a rage, *you're not my daughter anymore! All this is your own fault* since she did what was unspeakable. She's not to send them pleading notes or crawl back begging on her knees:

—And don't call yourself a Mormon now. May God have mercy on your soul!

The mattress has a funny smell, the window's opened up an inch; she's listening to street noise and a bit of phlegm in Daniel's throat. She's feeling fear and loneliness and mourning for her family and anger that they threw her out and never want her back again. Everything's so *all-at-once;* barely had a chance to breathe; where would she be sleeping now if Daniel hadn't married her? Three days ago she was a girl still living with her mom and dad, needed on the farm because her brothers had gone off to war. But she'd lost a lot of energy and couldn't keep her breakfasts down, and putting twos together Myrna's father finally did some math. Demanding that she tell so he could make the *bastard* marry her, Myrna couldn't meet his gaze when he assumed it was a Mormon boy. She watched his angry face turn red, the steam come out of both his ears; when she said her lover's name her father's color drained away. He suddenly stopped screaming at her, hand reached toward the kindling box; lucky that she turned so that he missed her swelling abdomen. She's thinking now she doesn't ever want to go back anyway: seen him beat her brothers but he'd never beaten her before. And she can't think why but Daniel has already bought some things for her: a table and some dishes and a picture in a picture frame. On the second evening he had kissed her when he'd said goodnight; in the morning he had breakfast ready when he woke her up. Tonight he's still curled on the floor, turned his face against the wall, head against his duffel and he's wrapped up in his overcoat.

—Daniel, aren't you kind of cold?
—Maybe just a little bit.
—Perhaps you'd like to sleep up here.
—Maybe just to warm up some.

He climbs into the skinny bed, fully clothed except for shoes, lies down with his back to her, blanket tucked beneath his ear.

—Aren't your clothes uncomfortable?
—I sleep like this when I'm on call.
—Maybe you should take some off.
—Maybe just my shirt and socks.

The first day he had seemed so bold, deciding what they're going to do; the only thing she had to choose was whether to say *yes* or *no*. It was seven in the morning when her father pushed her to the floor, at ten she's on the bus to Portland, by one o'clock Dan's found a room. It wasn't more than three before Dan laid out his engagement plans; by four they're at the courthouse and by six their dinner's being served. But they've been married three days and he still has on his boxer shorts, and Myrna's started thinking that perhaps he doesn't like her much. She puts an arm around his flank, finds out that perhaps he does; puts her belly to his back, says *you can kiss me if you want.* . . .

...

Hank was Brenda's passenger, his hand pushed tight against the dash; every time she took a corner, things went sliding back and forth. She was not sure where she was going, maybe somewhere along Alder Road; dispatch had some trouble breaking through the language barrier.

"They shouldn't let these people work unless they can speak English right. Every time I talk to one I feel like *I'm* the idiot."

Hank was biting on his tongue: *It's not the time for politics. Brenda Thompson's very nice, she's just a little ignorant.* When she turned on Alder Road she barely slowed the booster down, looking up the orchard rows to find whoever called for help. Brenda scanned rows to the east and Hank was watching westerly; down one row a tractor pulled a trailer with an orchard crew. So Brenda made the booster stop, jumped to set the tire chocks; right behind was Evan Smith out running toward the group of men.

"This must be the place," she said, noticing the injured man; Hank was horrified to see the rough way that they carried him. They'd picked him off the flatbed and were rushing him towards Evan's rig; Hank could see the head shake when they stumbled over gopher mounds. And if the man fell from a tree there were lots of things that could be wrong: a broken leg, a ruptured spleen, a massive subarachnoid bleed. Brenda grabbed the radio:

"Dispatch—Booster Seven-One—put Lifeflight on standby. . . . We're not sure, but this looks serious."

...

Myrna stands up from her chair—two seconds' worth of dizzy spell—thinking she can't spend the whole day wasting in her easy chair. She's really got to get a move on, going to make a casserole; Hank should be home soon from school and Daniel in about an hour. Passing through the dining room, she stops to push the window up, the warm breeze of the afternoon smells sweet of fir and fresh-cut grass. She's startled in the kitchen by how neat and clean the counters are, once more feeling dizzy that her sense of time is so far off. Monday she spent all day baking cookies for the PTA, Tuesday afternoon was bridge at Missy's new colonial. The only time her kitchen's neat is after Nona's been to clean, and Nona comes on Thursdays *so what happened all day yesterday?* She thinks sometimes she's going insane; her brain is like a colander, her memory the noodle water that she's pouring down the drain. Nona really is a gem, she even dusts behind the books, but after Nona's cleaned the kitchen Myrna can't find anything. She's looking for her baking dish that should be right beside the stove, but now that cupboard's full of crap that Nona's rearranged somehow. So she has to open every door, rummage 'round for what she wants, finally finds a casserole but not the one she's looking for.

She learned this from a magazine, a *quick-n-easy* dinner course: shredded cabbage, breakfast sausage, one can cream-of-mushroom soup. It bakes in only half an hour—*nothing could be easier!*—serve it with a can of corn on creamy mashed potato flakes. She turns the dial on the stove to let the oven start to heat; doesn't notice that the oven indicator doesn't glow. There's cabbage in the Frigidaire, sausage in the freezer box, but she can't find a single can of *stinking cream-of-mushroom soup!* She's looked all through the corner cupboard where the canned goods should be stored; in the pantry by the back door: Shredded Wheat and Cheerios. But she cannot find the mushroom soup; she buys a dozen at a time, for casseroles and onion dip and sauce for frozen vegetables. Maybe they got put down in the cellar bottom-of-the-stairs; sometimes Daniel lugs things there when she's run out of cupboard space. She opens up the basement door, light switch inside on the right; what she finds instead is a small closet full of winter coats. The dizziness comes back again, this time it makes the room go 'round: *Why would Dan install a clothes rod blocking off the way downstairs?* Someone's going to get hurt when they can't see where the steps begin; Myrna moves the coats to find that *all the stairs have been removed!* She suddenly feels nauseated, heart has started palpitating; someone's trying awfully hard to make her feel an idiot. She turns around expecting that her brothers will be standing by, wearing their shit-eating grins and stifling their belly laughs. But there's no one with her in the room, just the back door to the yard: *I'm gonna go find Martin and this time I'm gonna clobber him!*

The back door doesn't open and her rising panic grabs her chest; the dead bolt has been thrown and there's no key to turn the cylinder. She rushes through the dining room, the window curtains fluttering; nothing looks familiar and the entry dead bolt's locked as well. She's certain it has all been planned to make her do some stupid thing: Martin will have thought it out, the twins done all the dirty work. Since they've locked both of the doors, they're either trying to keep her in or deviously trick her into climbing out the dining room. She stops to listen for the sounds of whispered words and giggling; Earl and Edward sometimes give away their secret hiding place. But there's no sound from inside the house, no hands suppressing grunts and snorts; if Myrna could wait long enough she's certain they'll expose themselves.

...

Hank pulled out the medic bag while Brenda grabbed the board and straps; he told the men to hold on till they got the backboard underneath. There was nothing good about this scene: the body limp as wilted greens, like tulips in his garden when the gophers have been nibbling. He was thinking about ABCs, essentials of good trauma care: make sure the patient's breathing and his heart is pumping blood around. But they'd already committed sins by moving him from where he fell: every clumsy step they took risked severing his spinal cord. Now they'd placed him on the board and Brenda got the C-collar, Hank was checking pulse and breath while Evan got the oxygen. Hank called out in Spanish if somebody knew what happened here:

"Did anybody see him fall? Is anyone a relative?"

The foreman tried to answer all the questions Hank was asking him: yes, he had a wife and kid, but maybe they weren't married yet. He was certain the boy took no drugs; he drank a little beer sometimes; he fell because he worked too fast and tried to push himself too hard. Hank figured he was paralyzed, a massive bleed inside his brain, could see it stretching out for years, the feeding tubes and diaper change. Hank knew that there were two ways now: rush blindly toward this destiny, or slowly make a few "mistakes" and save a lot of suffering. But Hank could hear the ambulance's siren from two miles away, and it was just a twenty-minute flight to the nearest trauma hospital. Now Brenda helped as Evan bagged so Hank could use the radio to make sure dispatch knew *we need that helicopter right away!*

...

Myrna hears the siren, too, although it's not so loud this time: a different tone and rhythm from the siren she's remembering. But she's standing in the dining room, the curtains swaying back and forth, two flights up above the street that runs before the fire hall. And this is why she hates that noise: she never knows what it could mean—a bridge collapse, a burning school, a kitten in a maple tree. She doesn't see her brothers now, distracted by the distant sound, instead she's at the window with her hands once more around her ears. Of course Hank's started crying since it woke him from a needed nap, and she won't know what has happened till her firemen all straggle back. She's never seen them at a fire, only running off to them, dragging back all wet and black and smelling like old coffee grounds. Randal's had a nasty cough since the last time they went to a fire; Steven's put on extra weight and Marvin's back hurts all the time. She knows that they're all brave and strong and capable of anything, but Myrna can't help fretting now that they take such good care of her. It's like she's got a dozen brothers, treat her like she's one of them; Hank has got a dozen uncles, everybody dotes on him. Every time the siren wails—the bell clangs on the station wall—she doesn't know which of her friends most likely won't come back this time. Already she'd watched both the twins and Sam load up their duffle bags, anxious to go off to war *to kill our share of Japanese.* But *these* men go off twice a week, jolted from a dreamless sleep, jumping from the dinner table, racing for their rubber boots. Hank had cut his first teeth chewing on a chunk of fire hose; first three words he learned to say were *fire, lights,* and *siren.* The men taught her to cook and clean—unlike the way she'd learned at home: lots of beef and coffee and she'd never scrubbed a toilet bowl. The men don't condescend to her and only gently pull her leg; seldom try to challenge her authority on dirty words.

—*Myrna, are you in or not?*
—*These cards aren't worth a logger's fart.*
—*I thought something smelled kind of ripe.*
—*That's just your little buddy Hank.*

Randal picks his buddy up, pulls his diaper back to sniff, makes the face that men make when they first learn women *menstruate*. The firemen are middle-aged—someone's got to mind the store; they all have wives and kids at home and know what diaper pins are for. But this is where they draw the line and Myrna has to fold her hand, take her stinky little boy upstairs to do a diaper change. It's summer in the evening and her window faces south and west: the air's warm and the curtains dance and the sun's an inch above the hills. She's got her little boy all clean, his diaper off to let him dry, hoping for the moment that he doesn't tinkle on the floor. Standing by the window Myrna's watching strangers cross the street, realizing once more that her life's not like it used to be. She's miles away from Edgarville, the sawdust and the yellow pears, her brothers and her parents and the green beans that she had to can.

That's what she'd be doing now, the summer garden vegetables: thinning the tomatoes, putting traps in all the gopher holes. But she's twenty and not long ago she used to be a Mormon girl so even back one year she had been old for being single still. Where would she be if Frank hadn't dropped a trout into her well? There weren't a lot of Mormon boys to choose from in the area. Her parents talked of sending her to spend time with some relatives, or writing to the Bishop that they needed help with match making. There's a gentle tap against her door—she hadn't closed it all the way—and it swings to show her naked boy in the arms of Captain Richardson.

"I caught this fellow near the stairs. They move fast once they reach this age." Myrna's mortified to see her son's life flash before her eyes. She feels her heart up in her throat, not only from her negligence, but also from the crush she's had on the Captain for the past six months. He's younger than the other men, shoulders fill his uniform: handsome face and broad mustache and still has lots of hair to comb. He's different from the others, too, in that he's quiet and reserved: laughs at jokes but doesn't waste time playing cards all afternoon. He seems somehow mysterious: he never talks about himself; he'll lean against the bay door while he smokes a string of cigarettes. She's wondered if he has a family, wife and couple growing boys; the way he's holding Hank she knows he's handled lots of them before. He holds her naked son face out so if he pees it saves his shirt; he puts him on the bed and takes a diaper from the end table.

"You don't need to do that..." but he brushes Myrna's hands aside, tells her that he doesn't mind: she's done the really stinky part. Looking down she notices that Hank has got his flagpole raised; the captain only laughs when he sees how red Myrna's face has turned.

"It happens to the best of us . . ." and he tells her how he knows all this: "... the oldest of a dozen boys. I helped my mother out a lot."

Every word he says makes Myrna turn a deeper shade of pink, grateful when he folds the diaper, pins it neatly at the waist. She's so flushed now she has to move to catch the window's cooling breeze; the captain puts Hank on the floor and turns to come stand next to her.

"How much does your husband know?"—the breeze not nearly cool enough; apparently this man thinks he can ask her anything he likes. She only slightly shakes her head, staring out across the street, astonished someone said out loud what all the firemen must think. She'll never go downstairs again, never look them in the eye; she'd hoped they would ignore the fact Hank doesn't look much like his dad. And it's not even the milkman's hair or the jug ears of the garbage guy, but the squint of some *damn yellow chink* who *stinks of fish and laundry starch*. So they all think Dan's a *cuckold* and that she's *some Asian bastard's whore*.

—You're lucky that your husband's gone or there'd be a triple homicide.

But this is what he really says:

"I guess he'll find out soon enough. The men asked me to tell you that we'll help you any way we can."

...

Evan went to light some fusies at the makeshift landing zone; Brenda said she heard the distant echoes of the rotor blades. The ambulance would take the victim down to where the mill once stood: a half-an-acre concrete pad now sprouting weeds up through the cracks. Hank didn't want to tell the foreman that his friend may likely die; the surgeon had about an hour to fix the bleeding in his brain. Hank was not a medic and his doctor's license had expired; his only duty here was as the friendly Good Samaritan. The ambulance had driven off, the helicopter on its way, the victim had two IVs and a tube stuck down his trachea. Hank watched then as the orchard workers wandered off back down the rows, wondered if it wouldn't have been better if they'd let him die. Every time Hank thought of death he'd see the image of the boy, nine years old and gained some weight and waiting for somebody's heart. It wasn't always easy since the kid could get so on his nerves: question after question about every stupid little thing. They were sitting in the sushi place on stools before the carousel, watching as the plates went by around the long conveyor belt. Nathan was a little wired; they'd been out half the afternoon; took him to a movie that had not been quite appropriate. It starred a boy of Nate's age, but Hank hadn't read the whole review; now Nathan thought it wasn't fair they'd left before the credits rolled.

"How come that woman screamed so loud? What was that yellow slimy stuff? How come we had to leave so fast? I'll bet that bedroom really stank!"

"Nathan, let's just eat, okay? Here comes that octopus you like."

"I thought that part was cool the time that one guy cut that dog's leg off."

"You'll make me lose my appetite."

"Do people really bleed like that?"

"Nathan, keep your voice down please."

"I wish we could have seen the rest."

Hank looked sideways at the boy: *He needs a dose of Ritalin.*

"I'm sorry you saw any, Nate. That wasn't meant for kids your age."

Nathan had to catch his breath: a tinge of blue around his lips; excitement made his floppy heart beat fast and inefficiently.

"You want to lie down in the car?"

Nathan only shook his head.

"I could get the oxygen." But that would just embarrass him. The respiratory therapist had taught Nate how to purse his lips; it took a moment but he slowly turned back to his normal white.

"If I wait till I'm older . . ." and Nate had to pause for several breaths, ". . . then I'll be dead and never get to see the really gnarly stuff."

The Clean Slate
September 1997

THE ONLY PIECE of mill left was a giant slab of concrete floor, and it never was as clean as when the helicopter lifted off. The rotors blew the sawdust off, the gravel bits and scattered ash; George thought someone clever should convert it to a roller-rink. He could see an adolescent crowd, the boys and girls all holding hands, an image he remembered from an issue of *Life Magazine.* He used to yearn for such a thing when he had been about that age, but no one thought of roller-skates for kids in concentration camps. The photo-spread showed boys and girls, a spanking-new amusement park: ponytails and bobby socks and every face all clean and white. But if those kids had looked like George there would have been a barbed-wire fence and guards with guns in towers at every corner of the roller rink.

George didn't really mind that part—the gleaming strands of razor wire—because it was the first time in his life he felt like he belonged. At twelve he was a big threat to the national security, a menace to the patriotic citizens of Edgar Flat. He hadn't slept at all the night before they put them on the train; his brother had snuck out again, climbed back in at one a.m.

"Where'd you go, Frank?" George had asked.

"Never mind. And don't tell Mom."

That was all Frank said until he woke up George by shaking him, telling him to get dressed since the sheriff brought his deputies. A suitcase clutched in every hand, they walked out through their garden gate; a half-a-dozen neighbors stood to wave good-bye and wish them luck. They rode the train for two full days and didn't get fed very well and sleeping in a wicker seat was way beyond uncomfortable. But when they finally disembarked, George between his mom and Frank, he'd never thought in all his life he'd see so many Japanese. He was pressed on all four sides now by a crowd of black-haired immigrants, all the same except the soldiers spread out every twenty feet. George could hear the static-filled instructions from the loudspeakers, wondered why the guards did not use lariats and cattle prods. The sky was filled with Milky Way as they shuffled them into the camp, the desert night air cold so he saw steam from everybody's mouths. All that he could smell was dust and other people's nervous sweat; once the crowd spread out George saw the size of the internment camp. They wandered up and down the rows, the camp laid out in sectioned grids, their new home just a number on a paper someone handed Frank.

He watched as Frank pulled back the woolen blanket tacked across the door: tar paper and plywood walls, a lightbulb and a tin-box stove. At first it all seemed quiet, then the subtle sound of whispering, then as their neighbors got more bold he heard them like there were no walls. His mother sat down on one cot and put her face into her hands; Frank and George beside her till she told them she would be all right. Frank sent George to gather straw to stuff inside their mattresses; it didn't take an hour before George had a dozen brand-new friends. For George this was like summer camp, without the trees and swimming lake: he and Kay Fukui would play ping-pong every chance they got. His only chore was twice a day to sweep their dusty barracks out, make sure that his mother got a plate of what was served for lunch. For months there wasn't any school and no one told them what to do and half the adults that he saw looked like they'd like to kill themselves. There were no deep wells to tumble down and they couldn't get out past the guards: *So why not leave the kids alone? Let's hope this doesn't last too long. . . .*

And that was what reminded him, the taste of grit inside his mouth: the helicopter's rotors whipping up a little desert dust. Standing on the old mill slab, George felt like it was yesterday that he stood near the fence and watched the whirling of the dust devils. The dust got into everything, the bed sheets and the tooth powder; George still smelled the sweet stench of the overflowing shower stalls. After they were there a year, Frank's enlistment was approved; after Basic Training, Frank said he would go to language school. George stood in the settling cloud that formed inside the gates of camp, waving to his brother waving from the disappearing bus. His mom sat on their wooden stool, still inside their little room, hadn't had the strength to say good-bye to her departing son. But now the volunteers are gone, the helicopter lifted off; George spit dust out of his mouth onto the old mill's concrete floor.

...

The only person with George was this man who'd been confusing him: every time he turned around, this Hank had saved his life again. Every other day Hank came around to make sure he was fine, sat and asked him questions about what was growing up here like. So he'd told Hank all about the town, the first time that the mill burned down: it started in a sawdust pile: spontaneously burst in flames. There used to be a railway here—*the ol' Polygamy Express*—the road to Hooster just a skid of hairpin turns and muddy ruts.

 As far as Hank could figure, George might be his closest relative, not counting his mother since *she can't remember who I am*. George could be his uncle if what Myrna said was not a lie: verbal tics and wishful thoughts and random neurons firing. He hadn't brought it up with George because he couldn't know for sure: a crush his mother said she'd had when she was in the seventh grade. Hank wondered had George thought of this, had guessed who Myrna might have been: *that Mormon girl* his brother said he'd yanked out of the burning school. But Hank's existence only proved that Myrna had been indiscreet; she'd let a *Japanese* boy do what any other boy would do. Hank's father could be someone else and all Frank's DNA was gone; the only evidence was that their ears looked quite a bit the same. Even if his mother told him flat out who his father was, Hank could not believe a word because her belfry's full of bats. It didn't seem appropriate to ask George if his brother might have knocked up some poor Mormon girl then left before she was off her back. It already was an hour since Hank locked his mother in the house; he looked down at his watch and told George that he'd better hurry off.

 "Yeah, Hank, see you later," and George would have liked to say some more, but all he did was bend to pull a weed out of a concrete crack. He wanted to tell Hank that Myrna's brother was a bag-of-shit, that if he had a week to shout he'd still be listing expletives. George was only fifteen when the camp gates finally opened wide: Uncle Shige not sure yet if returning was a good idea. The *Hooster News* had full-page ads agreeing with that sentiment: *Go find someplace else to live! This valley isn't big enough!* The local Legionnaires had built an honor roll of all the names of valley men enlisted to help fight the krauts and Japanese. But they'd had to take it down again to scratch out seventeen of them: any name that even looked a little un-American. They'd scratched his brother off the list three days before the valley learned that Frank had died to save a dozen white boys in the Philippines. The only thing that gave some hope was there was word of mild dissent: a valley business here and there said that *they* would sell to *anyone*. A dry goods up in Hillendale, a larger Hooster grocery store, though a letter in the paper threatened they'd lose half their customers. So Uncle kept them in the camp till they heard from the pioneers: the young men who were not afraid of cars that drove by late at night. Occasionally a shot was fired, a rock thrown through a windowpane; a single wooden shed burned though it could have been an accident. But finally his uncle Shige said it was time to go back home; his farm was in the upper valley, two miles south of Hillendale. The neighbor who leased Uncle's farm had taken proper care of things: kept the tractor in the barn and sprayed the trees with dormant oil. He met them at the Hooster station, drove them home the twenty miles; told them it might be best if they lay low for a little while. The neighbor's wife had swept their house and brushed the cobwebs off the walls, put some staples in the kitchen, baked a casserole and pie. So it made it seem more personal when later they saw George's house: every window broken, all his mother's furniture was gone. The tractor wasn't anywhere, the door was missing off the shed, the only tool they found had been a broken-handled toothless rake. Uncle took George with him when he went to knock on Capo's door: Uncle wasn't tall and George was small for a fifteen-year-old. This big man pulled the door open, asks them *what the fuck* they want: *You've got plenty nerve!* he said, *get the fuck down off my porch!* Behind him George could plainly see an end table his father made, a mirror with a yellow frame that once hung in their living room.

Martin Capo stepped outside and slammed the door behind him closed, said they had a half a minute, then he'd let the dogs outside. *Don't cry to me about that farm—worthless filthy pile of crap—you fucking Nips can't farm worth shit. I should have torched the fucking place!*

Uncle slowly backed away—didn't need more enemies—told George as they walked off that they'd have to sell his father's place. But the farm was all that George had left—the work that Frank and Father did; if they could sell just part of it then George would fix up what was left. So they sold the extra twenty acres—for half the price they should have got—then paid off what was owed and used the rest to buy a tractor with. Uncle couldn't help much since their orchards were six miles apart; Aunt said there was no way she would let George live there by himself. So he made the long trek every day, six miles in about an hour; he had to walk one extra so he wouldn't step on Capo soil. The first month on the tractor barely got the weeds under control; the next month he turned sixteen raking out the irrigation ditch. The culvert was choked with blackberries, the irrigation box was smashed; four years of neglect infected half the trees with fire blight. He came back in the morning to find work he had to do again: a ditch filled with the same muck that he'd spent the last day shoveling. He looked down at the tractor marks that pushed the muck back in the ditch: the same ones that had backed into the irrigation box he'd fixed. George knew the tracks because they were the same ones that his brother made when he would drive their father's tractor up and down between the trees. The Capo farm was right next door, about a half-a-mile away, so no more than a couple neighbors would have seen him driving here. But who could he complain to who would listen to a Japanese? Who was going to take his word against a *real* American? Even if he had proof that the tractor once belonged to them, Uncle thought it best to let the bastard get away with it. *Best thing is to wait,* he said, *even if it's hard sometimes. If we can all be patient then one day they might forget we're here.*

Coffee-Almond-Fudge
September 1997

As Jessie pulled into the drive, she noticed that Hank's truck was gone, surprised how much her tension faded since she'd be alone inside. She'd never felt this way before, like home was not the place to be, that if she had a sleeping bag she'd sack out on her clinic floor. She was glad to go to work these days, to get away from Myrna's snarls, her husband's dark and broody mood, although he had her sympathy. Yesterday they sat and talked about each other's hectic day, but she knew there was something on his mind he wasn't telling her. They'd been together so long she knew just when he was going to sneeze or if he thought her salad dressing should have had more vinegar. So she knew he wasn't being honest when he said *I'm over it:* there was something but she wasn't sure she'd like to fight it out of him. She'd never not pushed on before, to talk out what the problem was, to find out why he'd acted like there was sand inside his underpants. It all seemed slightly uncontrolled, the way he managed Myrna now: the growing drawer of colored pills, the bruise on his mom's upper arm. But Jessie slammed that mental door and tried to think of something else: *My husband is the sweetest human being in the universe....*

Surprised to find the front door locked—she didn't have the dead bolt key—Jessie put her groceries down and walked around the other way. It was a warm and gorgeous afternoon, a hint the season soon will change; Trouble followed closely as she tried to find an unlocked door. She was home a half-hour early since her four o'clock had called in sick; Jessie thought she'd cook tonight and give poor Hank a needed break. She had to get the fish inside, the ice cream in the freezer chest: a pound of salmon for the grill, a pint of coffee-almond-fudge. They mostly locked the doors at night to keep Hank's mom from getting out: imaginary safety of a life out in the puckerbrush. *Why would Hank lock all the doors?* The mudroom's dead bolt had been thrown; the brass knob on the French doors to their bedroom also didn't turn. As she walked around the house she saw the curtains fluttering; if they were not home soon she'd have to crawl in through the dining room. It was all somewhat annoying to be locked out of her own damn house, the one time in a month she might have had the place all to herself.

He could at least have left a note. She wondered where they'd gone off to. *Maybe something's wrong* and Hank took Myrna to the hospital. She was trying not to get upset, to let this spoil her afternoon: doing something nice for Hank *but now he's ruining everything!* The salmon would soon start to smell and the ice cream would soon turn to mush and she needed to get the rice on to serve something starchy on their plates. Jessie made this simple plan to take some pressure off of Hank, *but what is wrong with him that he can't ever think of me for once?!* He didn't want to talk these days or even let her *try* to help; he said *there's nothing wrong* and yet their lives were both falling apart. They were living on this stupid farm surrounded by a bunch of hicks so Hank could take care of his mom by feeding her barbiturates. Their lives had been a crazy mess since Hank got too close to that boy: a way of compensating for the fact they couldn't have their own.

It suddenly occurred to Jessie why Hank might have locked the doors: not to keep intruders out but keep somebody safe inside. She stepped up to the open window, sill was level with her chin; knocking on the glass she called for Myrna through the opening. She'd climb in but was dressed for work: a silk blouse and a rayon skirt, and even though they're comfortable, her shoes weren't really up for this. They were brown suede with an inch of heel, soles slick as banana peels; if Myrna didn't answer soon she'd get the ladder from the barn.

Myrna's in her Lazy-boy, had to sit down for a while, exhausted from the effort of discovering the stairs were gone. But that's all been forgotten and she's on to more important things, like trying to recall the names of all her favorite firemen. Randal was an engineer who always chewed his fingernails; Thomas was a short man who had shoulders like a grizzly bear; Rudolf was a funny-guy—everybody called him "Rude"—only time his face is straight is when he's telling her a joke. She can't recall the Chief's name since he didn't hang out with the men and ate his meals at home because he only lived three blocks away. The men paid Myrna's salary—they each chipped in a buck a week—underneath-the-table since they're supposed to do the work themselves. But along with Daniel's check each month and not having to pay for food—and every cigarette she smokes is bummed off of a fireman—she saves well over half her pay and puts it in a bank account, just in case things don't work out should Daniel come back from the war.

She thinks about this all the time; Daniel said he's doomed for sure: *As soon as the war started I knew this is how I'm going to die.* . . . It was all part of the deal they made, why she'd agreed to marry him: a widow with an orphan or a slut stuck with a bastard child. It's not that she *wants* him to die, but the wait is driving her insane: every week another letter signed *your loving husband, Dan*. The *loving* part's annoying her—his face grows dimmer every day—although his letters all sound nice, and they'd had a three-day honeymoon. But there's something knocking at the window, someone calling Myrna's name; the only time that happens is when Frank Nagoya's visiting. But that was back five months ago and Frank's been sent off *God-knows-where*, and how could someone knock there when her room is on the second floor? She gets up from her Lazy-boy, more than just a touch confused, walks into the dining room and slams the stupid window closed.

...

Jessie barely saved her fingers, pulled back from the windowsill; at least she knew that Myrna wasn't half-dead on the bathroom floor. She knocked and called a few more times but Myrna wasn't answering; it was stupid not to have a key but she'd given hers to Lidia. She wondered where her husband was and how long she'd be stuck outside and why did Myrna think she had to slam the window closed on her? Everything was difficult: *This woman's going to drive me nuts! Why can't she just one time act like she's a normal human being?!* She might as well light up the grill, find something to eat ice cream with: from deep inside the glove box of her car she pulled a plastic spoon. *This will have to do* she thought and went back to the patio, poured a pile of charcoal bricks and doused them well with lighter fluid.

She hoped Myrna was safe inside, not doing something practical: trying to save the kitten she heard trapped behind the bathroom wall. But unless she broke a window there was no way she could check Hank's mom, so Jessie took the coffee-fudge and sat down in the wicker chaise. Of course she'd spoil her appetite, but she couldn't let it melt away; surprised to find it softened now to just-the-right consistency. Even with the plastic spoon the ice cream dished out easily, but still was frozen hard enough to feel the cold against her tongue. There was caffeine from the coffee and endorphins from the chocolate fudge; Jessie licked the spoon then scooped another dollop in her mouth.

Everything is just a trance. I choose to let things bother me. All I have to do is just decide to change this rotten mood.

She tried a new technique she'd learned to transform negativity: breathing in the bad and breathing out more pleasant energy. She took a breath of Hank's bad moods, the language Myrna liked to use, the speeding ticket that she got, the poor Tibetan refugees. Her exhale was a pleasant song, the warmth of early evening sun, the croaking of the creek frogs and the buzzing of the grasshoppers. She was breathing out the gentle breeze, the chirping little ditty birds, the smell of coffee-almond-fudge mixed with the smoky barbecue. Opening her eyes she saw the green leaves of the cottonwoods, the way the breeze moved through the trees like skin moves on a horse's rump. She let the bad fill up her lungs, then breathed out all this pleasantness; closing up her eyes she put a scoop of ice cream in her mouth.

The coffee flavor rich and smooth, the rippled-fudge the right amount, the almonds gave a perfect crunch: *I haven't felt this good in months.* The ice cream melted on her tongue and bathed her throat in cooling sweet; she looked to see the black briquettes were nicely white around the edge. Lidia said she was going out to dinner with some friends, but Hank should be back soon to fit his key into the cylinder. *Locking Myrna in the house is something I would never do. There's nothing going on here that is my responsibility.* She shook her head in mild dismay: *I wish I knew what's up with Hank;* taking in a breath she let more good out slowly through her mouth.

Myrna really should be safe so long as Hank switched off the stove and locked the sharp knives in the drawer and checked for falling blood sugar. But why would Hank have gone somewhere and left his mother vulnerable? *Perhaps he's finally fed up and he's run away with Lidia.* Wouldn't that be just her luck to be stuck with Hank's raving mom? *Though that would last an hour before she's packed off to a nursing home.* She needed watching all the time, a staff of smiling nursing aides, who all knew how to be polite to old people with failing brains. Jessie wouldn't dream of ever working in that kind of place: the litany of foul abuse and cleaning up the *accidents.* The staff would speak to the patients like they were all a bunch of three-year-olds: *Oh silly Mr. Henderson! Let's go put some clothes back on!* So Jessie had some sympathy for Hank not wanting to arrange for Myna to be locked up in the south wing out at Sunnyfield. But all the same it was getting to the point where she was dangerous: *One day she is going to burn the house while we're all fast asleep.*

It was then she heard the chopping noise, as if an orchard fan was on, the volume getting louder till it was practically on top of her. The helicopter's body had large medic symbols on the sides; it circled once around the flat, descending where the mill burned down. Instantly filled with regret, she'd thought Hank had done something wrong: he'd simply locked the doors before he'd rushed to help save someone's life. If they'd called the helicopter, it must have been quite serious: a toddler versus logging truck; a hunting rifle accident. She was nearly halfway through the pint when she started feeling kind of sick: *Why did I assume that Hank could act so irresponsibly?* He would have calculated risks—the chance his mom might hurt herself—against the likelihood that he could help save a *productive* life. If the call was urgent then she knew Hank couldn't *not* respond: ignore a cry for help to make sure Myrna didn't wet herself. She saw him rushing through the house to make sure all the doors were locked, stopping long enough to make his mother drink more apple juice. He'd then skid out of the driveway with the gravel flying through the yard, off to try to make up for the little boy he couldn't save.

...

Myrna's in the kitchen now, wonders who's the miscreant who knocked against the back door *just as I was . . . damn, now I forget!* There was something she was going to do, if she could just remember what: cook a roast or fix her hair or off to lunch with Madeline. She's thinking if it's Tuesday then there's Bridge Club in the afternoon, and if it's Monday she's supposed to be down at the library. Wednesday it's the Art Museum, Friday she delivers meals; Thursday she's in charge of selling gifts down at the hospital. But right now she's just awfully tired, as if she's been awake for days: *can't remember shit* and she could sleep against a bed of nails. But she knows she's got a list of chores she must have put down somewhere close; sometimes it's as if somebody's playing little tricks on her. If she could only catch him at it—has to be a neighbor boy—then she'd cuss the cretin out and cut him down a notch or two. *More likely I'm just getting old . . . unless this kid can walk through walls:* she keeps her doors and windows locked whenever she's alone inside.

She sits back in her easy chair, picks her floppy book back up: opens to the bookmark that is stuck halfway through chapter eight.

—*But even though she hates him so, he's caused a blooming of her rose, can feel a warmth ascending toward the center of her tortured soul. . . .*

Myrna puts the book back down while she wonders why she reads this crap, gets up from her chair so she can get on with her afternoon. But now that Daniel's passed away and Hank has such a busy life, it's hard to live all by herself and keep track of which day is which. If it's Monday she is late for reading to the little kids; if it's Tuesday Marsha will come honking in her Cadillac. She looks up at the kitchen clock: already after five o'clock; no matter what damn day it is she's late for getting dinner fixed. Dan gets home soon after six—*no, wait a minute . . . Daniel's dead!*—and up her spine a chill climbs then spreads outward through her shoulder blades. She feels the room begin to spin, a growing touch of nausea; she'd like to go lie down but can't remember where her bedroom is. She sits down in a kitchen chair—*we'd been married fifty years!*—and it's like they've been told once again his cancer has already spread.

Dan's too weak to leave his bed, the cancer's moved to lung and bone; Daniel says he doesn't want them putting in a feeding tube. He can't breathe if he's lying flat, so there are pillows stacked behind his head; the only medicine he takes is the *morphine* in an IV drip. *It's nice to know it's there,* he says, but he doesn't ask for very much; *the pain's not bad so long as I know I can treat it if I want.* Daniel isn't handsome but he's never looked this thin and pale, skin sags from the bones that used to hold her when they slept at night. She's trying to ignore the smell of urine and unhealthy sweat, of someone who's been lying in the same bed for the last two months. Dan tells her she should get some sleep, that he'll be fine all by himself: his bed now in the living room so he can see the city lights. There's a buzzer on his bedside table, water in a plastic glass, a bucket if he needs it and a white enameled urinal. Convinced he'll be fine for a while, her bed a few steps down the hall; they moved when Dan retired into a high-rise in the Portland hills. He asks her for a kiss good night, which lingers more than usual; drawing back he wears a smile she hasn't seen in years and years.

—*It's not the way I would have planned, but I'm glad I sat down next to you. How would we have met if I had gotten on a different train?*

Myrna was about to say that they met riding on a *bus,* but Daniel whispers he would like the morphine dose *turned up a notch.* Looking out the windows she can see the early signs of dawn: the middle part of June and so the nights don't stay dark very long. Out beyond the city lights, the mountain a dark silhouette, the long horizon just a smear of midnight blue on midnight black. The IV pump's confusing but Dan tells her what to set it at; he can't do it himself and so he tells her how the buttons work. She gets up from the kitchen chair, kisses Daniel's sleepy lips, slippers down the hall to figure out which bedroom door is which.

...

It was not five minutes later Jessie heard the helicopter leave, the increased whining engine sound that made the local coyotes howl. She watched as it rose straight up high above the ruined Edgar Mill, a phoenix flying quickly toward the Portland trauma hospital. She was hoping that it went okay, the patient not too serious, and Hank would be home soon so he could finally let her in the house. The coals had all turned ashen white, wafting heat waves through the air, so from her wicker chaise she saw the mountain ridges shimmering. She was sick from coffee-almond-fudge that now was half a pint of goo; she got up from the chaise to put the pound of salmon on the grill. Her husband should be doing this, the manly art of searing flesh; the yellow-jackets gathered quickly after she'd unwrapped the fish. She wasn't sure if they were more aggressive in the spring or fall, but knew that when she got stung she turned red and found it hard to breathe. They left the grilling fish alone but swarmed the slimy paper wrap; the last time she was stung she needed two shots of adrenaline. Trying to remember if the bee-sting kit was in her purse and how long it had been since she last checked the expiration date, she threw the fish-stained wrap away, far out from the patio, waved her hand before her face and pleaded to be left alone.

But the fish smell still clung to her hands so a few wasps kept on bothering and she couldn't go to wash them off and couldn't wipe them on her sleeves. She screwed apart a garden hose from a spigot near the flower bed, cursing when the water splashed across the brown suede of her shoes. The yellow-jackets left her to go scavenge off the paper wrap, but whenever she had been harassed it took a while to calm herself. She sat back on the wicker chaise, the sun now filtered through the trees, knowing Hank would be home soon: *The sweetest man in all the world.* She reached to take just one last bite of melting coffee-almond-fudge: didn't see the yellow-jacket on the back side of the spoon.

The Black Dress
September 1997

THOUGH GEORGE'S TRUCK was still in gear, his foot was firmly on the brake, stopped out on the dead-end where the road and gravel driveway met. He could barely see Hank's hidden house behind a massive cedar tree, its limbs drooped like the shoulders on the losing team in little league. This was what was on his mind: that he should turn around and leave: *Nothing that I have to say can't wait another couple days.* They'd been standing on the old mill slab, helicopter come and gone, all the other volunteers rushed home since it was dinnertime. But he and Hank had stood there staring at the last of Edgarville, just a cold foundation floor with ash filling the cracks and holes. He'd pointed out the railroad bed, where all the houses used to be: sawdust piles and fields of stumps, the big pond where they floated logs. Suddenly Hank turned to leave, said *hey, I'll catch you later, George!* and Hank jumped in his pickup, leaving George still deep in Edgarville. He knew that Hank was fifty-five, was born December '42: *That's six months after we were forced to go live in Camp Manzanar. If Myrna was a Capo then she would have been* that *Mormon girl . . . so when Frank said* farewell *he left her with more than she'd bargained for. So if Hank is Myrna Capo's kid and Martin's Myrna's mother's boy, then Myrna's Martin's sister and the mother of Frank's bastard child. . . .*

His impulse was to run and tell Hank everything he'd figured out: that Hank should call him *Uncle George* except when at the fire hall. But George was sitting in his truck, about to drive into Hank's yard, suddenly remembered that Hank's blood was not *pure* Japanese. Conjuring the way he looked, there were hints of Hank's Caucasian-ness: broader chest and taller frame and nose bent slightly out of shape. But even if he looked the part, that didn't make him trustworthy: Hank's genetic code was linked to George's mortal enemy. *If Myrna's Martin's sister then I can't assume Hank's innocent;* who could trust the nephew of a man who did what Martin did? When Frank died in the war the courts assumed George was his closest kin, but if Hank was his brother's child then George's farm belonged to him. And what if Hank already knew, and was scoping out what George was worth? The orchard and the house could fetch a hundred thousand dollars each. *So that's why Hank keeps coming 'round,* asking about George's past, stealing information that he'd use to prove who's farm it was. And here George was about to stumble straight into this bastard's trap: tell him he's his brother's son *and everything I own is his.* . . . Already George heard Martin Capo laughing from beyond the grave: even dead he'd found another way to twist the knife again.

But none of this fit in with George's theory of the arsonist: that every seven years Hank had come back to visit Edgarville. George was just about to leave, to turn around his pickup truck, to try to figure out why Hank had twice now rushed to save his life. But he saw Hank run out from the side yard, a woman carried in his arms, place her in the front seat of a brand-new silver SUV. Hank jumped in the driver's side: a massive cloud of gravel dust; George thought they'd collide but Hank had managed to swerve right and stop.

"Jessie's been stung by a bee. We're going to the hospital. My mother's locked inside the house. Please make sure that she's okay."

Then George was suddenly alone, a ring of keys thrust in his hand, the rumble of the V-eight sucking gas down as Hank raced away. The dust came in his open window, thin coat settled on the dash; George couldn't think what he should do but tend his brother's lover's needs.

...

In the kitchen Myrna's thinking *what the hell has happened here?!* All the cupboard doors are open, flour stuck to everything. There are pots and pans thrown on the floor and gadgets on the countertops: right before the Frigidaire, an oozing pile of shattered glass. The first thought that occurs to her is *Hank was trying to cook something...* imagining her young son to his elbows in a mixing bowl. But never in a hundred years would Hank make such a mess as this: ever since the age of four could crack eggs without breaking yolks. The only time she worries is when he thinks that she might get mad, always for some little thing she'd never give a damn about. It doesn't quite seem normal that he never tries to hide his crimes, seeks her out just to confess *I scuffed my brand-new tennis shoes.* It breaks her heart each time she sees her tenderhearted little boy trying to hide tears because he doesn't want to bother her. She's always thought he's much too easy, not like other mothers' boys: all she has to do is say *behave now, or it's back you go....* She wonders where he gets it from, couldn't be his Capo side: not one of her brothers ever thought twice about feeling bad. It must come from Hank's father, though she really barely knew the boy: lots of walks out in the woods, but mostly it was physical. So she never saw inside Frank's home, how neat he might have liked his room; never met his mom or dad but glimpses down an orchard row. Frank's father died before the war, but his mother should still be alive; she wonders if they would have bothered moving back to Edgarville. Remembering the newspapers, the hate spit at the Japanese: the Hooster Valley famous for the nasty *Welcome Home* they gave. Stores with signs *(Whites Only, Please!)* and homesteads having been destroyed: houses with their windows smashed and sheep kept in the dining rooms. She thought once if she's still around, that Hank should meet his grandmother; but second thought was that would just confuse things and upset the boy. And Lord-knows-what would happen if she ran into her family: her father so disgusted that his grandson is a *Lamanite.* Even Martin hated her, wouldn't even say *good-bye*: right outside the bus depot he told her what a whore she was. Her other brothers are all dead; one by one killed in the war: there's absolutely nothing now to bring her back to Edgarville. So her history is history, there's no sense telling Hank the truth; he'll start asking more questions then she'll never hear the end of it. The firefighters all agreed, the truth would only cause her grief, that she can tell Hank later when he's old enough to handle it. And Daniel—*bless his giant heart*—had taken everything in stride: looked at Hank, then scooped him up, said *hey there, buddy! Meet your dad!*

The kitchen is so awful she can't bear to even look at it; Nona comes tomorrow morning: *She can whip it back in shape.* When Dan comes home she'll tell him that he'll have to take her out to eat; tomorrow he can stop off for a doughnut on his way to work. Turning from the kitchen mess, she wanders through a bedroom door, slides the closet open to decide what she should wear tonight. *I might as well get dressed up sweet so Dan will take me someplace nice:* confused because her closet's full of clothes she doesn't recognize. But there are several things she rather likes, an outfit with a flowered print, a black dress with a bodice that would show off what she's got in front.

She thinks she'll try the black dress on, slides out of her morning clothes, pulls the dress over her head, pleased how nice the fabric feels. Looking in the full-length mirror, she thinks it's kind of flattering; her face is what looks pale and tired: her eye-bags need some camouflage. The bedroom has a master bath, cosmetics on the vanity, a dozen tubes of lipstick and assorted skin conditioners. She's done all this so many times she doesn't have to think too hard: foundation and mascara and a little dab behind her ears. Feeling she looks better now, she peeks into the jewelry box; she's never had her ears pierced but there's something for around her neck. Putting on a string of pearls—*perfect with a dress like this!*—she goes back to the closet to pick out a pair of decent shoes. There are at least a dozen different styles, the palette of a fashion queen; she can't decide between the dark-red pumps or something with a heel. She hears a knock at the front door, the sound of keys around the lock; she takes a last look in the mirror then goes out to present herself. But the man who's standing at the door is not her faithful husband Dan, but someone who looks Japanese and wearing dusty dungarees.

"Who the hell are you?" she asks, and George was slightly taken back.

"We've met once before," he said. "I'm Frank Nagoya's brother George."

He was staring at a woman who looked dressed up for a gala ball: a wedding or a birthday or some president's inaugural. As older women go this gal could nicely fill a party dress; George could see now why Frank might have thought that she was worth the risk. But it was nothing he was used to, seeing women dressed up to the nines; more often he kept company with pear trees and old hunting dogs.

Myrna's looking at this man: *Perhaps I didn't understand. . . .* Franklin's little brother can't be much more than a twelve-year-old. But he certainly resembles Frank; in fact, he's even handsomer: however many years have passed have added lots of character. It all makes Myrna dizzy like descending in an elevator: fifty stories straight down then that sense of heavy gravity. Then the elevator finally stops, the *one* lights with a ringing bell, the silver doors slide open and then all-at-once she's somewhere else. And of course Frank would come looking for her, now that Daniel's passed away; so much time has gone by and there's so much catching up to do.

"I thought we might go somewhere nice. Perhaps I'm slightly overdressed." George was thinking fast but not enough to know which way was which. Myrna's eyes were sparkling; she was flashing George the coyest smile: every indication she was honest as an apple pie. Hank had mentioned once or twice that *Mother often gets confused,* but from the way she looked he couldn't see what could be wrong with her. It was George who was confused now about what he was supposed to do, *but if she's all dressed up to go, I'll gladly take her into town.* He hadn't had a lady-friend since Janet Foster sold her house, moved to Arizona to be closer to her grandchildren. He looked down at his farming clothes—his jeans could stand all by themselves, his T-shirt stained around the hint of belly he had sticking out. Because she was so nicely dressed he'd have to take her somewhere swank; the nicest place in Hooster was the old Hotel Columbia. He'd need to find a coat and tie, dig out his only pair of slacks, perhaps put on that suit that he had only worn two other times.

"Is there something burning on the stove?"

"That's why I thought we should go out. . . ."

"What about your son's wife?"

"Oh, those two can take care of themselves."

So the hint of smoke he smelled was nothing he needed to worry about, and apparently this woman wasn't worried about Hank's ailing wife. It couldn't have been serious, or maybe had become routine: a bee sting meant a quick trip to the hospital emergency. He told her if she didn't mind, they'd stop so he could change his clothes, maybe take a second for a brief rinse in the shower stall.

"I'd love to see inside your house. It's always been a mystery. Martin told me once that Japs ate dog meat off the kitchen floor."

For just a moment George felt like his blood had turned to ice water, stunned that he would let himself forget who he was talking to.

"I used to like my brother, but he turned into a total ass. Right after you left he helped my father burn my bedroom set."

She's decided that she's going to tell Frank everything about her past: all that's happened since the last time she had helped undo his pants. She'll tell him about Daniel, how he promised he was going to die; how the firemen at the station taught her how to cook spaghetti right.

Outside by his pickup Myrna's watching while Frank dusts the seat; even though he's aged he still looks good inside his dungarees. She lets him help her up because the dress makes climbing difficult.

"If I'd known you'd be so spruced up, I'd have brought around my limousine."

The thought of that makes Myrna laugh: a limousine on Edgar Flat! More likely they'd be bouncing on the jitney down the railroad tracks. *What would it have been like if there hadn't been that stupid war—if I had stayed and married Frank and lived my life in Edgarville?* Her brothers might be still alive, but would they ever come around? Or would she live next door but they'd pretend she'd died and gone to hell? Her mother, every now and then, might sneak over to have a chat, when Father was in town and all his boys were trimming fire blight. And maybe after several years they might have loosened up a bit: first a nod and then a wave and then a *how's it goin' sis!?* But more important, what would it have been like living life with Frank? Learning to cook rice and fry those fishy tasting seaweed cakes? They'd have to sleep on skinny mats and make their pillows out of wood and bathe in a communal tub with other people's filth and germs. Frank's mother would have lived with them, bowing at her all the time, never understanding since she can't speak English very nice. At some point she would lose her face, embarrass the Nagoya name: have to get down on her knees and use the *harry-karry* knife. Then little Hank would grow up without Myrna's love and guiding hand, thinking it was normal to eat jellyfish and puppy dog.

George was taking Myrna home, so he could find some decent clothes; before they'd head to town they'd take ten minutes for a cocktail hour. He kept his liquor cabinet full, and knew he had a fifth of gin, a whisper of vermouth, and jars of olives kept inside the fridge. He helped her slide out of the truck—her dress hiked up above the knee—trying not to stare but she still had a decent pair of legs. Once they were inside he realized there was no place to sit: quickly took three leaning stacks of magazines off of the couch.

"Make yourself at home," he said.

"Alright if I just look around?"

"I'll just be a minute," as he gave her a martini glass.

It wasn't all that long ago that Hank gave her two tiny pills; not that she remembers but they haven't left her system yet. Already she feels quite relaxed, and she missed her normal midday snack: she fishes out the olive so there's something on her stomach first. *So this is what their house is like.* . . . Myrna's looking 'round the room: everywhere are piles and piles of different periodicals. She'd thought there'd be those woven mats, a table one foot off the floor: sliding doors of rice paper and funny hanging lantern shades. But except for all the magazines, it was a normal-looking home: a couch and a recliner made of leather-textured Naugahyde. There's an art print hanging on the wall, a maiden native Indian: buxom in a buckskin with big doe-eyes and black feathered braids. Centered in the living room: a console stereo-TV; a table with the kind of lamp bought cheap at someone's rummage sale. But if Frank has slightly tacky taste, he makes a mean martini drink; she's halfway through the glass before she knows how much she's feeling it. She's always been a featherweight: a few sips and she's giggling; she wanders through the kitchen looking at the stacks of catalogs. Opening the back door, there are pear trees where the yard should be, with no place for a swing-set or a playhouse or a swimming pool. If there were ever children here, all evidence of them is gone: no scribbled drawings on the fridge or pictures from the seventh grade. What's missing is a woman's touch, the curtains for the kitchen sink; the house has all the trappings of a sloppy lifelong bachelor.

The plumbing makes a sudden knock of the shower water turning off; she hears the sound of damp feet thumping on the wood floor of the hall. She wonders when the war was through, if Frank came back to Edgarville, found her gone then spent his best years hoping she'd come back again. He's waited for her all these years, that's why so many magazines: something to help pass the time till she became available. Following the echoed sound, the footprints thumping down the hall, she stops outside his bedroom door left open half-an-inch or so. She spies a single buttock and a left arm with a farmer's tan: he's finished drying off and throws the damp towel on the bedroom chair. She takes another sip of drink, pushes lightly on the door, which makes the faintest hint of squeak so Frank turns head-and-shoulders 'round. The last time that she saw him it was oh-so-many years ago: one of only three men she has felt such strong attraction for. Back then there had been silver moonlight shining past her windowsill: just enough so she could see to find his skinny belt buckle. And Frank's as handsome now as then, his chest perhaps a little thick, but still he's waited all these years to do what they once did again.

Quiet, Please
September 1997

BY THE TIME they got to Tucker Bridge, his wife was breathing easier; by Windmaster Convenience Store the hives weren't quite so angry red. The *epi* was a miracle—a quick shot in the outer thigh—and someone who was dying says *I'm feeling so much better now*. The problem was the drug's effects might only last a half-an-hour, and when they disappeared Hank's lovely wife might start to die again. So even though she was sitting up, Hank raced as if her breathing stopped, like he was driving taxi on the busy streets of Bangladesh. He was passing over double lines, leaning on the big car's horn:

"If you crash and we both die, Hank, you'll never hear the end of it. . . ."

Hank was nearly certain that his wife was going to be okay, that all she'd need was fifty milligrams of IV *prednisone*. But this stupid little brown sedan wouldn't pull over so he could pass, even with Hank's honking and their bumpers just two feet apart. A van went past the other way, he jumped in the oncoming lane, swung around the brown car yards before a logging truck went by. Jessie had her eyes closed and a hand tight on the panic bar, adding to her *epi* shot some natural adrenaline. She was feeling like she'd landed after parachuting from a plane, but now hung from a tree above a river full of crocodiles. Her heart was all aflutter and her chest hurt when she took a breath, but the air was going in and out and the itching wasn't quite so bad. If Hank had only slowed down she'd have felt like she'd survive the drive; if she could shift her trance to something other than a fiery crash.

They finally pulled into the space that was marked off for the ambulance; Hank helped Jessie from the car and through the automatic doors. The hospital was tiny, with perhaps a couple dozen beds; the ER was remodeled but was only Trauma Level IV. Hank had been inside before, when George first had his heart attack, and Jessie hit the deer and had to have her neck immobilized. They stood before the nurses' desk:

"My wife's in anaphylactic shock. She's had point-three of *epi* but she needs a dose of *prednisone*...."

The nurse remembered this guy from that time up in the ICU, when he tried telling her the finer points of taking EKGs. And now this guy came waltzing in and claimed his wife was going to die, whose only real problem was she'd married an embarrassment.

"You'll have to check her in out front," and she pointed back the way they came: *Toward those doors then to the right out to the patient waiting room.*

"Someone there can help you..." but he wasn't going to be put off.

"Listen. She's done this before. The *epi*'s going to wear off soon."

But Tamra was determined that he wasn't going to get his way, just because he was a man who knew some terminology. And his wife was *not* about to die, although she looked a little pale: the fact that she could stand meant that she had a decent blood pressure. If she had been with someone else, she'd have led her to a curtained room, taken vitals while the husband went to the admitting desk. But this man had been so arrogant, had made her feel an idiot: lecturing on vectors while she finished up a double shift. Dr. Smith was on tonight; he'd told her that he'd be back soon: off to get some food before they closed the cafeteria. So she was the one in charge now, with two patients waiting for their labs: a baby with a fever and a woman with a broken arm. Anybody else and she'd have smiled and been as nice as pie, but this time she refused to let this asshole push his weight around.

"Your wife is going to be just fine. But you'll have to do the paperwork. There's nothing I can do until they copy your insurance card."

Hank had nurses *up to here,* one tried so hard to ruin his life, the last thing that he wanted was to let this woman touch his wife. But Jessie needed steroids and a dose of antihistamine, and Hooster didn't have a better hospital across the street. Jessie took Hank's upper arm, said, "Let's

do what she tells us to," pulled him toward the doors then stopped, said:
"I'm not feeling very well."

Her voice was sounding hoarse and thick, her breathing thin and stridorous; Hank watched the blotchy hives as they were blossoming across her face. He picked his wife up once again, rushed her to an empty bed, yelling at the nurse to get the crash cart and adrenaline. The cart was only steps away, he broke the little plastic locks: the *epi* in the top drawer in a vial with a rubber top. The nurse gave him the right syringe, he quickly drew a half cc; Jessie got another stab, this time high on the upper arm.

"Get her on some oxygen. Use the non-rebreather mask! I need a sixteen angio. Get some blasted help back here!"

Thirty years ago Hank was a pediatric resident: up all night on-call for all the scut-work they could dump on him. Every kid who came in got a urine and hematocrit: three a.m. and Hank is spinning pee around a centrifuge. He had to read the chest X-rays before the early morning rounds, half-asleep he scribbled down their histories and physicals. But for six months of his intern year they barely let him touch the kids: the nurses didn't trust the first-year docs to take a temperature. Then one night about two o'clock a three-year-old pulled out his line; the nurses poked him six times but still couldn't cannulate a vein. The boy was in intensive care, battling a septic shock; he needed drugs to kill the bugs and push his tired little heart. The senior resident was there: already missed the biggest veins; Hank came in and said that he could do it if they'd let him try. The senior said *if you get in I'll take all of your calls tonight;* her next choice was to wake up the attending from his bed at home. Now everybody watched as Hank decided which needle to use, prepped the skin over a spot nobody'd thought to poke the kid. The toddler was a chubby thing, his mother pacing near the door; his thick layer of fat made it impossible to see his veins. A rubber strap around the thigh, Hank aimed deep for the saphenous: he knew that it was there because that was where the textbook said it was. It had been over an hour since the boy had any *dopamine:* his pressure barely holding from a thready tachycardia. Hank had to try to visualize: a pipe above the ankle bone, the needle plunging through the layers of skin and fat and intima. The whole room breathed a sigh when they all saw the little flash of blood, watched him test the line to make sure that it didn't infiltrate. The resident said *good job, Hank. Would you like to try the central line?* The nurses, for the first time, whispered *thank you, Doctor Davenport.* He'd been waiting for this all his life: the sense that he was finally real; he wasn't just pretending he was a doctor or his mother's child. *So this is what it feels like to be something other than a fraud:* competent and confident he'd found the place where he belonged.

For years he didn't mind he could be pulled out of his bed at night, that even on the weekends they could page him off the tennis court. Because he knew, no matter what, *they can't take this away from me:* his patients and the nurses were the family that he never had. He trusted that they trusted him to always do the best he could; that if he stuck a needle in he was going to get it in the vein. That was the contract that he made with children asking for his help: *I'll be there when you need me even if it's middle-of-the-night.* But he'd never had that growing up, the full blast of a mother's love: every chance she got his mom denied he was her flesh and blood. They'd be standing in the fabric store, with absolutely nothing worse than trying to be patient while she browsed though every pattern book. He was barely even five-years-old, trying not to act too bored, circling the tables touching all the different bolts of cloth. But she'd opened up another book—*it's going to be forever now;* underneath the table there was a cupboard with a sliding door. The cupboard held more bolts of cloth with room for him to climb inside, a hole drilled in the door to put his finger in to slide it closed. Looking back out through the hole he saw most of his mother's dress, the white skin of her slender legs: her purse and shoes coordinate. The cotton bolts were warm and soft: he woke up when he heard his name: the way his mom described him to the clerk now helping look for him. With a touch of panic in her voice, she said *he's only just so tall*; he couldn't be too far since *he was right here not too long ago.* Her voice was only steps away, Hank thought that this was just a game, that Myrna knew right where he was because moms always *know* these things.

...*black hair and a blue shirt and I think he's wearing tennis shoes....He doesn't look like me at all. His parents were both Japanese....*

Hank knew he was adopted but was not sure what that really meant, and he knew his mother was his mom because who else would make him brush his teeth? He was not sure what her words meant but they'd sounded slightly ominous: that nonadopted kids were supposed to look more like their moms and dads. Daniel's hair was reddish-orange, his chin perhaps a little strong; Myrna's eyes were dark but round; her dark hair with a natural wave. All she had to do was walk five feet and slide the door open: *Unless she's just pretending that she wants to find me right away.* He'd willed his mom to walk to him, put her finger in the hole, pull him out, a great big hug: *Oh, honey, it was just a joke!* But the panic rose up in her voice; the clerk said she'd look through the store, that Myrna should go next door and make sure he hadn't wandered there. *How long will she search for me before she goes back to the car, heads home to tell Dad they'll have to go pick out another boy?* Like deciding on a cat or dog, they'd head to the adoption pound; this time they'd be more careful picking out which breed they want to own.

...

Tamra wondered why she'd taken orders from this awful man, now that this woman's breathing didn't sound like she was going to die.

"Put her on the monitor. Eight liters of oxygen. Hang a bag of *Ringers* and then get some *methylprednisone*. . . ."

"Thank you for your help," she said, "but the doctor has to order that. When he gets back he'll look at her and order what he thinks is best."

"I *am* a fucking doctor!" and she thought she understood it now: *This must be that man who killed the young boy with the heart transplant!* It all made sense: he's Japanese, a new face in this little town, hiding from the world because of what a horrid thing he did. She took a step away from him, scared by what this man might do: kill his wife and try to make her death look like the nurse's fault. Without turning around she stepped the few feet to the nurses' desk, reached out for the phone and dialed the number for the overhead.

"Code red in Emergency," repeated in a nervous voice; half-a-minute later she heard footsteps running down the hall.

...

Jessie tried to change her trance, her current one no help at all, needing someplace quiet where the air was not so hard to breathe. She had the anxious jitters and there were all these people standing 'round; she tried to make them go away by concentrating on her breath. She found a space inside her chest, identified the feeling there: a tiny little poodle puppy anxious to go out and play. Cooped up inside all day long, it really, *really* had to go; its hyperactive walnut brain said run and run and run around! All she had to do was find a way to open up the door, let the puppy out so it could squat out near the rosebushes. But the front door had a dead bolt lock and her key ring held a thousand keys: she struggled for a breath while she jammed keys into the cylinder. Her mantra now was *quiet, please!* repeated every other breath; she picked the puppy up to try to hush its constant yapping bark.

—*Quiet, please*, she told the dog, but it didn't stop for very long.
—*Quiet, please*, and Jessie took a breath that didn't feel right.
—*Quiet* . . . and she held the air: the voice of people arguing.
—*Quiet, please* . . . and she could hear Hank call someone an idiot.
—*Quiet, please*. . . .
—Don't touch my wife!
—*Quiet, please*. . . .
—Let's all calm down. . . .
—*Quiet, please*. . . .
—So go ahead and call the fucking sheriff then!

She finally found a key that fit, that made the breathing easier; she let the dog out just to watch it run into the busy street.

The next sound made the whole room stop: the honking of the screeching cars, the grating *beep-beep-beeping* of Hank's fire beeper going off.

Flashover
September 1997

LIDIA THOUGHT with her luck this house had also caught on fire: halfway up the drive and she saw smoke come from the patio. Her day had not gone very well and her own house burned so recently that it took a second thought to think it was probably the barbecue. Lidia was home early from her dinner with her so-called-friends: the man they'd wanted her to meet was someone she'd already met. The man was plenty nice and had a good job selling auto parts, but when they'd dated once before there hadn't been a single spark. She wanted someone she could trust, a man she could raise children with, a steady paycheck every week, who knew enough to wipe his feet. But just as much she wanted to feel something when she looked at him: pitter-pat and short-of-breath; a soft throb from her ovaries. She wanted someone gallant who would open doors to let her through; someone with a motorcycle clenched between his muscled thighs. Somewhere there was someone who could help solve this dichotomy: a rogue who'd make her heart race who still makes it home by dinnertime. But this guy didn't ring her bell or set off any fireworks: slightly short and thin mustache and palm damp when his hand was shook.

As she'd turned on Collins Road she'd passed a dark-green pickup truck, would have sworn that Myrna was the woman in the shotgun seat. She pulled into the yard and saw the smoke come from the patio: Hank's truck in the driveway but no sign of Jessie's SUV. There seemed an awful lot of smoke for just a simple barbecue, but if the meat was marbled it would drop grease on the glowing coals. Before she got out of her car she stopped to put some lipstick on, freshen her mascara and make sure she wasn't smelling bad. The whole thing with the blind date made her tense enough for stinky sweat; she pulled out of her purse a tiny stick of anti-perspirant. Her hair she didn't worry about, pulled back in a long black braid; she got out of the car and smoothed the wrinkles from her panty hose. Going through this ritual was all for Myrna's benefit; when Lidia was dressed nice Myrna tried hard to behave herself.

Surprised to find the front door locked, she rummaged for the dead bolt key, then opened up the door to find *it's awfully stuffy-hot in here*. She stepped into the living room; Myrna wasn't in her chair. "Hola!" she said wondering if Hank was home alone today. It was like the heat was turned too high; she went to check the thermostat; the heat was off but still the dial read almost eighty-five degrees. She walked back to her bedroom so that she could put her purse away, opened up a button on her blouse to circulate some air. She peeked through Myrna's door to see if she might not be still asleep; stepped inside to smooth the wrinkles from her nice embroidered quilt. She opened Myrna's windows, though they only slide up half-a-foot; Hank had screwed some blocks in so she couldn't climb out late at night. Back out in the living room, she opened up a couple more; "Hola, Doctor Hank!" she called but didn't get an answer back. Perhaps he was up in the attic, making that strange crackling noise; going to the attic stairs she grabbed the knob and burned her hand.

"Joseph-mary-jesus-christ!" and she knew why it was hot inside: all that smoke she'd seen outside was not from grilling hamburgers. Instead of rushing out she ran to double-check no one was home: Hank and Jessie's bedroom empty, no one on the bathroom throne.

...

George was feeling dizzy now, his brain starving for oxygen: all his blood diverted to attend to more *important* things. This woman took his breath away: a certain way she did *that thing*; Janet Foster tried once but complained how much her jaw had ached. This had happened so fast that he hadn't had a chance to think; he was going to have to make her stop or risk another heart attack. She paused to look up at him, but things only went from bad to worse: standing up, she reached down to start pulling up her party dress. He watched as her nice thighs appeared, her lace-embroidered underwear, the soft flesh of her belly that was white as a nice cod fillet. He was trying to remember where he put his *nitroglycerin:* not quite having chest pain *but it should start any minute now.* Already she had proven he was not a *total* invalid; asked him in a whisper if he'd help undo the fastener. He hadn't been asked that in years (December 1983); in fact he'd done this so few times he couldn't do it very well. But the clasp seemed to undo itself, the garment nearly jumping off, sliding down her arms and getting hung up inches from his crotch.

...

Still in the emergency, Hank was flummoxed by which course to take: let his mother burn or trust his wife's life to these *idiots*. The second dose of *epi* had already shown some benefit: her breathing pretty easy for someone whose house was burning up. The call over his beeper had said *six-o-two Paul Partlow Road:* everyone got quiet when they saw the look change on his face. He'd held his beeper to his ear, praying for a fast response: that Evan Smith and Brenda Thompson might be in the neighborhood. He remembered giving George the key, asking him to check his mom; maybe George had let her out or maybe *both* were stuck inside. Or maybe George could not get close without a hose and Nomex suit: thirty feet away and watching Myrna bang the window glass. He was trying hard to think but there were images he had to stop: his mother looking like the pictures he'd seen in a trauma course.

When Hank came home and found his wife was near death on the wicker chaise, he didn't give a damn that he had knocked over the barbecue. He'd only looked behind to see which way the hot briquettes had spilled: looked like they spread harmless on the gravel of the patio. But he hadn't seen the glowing coal slide underneath the planter box, or twenty minutes later when the cedar siding finally caught. The flames then slowly climbed the wall, then underneath the overhang, sucked into the attic space and burned through half the roof supports. The fire didn't come inside until the gypsum ceiling fell, right behind poor Lidia while staring at the kitchen stove. Once one of the trusses broke the others went like dominoes; she could have gotten out then if she'd run straight through the living room. But she'd been through all this once before: losing everything she owned; instead of going out the front she turned left down the bedroom hall. All she'd wanted was her purse, her wallet and her ID cards, the old quilt off of Myrna's bed: protection from the raging fire.

...

Myrna's lying on the bed now, dying for a cigarette, wondering if Frank Nagoya thinks that she was worth the wait. She'd asked him *could I have a drink?* because her throat's a little dry; watched Frank get up off the bed and pull a pair of boxers on. He asks her what she'd like to drink: "A simple glass of water, please." She likes the way his legs look even with the thin red spider veins. He leaves the room, goes down the hall; she hears the running kitchen tap; she feels a chill and reaches down to pull the sheet and blanket up.

George was at the kitchen sink, filling up the water glass, swallowed one himself before he heard the siren going off. His pager wasn't turned on but was charging on the countertop; he flipped the dial to channel "B" to find out what was happening. He was standing in his underwear, listening to dispatch talk: *Structure fire, smoke and flames, six-o-two Paul Partlow Road.* The address seemed familiar, like he'd been called to that house before: remembering a winter day, a woodshed almost caught on fire. *Of course!* it was the Capo place, the house the arsonist forgot: catching everyone off guard by waiting till year *number eight. Who the hell is doing this?!* Perhaps they only now found out that Myrna was a Capo and she'd moved back to the family house. *But what if it's Hank Davenport?* He'd seen him run out from the house: carrying his wife could be a ruse to keep from being caught. How much could his heart withstand? The doc told him to slow way down: already done today more than he'd ever dreamed he'd do again. He'd been started on a pressure pill that kept his heart from beating fast, a blood thinner to make sure that his arteries would not plug up. But he couldn't stay at home and let this woman's house burn to the ground: climb back into bed pretending that it wasn't happening. He heard her from the other room, screaming like her hair's on fire, mixing with the high pitch of the siren from the fire hall.

"I hate that sound! I hate it!" since it triggers such a sense of dread: brave men running off to fight and never coming back again. The Captain's standing next to her at her window on the second floor, blushing from admitting that the men asked him to speak to her. She's got the vaguest kind of crush: he's handsome for an older guy; she's thrilled the way he holds her naked boy with such authority. And even though she's married she still feels completely unattached: Daniel told her when he left that he would not be coming back. But his letters now came every week, and she'd answered all of them so far; he often sent her photos of himself among the jungle fronds. He wrote once he was certain he was dying of malaria, but next week wrote his fever was a bug the men were passing 'round. His letters spoke of listening to bombs drop middle-of-the-night, expecting when he heard them whistle *next one's got my name on it*. Every time a letter came he'd write how close he'd come to death: mortar fire and hand grenades and jeep-rollover accidents. But Captain Andy's standing at the window right there next to her: flesh and blood and manly smells of after-shave and diesel smoke. She wants to lean against his arm, rest her cheek against his sleeve, when suddenly the siren blares and he quickly hands Hank back to her.

The fire was a *three-alarm:* a big blaze in a grocery store; the next time Myrna saw the Captain, it was at his funeral. It hadn't rained in two full months, but they hadn't rationed water yet, so the cemetery grass was green in the bright-white light of ten o'clock. He didn't die from too much smoke or pulling someone from the flames or crashing through a burning ceiling wrestling with a fire hose. Instead he's middle-of-the-street, talking to the Fire Chief: run down by some rubbernecker watching all the flames and smoke. He got a hero's funeral with fire streams and waving flags and all the men in full dress with their badges covered up with black. Myrna's standing three graves back, smearing tears across her sleeve: what's she going to do now that another man's abandoned her? Frank left through the window, and her father burned her bed and clothes, and even Martin told her she's a *worthless dirtbag little whore*. The only man still true to her she might not even recognize: twenty minutes with a judge; three awkward nights of honeymoon. Holding Hank beneath a tree, he smells like he could use a change; as the Captain's lowered down the mourning crowd begins to break. The smell of Hank's rank diaper makes her think she should back off a ways; a woman standing near asks Myrna if she isn't feeling well. Putting Hank down on the grass helps pass the wave of nausea; Myrna asks the woman if she knows those people near the grave.

—That's the widow and the kids. His four boys and his little girl. The oldest is a senior and the youngest is a three-year-old. . . .

...

Evan squatted at the door and listened to the burning house: a howling like his head was stuck in the engine of a jet aircraft. But the best part of a fire was in the belly of the blazing beast; nothing in his life compared to crawling through a burning house. It all was so immediate: no thoughts of stupid past mistakes, like when he was a probie and tried riding on the tailgate. The driver turned the corner fast, the left rear hit a *thank-you-ma'am;* they'd said he did a gainer before landing in the drainage ditch. But in a burning building it all narrows down to life-and-death: the battle between heat and flame and water from his nozzle tip. Even standing at the door, he was going to have to back off soon, watching as the flames tickled the ceiling of the living room. He was waiting for the flashover, when everything ignites at once: thirty years of fighting fire and he hadn't seen it happen yet. He should be helping Brenda with the woman she found in the grass, ten feet from the window she had shattered with a flower vase. The woman crawled through shards of glass she'd padded with a fancy quilt, ruined now by smoke and ash and bloodstains where her knee was cut. Brenda dragged her twenty yards and hooked her to an O2 mask; by then the house was so involved there was no chance they could put it out. Once she had some oxygen, the woman started sitting up; Brenda started wrapping gauze on superficial cuts and scrapes. Evan didn't want to ask if anyone was still inside: smoke from every window and the roof already falling down. Even if he thought that there was anyone alive in there, going in would only guarantee another life was lost.

Already there had been enough: the two men when the mill collapsed, Evan still not ready to forgive them such a stupid stunt. The rumors said George was at fault for sending them behind the mill when anyone with any sense could see it was about to fall. But Evan saw what really happened even though George took the blame: George told them to come back but they blatantly had disobeyed. Perhaps they thought that somehow they knew better than the Fire Chief, even though all they could do was save a pile of blackened bricks. George never said they'd disobeyed, thinking no one else had seen: didn't want their families knowing *they'd died of stupidity.*

He would have stuck up for the Chief if he'd wanted to defend himself, but all the accusations had been whispered behind George's back. And if George wanted everyone to think their deaths were all his fault then Evan wasn't going to be the one to tell them something else. And now if Evan had more men, he'd have them place defensive lines, set the water bins and hook the hard hose to the suction port. But Hillendale was miles away and Brenda had her first aid tasks and all the water in the truck would barely make the smoke turn gray. Knowing he might never see another fire as hot as this, he was hoping that for once he'd get to watch a room incinerate.

...

Jessie had her eyes closed and an IV in her elbow crease; Doctor Smith came off his break to order *methylprednisone*. The staff had finally calmed down after Doctor Smith had taken charge and Hank decided that the man was competent to treat his wife. She knew that Hank was pacing with his pager pressed against his ear, sorting out the static from the traffic at the fire scene. She didn't want to look at him, imagining his agony: knowing he felt right beside his mother in the smoke and flames. The poodle-puppy in her chest ran right out middle-of-the-street, smashed flat by the nine wheels on the left side of a semi-truck. But her breathing was much easier, no longer needing oxygen: trying not to think of who was locked inside their burning home.

She'd always thought they should have torn the house apart to start from scratch, instead of spending all that money fixing what they couldn't fix. She didn't know how Hank would ever manage to forgive himself; dispatch had asked Hooster to respond a second ambulance. *But no one else was home today!* unless a fireman was hurt: *All Hank needs is one more thing thrown on his dreadful pile of guilt.* If only she had had her key, did not react to bees and wasps, insisted that Hank never *ever* lock his mom inside the house. But there was something else she thought of that had crowned her own complex of guilt: that if Hank's mom was dead then *that's just one less thing to worry about.*

...

George was on his hands and knees, trying hard to catch his breath: *What a stupid thing to try to drag a hose line by myself!* He could have helped by offering to finish wrapping bandages; Brenda Thompson was a much more able-bodied fireman. Instead he grabbed the gated *wye* attached to the three-inch supply, dragged it from the engine to the east side of this ball-of-fire. Evan Smith was squatting staring through the front door of the house: suddenly occurred to George that *he might be the arsonist!* Why *else* would Evan stand and watch the fire raging through the house unless he was the very one responsible for starting it? No matter what the reason, Evan jumped when George had yelled at him; quickly got up off his knees and ran to grab a preconnect.

George had dragged the three-inch line out somewhere near three-dozen yards: every length of fifty feet weighed empty about eighty pounds. His strength came from adrenaline, like headlines in the grocery store: MOM LIFTS PICKUP OFF HER SON—DECLARED OLYMPIC CHAMPION. But all that left him suddenly, a massive pressure in his chest: a soaking sweat and dizziness and legs gave out from under him. Down now on his hands and knees, he was working hard to get some air, fighting for control over the sudden wave of nausea. He fell down flat against the grass, face turned toward the burning house, thinking if he had to die at least he got to see this part. The Capo place was now a box of leaping flames and billowed smoke; thankfully there wasn't anybody trapped inside the house. Martin died eight years before, from cancer somewhere in his gut; George thought he should say good-bye but Martin wouldn't talk to him. He'd always felt that dying gave his nemesis the upper hand, and learning that Hank owned his farm was Martin laughing from the grave. But as he lay there in the grass, a slight grin spread on George's face, realizing just who'd won the battle of the orchardists. He was going to die before he had to give his place away to Hank, and it didn't really count since Hank was half-a-kin to both of them. If Evan was the arsonist, then Hank was not involved at all, but if that were true then why did Hank wait so long to reclaim the farm? The pain was so intense that it was almost like it didn't hurt, knowing now that Martin Capo's last laugh had been premature. George guessed this was his final hour and he'd just pulled off the *coup de grace:* slept with Martin's sister and then watched the bastard's house burn down.

...

With all the noise the engines make and all the stench of truck exhaust, Myrna thinks it's good-a-time-as-any to go for a walk. Stepping from the pickup truck, still dressed in her nice black dress, she doesn't want it ruined by splashing mud or gently falling ash. She wishes she had better shoes; these pumps aren't very practical: not too big a heel but there's no traction from the leather soles. She wonders where she got them since she doesn't recognize the style, thinking, though, this black dress isn't bad for walking through the woods. The fabric has some stretchiness and the hem stops well above the knee so it's comfortable and doesn't interfere with taking decent strides.

From where the sun is in the sky—still above the western ridge—she should have time enough to make the round-trip down to Punchbowl Falls. Certain she's remembering right, it's only about half-a-mile, along a trail they'd made as kids that scrambles down the riverbank. It starts behind the Taylor's barn where no one but a kid would go: supposed to be a secret but now all the neighbors know it's there. The Taylor's barn looks like the old man finally got some paint on it; his 'coon-dog almost always runs out barking like a maniac. But the bitch must be inside the house, probably quite old by now, curled up underneath the table hoping for some dinner scraps. So she gets by unmolested and the path is where she thought it was: starts between a big rock and where Mr. Taylor burns his trash.

The trail is kind-of-steep at first, then cuts left sort-of-gradual, following a narrow bench she thought was longer than it is. She recognizes poison oak mixed in among the greenery, careful not to swing her arms or brush against it with her knees. The worst case that she'd ever had was when she was a nine-year-old, playing with a neighbor's dog that liked to run between her legs. The dog was mostly Labrador, friendly as a circus clown, running through the bushes and then dashing underneath her skirt. The itching was unbearable: at night they wrapped her hands in gauze; she couldn't walk for two weeks till the weeping rash had finally dried. Her mother offered sympathy, but her brothers' teasing wouldn't end: *Where'd you think that rash would be if that dog was half-again as big?!*

The path drops into denser trees, the poison oak not growing here, but now she has to step around the fallen branches on the ground. She sure would like some better shoes, something to protect her feet, wishing she were wearing her old pair of leather clodhoppers. With those she felt invincible, could go out anywhere she pleased: through the woods, across the streams, a pasture thick with dung and mud. It's been so long since she's been out to wander through the puckerbrush: never since her father made her douse her bed with kerosene. Once she left the Hooster Valley, never wanted to return; Daniel likes to hike and camp but that's what growing sons are for.

But now she's walking down the trail and can't imagine why she stopped: nothing in the world's as good as all day out all by herself. Already she can hear the falls echoed from the canyon walls; can't remember last when she smelled air so fresh it hurt her nose. Her brain is filled with memories: the tang of sap and pine needles, the must of last year's rotting leaves, the melting glaciers atomized. The path then goes from denser trees to angle through a slope of shale: scattered here are clumps of paintbrush red as mouths of fledgling birds. It's just as steep as she recalls, a hair this side of vertical: wouldn't have to bend to pick a nice bouquet of lavender. But she has to lean a bit to catch a glimpse of river far below, funneled through the canyon right above the spout of Punchbowl Falls. If she wished to end it all, she'd only need to take one step: at most she'd bounce a couple times while falling down a hundred feet.

The river here is glassy smooth but faster than a frightened horse; every drop of water like a lemming that can't help itself. Elsewhere on the river there are lots of quiet eddy swirls, places behind big rocks where a drop can sit and rest a spell. But once they hit the canyon walls their destinies have all been fused: paratroopers tied together pushed out of an open door. Looking at the rushing water: *That's what my whole life's been like. Nothing that I've ever done was more than just by accident.* Her whole life is this narrow canyon, perhaps a hundred yards in length, and she's a tiny drop mixed in with all the other drops of rain. Those rocks there mark the start of school, the day Frank pulled her from the fire; that crack there marks the birthday when the firemen baked a cake for her. Halfway down the canyon she is watching Daniel meet his son: Daniel caught her eye but then he never brought it up again. She can't believe she never got around to telling Hank the truth, but how could she explain when he'd been taught that lying wasn't right? They all said it was for the best, the neighbors will think she's a saint: *Sometime when he's older he'll see how the situation was.* She'd watched how people treated them at gas stations and grocery stores, that cop who pulled her over once for driving through a yellow light. He'd looked in through her window at Hank sitting as her passenger: ten years and he's old enough to know how stupid people are.

"You've got a handsome little houseboy...." and the cop's breath is unbearable, head stuck through her window and she wants to punch the bastard's nose. She's half-a-gulp of air away from letting out a string of words: *You pucker-butted-puny-little-flutter-fingered-cake-eater!* But Hank was quick to intervene: "She's really my adopted mom. My other mom and dad died when the bomb dropped on Hiroshima...."

She tries to think how old she is, how close her drop is to the falls; any time now she knows *I'll be plunging toward the pool below.* She must be right there near the edge, the falls where waters mix and swirl: the reason she's so dizzy and the world now makes no sense at all. Already she's forgotten all about her lovely afternoon; can't remember why she's walking down here in these stupid shoes. But she does remember years ago—Tuesday or the day before—hiking to the falls alone and thinking about suicide. She's deep inside the darkest angst of any average teenage girl—wondering if *they'll be sorry if I were to kill myself.* Thinking how her mom would feel, knowing she had been so cruel: making Myrna once more help her can *the God-damn-squeaking-beans! If anybody cared at all I'd have a nicer dress to wear;* if Helen is her best friend then *why wasn't she at home today?* But instead of leaping to her death to make them all feel terrible, she slowly scrambles hands-and-knees down to the pool below the falls.

She's never been so bold before: strips off to her underclothes, wades out through the sharp rocks till she can't touch bottom anymore. They're not supposed to swim down here because they might get *undertowed*: sucked down by the swirling current, never to come out again. But no one cares so why should she? *They'll never find me anyway*: just an ugly cotton dress and socks stuffed in her clodhoppers. The current's stronger than it looked; she's working harder than she'd thought; nearly to the middle something slimy brushed against her foot. Not sure but it felt alive: perhaps a little rainbow trout, or maybe a half-rotted leaf caught in the foaming turbulence. But then *that thing* touched her again, fingers grabbing anklebone: no one's ever swum so fast who only knows the dog paddle! Ever since, she's haunted by whoever's caught beneath the falls and how damn lucky she is not to be stuck down there with her now. Instead she's somehow gotten old, can't remember how or why, but someone must have cared because *this dress is so much prettier.*

She's certain that nobody in her family cared a lick for her: one little indiscretion and they quickly made her disappear. And Frank had not been any help, breaking down her willpower, tempting her with moonlit nights and horses made of polished jade. It was Daniel who had finally been her source for tender-loving care: gentle hugs and loved her son and never an unpleasant word. He'd once confided that he'd had a motive when he'd married her: shipping out in three days and he didn't have a family. He told her that she'd saved his life and that he owed her everything—that he'd have died for sure if he'd had no one to write letters to. Hank's the only one whose motives still remain a mystery: why had he been so *afraid* of misbehaving even once? Thinking back she can't remember ever having raised her voice; even if he'd needed it, Dan never could have hit his son. But Hank had acted so afraid of ever doing something wrong, trembling with his eyes big while confessing that his cocoa spilled. When he's home on vacation, Myrna thinks she'll finally ask him why: off at college, junior year, and dating some cute Jewish girl.

She's standing in a patch of light, the last before the sun goes down, wishing that these silly shoes had soles that weren't so slippery. She's thinking this might be the place to toss her anger overboard: life's been good so she forgives her family what they did to her. It might be best to stop right here than risk a nasty accident: halfway down a cliff a hundred feet above a waterfall. The hill's so steep she barely has to lean to rest against the slope: sudden overwhelming urge to close her eyes and fall asleep.

The Nickel
September 1997

THIS WAS NOT the first time Hank had witnessed the apocalypse: the now-charred wicker furniture all scattered on the patio. The big-sad-weeping cedar tree had lost the branches on one side, ghostlike in the darkness standing sentry over nothing now. The house of which he'd grown so fond was now a soggy pile of ash; the volunteers had made sure there was not one glowing ember left.

He was clueless where his mother was: somewhere out there in the dark; the Hooster Chief said there had been no sign of her inside the house. He wondered what that *sign* would be: a pile of black-enameled teeth? A greasy spot of ash shaped like the outline at a murder scene? Lidia had sworn she checked each room before the roof collapsed; nobody was home except for Trouble barking in the yard. Hank knew that the fire started when he tipped the barbecue, spilling half-grilled salmon and a pyramid of glowing coals. But the front door had been locked, she said, *so how did Mother get outside?* He'd handed George the key when he requested that he check on her. Hank could have asked George but he was racing to Emmanuel: Portland surgeons scrubbing to do urgent bypass surgery. So he told the sheriff he was going to run and check at George's house; meantime they should search the woods and orchards for a mile around.

Last time Hank had seen her she had fuzzy-slippers on her feet, wrapped up in a housecoat with pajamas hidden underneath. He couldn't think if Myrna got her evening dose of insulin: could see the vial he drew it from but can't remember giving it. He clearly saw that morning when he gave the shot in her left thigh: *cocksuckinglittlebagofshit* was what had come out of her mouth. But this afternoon he couldn't think what nasty thing she might have said, and if she got the shot then she'd be dead without something to eat. She'd drop into a coma when her blood sugar starts plummeting, fall into the ditch or stream or tall grass where she'd wandered off. He knew they wouldn't find her till her body was half decomposed, or someone's dog came home dragging a fuzzy-slipper in its mouth. But she still could be at George's house, napping on his cluttered couch; Hank put his foot down harder when he thought *she's there all by herself*. Remembering the candle Myrna left by George's bathroom sink; *God-knows-what* she'd light next with his house a giant tinderbox. He felt as if the nickel he had swallowed when he was a child had slid again and now was nearly blocking off his trachea. He felt the nickel all the time, though worse when he was stressed or tired: someone standing right behind him, strangling hands around his throat.

The nickel was the reason all his life he'd struggled to be heard; the nickel must have lodged about an inch below his vocal cords. It had always felt so tenuous, could turn and block the passageway: saying what he felt would make it shift and then he'd suffocate. If Hank could have screamed loud enough the nickel might have come back out; or maybe he'd have died with all that scream trapped deep inside his chest. That was how he felt right now, if only he could *really* scream, racing up the wooden steps past piles of George's magazines. The porch light had a motion sensor: startled Hank when it came on; the light was off inside the house although the front door was ajar. Just inside, he reached to flip the light switch on the papered wall, the bulb dimmed by the years of bugs collected in the frosted shade. At least there was no smoke or flame or food left burning on the stove; but George's couch held only two large stacks of unread newspapers. Afraid to even call her name, a sense that he might yell too loud, that if he opened up his mouth he'd choke as all the words came out. Walking through the dining room, he found another switch to throw; on the table all there was were more stacks of the usual. But he saw something that wasn't there: a boy sits eating cereal, mother in the kitchen fixing lunch for him to take to school. This house had been his grandparents', the title in his father's name: the man now in the bathroom shaving stubble with a razor blade. That's what would have happened if there hadn't been a second war: Hank would have grown up right here with Mom and Dad and *Uncle George*. His mind cleared all the mess away and brought in Myrna's furniture: pictures on the wall are photos from big family gatherings. His father came from down the hall, pulling up suspender straps, ready for some breakfast then a full day on a tractor seat. He was walking past behind his son, a rough hand through Hank's crew-cut hair, smooth shave pressed against Hank's cheek to breathe in Hank's spare molecules. *Why would someone do that if he didn't love the way I smell?* Drawn together from the fact they're made from the same flesh and blood? This fantasy was palpable: he felt his father kiss his neck; goosebumps on his arms and back, the nickel blocked his trachea. It trapped a big lung-full of air; he had to find his mother soon; he flipped the hall switch but the light just flashed then went back out again. But he found the bathroom three steps down: the sink where he'd have brushed his teeth, his foamy spit mixed with the spit of half-a-dozen relatives. She wasn't in the next room, either: single bed against the wall, desk and chair and bookshelf and a pennant from a baseball team. The nickel in his throat had grown: it felt like half-a-dollar now; this was where he would have slept: across from *Frank-and-Myrna's* room. He stepped across the narrow hall, switching on their bedside lamp: a rumpled sheet, some shoes and socks, his mother's bra and underpants.

His mind could not explain why all his mother's things were scattered there, except that he was finally waking from a long, unpleasant dream. But he knew that he was in the body of a man of middle age; knew that if he didn't scream he'd pass out on the bedroom floor. The noise he made was so loud that he didn't hear the ringing coin, landing in the corner rolling circles till it settled down.

Across The Hall
February 1998

HANK HAD HEARD from Jessie that they'd had to close the freeway down: too much snow and ice and double semis jacked across the road. She was at the Portland Sheraton, the conference ended yesterday: was bunking with three women in a room with just two single beds.

"It is a little crowded, but we're doing lots of giggling. The freeway won't be open till tomorrow at the earliest."

Hank had said *I love you* and *relax, you should enjoy yourself*: no sense rushing home because the power had gone off again. George had dealt another hand when all at once the house went still, sitting near the window so they hadn't had the lights turned on. Hank became aware of maybe half-a-dozen missing sounds: washing clothes and bathroom vents and humming from the Frigidaire. George said that it might have been a line dragged down by all the snow, but what was way more likely was that someone hit a power pole.

"Ten-to-one your beeper's going to go off any minute now. Hurry up and discard so that we can finish up this round."

But several hours had passed now and the cloudy sky had gotten dark, and Hank thought of his mother as he brought a set of candles out. He'd missed her for the past six months; they'd found her soon after the fire: search dogs and the sheriff flying circles over Edgar Flat. The things they gave the dogs to sniff were Myrna's rumpled underclothes; the only ones that hadn't burned Hank found on George's bedroom floor. Hank stayed at the road until the sheriff brought her body out, wanting to believe him when he said how peaceful she had looked. Hank had spent a half a day at Hooster's cemetery lot, searching through the markers for the graves of Myrna's family. His stomach tightened seeing all the names he'd thought his mom made up: stories about pranks and stunts that Earl and Edward played on her. Samuel died in '43, the twins in early '44, her parents just a month apart when Hank would have been eight years old. His uncle Martin was the only one to live past seventy, dying in the summer of the same year Daniel passed away. All of them were lined up and he could have placed his mother there; George had said his brother Frank was buried out in Arlington. But Daniel was the only one whose love Hank never doubted once; he mixed their ashes in one urn, then hiked down past the waterfall.

Ever since then Hank had lost that constant twitch above his eye, but every afternoon he'd think *it's time to give her insulin.* He didn't miss her scratching nails or being called a *peckerhead,* the dinner plates thrown on the floor and matches hidden everywhere. He missed what he had always missed: that sense of *unconditional,* what now he knew was always there but he'd chosen not to recognize. It took him over fifty years to learn that he was truly hers, to see that everything she did was done because she loved her boy. If Myrna hadn't cared she would have left him in an alleyway; if the neighbors knew they would have called Hank lots of other names. What Hank regrets the most is that he'd wasted all those years of love and hadn't learned the truth in time to change the way he loved her back. Jessie asked him once what he was feeling since his mother died, and what he'd said was that he wished he'd listened closer to her lies.

Now George congratulated Hank for how well he had played that hand, said that he was tired and that he thought he'd go lie down a while. Hank's pager had stayed silent and he'd thrown more wood into the stove, and George was stretched and snoring on the sofa in the living room. He listened as the house moaned underneath two feet of heavy snow, and lighting two more candles, he was glad he'd put a new roof on. He thought the nights were like this back three-quarters of a century: candle-glow and kerosene and shadows flashing on the walls. The candles weren't quite bright enough to let Hank read the newspaper; he thought he should be sleepy but he couldn't force his eyes to close. So he sat down in the comfy chair with Trouble snuggled at his feet, watching through the glass door at the fire dancing in the stove. Tomorrow he had clinic but he figured he should cancel it: ear checks and well-babies and some sutures needed taking out. His clinic was for children since they'd always been his specialty, but mothers began asking Hank to check their husbands' blood pressures. After only three months he could tell he'd need a little help, wincing at the thought that he would have to trust another nurse. He was glad that he was back at work with all the things he'd missed the most: swinging feet and bashful looks and screaming little three-year-olds.

As Hank was getting up to see if he could scrounge a late night snack, he was startled by the flash of headlights sweeping through the living room. He glanced out of the window but they'd passed the corner of the house; Trouble didn't bark although her tail was wagging back and forth. The deep snow muffled any sounds of gravel crunching under tires, his uncle undisturbed because he'd taken out his hearing aids. Why would someone bother coming up here through three feet of snow? *Jessie must be hurt and so the sheriff sent his deputies!* Suddenly Hank's palms were wet, his heart was pounding in his chest; he trembling grabbed a candle off the table in the dining room. He heard the scuffing feet of someone coming to the kitchen door: didn't bother knocking and the wind blew out Hank's candle flame. But he didn't need to see to know exactly who was standing there; the breeze that blew the candle out brought in a reassuring smell. He felt his heart melt in his chest, muscles in his neck relax, didn't know he'd had one till his headache all but disappeared.

"The freeway was still closed and so I drove up over Bennett Pass. I couldn't stand the thought of spending one more night away from you."

Jessie saw her husband standing backlit by faint candlelight; the man she used to love had slowly come back in the last few months. While George was still in rehab they'd had evenings all alone at home, sorting through the piles of all the catalogs and newspapers. Sitting at the kitchen table, snuggled on the vinyl couch, early into bed so they could have a little pillow talk:

—*Maybe Doctor Gary'd give you something for depression, Hank.*
—*Let's take a vacation somewhere nice and warm this wintertime.*

They'd talk about his mother's lie and what the truth had meant to him; she warned Hank that from now on *you must always tell me everything!*
—*I know you didn't mean it, but it felt like you'd abandoned me.*
—*Every time she cursed I really thought that I might strangle her.*
They'd sorted through Hank's guilt and pain for how he'd handled Myrna's care; he knew he wasn't perfect *but I really, really tried to be.* With the passing of Hank's mom, she'd learned something about herself:
—*Hank, when I grow senile you can give me all the drugs you want.*

...

The next day showed that they'd received at least another foot last night, and the dawn had crept up slowly through the snow that hadn't landed yet. Hank stood at the window while he wondered how long this could last and wishing that last summer George had got his tractor's snowplow fixed. But George had been so close to death he hadn't thought that far ahead, thinking more of where he'd find the energy for one more breath. Now Hank could hear George snoring from the bedroom right across the hall; George gave them his room because it really was his nephew's house. Hank still smelled the fresh paint of the master bedroom remodel, looking out a window that now had a stunning mountain view. But instead of at the snowy peaks, Hank stared out at the orchard trees, watching as the snow fell while he wondered what he'd do today. The new room held a queen-size bed and lots of space for Jessie's shoes, a stationary bicycle Hank used for hanging up his clothes. The whole house smelled of baking bread and two new rooms of carpeting, the odor from the wood floor's three fresh coats of satin urethane. The kitchen had new cabinets and a massive stainless cooking range; the master bath was tiled and had a matching porcelain bidet. But now with all the workers gone, Hank had no one to supervise; he'd cancelled the day's patients for his clinic up in Hillendale.

A hint of sun peeked through the clouds, but the snow had not let up at all; prediction was there'd be another foot before the storm went by. Jessie'd gone to stretch her legs and give the dog some exercise, strapping on a pair of skis to glide between the orchard rows. George was now five weeks back from his long stay in the hospital, four months in assisted living, strong enough to walk again. Hank thought when he woke up, George might play another hand of cards: any game he'd like to deal except for double solitaire.

It had taken Hank the past six months to sort out fact from fantasy: fifty years of dreaming that his father was a samurai. But Hank now knew his father had been practically a teenager, sneaking Myrna to the woods for unprotected intercourse. Counting backwards from his birth, the tryst had been a day in March: three months after all the whites stopped talking to *those stinking Japs*. The woods must have been cold and wet; perhaps they met in someone's barn; struggled with their clothes among the smell of mice and pesticides. According to the clipping that still hung up on the bedroom wall, his father died at twenty-four from wounds to chest and abdomen. Hank was only three then so he wouldn't have remembered much, even if he'd had a chance to meet the man who'd fathered him. The picture with the clipping showed a young guy in a uniform, somewhere between fully grown and worried when his voice would change. The resemblance was quite obvious, the ears and chin and bushy brows: wondered why his mother's genes had not had more effect on him. If Hank had looked more half-and-half he might have figured earlier that Myrna had been lying when she said that she'd adopted him.

He walked into the kitchen that was first built by his grandfather, roomy now that they'd cleared out the junk mail and the magazines. He'd stood at George's bedside on the day after his surgery: barely heard his own voice through the beeping of the monitors. He'd watched as George asked for a pen to write an affidavit out: *This man is my nephew and my older brother's only son.* He wrote that Hank owned all of it, the orchard and the family home, and George hoped Hank forgave the debt of fifty years of rent he owed.

...

Sitting at the table, George had dealt and sorted out his hand, teaching Hank a new game George had played since he was nine years old. It was better with three players but it still worked when they played with two: seven cards apiece and then one face up on the discard pile. The object was make runs and straights and try to get rid of your cards: twos and jokers wild but very risky to get caught with them. He used to play this game with Frank, their father sometimes joining in: passing cards and making jokes and crowing when somebody won. His nephew was now catching on to subtleties and nuances of when to pass a card back and to hold till his opponent's down. And this was now about all the excitement George could stand these days: took three breaks to catch his breath just walking through the living room. But overall he felt okay and liked what they'd done to the house and even though it's *healthy,* he ate better now that Hank was cook. With all his months in rehab, shuffling up and down long corridors, he'd had more time to really think who might have started all those fires. He'd crossed Hank off his list because they'd started when Hank was a boy, and Myrna wasn't likely because arsonists are rarely girls. He'd thought again of Evan Smith, but Evan wasn't smart enough; *whoever burned those houses was omniscient and omnipotent.* Except for even spacing and the owners were all *racist scum,* George never found a single fact that he could use as evidence. There should have been the telltale signs that gas was used to light a fire, or someone had stacked pallets in the corner of a dark garage. He'd searched for clipped electric wires or footprints leading through the yard or witnesses who sold someone a dozen cans of kerosine. Instead, he found extension cords run underneath the carpeting, plugged into the frayed end of an overburdened space heater. Every seventh year some family paid for such stupidity: *didn't get a permit for the wood stove Uncle Jed installed.* So what he had concluded on his long walks up and down the halls, was that the fires had all been fate and that there was no arsonist. The disappointment that he felt had almost been unbearable: that all those *stinking bastards* lost their homes to simple accidents. He'd wanted there to be someone responsible for all the fires, a superhuman hero seeking vengeance for the Japanese. The thought that there was someone out there slowly evening the score had made it easy to ignore the bad taste always in his mouth. Everyday he worried that he hadn't been quite good enough; that when he died he wouldn't get to pass between the pearly gates. The only hope he had now was that someday he would have the chance to ask God if *He* was the one who lit the fires of Edgarville.

...

George toyed with tossing down an eight to see if Hank was interested, knowing if he took it he was trying to fill an inside straight. Every time George looked at Hank he saw his older brother Frank; he had to chuckle thinking how his brother could have managed it. There'd been curfew and the threat from vigilantes driving 'round at night, barking dogs and loaded guns, the fact his lover's skin was white. George had some suspicion that his brother might have had a friend, but never would have thought Frank might have climbed over the *Capo's* fence. But given that he did, it all made sense now that George thought it through: Martin Capo knew who put his sister in the family way. All the trouble that he'd caused was Martin getting some revenge; her family would have thrown her out when they saw her clothes no longer fit. She must have been both scared and brave to give birth to a Japanese when up and down the coast they'd all been locked in concentration camps. Frank might not have ever known about his little replica, but George still felt ashamed Frank shirked a grave responsibility. He fanned his cards out once again and looked up at his brother's son, whose poker face was worthless as a fart inside a paper bag. Hank couldn't win without a straight, so George held back the nine of spades: he planned to stall until he had the cards to go down all at once.

Sitting near a pot of tea, Hank thought it had steeped long enough, poured it through a strainer into stubby, thick ceramic cups. He pushed one cup across to George who took it without glancing up, sipped the tea, looked at the cup, then said, "I kind of like this stuff."

"It's *bancha,* made with toasted rice," and Hank felt like he'd scored a point, slowly introducing George to food groups beyond *meat* and *starch.* Now George was eating whole grain bread and liked a lot more vegetables, and didn't seem to mind when dinner missed all the cholesterol. Hank had switched from scrambled eggs to big round bowls of oatmeal, dinner plates adorned with spears of bright-green steaming broccoli. He wasn't thinking just of George, but someone closer to his heart: genetically his own felt like a time bomb waiting to go off. His mom had died from Alzheimer's and problems with her blood sugar, his grandmother died early from a stroke in the internment camp. And his uncle's had three heart attacks and triple bypass surgery, all before he'd even reached the tender age of seventy.

"It does taste kind of *toasty,*" and Hank watched as George took sips of tea, then glancing at his own cards Hank discovered that he'd missed something.

He'd had his cards arranged all wrong and should have been collecting clubs, realizing all he'd need was one more to go down-and-out. He looked up at his Uncle George, the brother of his father Frank, trying not to show how much he hoped that George discarded right. But he wasn't very good at this and had to turn his face away, try to think of something else until George put his discard down. He looked around the living room, the mostly brand-new furniture: everything they'd owned had been destroyed when Myrna's house caught fire. But even with the new paint and the floors all sanded flat and smooth, the house still had the smell of all the years of people living here. The first scent was the wood smoke that leaked out when Hank would add a log, then the underlying smell that came from living with a dog. There were eighty years of cooking rice and fried foods they no longer ate, a thousand generations of the mice that lived inside the walls. Jessie wore a nice perfume, the faintest hint behind each ear: the same scent since they met and Hank still thought the best smell in the world. But there was something else he'd noticed that he'd tried for months to figure out: in the house some smell provoked a memory from childhood. He was hiding in the coat closet, his mom invited friends for bridge; he hated when they smoked and drank and Myrna started laughing loud. In the midst of coats and scarves that still retained some body warmth, felted wool and silken linings, air a little thick and sweet: he'd had a sudden sense it would be better if he ran away, that all these women playing cards thought Hank was something alien. The smell was simply *humanness,* the smell of people not like him: cigarettes and lavender and someone who forgot to bathe. But this was now his uncle's house, the home built by his grandfather; the same smell was produced by people Hank was now related to.

    The trees outside were all bent up from years of George's pruning shears; the garden on the south side had been tended by Hank's grandmother. Imagining her stooping down to weed among the radishes: a woman bold or timid who'd consent to be a picture bride. He couldn't quite imagine it: she's shown a grainy photograph; the next thing she is on a boat and life has been forever changed. His mother's life was much the same, though complicated by the fact that Myrna hadn't been the one deciding it was time to pack. If half of what she'd said was true, her family wished that she were dead: burned her bed and sent her off and never spoke to her again. Hank's amazed his mother found the strength to keep a half-blood kid, raise and love a bastard son through hateful stares and whisperings. It must have been a miracle that Myrna found a willing man to take the place of someone who'd been sent to an internment camp. It made Hank think of X and Y, the long strands of his chromosomes, the replicating genes that bridge the two sides of his family. Half had lived here in this house, their molecules still lingering: with every breath Hank filled his lungs with atoms of his next of kin. He shifted slightly in his chair, brushed crumbs off of the green felt cloth, trying not to smile and give away what he was thinking of. George had gently cleared his throat, then took another sip of tea, folded up his cards so he could neatly fan them out again. Hank looked at his uncle who was finally putting down a card: just the one to fill the run Hank didn't even know he had.

Acknowledgements
February 26, 2009

I would like to express my appreciation for the knowledge, patience, good will, and encouragement of all those who helped with the lengthy process of writing and publishing this novel. While each and every one deserves a mention here, I would be mortified to leave anyone off a list of names, and so will suffice it to say that their numbers were legion, their help was indispensable, and my gratitude is genuine and deeply felt.

The one person I *will* mention specifically is my wife, Beth. Her commitment to my writing has been constant and inspirational, and with this novel in particular, she has been both loving and long-suffering. She has always been, and shall remain, my one and only. —CJD

Sample Chapter

Himalayan Dhaba
By Craig Joseph Danner

Chapter One
The Patient

She's waiting out a sudden shower of fifty kilo bags of rice, a gathered clutch of angry chickens flapping like their heads are off. It's raining rolls of razor wire and wooden crates of tangerines, a blood-red set of luggage for a couple on their honeymoon. The driver honked through eighteen hours of blindly climbing hairpin turns; the bus hit every dog that dared to cross the road from Chandigarh. Mary's so exhausted she can barely stand among the crowd—she's praying that her bags are there, the one box in particular. At last she sees her canvas duffel sailing through the mountain air; she waves and yells to get the man to treat her box more carefully. But his ropy muscles flex and stretch across his shirtless arms and back, the sun gleams off the lines of sweat that trickle down his dusty flank. He doesn't look or heed her shout before he drops it to the ground—the box lands in the mud and dust: the sparkling sound of broken glass.

Trying not to get upset, she's swallowing her rising bile: *stupid idiot!* she thinks, though not referring to the man. She feels like everything she's touched has shattered in the past six months; *can't even get a goddamn-box of medicines down off a bus.* She knows that things are different here, she's not back home in Baltimore, but seven thousand feet above the plains of Northern India. The sun is beaming overhead, the sky the blue of early May; a soft breeze swings the evergreens, the mountains oh-so-beautiful. But the bus keeps belching diesel smoke and noise so she can't concentrate; three men are shouting in her face, each claiming his hotel is best. She'd like to turn around and leave, go find someplace to sit and cry—she's desperate for a private place to drop her pants around her knees. She has to shift from foot to foot, she hasn't gone since yesterday; the few times that the driver stopped, there wasn't any ladies room. Every muscle in her back is on the verge of spasming: sudden shooting, stabbing pains enough to take her breath away.

The closest man before her has a cancer growing on his lip; in all her years of practice she has never seen one half as big. Trying not to stare she shouts, "I'm staying at the hospital!" She sees the hope drop from his face, the pearly tumor glistening. The three men turn away as she attempts to gather up her bags; she thought, perhaps, there'd be somebody waiting for her when she came. She feels like she can't focus, like there's nothing under her control: a nauseating moment when she steps in something soft and dull. A half-a-dozen porters want to help her with her duffel bag, but all she sees are wasted arms on men who must weigh less than her. She doesn't want to feel this way, she thought that she had come prepared: she read the books and travel guides, the passages on culture shock. But she's never been so far from home or traveled overseas before; she's following her husband's ghost that led her to this wretched town. She makes herself meet one man's eyes, a porter with a crooked smile, her random choice because his shirt's the only one not torn with holes.

They are high up in a little town where tourists come to see the snow; the valley walls with peaks of ice are lined with fruiting apple trees. Her map shows that the road ends here, the last real town before the pass—further north are only arid mountains going on and on. But this town's rimmed by forests filled with evergreen deodar trees that rise up from the duff to try to imitate the mountain peaks. The buildings stand two stories high, their walls are mortared brick and stone; the town is just a couple blocks of alleyways and market stalls. The alley that they're walking down is filled with tourists from the plains: long-haired Western travelers and newlyweds with hennaed hands. The hotel signs are lettered in a half a dozen languages: *Stay Here for Your Honeymoon* and *Best Place for the Hippie Freaks;* Hindi, English, French and several others she can't recognize. But Mary doesn't have the time or energy to look about for anything except a place to let her aching bladder down. She'd like a clean, well-lighted place where she could trust them with her bags, a disinfected toilet and a sink to wash her face and hands.

Nothing looks too promising, the storefronts are all dark inside, the sidewalk lined with metal plates on stoves of hissing kerosene. These sizzling grills are saucer-shaped and large enough to sled on snow; she feels the spit of grease from brown samosas fried in smoking oil. She braced herself for beggars, but the impact is still visceral: a woman without legs has propped herself against a crumbling wall. On what's left of her lap she holds a plump and squirming two year old who vigorously sucks beneath a coarsely woven woolen shawl. This woman looks at Mary so their eyes meet for the briefest time—Mary has to look away or risk another crying jag. The wallahs in their canvas stalls—all shouting at her constantly—demand that she must stop and buy their cabbages and tangerines. And she'd like to pass this holy man, this baba smeared with human ash, who's blocking half the sidewalk as he browses through the marketplace. His begging bowl is pounded brass, his trident staff is tipped with bone; he hasn't got a stitch of clothes but dreadlocks filled with marigolds. She doesn't try to pass because she'd likely bump him with her bag—afraid she'd have to buy the goat he'd need for cleansing sacrifice. But then she sees a little cafe up another alleyway, a landmark from the photos that she memorized in Baltimore. It was where her husband took his meals, back a dozen years ago, *Himalayan Dhaba* painted on the sign above the door. It doesn't look much better than the other cafes that she's seen: built from poorly mortared brick, tiny windows thick with grease.

She motions to the porter that she wants him to wait by the door, signing with her hands, hoping he'll stay and guard her box and bags. She drops her backpack on the ground and feels a wave of urgency; she rushes through the cafe door and almost knocks the waiter down. He's a short and slender walleyed man dressed neatly in a Nehru suit—she's shocked to recognize his face, from another photo Richard kept. The picture shows her husband with his arm around this gentleman: Richard has a goofy smile, the waiter's eyes look here and there. The cafe is so dark inside she has to strain to look around: the room is twenty feet across, the tables don't look very clean. The cafe's barely half full with a funny mix of clientele; suddenly she's thinking that she should have looked around some more. Everyone has turned to stare; she feels a dozen sets of eyes: a ragged Western traveler, an Indian in suit and tie. She asks this man her husband knew: please, could she use the ladies room? He bows to her then wags his head, an answer she can't comprehend.

"*Mé-ré saath aa-i-yé,*" he says and gently takes her arm, leads her down the center of this darkly paneled restaurant. The room is close and filled with smoke, she smells the faintest hint of dope; the waiter guides her through the darkness toward the swinging door in back. He points her to a closet that smells like an open septic tank—ripping at her belt she barely gets her pants down fast enough.

The only light comes through a tiny window high up over head, and there isn't any toilet but a hole cut in the concrete floor. She's focusing on balance, trying to keep her pants up off the ground—horrified she'll tumble over, unsure where she's supposed to aim. At last her bladder's letting down, her feet not quite spread wide enough; her passport safe around her waist now jabbing in her pancreas. She'd made a promise to herself she wouldn't cry for two more days; tears have come so quickly ever since the day that Richard died. She feels them running down her cheeks, along the crease beside her nose, dripping from her chin into this hole between her hiking boots. She's worried that the porter won't be outside when she's finished here, and worried that she's never going to find the mission hospital. She's not sure why she's doing this, except her husband loved it here—she's thinking she should turn around for safe and sterile Baltimore. But there's nothing for her there now that she's left her home and quit her job, sold her house and practice in a clinic for the very old. She knows she'll find the hospital, it can't be very far away, and if the porter steals her bags she'll buy some other clothes to wear. There isn't any paper so she zippers up her wrinkled pants—doesn't trust the water in the pail to give her hands a wash. She wipes her eyes off with her sleeves, takes a breath of fetid air. She shakes her head and wonders *what-the-hell* she thinks she's doing here.

...

The alley's paved with graveled rock, the sunlight bouncing off the dust, and Mary has to squint to see, the restaurant was dark as night. The porter is still waiting with her bags beneath the dhaba's sign; she tells him with her red-rimmed eyes that she's feeling better than before. Now that she has peed and cried and hasn't lost all her supplies, this tiny village doesn't seem as awful as at first it had. The porter has a friendly face, his eyes are sparkling with life; she shows him once again the name of Doctor Vikram's hospital. She knows it's likely he can't read, especially her English script; his head moves in a way that Mary can't quite tell is no or yes. So she mimes as if she has a cough, walks like someone with a limp, finally rifles through a bag, pulls out her shiny stethoscope. The porter rolls his eyes and laughs, her destination obvious.

"*Achhaa-ji,*" he says, and picks up Doctor Mary's dusty bags.

He leads her from the restaurant, it isn't very far at all; he takes her down a winding maze of gravel paths and alleyways. As they walk she's looking round, a half-a-world away from home; she watches someone scrub a pot with dirt scraped straight up off the ground. But the sky today is cloudless and she's almost at her journey's end, anxious to meet Doctor Vikram, another one of Richard's friends. She's having a rare moment of her optimism blossoming: maybe she will like it here, this busy little tourist town. Her husband talked about this place, he worked here when he finished school: spent two months in these mountains just before they met in internship. He'd told her of the hospital, of Doctor Vikram Vargeela, a man from Southern India who runs the place all by himself. Richard called the man a saint, said Vikram had a magic touch—so long as you ignored the surgeon's tendency to preach too much. Rich said the place was beautiful with lovely terraced valley walls, a temple in the forest and the Himalayas all around. But he didn't mention how it smells, the nasty open-sewer stink, the beggars with their pleading palms and exudative skin disease. This is why she's come here, though, so useless since her husband's death: her love cut down in prime of life, a stupid biking accident. She cried herself to sleep for weeks, then made herself go back to work; just couldn't care enough about her aging patients' chief complaints. Her partners bought her practice for a price that was quite generous; she banked it with the million from the life insurance Richard kept. She contemplated suicide, but wasn't really serious; she tried to think what Rich would do if *she* had been the one to die. That's when Vikram's card came with his yearly Christmas newsletter which hinted for donations for his hospital in India. A way to keep her husband near, it felt like such a good idea: *supplies are low, the wards are full, could use a doctor volunteer.*

...

The compound has seen better days, with patchy bits of weeds and grass—she recognizes everything from Richard's color photographs. The buildings haven't changed at all, with roofs of rusty village tin, the windows glazed with wavy glass, the walls in need of plastering. She thought that this would feel familiar, as if she'd been up here before, but really it was Rich who worked here back a dozen years ago. Like all the buildings in this town, they're brick and rock and wooden beams—a painted sign in English points the way to the X-ray machine. The wards are both two stories high with wooden stairs and balconies, the courtyard beaten free of grass by years of patients' trampling feet. In the center of the yard there is a stunning, ancient walnut tree: massive trunk and spreading limbs, its canopy blocks out the sky. The porter drops her bags beneath it, speaks to her in Kullui; Mary doesn't know the coins so lets the porter keep the change. The man gives her his crooked smile and brings his hands before his face. Bowing he takes one step back before he turns to take his leave.

The hospital is tiny, with the buildings scattered randomly, dwarfed from east and west by massive Himalayan mountain peaks. She smells the sweet deodar smoke of someone cooking over fire, reminding her of camping in the pines of western Maryland. She wonders where the patients are, the lines that Richard once described—Vikram wrote that there was never time enough to see them all. It is sometime in the afternoon, perhaps the staff has gone to lunch; she set her watch in Delhi, though she could have turned the dial wrong. But *someone* should be hanging round, she knows they are expecting her; she sent a message yesterday: *arriving soon as possible.* The last time Vikram wrote he said there's always so much work to do—the clinic runs four days a week, with surgery the other two. Sunday is his day of rest, he preaches in the little church; she sees the tiny, empty building: a steeple and a crucifix. She tries to think what day it is, she left the States on Saturday; spent one night in the Delhi Hilton's musty air conditioning. She's guessing that it's Tuesday and it must be close to three o'clock—unlikely Doctor Vikram would take off to play a round of golf. So she leaves her bags beneath the tree with leaves the green of early spring, and wanders through the courtyard, through the echoing dispensary. The only sound she hears is someone's distant whistle off somewhere. She follows it in through a door, a painted sign to *Surgery*.

The hall is almost black inside, the walls are stacked with limp supplies: boxes with their lids cut off, the dust has never been disturbed. She's thinking it's incredible, the storeroom's loaded with antiques: surgical contraptions no one's used in half a century. She takes a cloth mask from a bin and holds it to her mouth and nose, then opens up a door that's marked the entrance to the surgery. It should be draped with braided rope, an old-time surgical museum: an overwhelming ether stink is sickly sweet and volatile. The table has a dozen cranks, a sheet draped over stainless steel; above it hangs an ancient lamp: a giant metal buttercup. Nobody's there, but still she hears the funny, tuneless whistling—and then a ringing echoed laugh, a soft and high-pitched giggle. It comes out from a little room, the next door that she opens up; she finds a tiny woman, someone Richard once had talked about.

"*Doctor-ji! Namasté!*" At last someone expecting her; she sent a photo of herself and Richard the first time she wrote. Padma can't be four feet tall, her body nearly bent in half: Rich had said he liked her best of all the people working there. Mary is amazed at how she looks just like her photograph: tiny little angel face and eyes benignly mischievous. Her spine has got a nasty twist, perhaps a childhood accident, but Mary's never seen a face as beautiful and radiant. Padma climbs down off a stool, her wrinkled apron stained with red from washing blood off rubber gloves so that they can be used again. She wangs her hands before her face: palms together, fingers straight; a man stands from a wooden bench: he's the source of all the whistling. She wonders if this could be Vikram—pleasant smile and slender hips—but he hasn't got the features of a man from Southern India. His face is more Tibetan-shaped, his eyes a little wide apart; in very broken English he says *Tamding* is his given name. Mary only knows a couple phrases of the dialect, studied from a worthless book, a numbing set of language tapes. She's not sure what his job is but he does what Padma tells him to: he helps her with her bags and shows her to the rooms that she's to have. They cross the dusty courtyard past the one-room missionary school; Tamding might be speaking English, but she doesn't know for sure. He's pointing out the landmarks, making jutting gestures with his chin; Mary only smiles and wonders anxiously where Vikram is.

He leads her to a building that could be a mom-and-pop motel: single-story cinderblock with doors all lined up in a row. She's got the last rooms on the end, the farthest from the hospital; Tamding opens up the door and shows her where she's going to live. *This won't do at all,* she thinks, her heart drops down another inch: the walls a shade of green like something growing in a swimming pool. She tries to see her husband here, how Richard thought it wonderful; the bed a musty block of foam, the kitchen doesn't have a stove; she looks into the bathroom: just another hole where she's to go. Tamding brings her bags inside and stacks them neat against the wall, wangs his hands before his face and goes out backwards through the door. She's glad, at least, to be alone, to have some time to recompose; her stomach gripped with anxious fear, she thinks *this was a bad idea.* Richard was the one who dreamed of coming back to India—never was the kind of man who needed to be comfortable. She wants her husband desperately, perhaps she would relax a bit: he'd take her out exploring, wander through the winding market place.

She lies down on the bed but can't relax enough to fall asleep; she wonders if the water in the tap is safe to brush her teeth. The only nice thing in the room is a sunny wooden window seat that overlooks an alley with a glimpse of snowy mountain peak. She pulls the curtains back to let some light into this gloomy space, wanders through the tiny kitchen, sniffs a hint of rat perfume. Then on a table by the bed she finds a letter with her name, held down at one corner with a textbook as a paper weight. She looks first at the massive tome, the English title on the spine: *General Practice Guidelines for the Rural District Hospital.* She flips through several pages filled with pictures of advanced disease: liver cysts from parasites she's hoping that she'll never see. She's thinking she won't be much help with everything so different here—Richard was the surgeon, could have operated anywhere. But Mary is an internist, knows medicines and lab reports: a specialist in geriatrics, treating grandpa's gout and stroke. She opens up the envelope, her name spelled in a hasty hand; it takes some time to read the words, decipher Vikram's doctor-scratch.

At first she doesn't understand, she has to guess some of the words; but then it all comes clear why there weren't patients at the hospital. And she thought that she hit bottom when she saw where she's supposed to live, but now she knows her heart can sink at least another couple feet. She's thinking now would be the time to quietly just disappear, leave a note for Vikram on the box of shattered medicines. But then she hears the whistling, the flute of Tamding's puckered lips—he's knocking nonstop on her door until she starts to open it. Breathlessly he's talking in a language she can't understand, motions with his hands so that she knows to quickly follow him. With no idea what's going on, she's led across the hard dirt yard; she's running through a list of what might be the worst that she could find. She's thinking it's a heart attack, a motorcycle accident—someone with a bleeding cut, an artery that's gushing blood. They cross beneath the walnut tree, the speckled light of twitching leaves; he leads her to a room that smells of nasty disinfectant spray. But no one's on the table that is centered in the trauma room, just a woman on a bench, a bundle cradled in her arms. The bundle's covered with a shawl and Mary's trying to catch her breath; the woman looks up briefly but then turns her eyes away. The woman's dressed in local clothes, a pattu made of homespun wool, a scarf ties back her long black hair, silver hoops pierced through her nose.

And Tamding's somehow disappeared so Mary's not sure where he's gone—doesn't even know exactly why he left her standing here. She doesn't have her stethoscope, she isn't in her long white coat; she couldn't even start to ask the questions that a doctor must. She's trying to imagine what required her so urgently; this woman isn't bleeding, isn't writhing round in agony. Mary tries to guess her age—she could be forty-five years old, she could be half of that but Mary finds it difficult to tell. Right then the woman looks at her, the saddest eyes she's ever seen; now Mary understands what made them call for her so urgently. Her heart skips several beats at first, a lump forms large inside her throat; she motions to the mother that she'd like to take a closer look. The mother pulls the shawl back so that Mary sees the baby's face—Mary has to swallow hard to keep her gasp from being heard.

The baby looks a hundred years, with sagging skin across the face: sunken eyes and fontanel, breathing at too slow a rate. She hasn't got a clue what's wrong: a birth defect or rare disease; she takes the baby from the mom as if she holds a hand grenade. With the baby on the table, she unwraps the musty woolen shawl; the skin hangs down like melted wax: a dying little baby girl. Her eyes are dry and glazed as if she hasn't blinked since she was born; doesn't cry or make a fuss, just stares and slowly gasps for air. In Baltimore there'd be a dozen nurses working frantically: X-ray techs and lab reports and respiratory therapists. All she'd have to do is give the orders to the nursing staff: stand and watch and make sure that the blood gets sent off fast enough. Mary hasn't slept in days, her thinking isn't very clear: this baby is dehydrated, should get some fluids into her. She's thinking meningitis, maybe *H. flu* septicemia: spinal tap and blood cultures; X-ray and a white cell count. She needs an IV right away, she'd like to put her on a vent; she puts an ear against her chest to listen to what noise she makes. She wants to know how long it's been, how old this ancient baby is; she needs to get the baby's weight to calculate the fluid drip. At last she hears the whistling of Tamding coming back this way; he steps in through the door and rattles something off in Kullui. She asks him for an IV drip; he only shrugs and wags his head. It's obvious he doesn't understand a word that Doctor Mary says. At last she hears another set of footsteps from across the yard—she sees a floating nurse's cap come sailing past the window frame.

The nurse who comes in through the door is not a day past seventeen: long black hair done in a braid, a ribbon tied-up in a bow. She says her name is Chidda and she'll try to help the best she can; the other nurses are at home, they weren't expecting her so soon. She says she's only worked a month, just graduated nursing school—that Doctor Vikram said he thinks that one day she'll be pretty good. But Mary doesn't have the time, this baby is about to die; already diagnosed the nurse's tendency to rattle on.

"I'm Doctor Mary Davis," she says, cutting off the chattering; starts listing off the things she'll need: an IV and a catheter. She's calculating in her head the dosages that she should give; she needs antibiotics that will cross the blood/brain barrier. This infant's running out of time, each breath could be her final gasp, and Mary isn't sure about the doses she's remembering. The nurse just stands in horror when she sees the withered infant girl, so Mary gets the feeling that this nurse won't do her any good. She starts into the list again, anxious that the work begin—mimes the way she'd try to stick a needle in the baby's vein.

"If you can't help, I understand. *Just find somebody else who can!*"

The nurse then turns around and leaves, comes back in with an IV tray; puts it down then backs away, not volunteering for the job. Mary hasn't started IVs since she finished Internship; she's used to having IV techs and nurses with experience. She quickly asks for sterile gloves, a swab or two of Betadine; she'll need a couple culture jars, plus red and purple vacuum tubes. Mary's nervous she won't find a vein before the baby dies; asks then for a tourniquet to strap around the baby's thigh. She's slapping at the leg to see if she can raise a purple vein—baby so lethargic that the slapping doesn't make her cry. She looks up at the nurse to see if she has brought the things she needs; nurse is still just standing staring at the walnut tree outside.

"I'm sorry," Chidda says this time, "but everybody else is gone."

The nurse sounds like she's going to cry—she says that she is all alone; when Doctor Vikram left he said that they should close the hospital. They can't get any X-rays since the tech has gone to Chandigarh, off to search for parts to fix the broken autoclave machine. They can't do any cultures since they haven't got a micro lab; she thinks the spinal needles are still waiting to be sterilized.

"And we don't have any *bata-deen*. I'm not sure what it is you need."

Mary's hands are shaking, thinks this baby can't be three weeks old; the baby doesn't have the strength to keep on gasping any more.

"I need something to clean the skin," and Mary's also on the verge; she's slapping at the other leg, still desperate for a decent vein. Chidda brings a cotton ball that's soaked in something horrible; slowly mops the knee and thigh till Mary knocks her hands away. The baby is so deep in shock her veins have all nearly collapsed; with fingers trembling Mary blindly sticks the IV needle in. She knows that there's a big vein somewhere near the outside of the shin; after several tries she finds it: tiny flash of something red.

"Damn it! I need tape!" she screams, her patience finally wearing out; she knows this baby's going to die and everything will be her fault. Vikram's letter said the staff would help her any way they could; all she needs to do is ask: *the nurses are all excellent.* And this was what he'd written in the letter underneath the book: that he would keep her in his prayers, that Richard would be proud of her. *I'm going home to Kerala. My father's taken gravely ill. I'll be back in a month or so. The hospital depends on you.*

She knows that she's not up for this, she hasn't got much in reserve—she came this far to find a ghost to hold her hand and comfort her. She looks down at this tiny girl, while Chidda draws the saline push; this dying baby's face holds all the sadness in the universe. She knows that she will have to stay, if only for a couple days: *she'll live but only if I keep this needle safe inside her vein.*